I turn to run—there's no [illegible] in a straight sprint. Bu[illegible] [illegible]nage two steps before he grabs the back of my jacket.

For a second, it's like we're locked in an insane dance. I'm bending over backwards, leaning into his body. He's dropping his shoulder towards me, the blade close behind it.

I twist to the side, ripping free of his grip, only just managing to stay on my feet. He laughs again. Little needles of terror are shooting through me, but there's something underneath it too: anger. I delivered the cargo clean. *I finished the damn job.* And now Darnell wants me gone? Like I'm a loose end that needs to be snipped off?

No way. Not today.

The guard reaches out for me. He's a good fighter, and fast, but he's easy to read. He wants to pull me in and drive the knife into my belly. So instead of leaning back, like he expects me to, I drop, swinging my right leg in a wide arc.

He spots the move, dodges back, but not before the edge of my shoe clips his ankle. It's just enough. He stumbles, tries to stay upright, then crashes to the ground. His right foot hits the ground, bounces up, comes to a rest on the power box where the wall meets the floor.

I don't let myself second-guess it. I jump as high as I can, and bring both feet down on his kneecap. There's a thin snap, like someone breaking a stick of celery, and then the guard is screaming.

I stumble off him, grab my pack, and run.

TRACER

ROB
BOFFARD

REDHOOK

www.redhookbooks.com

Redhook Books/Orbit
Hachette Book Group
1290 Avenue of the Americas
New York, NY 10104
www.orbitbooks.net

Printed in the United States of America

First U.S. ebook edition: July 2015
First U.S. mass-market edition: June 2016
Originally published in Great Britain by Orbit

10 9 8 7 6 5 4 3 2 1

Redhook is an imprint of Orbit, a division of Hachette Book Group.
The Redhook name and logo are trademarks of Hachette Book Group, Inc.

ISBN: 978-0-316-26527-0

For M. O. R.

Seven years ago

The ship is breaking up around them.

The hull is twisting and creaking, like it's trying to tear away from the heat of re-entry. The outer panels are snapping off, hurtling past the cockpit viewports, black blurs against a dull orange glow.

The ship's second-in-command, Singh, is tearing at her seat straps, as if getting loose will be enough to save her. She's yelling at the captain, seated beside her, but he pays her no attention. The flight deck below them is a sea of flashing red, the crew spinning in their chairs, hunting for something, *anything* they can use.

They have checklists for these situations. But there's no checklist for when a ship, plunging belly-down through Earth's atmosphere to maximise the drag, gets flipped over by an explosion deep in the guts of the engine, sending it first into a spin and then into a screaming nosedive. Now it's spearing through the atmosphere, the friction tearing it to pieces.

The captain doesn't raise his voice. "We have to eject the rear module," he says.

Singh's eyes go wide. "Captain—"

He ignores her, reaching up to touch the communicator in his ear. "Officer Yamamoto," he says, speaking as clearly as he can. "Cut the rear module loose."

Koji Yamamoto stares up at him. His eyes are huge, his mouth slightly open. He's the youngest crew member, barely eighteen. The captain has to say his name again before he turns and hammers on the touch-screens.

The loudest bang of all shudders through the ship as its entire rear third explodes away. Now the ship and its crew are tumbling end over end, the movement forcing them back in their seats. The captain's stomach feels like it's broken free of its moorings. He waits for the tumbling to stop, for the ship to right itself. Three seconds. Five.

He sees his wife's face, his daughter's. *No, don't think about them. Think about the ship.*

"Guidance systems are gone," McCallister shouts, her voice distorting over the comms. "The core's down. I got nothing."

"Command's heard our mayday," Dominguez says. "They—"

McCallister's straps snap. She's hurled out of her chair, thudding off the control panel, leaving a dark red spatter of blood across a screen. Yamamoto reaches for her, forgetting that he's still strapped in. Singh is screaming.

"Dominguez," says the captain. "Patch me through."

Dominguez tears his eyes away from the injured McCallister. A second later, his hands are flying across the controls. A burst of static sounds in the captain's comms unit, followed by two quick beeps.

He doesn't bother with radio protocol. "Ship is on a collision path. We're going to try to crash-land. If we—"

"John."

Foster doesn't have to identify himself. His voice is etched into the captain's memory from dozens of flight briefings and planning sessions and quiet conversations in the pilots' bar.

The captain doesn't know if the rest of flight command are listening in, and he doesn't care. "Marshall," he says. "I think I can bring the ship down. We'll activate our emergency beacon; sit tight until you can get to us."

"I'm sorry, John. There's nothing I can do."

"What are you talking about?"

There's another bang, and then a roar, as if the ship is caught in the jaws of an enormous beast. The captain turns to look at Singh, but she's gone. So is the side of the ship. There's nothing but a jagged gash, the edges a mess of torn metal and sputtering wires. The awful orange glow is coming in, its fingers reaching for him, and he can feel the heat baking on his skin.

"Marshall, listen to me," the captain says, but Marshall is gone too. The captain can see the sky beyond the ship, beyond the flames. It's blue, clearer than he could have ever imagined. It fades to black where it reaches the upper atmosphere, and the space beyond that is pinpricked with stars.

One of those stars is Outer Earth.

Maybe I can find it, the captain thinks, if I look hard enough. He can feel the anger, the *disbelief* at Marshall's words, but he refuses to let it take hold. He tells himself that Outer Earth will send help. They have to. He tries to picture the faces of his family, tries to hold them uppermost in his mind, but the roaring and the heat are everywhere and he can't—

1

Riley

My name is Riley Hale, and when I run, the world disappears.

Feet pounding. Heart thudding. Steel plates thundering under my feet as I run, high up on Level 6, keeping a good momentum as I move through the darkened corridors. I focus on the next step, on the in-out, push-pull of my breathing. Stride, land, cushion, spring, repeat. The station is a tight warren of crawl-spaces and vents around me, every surface metal etched with ancient graffiti.

"She's over there!"

The shout comes from behind me, down the other end of the corridor. The skittering footsteps that follow it echo off the walls. I thought I'd lost these idiots back at the sector border – now I have to outrun them all over again. I got lost in the rhythm of running – always dangerous when someone's trying to jack your cargo. I refuse to waste a breath on cursing, but one of my exhales turns into a growl of frustration.

The Lieren might not be as fast as I am, but they obviously don't give up.

I go from a jog to a sprint, my pack juddering on my

spine as I pump my arms even harder. A tiny bead of sweat touches my eye, sizzling and stinging. I ignore it. No tracer in my crew has ever failed to deliver their cargo, and I am not going to be the first.

I round the corner – and nearly slam into a crush of people. There are five of them, sauntering down the corridor, talking among themselves. But I'm already reacting, pushing off with my right foot, springing in the direction of the wall. I bring my other foot up to meet it, flattening it against the metal and tucking my left knee up to my chest. The momentum keeps me going forwards even as I'm pushing off, exhaling with a whoop as I squeeze through the space between the people and the wall. My right foot comes down, and I'm instantly in motion again. Full momentum. A perfect tic-tac.

The Lieren are close behind, colliding with the group, bowling them over in a mess of confused shouts. But I've got the edge now. Their cries fade into the distance.

There's not a lot you can move between sectors without paying off the gangs. Not unless you know where and how to cross. Tracers do. And that's why we exist. If you need to get something to someone, or if you've got a little package you don't want any gangs knowing about, you come find us. We'll get it there – for a price, of course – and if you come to my crew, the Devil Dancers, we'll get it there *fast*.

The corridor exit looms, and then I'm out, into the gallery. After the corridors, the giant lights illuminating the massive open area are blinding. Corridor becomes catwalk, bordered with rusted metal railings, and the sound of my footfalls fades away, whirling off into the open space.

I catch a glimpse of the diagram on the far wall, still legible a hundred years after it was painted. A scale picture of the station. The Core at the centre, a giant sphere which houses the main fusion reactor. Shooting out from it on either side, two spokes, connected to an enormous ring, the main body. And under it, faded to almost nothing after over a century: Outer Earth Orbit Preservation Module, Founded AD 2234.

Ahead of me, more people emerge from the far entrance to the catwalk. A group of teenage girls, packed tight, talking loudly among themselves. I count ten, fifteen – *no*. They haven't seen me. I'm heading full tilt towards them.

Without breaking stride, I grab the right-hand railing of the catwalk and launch myself up and over, into space.

For a second, there's no noise but the air rushing past me. The sound of the girls' conversation vanishes, like someone turned down a volume knob. I can see all the way down to the bottom of the gallery, a hundred feet below, picking out details snatched from the gaps in the web of criss-crossing catwalks.

The floor is a mess of broken benches and circular flowerbeds with nothing in them. There are two young girls, skipping back and forth over a line they've drawn on the floor. One is wearing a faded smock. I can just make out the word Astro on the back as it twirls around her. A light above them is flickering off-on-off, and their shadows flit in and out on the wall behind them, dancing off metal plates. My own shadow is spread out before me, split by the catwalks; a black shape broken on rusted railings. On one of the catwalks lower down, two men are arguing, pushing each other. One man throws a punch, his target dodging back as the group around them scream dull threats.

I jumped off the catwalk without checking my landing zone. I don't even want to think what Amira would do if she found out. Explode, probably. Because if there's someone under me and I hit them from above, it's not just a broken ankle I'm looking at.

Time seems frozen. I flick my eyes towards the Level 5 catwalk rushing towards me.

It's empty. Not a person in sight, not even further along. I pull my legs up, lift my arms and brace for the landing.

Contact. The noise returns, a bang that snaps my head back even as I'm rolling forwards. On instinct, I twist sideways, so the impact can travel across, rather than up, my spine. My right hand hits the ground, the sharp edges of the steel bevelling scraping my palm, and I push upwards, arching my back so my pack can fit into the roll.

Then I'm up and running, heading for the dark catwalk exit on the far side. I can hear the Lieren reach the catwalk above. They've spotted me, but I can tell by their angry howls that it's too late. There's no way they're making that jump. To get to where I am, they'll have to fight their way through the stairwells on the far side. By then, I'll be long gone.

"Never try to outrun a Devil Dancer, boys," I mutter between breaths.

2

Darnell

"So you don't have it?"

The technician is doing his best not to look at Oren Darnell. He frowns down at the tab screen in his hands, flicking through the menu with one trembling finger.

Darnell's nose twitches, and he takes a delicate sniff, tasting the air. He's always had a good sense of smell. He can identify plants by their scent, stripping them down into their component notes. The smell of the bags of fertiliser stacked along the walls is powerful, pungent even, but he can still smell the technician's sweat, hot and tangy with fear. Good.

"I know it was here," the tech says, shaking his head. He's a short man, with a closely shorn head and a barely visible mask of stubble on his face. "Someone must have signed it out."

He glances up at Darnell, just for a second, then looks down again. "But it doesn't make sense. That shipment was marked for your use only."

Darnell says nothing. He reaches up to scratch his neck, glancing back towards the door of the storeroom. His guard Reece is lounging against the frame, looking bored. He catches Darnell's eye, and shrugs.

"Don't worry though, Mr Darnell," the tech says, snapping the tab screen off and slipping it under his arm. He pushes it too far, and has to catch it before it falls. "I'll find it. Have it sent right up to your office. Bring it myself, actually. You leave it with me."

Darnell smiles at him. It's a warm smile, almost paternal. "That's all right," he says. "It happens."

"I know what you mean, Sir," the tech says, meeting Darnell's smile with one of his own. "But we'll get to the bottom of—"

"Do me a favour," Darnell says. He points to the back of the storeroom. "Grab me a bag of micronutrient, would you?"

The tech's smile gets wider, relieved to have a purpose, a job he can easily accomplish. "You got it," he says, and scampers across the room, already scanning the shelves for the dull orange bag of fertiliser he needs. He sees it on the top shelf, just out of reach, and is standing on his toes to snag the edge when something whistles past his head. The knife bounces off the wall, spinning wildly before coming to a stop on the floor. The tech can see his own expression in the highly polished blade. A thin whine is coming out of his mouth. The tab screen falls, shattering, spraying shimmering fragments.

"I always pull to the right," Darnell says as he strolls towards the tech. "Don't hold it against me, though. Throwing a knife is hard – and that's with a blade that's perfectly balanced."

The tech can't speak. Can't move. Can't even take his eyes off the knife, the one that passed an inch from the back of his neck. The handle is hardwood, shiny with oil, the grain smooth with age.

"It's all in the arm," Darnell says. "You can't release it until your arm is straight. I know, I know, I need to get better. But hey, you don't have anything to do at the moment, right? Why don't you stay and help me out? It's easy. You just have to stand real still."

He points at the knife. "Pick it up."

When the tech still doesn't move, doesn't do anything except stand there shaking, Darnell gives his shoulder a push. It's a light touch, gentle even, but the tech nearly falls over. He squeaks, his hands clenching and unclenching.

"Pick it up."

"Boss." Reece is striding towards them, his hands in his pockets. Darnell glances up, and Reece jerks his head at the door.

Darnell looks back at the tech, flashing him that warm smile again. "Duty calls," he says. "Truth be told, it's hard to find the time to practise. But don't worry – when I get a moment, I'll let you know."

The tech is nodding furiously. He doesn't know what else to do.

Darnell turns to go, but then looks back over his shoulder. "The blade hit the wall pretty hard. Probably blunted it up good. Would you make yourself useful? Get it sharpened for me?"

"Sure," the tech says, in a voice that doesn't seem like his own. "Sure. I can do that."

"Kind of you," Darnell says, striding away. He exchanges a few whispered words with Reece, then raises his voice so the tech can hear. "Good and sharp, remember. You should be able to draw blood if you put a little bit of pressure on the edge."

He sweeps out of the room, Reece trailing a few steps behind.

3

Riley

I slow down slightly as I enter the Level 5 corridor. Drop-off is way up the ring, at the Air Lab in Gardens sector. With each sector in the ring three miles long – and with six sectors in all – it's a long way to go. Unless you're a tracer, with the stamina and skill to get things where they need to be. I don't mind the distance – heading to the Air Lab means I get to see Prakesh.

I smile at the thought, before remembering that he's not there today. It's a rare day off for him, one he was boasting about when I saw him a couple of weeks ago.

The package snuggled next to my spine – the one the Lieren want to jack in the hope it's something good – is going to Oren Darnell, the man who runs the Air Lab. It was given to me by a merchant in the Apogee sector market. The merchant – Gray, I think his name was – paid with six fresh batteries, slapping them down on the rusty countertop of his stall, barely looking at me. Totally fine with that; pay is good, so your package gets delivered.

As I enter the corridor I reach back over my shoulder for the thin plastic nozzle protruding from the top of my pack, jamming it into my mouth and sucking down water from the reservoir. It's warm, and feels viscous in my mouth. There's not much, but it'll keep me going.

I'm in Chengshi sector, between Apogee and Gardens – just over halfway to the drop-off. I'll have to stop to refill somewhere in Gardens, because there's no chance of getting any water from Darnell. I might be bringing him a package, but asking that guy for water is almost as deadly as jumping off a catwalk blindfolded.

The corridors here are darker than before. I have to pay more attention to the surface as I run towards the next turn, watching for the places where the steel plates are twisted and bent. Surprisingly, there's a working screen here, grimy with dust but still showing a cheery recruitment ad for the space construction corps. A smiling spaceman, clad in a sleek black suit with the visor up, wielding a plasma cutter as he manoeuvres himself around a construction ship's arm. The video fills the corridor with soft blue light, and as I turn the corner, I close my eyes for a split second. The light filters through my lids, flickering a warm orange.

I've never been there, but sometimes I like to imagine myself on Earth, running across fields of grass, under a sky so blue that it hurts to look at it. The sun, warm on the back of my neck as I go faster, and faster, and faster. Until I'm no longer running. I'm airborne.

I open my eyes.

Just in time to see the metal pole swing out from behind the corner and slam into my chest.

For a second I really am airborne, lying prone in mid-air. I crash to the ground, my bones feeling like they're going to vibrate out of my skin. I try to scream, but all I can manage are thick, wheezing gasps.

The one with the pole is just a fuzzy black blur; he twirls the weapon in his hand, like he's out for a stroll. Another spasm of pain crackles across my chest, and I begin to cough: a deep, hacking, groaning noise that causes the pain to spread to my abdomen.

"Good hit," says a voice from the left. There's laughter from somewhere else, behind him.

Then there are six of them looking down on me. More Lieren – different from the ones who were chasing me. I cough again, even worse this time, like there's a dagger in my chest.

The one that hit me looks around nervously. I glimpse a dark red wolf tattoo on his neck. "Come on," he says, looking back down the passage. "Get her pack."

Someone wedges a boot under the small of my back and flips me over, forcing another cough out of my body. A foot on the back of my neck slams me into the floor before two others take my arms, yanking them backwards and sliding my backpack off.

My mind is racing. There should have been other people in this corridor by now. I can't be the only person here. Even if they didn't intervene, they might be the distraction I need to get away. And how did the Lieren set this ambush in the first place? They were behind me. I only came this way because the catwalk was blocked, and I had to...

Oh. Oh, that's clever. The group of girls on the catwalk. They were sent directly into my path, either paid or forced to do what the Lieren wanted. They knew they weren't fast enough to catch me, so they funnelled me right to them. I've run cargo to the Air Lab before – they'd know the routes I take, where I'd go and what I'd do when I was chased. Played like a fool, Riley.

"Anything else we can get? Her jacket?" I hear one of them say. Anger shoots through me; if they take my dad's jacket, I'll kill them. Every one of them.

"Nah, it's a piece of shit. The cargo'll be enough."

They yank the pack off and force me back down.

Someone reaches into my jacket pockets and grabs the batteries. The boot is lifted off my back. I raise my head and see the kid with the pole tossing a battery up and down, a weird little grin on his face. He has my pack dangling from his other hand, and he and the other five are already moving away.

I push myself to my feet, chest aching with the effort, forcing myself to stay silent. I gain my balance, then start towards them, shifting onto the balls of my feet to lower the noise in the cramped corridor. Quick steps.

It's the one with my pack I'm after, and at the very moment he realises I'm behind him, I bring my right hand up in a lunging strike. I've balled my hand into a fist, with the knuckle of my index finger protruding slightly, and I'm aiming right for the base of his skull. Amira's tried to teach me about pressure points before, but this is the first time I've ever had to put it into practice.

My strike is true, hitting the tiny pocket of flesh where the skull joins the spine, and I feel something under my fist crack. He makes a strangled sound, and flies forward, my pack falling from his hand.

I have about half a second to appreciate my victory. Then one of his friends steps forward and socks me in the eye so hard that I just go somewhere else for a while.

When I come back – seconds later? Minutes? – I'm pushed up against the corridor wall, two of the Lieren holding me in place. My face is numb, and there's blood in my mouth; I can taste the metallic edge, sharp and nasty. The one I attacked is still out on the ground. As I watch, he groans, twitching under the flickering lights.

The Lieren with the wolf tattoo is standing in front of me, rearing back for another hit. If this one connects, it's goodbye Riley.

He throws the punch. I wrench my head to the side,

and his fist slams into the metal wall, sending a resonant clang rattling around the corner. He pulls it back with a cry of pain. A flap of skin hangs off his middle finger, blood already welling up around the edges of the wound. His buddies relaxed their grip in surprise for a moment when I dodged, but not enough for me to break free, and now they force me back against the wall. "She's got some fight in her," growls one.

Tattoo is holding his wrist and shaking his hand back and forth. "You missed," I say. "Can't even hit someone standing still, can you?"

"Is that right?" he says, wiping his mouth with his uninjured hand.

"Yeah. Maybe you have these guys let me loose, and we go a few rounds. You and me. See who's faster."

"Think so? You're kind of small for a tracer. What are you, fifteen?"

"Twenty," I spit back, instantly regretting it.

"She's ugly, too,' says one of the Lieren holding me. "Like some nuke mutant from back on Earth."

"Maybe she's got some cousins down there right now. New life forms."

There's laughter, cruel and sharp. I try to keep my voice calm. "Listen to me," I say. "That cargo is going to Oren Darnell. I'm under his protection in Gardens. If you take my cargo, you'll have to answer to him."

"The hell is Oren Darnell?" says the one holding my left shoulder.

"Don't you know anything?" says the Lieren with the tattoo. "He's in charge of the Air Lab." But no fear crosses his face – instead, he looks amused, still flicking his wrecked hand. Not good.

"He's got gang connections," I say. "Death's Head. Black Hole Crew. You sure Zhao would want you to jack cargo going in their direction?"

I'm half hoping that mentioning the name of Zhao Zheng, the leader of the Lieren, would have some effect. But Tattoo just laughs. "Rumours, honey. That's all there is to it."

"It's the truth. I..."

And then Tattoo pulls out a knife, and the words die on my lips.

4

Darnell

Darnell marches across the Air Lab, his heavy footfalls ringing out across the metal walkways. He doesn't need to check that Reece is following him; the guard is always close by, always there when Darnell needs him. His footsteps are as silent as his boss's are loud.

There are algae pools lined up along the walkway, each one thirty square feet, with surfaces like murky glass. Darnell leans over one of them, idly running a finger along the slime.

"So what's so urgent you had to pull me away?" he says.

Reece stops a short distance away, his arms folded. He glances left and right. There are plenty of other techs on the floor of the cavernous Air Lab, tending to trees or crossing the floor in tight groups, but there's nobody close to where he and Darnell are.

"Well?" Darnell says, staring intently at the viscous water.

"What's going on, boss?" Reece says.

Darnell says nothing.

Reece unfolds his arms, hooks his thumbs in his belt.

"This isn't some gangster who hasn't paid us his water tax," he says. "That was one of your employees. I can cover for you on most things, but even I might struggle to square that one."

Darnell swings himself upright, pointing a finger at Reece. A tiny thread of algae comes with it, swinging back and forth. "You getting scared, Reece?" he says, stepping away from the tank. "You think I'm going too far?"

The guard doesn't flinch, just refolds his arms.

"If I'm going too far," Darnell says, "then maybe you should stop me. How about it, Reece? Want to try?"

Reece's cool eyes look back at him. Despite his anger at the insubordination, a part of Darnell marvels at Reece's refusal to get scared. It's why he's kept him around so long.

"You've been distracted, boss," Reece says. "For like a month now. And I've never seen you flip out on one of your own techs before, not like that. Whatever's going on, you should tell me so I can—"

"*Should?*"

Reece stops dead.

"You just make sure that shipment gets here," Darnell says. He sweeps his arm around to indicate the rest of the hangar. "Isn't that what you do? I'm in charge of the Air Lab, Reece. I'm responsible for every molecule of oxygen that you suck into your lungs and every molecule of CO_2 that comes out of them. You need to make sure I have everything I need to do it. That's what you need to do."

"I'll handle it," Reece says.

"Excellent," Darnell says, resuming his march towards the control room, his mind already elsewhere. He's got bigger things to worry about, like the other shipment: the little package Arthur Gray is supposed to deliver. If someone diverts that, they'll have a lot more to worry about than his shitty knife-throwing.

5

Riley

It'd be nice to say it's a beautiful blade. It's not. The handle is patched and frayed, and the steel is laced with rust. If the cut doesn't kill you, the infection will.

Tattoo holds it up, the metal catching the edge of the light. "You know," he says, "we just wanted a score. We weren't really planning on killing you."

He rotates the knife, angling the point towards my eyes. "But now, we have to take something back. You can't hurt one of us, and not expect to get it back in return. You understand, right?"

I try to say something, but I can't look away from the blade. He leans in close. The point is now inches away. "What'll it be? Left ear, or right?"

"Let me go," I finally say. It's almost a snarl. But the knife remains steady, its tip hardly wavering at all as it creeps towards my face. He starts flicking it gently back and forth. I can feel sweat soaking my shirt at the small of my back. I yank my body to one side, but the Lieren holding me are too strong. One of them plants a hand on my forehead, pinning me in place. "You might want to stay still," he says.

Left, right, left, right.

There's a yell from behind Tattoo. He straightens up, irritated, and looks back over his shoulder. One of the other Lieren, tall and gangly with sallow skin, is holding my pack. It's open, and he's frantically beckoning his buddies over.

With a sigh, Tattoo drops the knife from my face and walks over to him. "And now? What's the matter with..."

His voice falters as he looks into the pack. He turns, blocking my view, holding a whispered conversation with his partner.

I don't have the first clue about what's in my pack. We never do. It's one of the reasons why my crew gets so much work. You can send whatever you want, and you can trust us to never know about it.

I feel a flicker of hope: for the first time, it looks like it might just save my life.

After a minute of hissed back-and-forth with his friend, Tattoo signals to the ones holding me against the wall. Abruptly, they let me go. I collapse against the wall, try to rise, but my legs have stopped listening to me.

Tattoo is staring at me with an odd look on his face. He walks over, leans close, whispers: "This isn't finished."

He holds up a battery, bringing it as close to my face as he did the knife. "And we're keeping these."

The one who opened the bag lets it fall, and it lands with a thump on the floor. With a gesture from Tattoo, the Lieren set off down the corridor. One of them grabs the man I took down with the pressure-point strike, swinging him over his shoulders like a crop bag.

I don't want to, but I stay down until they're out of sight. I'm shaking, and it takes a minute for me to steady myself. Then it takes me another minute to rise – I nearly lose my balance when I do, and some blood droplets patter onto the floor ahead of me. My face is humming with pain, and my eye socket is on fire. But I can't worry about that now. I've lost too much time already.

As I move to grab my still-open pack and zip it shut, I can't help but see what's inside. It's the box Gray gave me to deliver – barely the size of a fist, like something you'd keep a small machine part in. The top of the box has been opened up by the Lieren. Inside is something wrapped in layers of opaque plastic padding – a blurred shape, vaguely familiar.

And from the bottom right corner of the box, slowly leaching into the protective foam, I can see a thin trickle of blood.

I want to close the bag, to zip it shut and finish the job and not think about the thing in the plastic, but my hands falter. The blood is still there, pooling on the foam. The corridor is deserted.

I have to know.

Slowly, I push a finger into the plastic wrapping. It's thick, clammy-cold against my skin. The wrapping is tight against the cargo, the edges catching as I lift it up. But then my fingers brush against something soft and slick, and the blurred shape in the bag leaps out at me.

I'm staring at it, willing myself to look away, but there's no mistaking it.

It's an eyeball. I've been carrying an eyeball.

6

Darnell

Darnell has a table at the back of the darkened control room, surrounded by battered chairs. Every tech who works there knows not to move them, not even an inch, or to say anything about the suffocating temperature their boss likes to keep the room at.

He's sitting at the table, going through reports, when Reece brings the storage technician in. The man hovers off to one side, a small box under his arm, waiting for Darnell to notice him.

Eventually Darnell waves him over. The tech scurries across the floor, holding the box out in front of him like a shield. The heavy lettering on the front reads AIR LAB CONSIGNMENT 6/00/7-A MOST URGENT.

"Found it, Sir," he says. "Just got misplaced, that's all. Temporarily."

Darnell barely glances at him. "And the knife?"

The man swallows. With a trembling hand, he pulls the knife out of his pocket, careful to hold it by the blade. He places it flat on the table, lined up next to the box.

Darnell tilts his head. "You got fingerprints on the blade."

"I..."

"You sharpen it, like I said?"

"Yes, Sir. Like you said."

An urge takes Darnell then, hot and demanding: the urge to test the knife's sharpness by sliding it into the man's stomach. His fingers twitch. It would take less than a second. In and out.

Instead, he waves the man away. The tech backs off, nodding like his neck is already broken. Darnell returns to his reports, scowling. As much as he hates to admit it, Reece's words have stayed with him. He needs to be more careful. He's worked too hard and waited too long to get distracted now.

He tears the top off the box, wiggling his hand inside. His fingers brush machined glass, and he pulls out a tab screen – smaller than the regular units, with a bulbous antenna poking out the top. He switches it on, flicking through the menu options. A smile creeps across his face like oil moving through water. His connection in Tzevya sector did his job.

The storage tech nearly trips over the door as he leaves the control room, and the thunk of his foot on the metal lip makes Darnell look up. He's pleased with himself for not giving in to his urges. Besides, the tech will get what's coming to him soon enough. Along with Reece, and the other techs, and everyone else on Outer Earth, if he can just keep it together. Discipline, that's the key. Control.

7

Riley

A dry heave builds in my throat, boiling up from my stomach. My hand jerks, and the box is jolted sideways. It slips out of the pack, and the thing slides out of the plastic and hits the floor with a muffled plop.

It rolls in place, the trailing optic nerve stuck to the floor on a meniscus of blood. It's not looking at me, but I can see the iris, dark blue, surrounding the inky-black dot of the pupil. I have to force myself to look away, and as I do the heave becomes a full-blown retch. Doubling over, I push it back, forcing it down.

You will not throw up. Not here.

Never look at what you carry. It's the one big unbreakable, the one thing Amira has told us over and over again. There's a reason for that: it gets us work. People trust us. We're not going to steal your cargo, or even care what it is.

Plus, not knowing keeps us alive. Tracers, us included, sometimes carry bad things. Weapons, contraband, drugs concocted somewhere in the Caves and destined for sale in a distant sector. Be nice if we could live off doing hospital runs, but we can't. It's better if we don't know. Realistically, I know I could have been carrying severed eyes for years and never known. But actually seeing it, touching it...

Crouching, I use a corner of the plastic to grip the nerve, gently tugging at it. The iris rolls towards me, and I force myself to look away. The retch comes again, and I have to close my eyes and inhale through my nose for a few seconds, before looking back. More details begin to jump out. Tiny, milky-smooth clouds in the pupil that I hadn't noticed before. Thin arteries, running off the iris like fine pen lines.

Movement. Voices. Without thinking, I grab the eyeball. It's soft and pliable in my grip, like putty.

Don't squeeze it too hard or it'll pop.

I have to force back another heave. I shove it back into the box and zip my backpack shut as the owners of the voices come round the corner.

Two stompers. They're officially known as Station Protection Officers, but nobody calls them that any more. I'm surprised to see them; there aren't too many around these days.

A few times a year, you hear stories about gang bosses joining forces, declaring open season on any stomper foolish enough to walk into their territories. It always ends up with plenty dead on both sides – but when it comes to new members, people always seem to be more willing to join up with the gangs. The sector leaders do their best, showing face in the bars and the market and the mess halls, looking for recruits to the stomper corps, but they always have to go back to the council in Apex with bad news.

The stompers walking towards me are dressed in thick grey jumpsuits with the station logo – a stylised ring silhouette – stitched into the top pocket. The noise of their boots is heavy in the cramped space. On their hips rest specially modified pistols: guns with ammunition designed to go through flesh and bone, but not metal. We call them stingers.

I've seen the one on the left before – Royo, I think his name is, a bear-like man with dark skin and a shaved head. His partner is just as big, with a shaggy beard. In different circumstances, he'd probably look jovial, but as he locks me in his gaze I see that his right eye is glass, dead and inert in its socket.

Left, right, left, right.

They take in the scene. A blood-splattered floor, and a tracer who looks like she just had a head-on collision with an asteroid. "What's going on here?" says Royo, but even as the words are out of his mouth I'm bolting past him. His partner makes a grab for me, but I'm too quick, slipping under his arm. "Cargo delivery!" I say over my shoulder.

I'm expecting them to give chase, maybe even draw on me. But they don't follow, and I heave a sigh of relief. Maybe they figure a beat-up tracer isn't worth their time. Good news for me. I have a lot of ground to make up. My collarbone seems OK, but my face is throbbing again, and prickly waves of pain are spreading out from where I got punched.

A million thoughts are crowding for attention. Part of me wants to drop the box somewhere and run, pretend that I'd never taken the job. I turn that option down in seconds – I don't even want to think what will happen if Darnell doesn't get his eyeball. He'll probably use one of mine as a replacement. And if he decides to take revenge on the Devil Dancers...

But can I really deliver the cargo? Pretend I never saw the eyeball, walk away, and hope everything goes back to normal? Is that even possible now? Every time someone hands me cargo, or asks me to turn around so they can put it in my pack, I'm going to be thinking about today.

But it's not a choice. Not really. I have to finish the job. There's a chance that Darnell will find out that I saw my cargo, but it's a lot less risky than abandoning the job completely.

Every time the pack jolts, every time the cargo shifts against my back, a fresh wave of horror rolls through me.

I pass the mining facilities Chengshi is known for. Their kilns and machines are silent, and the rooms that hold them spill no light into the corridors. They won't be up and running again until the next asteroid catcher ship swings into orbit alongside the station. I don't really like running here; I always seem to come out with streaks of grime on my skin and clothes. I tell myself to keep going, that it can't be more than a mile to the Gardens border.

There are more slag rooms, dotted here and there with rundown habs, all locked up tight. Several times I have to react quickly to stop myself smashing into people in the corridors. Some lie sprawled on the ground, their possessions arranged in haphazard piles. With no hab units willing to take them, they have to sleep where they can.

I'm struggling to run at full speed after the attack, so I slow back to a jog. As I do so, I turn the corner and nearly collide with a tagger.

He's painting something onto the wall – I catch a glimpse of it as I dodge past, a slogan. "It's the only way." The phrase doesn't make any sense, until I remember where I've heard it before. At a demonstration in one of the galleries, where it was being chanted. But what were they protesting about again?

The tagger catches sight of me. "We need to control the birth rate," he says, his voice on the edge of a shout. "Humans were never meant to keep existing…"

Ah. That was it. Voluntary human extinction.

"Out of the way," I say, all but hurling the words in his direction as I flash past.

I've heard it all before. How we need to stop having children to restore balance to the universe. Voluntary euthanasia. If I let the tagger stop me, he'll end up telling me all about how Outer Earth shouldn't even exist, that it was a pissing contest between Earth governments that got too far along to kill. Population overflow, they called it. I know the story like every person on this station.

Of course, a massive nuclear war a few years later didn't help either.

But that was a long time ago, and I just don't care that much. I turn around, and flip the tagger a raised middle finger. Then I keep running.

Soon, I'm jogging under the sign that marks the border between Gardens and Chengshi. I look up as I pass underneath it. A long time ago, someone took a spray-can, crossed out the words Sector 2 and drew crude pictures of flowers and trees in green paint around it.

You can cross sector borders on nearly all the levels, but for some reason, I always find myself on this one. Gardens is cleaner than Chengshi – better maintained, with much less graffiti and dust. Most of the sector is given over to the Air Lab and the Food Lab, the places which give Gardens its name. They're behind a set of enormous airlock doors at the bottom of the gallery. I can see the two guards on duty today: Dumar and Chang. Chang's new – a couple of weeks ago, he refused me entry, and I had to wait for Prakesh to come out for a break before I could get in – but Dumar's been working there for years. He's a stocky guy with dark eyes and a huge, black, knotted beard. He raises a hand as I approach, less a command to stop than a friendly greeting. But I can see his hand resting, as always, on his stinger holster.

"Back again?" he says.

I force a smile. "Good to see you too, Dumar."

"I swear, one day you're gonna go in there and grow roots, you visit so often."

"Hey, I just visit. You work here."

We've been exchanging the same lines for years. He gives a good-natured grunt as he turns to his control panel. Behind him, Chang sniffs. Prakesh once told me that on his first day he attempted to body-search every tech who came through the door.

Dumar eyes my pack. "You doing a delivery?"

I swallow. "That's right. Up to Mr Darnell."

He shakes his head. "You want to be careful with that one," he says. He seems about to go on, but Chang flashes him a dark look, and he falls silent.

Dumar presses a few keys, and the outer airlock door hisses open. I step through. "Have fun," he says over his shoulder as the door closes behind me. As I wait for the inner door to open, I run a hand through my hair. As usual, it's greasy, caked with grit, uncomfortably sticky. I try to keep it short, but it doesn't help all that much.

I can see myself in the reflective metal door. My hair frames a face shiny and gleaming with sweat. I try not to look into the reflection's dark-grey eyes. Instead, I focus on the body, stretching my arms out to the sides, shaking my legs out. The jacket is bulky, but the body underneath it is lithe and supple, muscles sculpted from endless running and climbing and jumping.

There's a buzz, then a brief flash of purple light – ultraviolet, designed to zap any surface bacteria. I don't know why they bother. I'm not even sure it works. The door in front of me hisses open, vanishing into the wall.

You get to the Air Lab by going through the Food Lab. I can dimly see the shapes of the crops through the opaque plastic domes in the hangar: corn, tomato plants, beds of lettuce, beans, all bathed in a soft, green glow from the grower bulbs. There are no main lights in the

Food Lab itself; the path ahead is softly lit by the ambient light, and a gentle hum emanates from the large aircon units on the walls. The hangar seems to stretch on for miles, and in the distance I can see the lights of the lab complex where the techs work to make the crops more efficient, easier to grow.

Beyond the greenhouses is the insect colony: what I've heard the lab techs call the buzz box. Tiny beetles and little silkworms can't make much noise on their own, but get millions of them in one place and the hum they generate can shake your stomach. Still, they taste OK. Especially the fried beetles they do in the market sometimes. Crunchy and salty. Much better than the mess hall stuff.

I turn right, by a greenhouse labelled Soja Japonica, and head down the rows. Before long I'm walking through a door and then the space above is filled with a thick green canopy. The trees are a special breed of oak, enormous, designed to suck in carbon dioxide and pump out as much oxygen as possible. And some of them are old – much older than the techs who work on them. Over the years, their roots have broken free of their metal prisons, pushing up through the floor. I have to step over a couple as I move between the trees.

Unlike the Food Lab, the Air Lab is brightly lit, huge lights beaming down from the ceiling. I stop for a moment under a tree with a thick, gnarled trunk, and tilt my head up, watching the rays of light filter through the branches. The air is cool. Were it not for the fact that the floor under my feet was metal grating, and that I was surrounded by huge pools of algae, nestled between the trees, I could be somewhere on Earth. If the nukes hadn't turned most of the planet into a burning wasteland before I was born, maybe I would be.

Of course, by then there weren't many trees left anyway.

The Air Lab is just as big as the cavernous Food Lab – it has to be to provide enough air for the station. I head towards the back, to the control rooms, towering over the trees. It's tempting to just drop the cargo off at an office somewhere, maybe the storerooms, just to avoid Darnell. No chance. I deliver the cargo right into its recipient's hands, or I don't deliver it all.

No matter what's inside.

I climb the clanking metal stairs, wondering how a place in which I can find someone as good as Prakesh is also home to a person like Darnell. As I reach the top, I spot the usual guard outside. He's a short man, wiry, with a grim face and a grubby, knee-length coat. He gives a nod when he sees me, and hauls open the door to the main control room – after so many runs, he's used to me by now.

Stepping through the door, I'm blasted by a wave of heat. The convection fins on the hull keep the station cool – most of the time – but Darnell likes to keep the temperature up. He likes to make visitors uncomfortable.

I can feel the sweat begin to run again, pooling at my waist. I'm dying for water – I burned the last of my pack supply on the final stretch here – but you don't ask Oren Darnell for a drink.

The control units around the walls hum away quietly, attended to by white-coated techs who have shrunk into their chairs like beetles. In the centre of the room are two large drums of water, sloshing gently – just the sight of them makes my tongue jump, like it's touched an electric wire. Darnell is seated at the back, deep in conversation with one of his lieutenants.

The air is thick with dry heat. In the background, a clanging starts – from one of the water pipes somewhere else in Gardens, maybe – but it only lasts a moment before the door swings shut behind me, reducing the sound to a muted boom. Right then, Darnell looks up and sees me.

He's a giant of a man, with thick arms and a chest like the hull of a ship. He dresses well: a tight-fitting black shirt and slim black pants made from a smooth fabric. I don't know what to do with my hands, so I busy myself removing my pack. The straps feel rough and unyielding, my fingers clumsy.

"Riley Hale," he says. His voice is soft and high-pitched, like a child's. It sounds strange, coming from someone so enormous. He moves towards me in long, languid strides, and his eyes rove across my body, passing over my battered face. "A pleasure to see you again. I trust you are well?"

I shrug, trying to avoid his gaze. Instead, I reach into my pack, and pull out the box.

Darnell gestures to a tech, who steps forward and takes the box from me, reaching out to grab it before shrinking away, as if I might bite his arm off. I made sure I sealed the box shut before I got here – there's no evidence that it's been opened.

The tech hands it to Darnell, who quickly breaks the seal, glancing inside. My stomach churns. Darnell nods, reseals the box, and hands it to the tech, who spirits it away to the back of the room.

I'm still watching the box when I realise that Darnell has taken a step closer. Before I can stop him, he runs a finger delicately across my bruises, around the side of my eye. I have to force myself not to flinch.

"These are fresh," he says. "Tell me who did this."

"It's nothing," I say, trying to turn away. He doesn't lift his hand from my face, and the light pressure forces the words out of me. "Just another gang thinking they could jack the cargo."

"But you fought them off."

"Of course," I say, taking a step back. His hand drops from my face. "Cargo this important, it's—"

"Important?"

I keep my expression as neutral as I can. Inside, I'm screaming at myself. The words just tumbled out of me, knocked loose by his touch, the feeling of his smooth fingers on my skin. Darnell is looking at me, his eyes narrowed.

"Yeah, important," I say. Amazingly, I manage a casual shrug. " 'Cos it's you, you know. You're not just a regular client." The words sound forced even as I say them, but I keep my voice steady.

Darnell doesn't move. For a good three seconds, he simply stares at me.

Then he smiles. "Well, if you ever decide you'd like some payback, you just let me know. I don't imagine today was the first time you've run into trouble."

I try not to exhale. It's all I can do to shrug a second time, like it's nothing.

Darnell raises his eyebrows in mock alarm. "But I'm being such a terrible host. Something to drink?" He gestures to the water in the drums.

"Thanks," I say, finally meeting his gaze. "I'm good."

He chuckles. It's an odd sound, gravelly and brief, like a bare foot stepping on broken glass. "On the house, Riley. No charge. And look..." He strides over to the drums and draws a handful of liquid to his lips. "It's clean. Didn't even spike this one."

A few drops leak out of his cupped hands, splashing back into the drum. I'm conscious of my tongue, large and dry in my mouth, like a hunk of old resin.

One of Darnell's men appears at his side with a tin cup, and he fills it and hands it to me. I pause, but only for a moment. The water is cool and sweet, with just a faint hint of the metal in the drum. I've raised the cup with both hands, and tilt it to catch every last drop.

I hand back the cup and wipe a hand across my lips.

All of a sudden, I want out of there, bad. I nod thanks, taking my pack and turning to leave – job done, cargo delivered, time to go.

Darnell clears his throat behind me. "Riley."

I look back over my shoulder. He goes on: "You really should think about making our arrangement a little more..." He searches for the right words. "More full-time. I could use your talents."

"Sorry," I say. "I like what I do."

"I wasn't suggesting you stop. I could use a tracer in-house. Someone who worked exclusively for the Air Lab. For me."

"You've got crews in Gardens. Hire one of them."

"Them?" That laugh again. His eyes are ice crystals. "No. They don't know what it means to work for something. But you..."

"Like I said. Not interested." I step towards the door, but he clears his throat again, and this time the noise freezes me in my tracks.

"I usually only make an offer once, Riley. But I'll let you think about it. Just let it roll around in that little head of yours. I could give you protection. Imagine: no more black eyes."

I say nothing. His smile doesn't change. "You be safe now."

He turns away, striding back to the table, like he's already forgotten about me. I turn to go, ignoring the eyes of his techs, burning into my back. On the catwalk outside, the guard gives me a lazy mock salute before gently pushing the door shut.

8

Riley

I'm almost at the bottom of the stairs when I collapse.

I don't know whether it's the shock catching up with me, or simply the beating I took from the Lieren, but one second I'm taking the last few steps, and the next I'm lying flat on my stomach. The metal flooring is cool against my cheek. It feels good.

Hands on my back, then around my shoulders, lifting me up. Someone is saying my name, and then I'm looking into the face of Prakesh Kumar.

He's taller than me, his arms strong from digging in the dirt every day, and before I know it he's sat me on the edge of an algae tank. "Gods, Ry, what the hell happened?"

His hands are already reaching towards my face, but I brush them away. His walnut-dark skin is calloused, flecked with grains of dark soil.

"Thought you were off today," I say. I have to focus on each word, form them carefully so I don't slur.

"Cancelled. They needed extra hands. What happened?"

"I'm OK," I say. "Just had a little problem on the run."

"A *little* problem?" He moves his hands up again, and I have to push them away more firmly.

"I said I'm fine," I mutter.

"You don't look fine. You don't even look close to fine." He folds his arms, eyeing my bruises. On the other techs, the white lab coats look bulky, almost baggy, but Prakesh wears his well, square on his shoulders over a rough cotton shirt.

I keep my voice low, in case anyone is listening. "Ambush. Lieren. They were trying to jack my cargo. Managed to fight them off..." I have to stop as a cough bursts up through my throat, doubling me over.

Prakesh's hands are on my back, steadying me. "Easy. Easy. Just sit here, OK? I'll get some water." I try to push him away again, try to tell him that I already had some from his boss, but this time he pushes back, his hand holding steady between my shoulder blades. "No. You're hurt. You can take some water. I'll be right back."

He leaves, and I sit back down heavily on the edge of the tank. After a minute, I'm feeling less woozy, and stumble over to one of the nearby trees. Steadying myself against it, I sink down onto the soft, loamy soil. Prakesh will probably shout at me for sitting on something as precious as his good soil, but I don't care. I'm just happy to be off my feet. I lick my lips. The crust of blood on them cracks just a little, like old glass.

My thoughts drift back to when I met Prakesh. Back when we were in school, we had to file into a cramped room with hard chairs and harsh lights. When you're little, it's kind of fun – you don't spend as much time there, and you're mostly being taught how to read and write and count, and sometimes even draw pictures if the teacher had some coloured pencils.

But when you get older, the classrooms get more packed, and there's less space on the chairs. What you learn doesn't make sense, either: the teachers would show us pictures or videos of life back on Earth: animals in captivity, blue-green oceans, huge collections of buildings called cities. They'd try to teach us how it all worked. I remember looking at something, some animal – a huge, improbable thing with a massive, tentacle-like nose and horrible, wrinkled, grey skin – and trying to picture it in real life, as it would have been back on Earth. I couldn't do it. I just couldn't see it. I knew what it looked like but I couldn't picture it. And the name: elephant, like something out of a scary story. The letters in a weird order, a word light years away from anything I knew.

I got angry and started punching the tab screen in a fit of stupid rage. I remember the thin glass on the screen cracking, the tiny sting as a piece cut me and the elephant vanished. I was seven.

I hadn't really paid much attention to Prakesh up until then. I'd sort of known who he was, sure, but I'd never spoken to him. But for whatever reason, he was sitting next to me that day, and as my hand came down for a fourth time to smash the screen he caught me, grabbing my wrist. I looked at him, startled: I expected to see fear, even anger, but his eyes were kind. He reached across, and gently plucked the piece of glass out of my hand. As I watched, a thin dot of blood appeared, seemingly out of nowhere.

And then the teacher grabbed me by the scruff of my neck. He tossed me out of school right there, ordering me to go home. But as I stood in the corridor, the real pain just starting to creep into my hand, I realised that for the first time, I wanted to get back in.

It didn't last. My mom begged them to let me come back, and after a while they did, but I just couldn't concentrate. Prakesh was friendly, and we started spending more time together, but it wasn't enough. When my mom died, a few days after my fourteenth birthday, I told Prakesh I was finished. Not surprisingly, the school didn't come looking for me.

I didn't see him for a long time. It's funny the way this place works. We're packed in so tight, a million people in this little steel ring that was only designed to hold half that, but you can go years without seeing someone. And then, a few months ago, a woman asked me to deliver a package to her son in Gardens. I almost didn't recognise Prakesh at first, but he remembered who I was. He was just a food tech then, another guy in a white lab coat. But he showed me around, gave me some water and some fresh, crisp beans to eat, told me about his work. I realised how much I'd missed him.

Prakesh comes back, bearing a thick plastic flask. He mutters something under his breath when he sees me sitting against the tree, but doesn't protest. Instead, he drops to one knee and hands me the bottle, and I raise it to my lips, drinking deeply. The water is deliciously cold, so cold it almost stings, and before I know it I've drained the bottle.

"You're not done yet," he says, digging some baby tomatoes out of the pocket of his lab coat. As he passes them to me, our hands touch, the warm skin of his fingers brushing mine.

I eat two tomatoes before I stop suddenly, another halfway to my mouth. "This isn't the genetic stuff, is it?"

"Genetic stuff. I love how your mind works sometimes, Riley," he says, and takes a bite himself. "No, this is good old natural veggie. We won't have results on the genetic stuff for another year at least. But once we do—"

"You'll be able to grow millions of plants in a nanosecond and feed the entire station in a day and use your science skills to give me biological rocket boosters so I can fly away. I know, you've told me before."

He scratches the back of his head. "Well, we did have a breakthrough yesterday. We actually got an entire soybean plant to sprout in twenty-four hours. Of course, it would have killed anyone who ate it, but it's a long way from the kids' stuff they were doing before. And gene work isn't the whole picture – the plants need the right minerals to grow. It's been months since we had an asteroid catcher bring back a haul, and the stuff we got from Mars and the moon isn't doing the job."

"Forget the minerals, then. Start doing the genetics on human beings. We don't need minerals to function." I hold up the last tomato, then pop it into my mouth. "Just give us the odd tomato to eat, and we're good to go."

"Yes, because hominid genetic modification worked out *so* well last time. Or don't you remember school history?"

"I think I missed that class."

He looks down, then back up at me, his eyes clouded.

"What?" I say. And then, annoyed: "What?"

"What really happened, Ry? On the run?

"What do you mean?"

"So you managed to fight off an entire crew by yourself? In an ambush? Bullshit, Ry. You got your ass kicked, and now you're lying to me about it."

"I'm not."

He raises his eyebrows. Usually, I laugh at him when he does this – it makes him look like someone's just told him a rude joke – but this time, I can see the frustration in his face. His one hand is digging in the soil, and the dark grains are squishing out from between his fingers. I don't even think he realises he's doing it.

"Why do you always do this?" he says. His voice is quiet, but there's no mistaking the anger. I always forget how quickly his mood can change. He may have stopped me from smashing the tab screen, back in that school room, but as we've got older it's like all my anger has slipped into him.

"Do what?"

"I try to help, and you just shut me out."

"I don't need help." The words sound stupid and petulant, even as I say them. "I can take care of myself, thanks."

"Really?" he says, jabbing a finger at my face. "Is this taking care of yourself?"

"Well, what do you want me to do?" I ask, my voice rising. "You want me to stop running? Other gangs are part of the job, Prakesh. You live with it."

"It's not worth it. Not for this. There are other jobs you could do."

"Oh yeah? Like what?" I pull myself to my feet. The ache in my arches wakes up, starts growling.

He rises to meet me, springing off the tree with frustratingly easy grace. "Anything. You're smart, you could get a job anywhere on this station. But running? For what?"

"For your information, I actually like running."

"I know," he says. "But there's nothing else in your life. You run, and that's it. And if you get hurt like this again? What are you going to do?"

I glare at him. "There's plenty of stuff I do when I'm not running."

His laugh is bitter. "Riley, come on. After all this time, I've never seen you do anything else besides run and play cards. Putting your life in danger for what, a few batteries? Some stolen food? It's not worth it."

"Better than working for nothing in a greenhouse all day," I say. The second the words are out of my mouth, I want to pull them back. Prakesh, however, absorbs them without comment, simply staring at me.

After a while, he says, "What we do here keeps people

alive. In case you haven't noticed, there aren't a lot of us left. And without air, without food, there'd be a lot less. So you can come in here and drink my water, and if you want to get angry with me for it, that's fine. But don't ever tell me I'm working for nothing."

We stare at each other. Our outburst has attracted the attention of another tech, a timid woman with shocking-red hair who's walking nervously towards us. "Is everything all right, Prakesh?" she says. "I can call security if…"

"No, Suki, we're good here," he responds, but he doesn't look away.

"And I was just going," I say, breaking his gaze and shouldering my pack.

His hand is on my shoulder. "Riley, listen…" But I shrug it off and break into a run, leaving them standing beside the tree. Before long, I'm outside the Forest, dashing past a startled Dumar. Letting the rhythm of my movement calm me as I run back into the galleries. People are waking up, walking from their quarters to the mess, to school, to their jobs. As I run, my own anger fades, like a handprint evaporating from a pane of glass, and I lose myself in the crowds.

9

Darnell

The door to Oren Darnell's office is a slab of thick metal, its hinges ringed with rust. It's half open when he arrives, and he shoves it to one side. The bang when it hits the wall is loud enough to shake the giant window that overlooks the Air Lab. One of the control room techs has followed him, wanting to ask him something, and he has to dodge out of the way as it bounces back.

Darnell doesn't even glance at him. "Get out," he says over his shoulder.

The tech knows better than to persist. He scurries out, pulling the door shut behind him. Just before it closes, Darnell bellows, "And tell Reece I want to see him. Now."

The door wavers, then snicks shut.

Darnell turns back to the window. Despite what the tech might think, he isn't angry. He's excited. So excited that he feels like laughing out loud. He smiles instead, his teeth reflected in the window. He flips open the box, upends it, and rolls the eyeball around in his hands. It leaves his palms slightly sticky, but he barely notices.

It's taken so long. So many years of watching and

waiting, of having to associate with the filth that make up most of the station's population. Of having to pretend to the council and the techs and the countless functionaries that he gives a shit about the station's air quality. No more. The eyeball is the final detail – and at long last, he can give this rotten wreck of a station everything it deserves.

He tells himself to stay calm. There are still certain things to take care of. Riley Hale, for example. She hadn't even entered his thoughts as "a thing to take care of" until she walked into the control room. It wasn't just the bruises. Riley Hale had delivered goods to Darnell a dozen times, and he'd never seen her on edge. Not until this particular delivery. Her entire body was tense, like she was plugged into a power socket. So yes, he knew she'd seen inside her pack, even before she made that crack about the cargo being important.

Darnell had wanted to wrap his fingers around that pretty throat right then and there when she turned him down, take care of the problem as soon as it presented itself, but he told himself to hold back. It wouldn't do to kill someone in the Air Lab. Just as it wouldn't do to let her walk free. He's much too close to let things like that cause problems for him.

And he was fair. He gave her a chance to join him. Of course, it won't matter one way or another – she, and he, and everyone else on the station have a lifespan measured in days. But it might have been fun to bring her over. With her speed, she'd have been exceedingly useful. Now, she's just a liability.

He's pleased at the eye's condition – Gray had told him that he'd inject it with a compound he'd developed, some sort of preserving fluid to slow decomposition. He bounces it in his palm. It makes a very soft squidging sound, as if he's handling rotten fruit.

Movement, right at the edge of the Air Lab. It's Hale, sprinting silently down the path between two enormous oaks, heading right for the exit. Darnell can just see the edge of her jacket, flying out behind her.

He seals the eyeball back in its box and sits down at his desk. It's wood, carved from a dead tree – as far as Darnell knows, it's the only piece of wooden furniture on the entire station, maybe even the only piece left in existence. He keeps it polished, shiny with oil.

The desk is dominated by a bonsai tree: a Japanese boxwood, no bigger than his head, with a thin, twisted trunk and puffs of bright green leaves. Darnell keeps a set of shears on his desk, short and stubby, and he reaches for them now. He leans in, grips a twig, and cuts. A single tiny leaf drifts to his desk. He moves, leans forward, cuts again.

Once, there were hundreds of thousands of boxwood trees across Asia. Beautiful trees, with thick, green foliage. All gone. But maybe, Darnell thinks, they might grow again. If no human beings are around to interfere, to cut them down, to destroy their habitats.

The door hinges creak. Reece enters, his long coat sweeping around his legs. Darnell doesn't look up. "You know that tracer, came in earlier?" he says.

"Uh-huh."

"She was ambushed on her way over here. Some gang or other. They'll need a visit. Make her tell you who they were. Be persuasive."

"What about the tracer?"

"Kill her."

10

Riley

I make it as far as the Gardens border before I have to stop. I can feel every muscle in my legs and abdomen, white-hot filaments criss-crossing my body. When I slow to a jog, a stitch springs up in my side, biting deep. My body begs me to bend over, to relieve tension on the muscles, but I force myself to stay upright, breathing long and slow through my nose. My eye socket throbs with pain.

I did it. I finished the job, delivered the cargo, got away clean. I have no idea how the hell I pulled that off, but I did it.

No more jobs today. I am going home, and then I'm going to sleep. Probably forever.

I'm on the bottom level of the sector, and the corridor is blissfully deserted. I let myself lean on the wall. The metal is cold and oily under my palm, so I rest my shoulder on it instead. Then I turn so I've got my back on it. And before I know it, I slide right down the wall. There's a low power box jutting out right where the wall meets the floor, and I sit down on it, my legs splayed out in front of me. My breathing has slowed, and the heat in my muscles has gone from white hot to a sullen red. It'll do. At least until I can get back home.

I can still hear the crowd from the distant corridors behind me. The noise is given a metallic edge by the time it reaches me, twisted and bent by the floor and walls, so that it sounds like a weird alien monster roaming the station.

It takes me a minute to realise that there's another sound too. Footsteps. My eyes fly open, just in time to see a figure stepping towards me, silhouetted by the flickering fluorescents.

The figure stops, raises his hands. "Woah, hey, be cool. I just wanted to ask if you had some food."

I blink. The voice is weirdly familiar. Then my eyes adjust, and I see that it's the tagger I saw earlier. The one I blazed past in the upper-level corridors, just before the border, while I was running to the Air Lab. He's younger than I first thought, little more than a kid, with a bad case of acne and dark hair that sticks to his forehead. His paint can is tucked in his waistband.

If he recognises me from before, he gives no sign, just gives my pack a pleading look. I'm about to tell him to get lost, but then I remember that I already flipped him off once today, and feel kind of bad.

"Sure," I say. I'm almost certain that my bag's empty, but there's always a chance that half a protein bar or something got lost in the bottom. Part of me knows I should stay alert, but surely not even I would be unlucky enough to get jacked twice in one day.

"Thanks," he says, as I zip open my bag and rummage through it. "I haven't had anything to eat all day, and I can't go to the mess hall until I find a job, so – hey, what—"

His words turn into a horrific, bubbling scream. I jerk my head upright just in time to see a flash of metal at his throat, followed by a dark spurt of blood. I bolt to my feet just as the figure behind the tagger shoves him to the side.

I react on instinct, leaning backwards just as the knife flashes out at me. I get a half-second look at my attacker's face – it's Darnell's guard, the one who let me into the control room. What the hell?

He slashes at me again, and I manage to grab his arm, just below the elbow. The tip of the knife nicks my neck, and I hiss in pain. The guard twists away, laughing, then attacks again, driving me back down the corridor. Behind us, the tagger's body twitches as he bleeds out.

I turn to run – there's no way this guy can beat me in a straight sprint. But I barely manage two steps before he grabs the back of my jacket. For a second, it's like we're locked in an insane dance. I'm bending over backwards, leaning into his body. He's dropping his shoulder towards me, the blade close behind it.

I twist to the side, ripping free of his grip, only just managing to stay on my feet. He laughs again. Little needles of terror are shooting through me, but there's something underneath it too: anger. I delivered the cargo clean. *I finished the damn job.* And now Darnell wants me gone? Like I'm a loose end that needs to be snipped off?

No way. Not today.

The guard reaches out for me. He's a good fighter, and fast, but he's easy to read. He wants to pull me in and drive the knife into my belly. So instead of leaning back, like he expects me to, I drop, swinging my right leg in a wide arc.

He spots the move, dodges back, but not before the edge of my shoe clips his ankle. It's just enough. He stumbles, tries to stay upright, then crashes to the ground. His right foot hits the ground, bounces up, comes to a rest on the power box where the wall meets the floor.

I don't let myself second-guess it. I jump as high as I can, and bring both feet down on his kneecap. There's a thin snap, like someone breaking a stick of celery, and then the guard is screaming.

I stumble off him, grab my pack, and run.

11

Prakesh

The glass beaker smashes against the wall. In the silence that follows, the only sound is the gentle hum of the lab's DNA thermocycler.

Prakesh Kumar looks away from the mess of glass, furious with himself. Glass beakers aren't easy to replace. Still, at least he can clear it up before anyone notices. He's by himself in the mobile lab, on the opposite end of the hangar to the main control room. Not that it bothers him. He likes working alone.

Especially when he decides to vent some anger by smashing things.

He grabs a bucket from a nearby tool shelf and crouches down, picking the big pieces off the floor and dropping them inside. Damn thermocycler. He couldn't get it to work – the temperature wouldn't rise, and he had to reset the system three times to get it to budge even a little. By the time he got it working, every muscle in his body felt like it was on an electrical circuit. He didn't even realise what he was doing until the glass was in jagged pieces on the floor.

Except it's not the thermocycler Prakesh is angry with.

Not really. It's a machine. He can understand machines, just like he can understand trees, or algae. When they stop working there's always a solution that you can use to set the problem right – a system reset, a different kind of fertiliser. They're not like human beings.

When he's filled the bucket, he pushes it under the table, telling himself he'll deal with it later. He stands and rubs his eyes, amazed at how tired he is. It'll take a couple of hours before he can send the results for gel electrolysis. Time for a break.

He steps out of the lab, shutting the door behind him, and walks back to the control room, zig-zagging down the walkways between the trees. There's no one around, not even Suki, who's known to stay way past the shift change. No one interrupts him as he walks down the hangar.

Riley's back in his head. He always ends up on the same image of her: the first time she came back to the Air Lab to visit him, after that first delivery. She was jogging to a stop, her hair flying out behind her, a smile playing across her face. He remembers thinking that he'd never seen anyone so at ease with speed, so in love with movement.

Not that it matters. *She won't let you in*, he thinks. *She won't even let you help her when she gets hurt. You're a friendly face to her, someone who can get her some food when she needs it. Nothing more.*

The locker room is at the back of the main lab. The floor is grimy with tracked soil, the lockers bent and rusty. The one Prakesh uses doesn't even shut properly any more, but the only thing he keeps in there is his lab coat, and anybody who wants to steal that is more than welcome. He slips it off his shoulders and shoves it in, shutting the door with a bang. Then he rests his head on the metal and shuts his eyes, just for a second.

When he turns around, Oren Darnell is standing there.

He's standing with his arms folded, his face expressionless. He's close enough for Prakesh to pick out the pores on his skin.

Prakesh tells himself not to freak out. He knows Mr Darnell's reputation – everyone does – but he's not in the habit of messing with the techs. Not unless they cross him. He needs them to keep producing results, so he can stay in the top spot at the Air Lab. Prakesh meets his eyes, even though he really doesn't want to.

"Something I can help you with?" he says.

Darnell doesn't answer. Instead, he grabs Prakesh's shoulders, slamming him up against the lockers. They creak and groan, juddering against his back. He's too stunned to speak, caught too tight to move. His shoulders feel like they're trapped in a vise.

"Where is she?" Darnell says quietly. He could be asking for an update on the electrolysis results.

Prakesh swings his arm up, trying to hit Darnell across the side of the face. Darnell knocks it away, his hand swinging back. Prakesh's anger vanishes, replaced by bright terror. He tries to hit Darnell again, but the lab boss grabs his wrist.

"Do that again, and you'll lose the arm. Where is Riley Hale?"

Prakesh tries to answer. He might as well try to make trees grow using his mind. All the stories, all the little rumours he's heard when he's taking a break with the other techs, are popping up one after the other. It feels as if they're clogging his throat, sealing it shut.

Darnell sighs. He jabs his forearm into Prakesh's neck, banging his head back against the lockers.

Prakesh claws at the arm, desperate for air. There's a tiny sting in his neck. It grows and grows, the pain flooding through his body. He has to scream, he has to, but Darnell clamps a hand over his mouth.

"You're not going to like what happens when you wake up," he says. He's at the end of a very long, dark tunnel, and by the time Prakesh figures out what the words mean, he's gone.

12

Riley

Too close. That was way too close.

Every stride brings another image flashing up. The tagger standing above me. The glint of metal. The sound of his scream, like water burbling through a rusted pipe. If he hadn't been there, if I hadn't stopped in that exact spot...

No. I can't think about it like that. Darnell's guard killed the tagger because he was in the way. If it wasn't him, it would have been someone else. I was the target – and since not even Darnell would risk murdering me in the middle of the Air Lab, he sent his goon to do it for him. It's a good thing I left before...

Oh gods – *Prakesh*.

I'm already running through every memory I can think of, trying to remember if Darnell had ever seen us together. I don't think so. But the last words Prakesh and I said to each other are running over and over in my head.

I should go back. No. No way. I can't show my face in Gardens until I've figured this whole mess out. Stompers? Not a chance. They'll throw me in the brig along with Darnell.

Amira. She'll know what to do.

I keep running, fast as I can, doing my best to push everything else away. But the anger I felt when I was attacked is still rolling in my stomach. It's not just anger at Darnell. It's anger at the ugliness of the station. The dirtiness of it. It's like I've ripped back a scab, one so old that I'd almost forgotten it was there. I feel like I've had a look at the raw flesh underneath.

Enough. Focus on running.

Movement helps. It always does. I let my muscle memory take over, and in no time at all, I'm in the upper-level Apogee corridor that leads to the Nest.

For most people, there are only six levels on Outer Earth. But there are things in this place you won't find on any official map. Vents, wiring ducts, sewerage pipes. And storage units that a person can easily stand up in. These are places that the rest of the station has long since forgotten about. But if you know where to look, you can score yourself a very handy base.

I have to look for a moment to spot the hatch in the ceiling. In the dim light, I can just make out the yellow warning label, its Hindi and Chinese script almost illegible. I break into a run, willing my body to go a little further. It's nine miles from the Air Lab to the Nest in Apogee, and I can feel every single one of them in the arches of my feet.

As I run up to the hatch, I jump towards the wall, launching myself back off it in a reverse tic-tac towards the ceiling. I flatten my hand against the hatch as I pass underneath it, and push – it glides silently upwards and away, the hydraulics Carver built into it working perfectly. I land, and then immediately leap towards the opposite wall for another tac, pushing off and backwards in one smooth move.

I fell on my ass hard the first few times I tried this.

As I jump, I reach up and behind me, grasping the lip of the opening. I relax into the movement, letting my body rock backwards, and then using the forward momentum of the swing to haul myself up through the hatch.

I roll onto my side as I do so. My body screams at me to stay there, but I ignore it, forcing myself to my feet.

The hatch slips back into place with a tiny hiss. The entranceway is almost completely dark, the only light coming from a tiny digital keypad bolted onto the wall behind me. It's the perfect security system: getting up into the storage unit requires either something to stand on, or the moves of a tracer, and even then you've got to know the access code to the inner door. Whoever designed this part of Outer Earth probably didn't plan on it being used this way, but it's worked out pretty well for us.

I have to fiddle with the 9 for a bit before the number appears on the display: the unit's old, salvaged from a discarded piece of machinery, and although Carver works hard to maintain it, it's slowly wearing down.

The keypad soon gives two welcoming beeps. I push on the door, but instead of swinging open, it remains locked shut. Frowning, I look at the keypad. Right before the display resets itself, I catch sight of the code I entered. It was correct.

I do *not* have time for this.

I punch it in again, but still the metal door refuses to budge. I'm about to enter the code a third time when I realise exactly what the problem is.

"Carver, open this door!" I shout, not caring if there's anybody in the passage below to hear me. I hammer on the metal, and the sound sets my ears ringing.

There's movement from the other side, and then a voice: "That kind of tone won't get you anywhere. Say please."

The attempt to control myself lasts perhaps two seconds. "I swear, Carver, if you don't open this door right now, I will tear it off the wall and make you eat it."

I hear muted laughter, and then the click of the lock being released. The door opens, and as I step through into the Nest I reach for the first thing I can see – in this case, an old battery lying on a nearby chair – and hurl it across the room at Aaron Carver. As much as I wish it wasn't the case, his reflexes are as good as ever. The battery smashes harmlessly into the wall with a clang before bouncing out of sight.

There's a small box in his hand, and I can see the thin wires snaking across the floor to the entrance. He's perched at his workbench, a mess of something black and spiky on the table in front of him. We have him to thank for our super-light backpacks. They're better than the canvas packs we used to use – with those, the cargo would be shaken to pieces inside of ten minutes.

None of which stops him being incredibly annoying.

There's a gasp on my right. Then a voice, high and musical: "Who beat up your *face?*"

I look round to find the Twins: Yao Shen and Kevin O'Connell. Yao is on the right, sitting cross-legged on the floor, staring goggle-eyed at my bruises. She's a wispy, elfin thing, with curious eyes and a tiny bud-shaped mouth. When I first saw her, I thought she was way too young and fragile to be a tracer, but she's got some serious moves: the bigger the jump, the harder she throws herself at it.

Kev is seated next to her. While Yao is tiny, Kev is enormous: a bruiser with upper arms that look like thick steel cables. There's a book next to his knee – *the* book, rather, a copy of *Treasure Island* that we've each read so many times the jacket has disintegrated and most of the pages are torn.

The Twins take jobs together, run together, fight together. From what Amira has told me, they aren't lovers, but sometimes I find it hard to believe. I once referred to them as the Twins for a joke, and the name stuck.

I rub my eye socket absently. "Got in a fight," I say, in answer to Yao's question. "Where's Amira?"

"Out on a job," says Carver. He's also staring at my face, his eyes narrowed. As usual, he's wearing a sleeveless T-shirt – red today – and his blond hair is perfect, the goggles on his forehead positioned just so.

"Who'd you get in a fight with?" Yao asks, squirming to her feet. "Everyone on the station? Did you win?"

"I'm fine." Now that I've stopped running, the anxiety has come rushing back. Does Darnell know which crew I run with? Does he know where we live? If they get here, can we fight our way out? And Prakesh...

"Don't look fine," says Kev, his voice rumbling. He starts to get to his feet. It's like a crane arm on a construction ship unfolding, with heavy joints locking into place.

"We should go find 'em," Yao says. "Who were they, Riley? I'll tear their legs off and play catch with their kneecaps."

"Yao, be still," Kevin says, without looking at her. Yao pouts and subsides, but she's still looking at me, anger and worry on her face.

"Leave her alone, kids," says Carver, turning back to his workbench and picking up a soldering iron. "She's good. What're a few bumps and bruises to someone like Riley Hale? It's all part of the job."

I've put up some pretty thick walls in my mind to keep it together today, but Carver's words go right through them, like they're nothing more than cloth. Without another word, I walk over to his workbench. He's set a bunch of parts to one side, neatly arranged on the scarred surface, and I slam my fist down right in the middle. The parts scatter, jingling as they bounce off the bench.

"The hell—" Carver says.

I get right in his face. "Do you know what I've been carrying all day? An eyeball. Ripped from someone's skull. I've gone through ambushes and assassination attempts, and I'm a little wired right now. So do me a favour, and don't tell me what is and isn't part of the job."

Carver is looking at me like I've gone insane. Kev and Yao are staring, open-mouthed.

"Well," says a voice. "I'm so glad things didn't fall apart while I was gone."

Amira Al-Hassan is standing by the door, her arms folded, her eyes locked on mine.

13

Riley

If she hadn't spoken, none of us would have noticed Amira come in. She's deathly quiet, always has been, and runs as if her feet aren't touching the ground. The jumps that I stumble and crash on, she lands with gentle ease, soft and hushed as a kiss.

She has to bend her head slightly to come through the door. Amira's older than me by a good ten years, and is dressed simply, in a grey tank top and cargo pants. Around her neck is a faded red scarf, the frayed ends falling down her back. Her pack hangs loosely from one hand.

She walks over to Carver's bench, taking in my bruises. "This is a story I have to hear," she says, before reaching inside her pack and pulling out a box of protein bars. "I got these from the job. Let's have some breakfast."

"Yeah," says a dazed Carver, getting to his feet. "Good idea."

I sit down on the pile of mattresses in the corner. It was a little hard to stay standing – my body seems to give up all at once, the strength flowing out of my legs. My dad's flight jacket bunches up around me, the sleeves pushing down over my hands.

The Nest doesn't look like much. It's just two narrow interconnected rooms, low ceilinged, with hissing pipes scaling the walls. The room that houses Carver's workbench is where we tend to hang out – the other one has an air shower and chemical toilet, which he's hooked into the main system. People who come here say the place smells. It probably does, what with five Devil Dancers living right on top of each other – the Nest being the size it is, it's not really up to holding a lot of people. But I don't think I've noticed a smell for years. It's home.

My gaze strays to the colours on the wall by my head. Abstract shapes in shades of red and green and black and gold. Yao's mural. None of us are really sure what she's painting – sometimes, I don't even think she knows. The homemade tattoo ink she traded for might have been too old and toxic to go into skin, but it works great on the walls – even if Carver did complain that he'd been wanting to trade for a new wrench instead.

Amira tosses me a protein bar, and I catch it without thinking. "So, Riley," she says, arranging herself on Carver's chair. "Let's hear why you're carrying body parts. And how you *know* you've been carrying body parts."

The gummy, chewy protein slabs taste faintly sweet and stick to the teeth in stubborn little clumps, but they keep you going forever – after even one, you feel like you've had a full meal. They're hard to come by, so we dig into them, washing them down with gulps of water from our stash. We prefer food we can get ourselves to anything from the mess halls; the food there is barely edible, cooked into mush, and some of the workers won't let you eat if you don't have a sanctioned job. Being a tracer doesn't count.

Between bites, I tell them what happened – the chase,

the ambush, Darnell, all of it. Amira doesn't speak while she eats, using her left hand to take large bites of the protein bar. Her right hand rests on the workbench, and I notice that the stumps where her index and middle fingers used to be are raw and red. She's been rubbing them again; most of the time, she doesn't even realise she's doing it. Her little souvenirs from the lower sector riots, years ago. From running the Core without a thermo-suit, going from Apogee to Apex via the sub-zero hell of the fusion reactor, carrying a bomb on a delay timer. Anarchists had set it up, but she managed to pull it free and run.

Frostbite might have taken her fingers, but after she jettisoned the bomb from the dock on the other side, Amira was a hero. She was offered a seat on the council, where her parents before her had sat. But I guess after running the Core, council politics don't do it for you.

Hence the Dancers. Hence, us.

After a hundred years, it's got a lot harder to replace or fix anything on the station, so transporting objects and messages is tougher than it used to be – especially with gangs waiting to snatch them. Tracers are the network that allows it to happen, and the Devil Dancers are among the best crews on Outer Earth. There are plenty of others, but under Amira's leadership, we've developed a pretty solid rep.

When I finish my story, the crew sits in silence for a moment, and then everyone tries to talk at once. Carver and Yao are angrily demanding we bring the fight to Darnell, but Amira raises a hand, and they reluctantly calm themselves. Carver, muttering obscenities, turns back to his bench, grabbing his goggles and pulling them down roughly over his eyes, making his hair stick up in strange directions. Amira just stares at me, and this time there's a flash of reproach in her eyes.

"Not good," Kev says to Amira, giving an uncharacteristic shudder.

Yao agrees, nodding furiously. "There was that woman who went missing a while ago. She worked in the mess. And I did that run to Chengshi and heard about a sewerage tech who went missing. I didn't think about it before, but what if it's the guy who gave you the cargo?"

We all stare at her. She has a damn good point.

"Imagine if we caught the guy," she says, her eyes glittering.

"Are you insane?" The goggles have been yanked off, and Carver is staring at Yao as if she's grown an extra head. "Are we actually talking about going after someone who sends eyeballs by special delivery? No. Hell no. I like breathing. And by the way, nice work, Riley. I always enjoy ending my day with a fight to the death against the minions of a psychotic lab boss."

"I *wasn't* followed," I say. It's almost a snarl, covering up the uncertainty I feel.

Amira has remained silent, her hands clasped before her, tilted back with the fingertips just touching her lips. She looks at me. "We're not supposed to know what we carry," she says. "That's the job. That's the only way we survive, and you know it. You should never have looked in your pack – I trained you better than that."

A hot flush comes to my cheeks, but I hold her gaze.

She shrugs. "You got us into this, Riley. What do you think we should do?"

I take a deep breath, trying to push my thoughts into some sort of order. "Darnell's going to want revenge," I say. "The man he sent after me won't be the last. That means everyone here is at risk."

"So what? We can take 'em," says Carver. Amira raises her hand, silencing him.

"It's more than that though," I say. "We shouldn't have to do this. We shouldn't have to be a part of whatever... sick game this is."

"Mmm," says Amira. "So what do you suggest?"

"Right now, we're the only people outside of Darnell and the guy who gave me the package—"

"Gray."

"Right. Gray. Outside of them, it's just us. So we bring the fight to them. Let them know we don't go down easy – starting with Gray."

"Why not hit the big bad guy first?" says Yao, but Amira interrupts. "No, Riley's right," she says. "This merchant – this Gray – he picked us because he knew that we do not wish to know what we carry. He took advantage of our trust." She shakes her head. "I won't allow that. Attacking Darnell isn't the answer – not right now, anyway – but we can take care of Gray ourselves. Send a message."

Yao is gagging. "I think I ate one of his onions the other day. What if he fertilises them with *human blood*?" Carver rolls his eyes.

Amira glances at me. "We're probably going to have to deal with this head-on at some point. Riley – you've dealt with Darnell more than the rest of us have. Anything we need to know?"

I let out a long breath. "He's nasty. Keeps a low profile, but he practically runs some of the gangs up there. Water points mostly – he's got connections, so he shuts them down until people have something worth trading."

"So it won't just be him we're facing?"

"Probably not."

"Stompers?" says Kevin, echoing my earlier thoughts.

Carver throws his arms up. "Great idea, Kev. Because we have such a great relationship with the stompers anyway."

"No stompers," says Amira. "This is our problem. We'll deal with it." She turns to the Twins. "We'll need as much intelligence as we can get. I want you to go to

Gardens and find a way into the Air Lab. Observe Darnell, see what he's doing, and report back. If he really is going to come after us, we need to know about it."

With only the briefest of shared glances, the Twins head out, dropping through the hatch. I can hear their soft footfalls disappearing down the corridor.

Amira turns back to us. Her eyes are cold slits. "We're going back to the market. Time to meet this Arthur Gray."

She jerks her chin at my bruises. "Are those going to be a problem?"

I shake my head. "I'll live."

"Good."

When we drop out the hatch, the corridor is quiet, with no sound save for the rumble of the station. But as we start jogging towards the gallery, there's a shout from the far end of the corridor. Someone yelling my name.

I whirl, bracing myself for the worst – the Lieren, or another attack from Darnell – but then I see it's a tracer, sprinting towards us from the far end. He's an older guy, one I've seen around, with flecks of grey in his shoulder-length hair. Not someone I know.

"You're Riley Hale?" he asks, jogging to a halt.

I nod. "That's right." My fists are curled into tight balls. With an effort of will, I force them apart. Carver and Amira are a little way ahead of me, looking back quizzically at the new arrival.

"Cargo for you," says the tracer, reaching into the pocket of his jacket. He thrusts something at me – it takes me a second to realise what I'm looking at.

"Is that – paper?" says Carver.

Outside of our copy of *Treasure Island*, I don't think I've ever seen a sheet of loose paper. It feels strangely soft in my hands. The tracer gives a curt nod, and takes off in the direction he came from.

"What is it?" Amira asks.

My stomach is doing that long, slow roll again, and the noise as I unfold the paper is too loud in the cramped corridor. I read the message, written in a tiny cursive script, and my heart starts thudding again in my chest.

"Riley?" says Amira.

I thought Darnell would send more people after us. But this is worse. Much, much worse.

Dear Miss Hale,

You will die quickly. Prakesh Kumar will not. I suggest you trade your life for his. And when you come back to the Air Lab, come alone.

Warmest regards,

Oren Darnell

14

Darnell

The foreman tries to tell him that the monorail is full. The man is new, barely a month into the job, and all he's concerned about are the food shipments to Chengshi and Apogee and New Germany. He doesn't notice the other workers edging away from him, doesn't see the averted eyes or the sudden interest in train schedules and food manifests.

Darnell puts an arm around the foreman. "What's your name?"

"Judd, Sir." The foreman's words come out a little muffled, mostly because his head is buried in Darnell's armpit.

"Judd. OK. Do you know my bodyguard? Goes by the name of Reece?"

Judd tries to shake his head, doesn't quite manage it.

"He got his knee snapped in two a couple of hours ago. Mostly because he didn't do exactly what I asked him to do."

Darnell lets him go. Judd stumbles away, staring at his boss. Darnell points to the crate behind him – a big, sealed metal box on a wheeled pallet, labelled Soja Japonica. "Load my crate, Judd," he says.

He can see the questions in Judd's eyes – like why another crate of soybeans needs to be loaded onto a monorail already full of them. Or why Darnell wants to accompany the shipment personally. But by the time Darnell climbs aboard the back monorail car, his crate is loaded and strapped down. With a rumble, the train pulls out of the loading dock.

It's black inside the tunnels. The big halogen bulb on the train's cabin doesn't reach this far back, and Darnell has to hold on to the crates for balance. There used to be dozens of monorails trundling around the inside of the ring – it was the station's public transport system. But it became impossible to maintain, and now monorail use is restricted to food shipments and council use only.

The train passes an abandoned station, the platform thick with dust. There's evidence of human habitation – pieces of trash, a clean space in the dust where someone might have bedded down – but it's empty now. Just before the darkness swallows them again, Darnell spots the mark on one of the tunnel supports. A rough white cross, spray-painted on the metal.

Darnell gauges the train's speed. Slow enough. Working quickly, he uses his knife to cut through the straps that tie the crate to the train car, then hauls the lid off. Prakesh Kumar is inside, still unconscious, his body twisted awkwardly.

Oren Darnell reaches in, lifting the comatose technician up. Then he hurls him off the train.

Prakesh bounces off the side of the tracks, rolling to a stop. Darnell sees his mouth twitch, form a groan of pain, but he doesn't wake up, and the sound is lost in the rumble of the monorail. Darnell jumps, landing squarely on the side of the tracks.

He nearly falls. Even overloaded and moving slowly, the monorail shakes the tunnel. The surface under his feet vibrates, like it's alive. But he just bends his knees a little more, leans into it, and lands clean.

He reaches down, grabbing Prakesh and swinging him across his shoulder. Arthur Gray calls the stuff quicksleep. Darnell likes to carry some in his pocket, a small pouch filled with tiny capped syringes.

He stills himself for a moment, letting his eyes get used to the darkness again. He quickly spots the door, recessed slightly into the wall of the tunnel. He walks over to it, activates the entry keypad, sending a dull white glow into the tunnel. Gray didn't want to give Darnell the code to what he calls his work room. Darnell made him change his mind.

He punches it in, and the door locks disengage, the sound echoing around the cramped tunnel. The passage beyond the door is dimly lit, the metal walls pitted and scarred. Hefting his loads, Darnell heads down the passage. After he dumps the idiot tech, he can head back to the Air Lab, and await the return of Riley Hale. He won't even have to dose her. She'll come with him willingly, if she knows what's good for her. He can give her to Arthur Gray as a…

Darnell stops, listening closely.

The door hasn't clicked shut behind him.

He looks over his shoulder. The door is slightly ajar. His eyes move to the bottom, where the toe of a shoe is positioned in the space between the frame and the door.

Darnell charges. He uses the tech's body as a battering ram, slamming into the door. It flies open, sending the owner of the shoe stumbling backwards. Darnell lets go of Prakesh, hurling him outwards, and his pursuer crumples under the dead-weight, crashing onto the track.

Movement. To his right. A figure leaps at him, barrelling out of the darkness. Darnell back-hands the attacker. She cries out, and blood spatters across his hand. He can't see it in the darkness, but he can feel it, hot and sticky, and it brings a smile to his face.

The first one is up. Darnell can't see his features in the darkness, but he's enormous, with arms like tree trunks. For a split second, Darnell hesitates. But as the man gets to his feet, he makes the mistake of glancing down in horror at the tech's body.

Darnell lifts two syringes out of his pocket, flips the caps off. They bounce away across the floor. The first needle only scratches the giant, but it's enough to get some quicksleep into his blood, and in seconds he's stumbling, throwing uncoordinated punches. Darnell dodges, dodges again, then plants the needles right in the giant's chest.

The man collapses almost instantly, dropping first to his knees, and then flat onto his face. There's an incoherent yell of fury, and then the little one is back.

She rushes towards Darnell, her shoulder low, aiming for his legs. He snags her by the neck before she can get close, lifting her up. She kicks out at him, tries to scratch the exposed skin on his arm, but it's no use. His hand goes all the way around her neck, locking her in a vice.

There's some light coming from Gray's passage. Darnell can just make out his attacker. She's a tiny woman, her skin spangled with colourful tattoos. High up on her neck, curving around to her throat, are two words in a delicate, curlicued font. *Devil Dancers.*

Riley Hale's crew. So.

Her struggles are getting more urgent. Darnell's fingers clench. A little more pressure, and her fragile spine will snap. And there's his blade, tucked in his belt. A single short cut will open her throat.

No. Better to keep his options open – for now. Darnell

pulls out another syringe. He takes the cap in his mouth, grips it in his teeth, pulls and spits. The girl's eyes go wide, and then he jabs the needle into her neck and they defocus, the irises rolling back.

He drops her, and the tunnel is silent again.

15

Riley

I read the note again. And the horrible sick feeling in my chest begins to grow. Anger blooms like a poisonous flower.

Trembling, I pass the paper to Amira, and she and Carver scan it. When she looks up, her face is grim. "We should stick to the plan," she says quietly.

I stare at her. "Stick to the . . . no. I have to fix this. I'm going back to the Air Lab."

"He'll kill you if you do."

"He'll kill Prakesh if I don't."

"Slow up, Riley," says Carver. I'm expecting a wisecrack, but his voice is calm. "Amira's right. You don't just rip out someone's eyeball or hold kidnapped techs in the Air Lab – he'll have somewhere quiet and out of the way. And if you show up in the Labs, he'll kill you *and* Prakesh."

"So what do we do?" I say. My voice cracks on the last word.

"We stick to the plan," Amira says again. "We find Gray. We track him. He leads us right to them."

Another burst of guilt as I remember that we sent Kev and Yao over to Darnell's. "What about the Twins?"

"They can handle themselves," Amira says.

She doesn't wait for a response, taking off down the corridor in a run. After a moment, Carver and I join her, running in tight formation. As we turn the corner, we see more people in the corridor ahead, right in our path.

Amira yells over her shoulder, "Riley, point!" and I accelerate, bursting ahead to overtake her.

There's an art to running in a group. You have to move in single file, creating as narrow a profile as possible. Even then, you have to know when to break formation to cut through the crush of people. The fastest tracer sets the pace and the route, and I pick the quickest one I know, heading back past the mess hall and into the maze of corridors on the bottom level.

There are crowds we have to fight through by the habs – the ones in this part of the sector are dorm-style, designed to hold a lot of people. There aren't any mining or factory facilities in Apogee, and over the years more and more people have moved in. There are plenty of families here, which means the corridors are always crowded and noisy – mostly with kids, no matter what the hour is.

As we descend, I come round a corner on a stairwell to find a ball flying right at my head. I have to spin to the side to avoid it, nearly colliding with the wall. Amira knocks the ball back without stopping – it's nothing more than rags held together with tight strips of cloth. The kids are in a tight group at the top of the stairs, and one of them catches the ball above his head, a huge smile on his face. I have to suppress the urge to shout at him. How can he be so happy when Prakesh is...

I fight it off. Let my movements and the rhythm of my breathing take over. Every so often, when the crush forces us to break out of single file, I'll catch a glimpse of the other two Dancers cutting in alongside me.

I might have pure speed on my side, but Amira moves with a devastating economy, each foot placed exactly, perfectly balanced, her shoulders tilted back and her eyes on the horizon. Her scarf billows out behind her, the faded red material catching the light.

Carver's technique is less precise, but his sheer brute strength and long arms mean he can take the biggest of jumps with ease. As we near the market, we reach a small open area, where the passage we're in narrows to a dead end by a bank of terminals. Another walkway runs parallel, above and to the left. Amira and I have to tic-tac off the opposite wall to reach it, but Carver just flings himself upwards in one huge leap, hauling himself over.

Sometimes, the crush of the crowds forces us away from each other, but we always link back up. Just when I think I've got ahead of them, Amira will appear, or Carver, shooting out of a darkened passage where the lights have burned out, or slipping through a crowd. It feels horribly wrong to be running away from where Prakesh is, but Amira's right. The only way is to stick to the plan.

The crush gets thicker the closer we get to the market. More and more often, we're having to spread out to find the gaps. But we've made good time, and we soon reach the huge hangar doors marking the entrance. Merchants have spilled out the doors, their makeshift tables jumbled together. The air is hot, thick with smoke from improvised forges and furnaces. I can smell iron, and spices.

My throat is parched, and I'm grateful when Amira pulls a small flask out of her pocket and passes it over. There's not a lot, but we manage a few gulps between us. We passed a few water points on the way over here, but I didn't think to stop at any of them. They're all over Outer Earth: machines set into the walls of corridors and galleries where you can get clean water, purified from recycled human waste, connected by a nerve system of pipes and filters that extends across the whole station. It's nasty when you think hard about it, but it's also the only source of water we've got.

"What now, boss?" says Carver as he passes the flask back.

Amira takes a final swig and runs a hand across her mouth. "We go in. Riley, stay out of sight, no matter what. Wait a few minutes before you follow us."

"Got it."

Amira and Carver move off, walking slowly through the massive doors. Soon, they're lost in the sprawl. I wait a few moments more, then follow, ducking my way under an awning and cutting to the left.

The hangar is enormous – they used to build ships here. The noise rises to ear-splitting levels as I enter, not only from the bustling crowds but from the merchants trying to shout over each other. Everywhere, people barter vegetables, scrap metal, batteries, machinery, tiny packets of spices haggled over in dark corners. Beetles sizzle on fat-caked metal. There are piles of silkworm larvae, barely cooked, served in dirty cloth bags. I had some once, and I'm glad it was only once.

To the right, a burst of sparks shoots out across the stalls as a man demonstrates a homemade plasma cutter, filthy goggles pulled down over his eyes.

There's at least one market in every sector. People used to rely completely on the mess for food, back when everybody had a job and showing up for work was the only way to get on the food list. They'd go to work at the Gardens, or lifting crates in the ship docks, or on maintenance crews assigned to maintain the pipes and power lines. But when the number of people here grew larger than the amount of available jobs, people started taking care of themselves.

"Riley," someone says, and I turn to find Old Madala grinning at me.

Short and stooped, he's lost most of his teeth, save for the odd fuzzy, yellow stump. The left sleeve of his overalls is tied at the shoulder, flopping loosely in place of his missing arm. He's a regular client, a vegetable grower – our last run for him netted us a thick bunch of sweet, crunchy carrots. I don't even think he has another spot on the station; he just seems to sleep under his table, relying on the other merchants to keep an eye on his goods.

His toothless smile widens. "You not come see me for long time there," he says in his odd patois. "Where you been?"

"Just busy. Around. Thanks for the carrots, by the way."

"You want some more? I got a job for you, if you like." He holds up his hand, and I see he's carrying a small parcel, wrapped in tattered oilcloth.

I shake my head, forcing myself to stay calm. "No, I'm on another run right now, but I'll tell Kev to come find you."

"OK, no problem. But come by soon, eh? You don't want to leave an old man lonely now, do you?"

He gives a lascivious wink. Coming out of anybody else, it would be creepy, but Madala has this way about him that makes it hard to get angry at him.

"I will," I say, and lean close. "Listen, I want to ask you something."

He raises his eyebrows quizzically. "Information? I tell you things? Gonna cost you, you know."

I pout. "Oh come on," I say. "We've been doing business for a long time. You can spot me this one."

He barks a short laugh. "True. True. What you wanna know?"

"Anything you can tell me about the guy who sells onions over by Takashi's. Gray."

His expression is puzzled. “Gray? Nothing here. Not much I know ’bout him. He stay quiet, keep his business his business, you know? I never get any trouble from him. S’good. We need more like that.”

“Do you know where he lives?”

Madala rubs his chin, then jerks his finger upwards. “Up on top levels, I think. But thinking now, my friend Indira, she live there too. Take her long time to get up and down every day, not good with her leg.”

I interrupt him. “What’d she say?”

He looks me in the eye. “He never there. He never go back. I think he sleep somewhere else maybe.”

I grip his hand and squeeze. “Thanks, Madala. We’ll come find you when we’re done, all right?”

He winks again before turning and moving back into the smoke, ducking under another shower of sparks.

I move along the wall of the hangar. Ahead of me, two musicians have set up: a man carrying an ancient, battered guitar, and a young girl, barely a teen. She’s singing, and a small crowd has started to gather, drawn by her voice. Her song is fragile, brittle, but it carries over the wallah of the market.

I want to stay and listen – she’s singing in Hindi, a language I can only mutter a few words in, but her voice is haunting, soft. There’s no time to stop. Not now. So I push through the group of people who have gathered to listen.

And as I do so, I feel eyes on my back. I turn, expecting danger, but finding no one. It’s a moment before I catch sight of a woman, staring at me through the crowd. She’s around sixty, her head covered by a blue scarf, and she has the oddest expression on her face; deep sadness mixed with…something else. Before I can react, she vanishes, turning back into the crowd.

Whoever she was, she can wait. I force myself to keep

moving, pushing through the crowd, away from the singer.

As I move towards the back of the hangar, I pass under the massive outline of the station spray-painted on the wall. Not for the first time, I wonder how they even conceived this place. It would have been so much easier to build a city on Earth, underground maybe. But Outer Earth is what happens when a bad idea gets a lot of backers. People can be pretty stupid sometimes. Especially if they're in government, and have something to prove.

Split the ring into six sectors, running clockwise from Apex through Gardens, Chengshi, Apogee, New Germany and Tzevya, all the way round the ring. The names are old, given to the sectors by the first people who came here. Some of the names are hangovers from where they lived back on Earth; places that don't even exist any more. I sometimes wonder what old Germany was really like. What it would have been like to live there, or in China, where the word Chengshi came from.

Run a monorail round the inner edge of the ring, and there you go: one space station, three hundred miles above the Earth, fit for habitation until the sheer amount of population growth pops it like a grape.

It's weird to think that the floor below us is really the outer wall of the station. Thanks to its ring shape, the floors of Outer Earth are all slightly curved, although the curve is so imperceptible that you have to concentrate hard to see it, even when you're running around it – that'll happen when the ring itself has an eighteen-mile circumference. The higher you go, the closer you actually get to the centre of the ring, although the distance is relatively so small that you can't feel any change in gravity.

The spokes running out from the Core meet the ring at Apogee and Apex. Enter the path to the Core, through the ceiling of Level 6 in Apogee, and keep running, and pretty soon you'll be in zero-G. The further in you go, the lighter you get.

Through the haze in the market, I see Takashi's Bar, at the far end of the hangar. It used to be a reclaimed office, the only actual building in the hangar. Takashi himself died in the riots years ago, but the bar kept his name, and it's been selling homebrew for as long as I can remember – as well as a regular supply of super-pricey weed, if you know who to talk to.

Takashi's is right up against the wall of the market – right where the escape pods used to be. People have taken them over the years, cutting themselves loose, refusing to believe that there's nothing left on Earth to go back to. Most of the pods had been stripped for parts before they even got there, their fuel tanks drained dry. Didn't stop people from taking them.

The last one was shot out of Outer Earth decades ago. There are ghost stories about them: pods that never made it back home, that are still floating through the void.

I tear my eyes away from the gaps in the wall. And it's then that I see him. Arthur Gray.

I didn't pay a lot of attention to him when I picked up the cargo. He has a face you'd forget instantly if you passed over it in the crush. He's nearly bald, with just a few thin wisps of white hair around his ears. His tunic is stained brown, although the stains are liquid somehow – more sweat than grime.

Gray is leaning over his table, a dirty box of onions behind him, deep in conversation with a buyer. I duck behind a stack of crates, and watch as they talk. He and the buyer reach some kind of agreement, and strike palms. And then, Gray smiles, and it's all I can do not to run screaming towards him, leaping over the table and wrapping my hands around his throat. Because his smile is the most awful thing I've seen.

I'm halfway through calculating my jump distance and working out whether I should skip the chokehold and just kick him in the face when I realise that Gray is packing up. He's closing his boxes, pulling an old, rusty chain over them and clicking a solid padlock shut. He busies himself with securing the boxes to a nearby wall strut.

Amira and Carver. Surely they'll have seen him too. But as I scan the stalls again, I can't pick them out of the throng.

Gray heads off through the crowd, moving with surprising speed. I look around, expecting to see someone slip from their hiding place and give chase, but there's nobody. He's heading for a gap between two stalls piled high with scrap; in seconds, he'll be gone, vanished into the crowd. Amira might have warned me to stay hidden, but I can't let him slip away.

The part of my mind still working properly is screaming at me. There's no proof he even knows Prakesh exists. Following him could be a giant waste of time – and besides, you can't risk getting near him. Let Amira and Carver do it.

I step out from behind the crates, and take off into the market, after Gray.

16

Darnell

By the time he's finished dragging the two tracers and the technician inside, Darnell is dripping with sweat. It sticks his shirt to his back and runs in rivulets down his chest.

The big one was the worst. Darnell couldn't lift him up; he had to grab him under the arms, pull him down the passage. He's in an ugly mood. The joy he felt when he received the eyeball has burned away.

He straightens up, his shoulders aching. Gray's work room doesn't have a lot in it – a few benches, a couple of mobile storage containers. A big metal table, suspiciously clean. Darnell's gaze falls back on the unconscious trio. Should he restrain them somehow? He knows where the cuffs and the zip ties are, in the storage area at the back. Gray once showed Darnell what he called his toys; the knives and pliers and handheld blowtorches, all arranged on neatly labelled shelves.

He shakes his head. He needn't bother with restraints. He's seen quicksleep in action before – they'll be out for hours, which gives him plenty of time, and even when they wake up, they'll be too groggy to do anything.

Gray. The man is meticulous. Fastidious, even. But even meticulous men make mistakes, and Gray's mistake has made things exceptionally complicated. Darnell is so close to his goal that he feels as if he can reach out and touch it. But he has only got this far by being meticulous himself, by minimising error.

He licks his lips, and looks back at his prisoners.

Even small mistakes can have consequences that spiral out of control. He can't risk those mistakes. And he definitely can't risk someone like Gray making them for him.

He pulls a metal chair off a stack on one side of the room, and sits down heavily. He'll need to get back to the Air Lab soon, to take care of Hale. But first, he's going to have a little talk with Arthur Gray.

17

Riley

The worst thing a tracer can do is run in the dark.

There are parts of the station we call black runs: areas where the lights have burned out and plunged the surroundings into darkness. It's not just about injury; it's the gangs too, lurking in the shadows, just waiting for a rookie tracer to take an easy shortcut.

And the number one place to avoid? The darkest part of Outer Earth? The monorail tracks running around the inside of the ring.

Unless a food train is coming through, the tunnels are black as death – cold and silent. When the station started getting really crowded, people tried sleeping in the tunnels, but after a few got crushed under the monorail, everybody else got the message.

I have a feeling in my gut that the tracks are exactly where Gray is going. I should wait for Amira. But there's no way I'm letting Gray get away. Not when he might be my only link to Prakesh. I keep my distance from him, trying to blend into the stream of people in the market. I've never had to tail someone before; usually, I'm running away from trouble, not towards it.

To get to the tracks, you've got to climb to the top level and enter via one of the old platforms. Gray pauses at the market entrance, and I tense, ready to slip behind a nearby stall if he turns around. But instead, he tilts his face upwards for a moment, then resumes trudging, heading out towards the nearby stairwell. He begins to climb, taking long, purposeful strides.

Still no sign of Amira, or Carver. I swallow hard, and keep on him.

The crush thins out as we ascend, and by the time we reach Level 6, the stairs are all but deserted. As I suspected, he heads straight for the monorail platform, climbing the last set of stairs onto track level. This time, I hang back until he's out of sight.

I count to ten, then quietly climb the stairs to the platform.

I haven't been here in a while, and I'm surprised to find that the digital readouts still work. There are luminous orange holograms above the tracks, meant to indicate when the next train will arrive. They're just flashing gibberish now, endless lines of meaningless code, but they bathe the platform in a warm glow. A couple of the fluorescent lights are working, too – not even flickering. The floor is made of black steel plates, and the walls are lined with dusty benches. Metal columns sprout from the ground beside the tracks.

I close my eyes and listen. There – very faint: the sound of footsteps, heading off down the tunnel to my left. Gently, I lower myself from the platform to the track below. The light from the platform ends where the tunnel begins, cut off, as if it's run up against an invisible barrier. My hand rests on the edge on the platform.

Terror grips tight. I've seen nothing of Carver or Amira since I left the market. I'm breaking every rule we have: never go into the tunnels, never run in the dark, and never go off on your own to tail someone while breaking the above two rules.

I take a deep breath, and step into the darkness of the tunnel.

I have to force myself to pause so my eyes can adjust. In the distance, I can hear Gray's footsteps, getting fainter and fainter. Even so I wait until I can make out the edges of the track, then slowly make my way along it. I've shifted onto the balls of my feet, trying to move as silently as possible. If a train comes along, I'm finished, but I calm myself by thinking that if Gray has a hideout here, then he'll know when it's safe to walk the tracks.

Air whistles down the tunnel. In the darkness, I place a hand on the wall to steady myself. The sound of my fingers on it is dull and faint, the metal slightly greasy to touch. The walls of Outer Earth are several yards thick to protect us from radiation, but it still feels as if the vacuum is sucking at my hand, inches away, scrabbling at the wall. It's so easy to forget that we're in space, that the station is just a tiny metal capsule floating in the void.

The footsteps have stopped. I freeze, listening hard. How long have I been walking? Is he still ahead of me?

But then I hear his breathing, haggard and rough, right next to me, and it's all I can do not to scream. Instead, I quickly flatten myself against the tunnel wall. I can hear him moving now, a faint rustle of cloth, then the tiny glow of a keypad. He's up ahead on the opposite side, his back to me. The beeps as he punches in the code seem as loud as klaxons. There's a click, and suddenly light floods the tunnel. He steps through, and the door shuts behind him with a resounding slam, plunging the tunnel into darkness again. When the echo fades, there's the only sound of my heartbeat, so loud that I'm sure he must be able to hear it behind the door.

I hop the tracks, and run my hands over the keypad, mentally kicking myself for not thinking this far ahead. *Of course* he'd have a lock on the door. He wasn't just going to leave it open for anybody to find. I look around, my eyes searching the gloom for anything that could help, but see nothing. Carver would know how to hack this thing, and if I'd waited for him . . . I swear under my breath, and I'm about to turn back to the keypad when I glance up, and stop dead.

Surely not even I can be that lucky.

One of the plates in the roof is loose. There's just enough light to see that it's pushed very slightly to one side, with darkness beyond the opening.

I have no idea where it goes, or if I'll even be able to squeeze through, but it's the only option I've got. Getting into it is going to be tricky. I consider tic-taccing off the wall, as I would to enter the Nest, but that's no good. It'll be way too noisy. No, there's got to be another way.

I look around, and see the struts on the wall next to the door. They're old and rusted, but look like they'd support my weight. I brace my hands on the outer lips of the strut closest to the hatch, then lean back experimentally. The rust bites into my palms, and the strut groans slightly, but it holds.

I lift my feet onto the wall, and start to pull myself up, hanging back off the strut, my arm muscles flaring in protest. When I reach the top, I very carefully reach one hand back. My fingers catch the edge of the roof plate, lose it, catch it again and pull it towards me. With a creak of old metal, the loose plate slides across the opening.

I tense, take two quick breaths, then throw myself backwards, grabbing the lip of the opening with both hands. Part of the edge is jagged, slicing into my right palm. Hot blood runs down my wrist, and I have to stifle a howl of pain as I swing backwards. I force myself to use my momentum, and as I begin to swing forwards I pull myself up in one movement.

I'm forced to my stomach almost immediately. The

crawlspace above the opening is tiny, enough for me to lie prone but no more. It's thick with wires and cables, and everything has a fine film of dust which tickles my nose. I run my thumb over the wound in my hand, hissing with pain: it's cut deeply in a ragged line, just where the fingers meet the palm.

One more injury to add to the list, I think. *Racking up quite a score there.*

The sound of air rushing down the tracks has vanished. I have no idea if the crawlspace even follows the path Gray took; it could diverge, or swing off in a different direction entirely. Worse, it could split into multiple paths. And – I taste another dose of bitter fear at the thought – there's no way to turn around. The only way out of here is backwards.

I've never had a problem with enclosed spaces – when you live with a million other people in close quarters, you sort of get used to the idea – but the tunnel ahead seems to tighten as I look at it. My throat twinges – the familiar thirst, biting down again. I shake it off, and begin to crawl, using my arms to pull my body forwards. My jacket hisses as it rubs against the side.

My fingers scrape a wall ahead of me that I can't see. I run my hands along it, and discover that the path turns sharply to the right.

There's no way I'm going to turn the corner prone. I push my body up, leaning hard onto my left side. The zipper of my jacket digs into my waist, an unexpectedly sharp pain that I can do nothing about. I concentrate on slowly inching forward, pushing past the turn: first my head, then my shoulders, squeezing through. A skein of dust falls onto my face from the roof of the tunnel, tickling my nostrils.

Something moves under my hand. Something alive.

Forcing back a shriek, I rip my hand away, and in the

darkness I hear a tiny flutter, a skittering sound as something crawls along the metal. A bug. A beetle, maybe. One that got lucky and escaped from the buzz box. I shudder as I imagine them breeding, forming colonies in the blackness of the vent systems. The fear is back, fighting for control.

I'm halfway around the turn, about to reach my arms out and pull my legs around, when I feel it. The vibration. It's only slight at first, a tiny tremor in the back of my heels, which are forced into the far wall. But it rapidly grows, and the entire crawlspace begins to rumble and shake. The noise is huge, a low rumble that takes hold of a deep part of me and shakes.

The train. A monorail passing on the tracks behind me. I'm in no danger, but every fibre in my being wants to scream. I try to clamp my hands over my ears and shut off the insane noise, but they're pushed ahead of me, and I can't get them back far enough. I lie, trembling, until the train passes, its behemoth rumbling replaced by a high-pitched whine in my ears.

I remain still, breathing hard for a moment, before reaching out and pulling myself round the corner. The crawlspace is still completely black, and I realise that at some point, if I can't find a way to Gray, I'm going to have to push myself backwards down the tunnel.

I've been crawling way too long. I could be anywhere, maybe even near the outer hull, unprotected by the thick shielding and getting a dose of lethal radiation. I pause for a moment, panting, the exertion of pulling myself along seeming to catch up with me in one awful moment. Thick, sour saliva coats my mouth. I swallow, and as I do, I hear them: voices. Very faint, but there.

I stop, hardly daring to breathe. For a moment, I think I've imagined them, but then they catch the edge of my hearing again. I force myself forwards, pushing on through the blackness. The voices get louder. I can't make out the words. One of the speakers is Gray, I'm sure of it. But who is he talking to?

Around another corner, I see a tiny shaft of light, piercing the darkness of the tunnel and revealing grimy, dirt-blackened walls. The light is coming from a small chink in the tunnel's bottom panels, a gap which looks like it wasn't welded properly and which came loose over time. The voices are louder now; I still can't make out who Gray is talking to, although I have a good idea who it might be. Slowly, I pull myself along to the gap, and look through.

A room. Brightly lit, with the usual plate-metal floor. A storeroom of some kind. Gray is there. He has his back to me, and he's talking to his companion, a blur at the edge of my vision. I can finally hear his words, coming up through the gap in the tiles. "I did what you wanted," he says.

The other person in the room replies, "No, you didn't. You screwed up, Arthur."

I know that voice. It's the same fluty, gentle tone that offered me a job barely hours ago.

Oren Darnell steps forward, into my field of vision. And as he does so, I catch sight of Prakesh.

He's behind Darnell, sprawled on the floor – not bound, but unconscious. My breath catches in my throat. Not just because of him.

Lying next to Prakesh are Yao and Kevin.

18

Prakesh

Prakesh doesn't realise he's awake until he hears the voices. They're muffled, metallic, but as he slowly fights his way out of the darkness, they become clearer.

"I ask you for one very simple thing, and you can't deliver," a man says. "I don't have a lot of respect for people who can't keep their promises."

That's Mr Darnell, Prakesh thinks. The thought is fuzzy, indistinct. His eyes are closed. He tries to open them, but it's like they've been glued shut. For some reason, he finds this very funny. Not that he can laugh; there's an ache in his throat, a hot ring above his Adam's apple. It doesn't seem important.

"You wanted him dead, he got dead!" says another man. And that's when Prakesh remembers everything. Remembers his boss's hands around his throat. He is suddenly awake, more alert than he's ever been, but his body refuses to obey him. His eyes remain stubbornly shut.

"I also wanted his left eye delivered in such a way that it didn't attract the attention of *every tracer on Outer Earth*," Darnell says. "You should have brought it to me yourself, instead of using a little delivery girl to do it for you. Now I have to kill a lot of people to make this go away."

This is all wrong, Prakesh thinks. With an effort of will, he finds that he can force his eyelids open a crack. Sharp light lances through, and he closes them again. Pain stabs deep into his skull, takes up residence, starts beating out a drum line.

"Don't worry about them," says the other man. He sounds confident, but his voice tremors ever so slightly. "The quicksleep did the trick, didn't it? We can deal with them whenever we want."

"They belong to the same crew as the tracer you hired," Darnell says. "It's not just them. Are you beginning to understand the problems your failure has caused?"

"But you got the eye, didn't you?" A sullen note has crept into Gray's voice. "You can crack the scanner. So what's the problem?"

It's all Prakesh can do to open his eyes again. He focuses every ounce of energy he possesses into the muscles around his eyes. He makes them stay open. Slowly, with every moment bringing agony, Prakesh lets the light in.

He's on his back, staring up at the ceiling. He can just make out Oren Darnell, upside-down above him, and he can see the person he's talking to – a bald man, his skin shiny with sweat.

Darnell's eyes are cold and black, and the face they're set into seems made of steel. "Do you know why you've been left alone for so long? Why the stompers never cottoned on to this nasty little habit of yours?"

The other man moans, sweat dripping down his face.

"We spent a long time recruiting sleepers," Darnell says. "People we could count on. And you – you were the only one who knew about killing."

It's then that Prakesh sees movement. Up in the ceiling. There's a smudge on one of the plates – no, not a smudge, a gap. And there's something behind it. An eye. Someone is watching them. Someone is looking down. The eye isn't focused on him; it's looking away, flicking between Darnell and his accomplice. Prakesh wills his eyes to stay open, wills the other eye to look at him.

The eye shifts. Prakesh gets a quick glimpse of a nose, the edge of a mouth. And at that moment, the person in the ceiling snaps into focus.

No, Riley, Prakesh thinks. *Don't come in here.*

"You could have been very useful in the days to come," Darnell says.

"I still can!"

"I disagree," says Darnell, and whips a knife into the side of the man's neck.

Prakesh can't scream. He can't do anything. As blood spatters onto the floor, dotting his cheek, he feels his grip on his eyelids slipping. Then it fails completely, and the world goes dark.

19

Riley

The move is so quick, so immediate, that it takes a second for me to realise what Darnell's done. Gray gives a horrible, strangled cough, as short and sharp as the blade itself. Darnell pulls it out, with a horrible sucking sound that reaches up into the crawlspace like a long, black tendril. I have to bite my tongue to stop myself from crying out.

He pulls a rag from his pocket and wipes off the knife, running it gently down the blade. His expression is calm, a thin sheen of sweat on his forehead, and with a sickening feeling I understand that the sweat isn't from guilt or apprehension, just exertion. He looks as if he's just hefted a heavy crate.

At his feet, Gray shudders and jerks as he dies. A gout of dark blood is spreading across the floor.

I've got to get in there. I'm the only person who knows where Prakesh and the Twins are. Going back isn't an option; it'll take far too long to squeeze myself backwards in the black crawlspace, and even then I'll be stuck facing the locked door with no other way to enter, while Darnell does to them what he did to Gray. I'll have to keep moving forwards, but even as the thought occurs I realise with a start that I can't do that either. The crawlspace I'm in goes right over the middle of the room, and I can't move along it silently enough. If I make even the slightest noise while pulling myself along, I'm done for. I see the knife rammed upwards through the thin metal and into my stomach. Darnell could do that and walk away, leaving me to bleed out in the duct, with no one to hear my screams.

Through the gap, I see him turn to the Twins, his knife in hand, and my heart leaps up into my throat. But all he does is look at them for a long moment before striding out of view, stepping over Gray's body as he does so. I hear the door below me open, and close again. Faint footsteps echo up into my crawlspace as Darnell heads back towards the tracks.

Very quietly, I take a few deep breaths, and then pull myself forwards through the tunnel. The noise of my elbows and knees banging the metal seems far too loud, but I'm pretty sure that Darnell won't hear them, and before long I've reached the wall at the other end of the room.

I badly want to rest, to lie in the tunnel and let my aching arms and legs take a break. No chance.

Ahead of me, the tunnel splits in a T-junction, and I impulsively take the right fork, bending my body past the turn, my fingers feeling ahead of me for changes in the tunnel floor. And suddenly, my fingers collide with something: a raised knot in the floor, gritty with rust. I pause, and slowly move my hands over the surface. I thought my eyes would adjust to the dark, but after the piercing light of the peephole I'm blind again.

My fingers feel out another knot. It's a hinge. I've happened on a trapdoor, another entry into the crawlspace, and relief floods through me. I hurriedly scratch around, locate the outer edge and pull it up. By now I'm beyond caring about how much noise I make. I just want out.

A little light brightens the tunnel, coming from the room below. I pull myself forwards, past the open trapdoor, then gingerly lower my legs backwards into it. It's still too dark to see where the floor below is, or even what I'm dropping into, so I take it as slowly as I dare.

I quietly move down to a hanging position, and let go. My feet hit metal, and I drop to a crouch, scanning the room. The light is coming from a tiny crack under a door to my left, and I can see that the room I'm in is another storeroom, stashed with old electrical equipment. Puffs of cold air are coming from vents set low in the wall, but there's no way of knowing if it's air conditioning, or just the breathing of the station. Despite that, the room has an odd smell – thin, unpleasant, almost chemical.

There's a row of big lockers lining the back wall, and stray wires and tools lie stacked on shelves around the room, dimly visible in the low light. This place would be a goldmine for the guys in the market.

The pain in my right hand flares, and I clutch it to my chest. Opening it gingerly, I run a finger along the gash. It's already crusted with dried blood and dirt, and even the slightest touch makes me wince. But I can't worry about it now. By my reckoning, the crawlspace has dropped me into a room just off the one where Gray and Darnell were talking. I drop to one knee and lower my head, tilting it sideways and squinting to see under the door. Nothing: just a bar of blinding white light.

I don't want to go into that room.

The thought of finding Darnell there causes little electric shocks to rocket up my spine, and as I slowly raise myself up, I have to struggle to control my breathing. I should have waited for Amira and Carver. Three of us against Darnell might even the odds; hell, Carver alone could probably take him down with a little luck. But me?

And that's just it. Right now, there's only me.

Slowly, I pad towards the door. What if it's locked? Sealed by a keypad on the other side? No. Can't think about that now. I have to get to the Twins. I push my ear to the door, listening intently. Unlike a lot of the doors on the station, this one isn't electronic. It has an old-fashioned handle, caked with dust.

For what feels like a whole minute, I listen, but there's not a single sound. Very slowly, I reach towards the edge of the door, grasp the handle, and pull.

With a click that's too loud, way too loud, the door clacks off its lock. Dazzling white light shoots through the crack, blinding me for an instant. I blink several times, and very carefully step into the room.

The place is sparsely furnished, with workbenches pushed up against the far wall. It must have once been used by repair techs working on the monorail. Gray's body is on the other side of the room, and I do my best not to stare at it.

The Twins and Prakesh are on my right. Yao's face is swollen and bloodied. She must have fought when Darnell hit her with the quicksleep.

I scan the room once more, and run to them, sliding to my knees as I reach Prakesh. I'm more terrified than I've ever been in my life. The fear digging into me is like a creature perched on the back of my neck, running its claws along my shoulders.

I reach out a hand, gripping his shoulder. "Prakesh," I hiss.

His eyes flicker open, and at that moment, huge, damp hands close around my throat.

20

Riley

His grip is steel. I claw at his enormous hands, desperately wanting to scream, but all that comes out is a horrified wheeze. How could a man so enormous be so quiet?

His hands tighten, those wet fingers crushing my windpipe. A dull ache starts in my chest, sharpening as he squeezes. He lifts me right off my feet, before spinning me around and slamming me into the wall above the Twins.

His expression is not one of anger, but something even more terrifying: joy. He grins, showing huge teeth. They're pearly-white, dazzling in the fluorescent lights, and it's that fact – that he's somehow managed to keep them clean and pristine – that makes me lose it. I pummel at his arms, try to squirm out of his grip, but his smile just gets bigger. My feet are dancing, trying to kick him, but he's way out of range, holding me at arm's length against the wall.

"You should have taken my offer," he whispers. He flicks his eyes to the ceiling. "I knew you were there the whole time. I didn't even have to come and find you. You came right to me."

He leans in slightly closer, and I take the chance, swinging my hand up and raking my nails across his face. I keep them cut short, but they're still ragged and uneven, and they open up three thin cuts across his forehead. He swings his head to the side, but can't avoid the strike, and when he turns back the childlike joy has been replaced by fury.

In a rage, he hurls me across the room. I wasn't expecting it, and there's no time to drop my shoulder before I hit the ground. The impact knocks what little breath I have right out of me. My head collides with the wall, causing another starburst of pain.

But I can breathe again, and the oxygen rushing into my lungs fuels my anger. I push off the ground and spring up, woozy but alert. I am *through* getting my ass kicked.

Darnell crosses the room in a matter of seconds, his footfalls booming on the metal as he breaks into a run. His left arm is pulled back, level with his waist, winding up a gut-punch. But he's coming too fast to control himself: I feint right, then drop into a crouch and throw my left leg out. He sees the move, tries to dodge, but his back foot catches my thigh and he ends up smashing into the wall.

He roars, but he's off balance, and as I spring backwards from my crouch I bring my other foot up and kick hard, aiming right for his crotch.

But for a giant, Darnell is obscenely fast. He grabs my ankle in that tempered-steel grip, and in one movement he regains his balance and yanks me towards him.

My heart is full go, pounding in my ears, and I'm more scared than I've ever been in my life. I see his hands on my throat again, and terror surges through me. If I can get away and get a little head start, I might just be able to find help.

I twist to one side, throw my torso upwards – and sink my teeth into his calf.

The thin fabric of his trouser leg rips under my bite, and he howls in agony. Burning-hot blood explodes in my mouth. Every instinct is to let go, and I can feel my gorge rising, but I force myself to hold on.

He kicks out with his other leg, and connects with my bruised collarbone. He couldn't have had a better hit if he'd planned it. A grinding agony flares in my shoulder, and I let go of his leg, crying out. My face is sticky with blood. I try to get to my feet, but the balance has been knocked out of my legs.

Through eyes blurred and wet, I see the kick coming in, and this time there's no bracing for it. His massive boot connects squarely with my stomach, and every atom of air inside me explodes from between my lips.

I lie there, heaving, and Darnell flips me over. He straddles me, and with a sound like a dying breath, draws a knife from his belt. His breath is hot, ragged with effort. A short laugh crawls out of his mouth.

I summon up every piece of energy I have and spit right in his face. The move costs me, and a fresh wave of heaving rolls through my chest. Darnell flicks the spittle off his cheek. I hear it patter softly on the ground. "That's the spirit," he says. And with that, he flips the shank in one effortless movement, and raises it above his head to stick me.

There's a bang, and Darnell is knocked sideways. I see the hand holding the blade, twisted backwards in the air. And then Darnell's gone, and the world is filled with noise and movement and shouting voices. Hands grip my shoulders, hoist me up. For a moment, the room seems filled with a dazzling white light.

Amira is there, mouthing words I can't quite hear, gripping my shoulders. Behind her, the room swarms with stompers and medics, a buzzing cacophony of grey and white jumpsuits. Darnell is on his stomach, his arms being restrained behind him, blood leaking from a stinger wound below his left shoulder. He's shouting, swearing revenge. A stomper aims a kick at his chest; he curls into a foetal position and falls silent.

Yao is sitting up, and one of the medics – a young woman with blonde hair split by a streak of electric blue – is shining a light in her eyes. Kev and Prakesh are blinking in the light. Nobody seems to be looking at the body of Gray, sprawled in the middle of the room.

"The blood," says Amira. "Riley? Riley, where's it coming from?"

It takes me a moment to realise she's talking about Darnell's blood, splattered on my face. "Not mine," I say. "It's not mine."

"You should have waited, damn you," whispers Amira. I just catch her voice above the chaos. I manage to sit up. Carver is standing by the door, and there's a weird look on his face – pleased and appalled at the same time.

I jump up and run to Prakesh. A medic pushes me back, but I dodge under his grip. I want to look everywhere on Prakesh's body at once, desperate to see if he's been hurt. He pulls me into a hug. I freeze up on instinct, not used to the contact, then I hug him back. It seems crazy not to.

"I'm sorry," I say. "I'm so, so sorry. This was all because of me, I…"

"I'm fine," he whispers in my ear, his voice hoarse. "It's OK. Let them do what they need to do. We're good."

I squeeze him tight, then do as he asks, dropping back. Kev gives me a bleary thumbs-up.

Amira explains how they saw me start tailing Gray in the market; they'd been hidden close to his stall, and when I started the pursuit ahead of them, she decided that rather than try to intercept me, they should hang back and follow me as a fail-safe. "Darnell might have seen us if we'd crossed paths with you," she says.

I stare at her, an unsettling thought occurring. "You used me as bait."

Her gaze is steady. "You left us no choice. You always were impatient."

They'd come up behind me in the tunnels, and when they saw how I'd gained access through the roof, they decided not to follow me – "Three people in the service ducts would've been a bad idea," Amira says – and it was then that they'd decided to find the stompers. It was a gamble that paid off.

A medic comes over and crouches down to my level. He's an older guy with a craggy face, but his eyes are friendly, and Amira steps back so he can look at me. I get the light-in-the-eyes treatment too, and he runs a hand over my collarbone, my stomach. "Bruises and some shock, but nothing major," he says. "You are one lucky kid."

I gesture to the Twins. "They got hit with something. Quicksleep, I heard him call it."

He nods. "We've seen similar things before. It was a powerful strain he was cooking, but it'll wear off."

He lifts up my hand, and mutters something before rummaging in his tattered shoulder bag and taking out an injector. He notices me staring. "Disinfectant," he says. "It'll keep that cut from going bad."

"Does it hurt?"

"Let's find out," he says brightly, and squirts a jet of white foam into my palm. The sting is so sudden and strong that I have to stop myself from lashing out, but after a moment the pain fades, replaced by a throbbing warmth. The foam bubbles, and seems to sink into the cut, forming a hard, white crust. The medic stands, holds out his hand, and, despite the shock, a wave of elation surges through me. I reach out with my good one and grab it, and I'm pulled roughly to my feet.

"Captain," a voice shouts from the storeroom. "We've got bodies back here."

The lockers. That thin smell. I have to work very hard not to ask if one of them is missing an eye.

A stomper steps out from behind the medic, and I'm surprised to see that it's the one I met in the run to Darnell's. Royo. His expression is still gruff, but as he looks me over it softens very slightly.

"You owe these two big time," he says, looking at Amira and Carver. "We wanted to arrest them for going into the tunnels." His voice is rough, as if a statue, heavy with dust and grit, had learned to speak. "Can any one of you tell me how we ended up arresting the chief of the Air Lab instead? Anyone? Not that I wasn't looking for a reason before."

I do most of the talking: I have to tell him the entire story, and then I have to repeat it when his boss – a bigger, uglier version of Royo named Santos – comes over.

I tell him that I've delivered cargo before, but never knew what it was. When he hears that, Royo gives me a long, hard stare – enough to make me trail off for a moment. Finally, he utters a non-committal grunt. He's probably got every right to take us all in for assisting in criminal business, but he says nothing, and I decide not to chance it.

After a few more questions, Royo turns to leave, but turns back to offer his hand. His grip is firm. Carver has sauntered over, and does a double take at the sight of a tracer shaking hands with a stomper. I laugh, despite myself.

"So we're good?" Carver says, looking sideways at Royo. It doesn't look as if he trusts him all the way.

Royo releases my hand, and looks at him. "You just created a massive power vacuum," he says. "Now every gang on Outer Earth is going to try get a piece of the water points. Which means we're going to be working overtime to stop them killing each other."

He pauses – and I swear I see the ghost of a smile slip across his face. "But in my experience, that usually takes a few days to happen. If we can get in there and show some face, maybe we can disrupt things. Anyway. I don't usually trust you tracers, but you did good today."

"And what's that worth, exactly?" asks Amira. Royo shakes his head and turns away, his good humour exhausted.

Behind him, Darnell has been pulled to his feet, and all at once his voice is back. "Your world's going to end!" he screams. More stompers have to rush in to hold him. He strains at his cuffs, muscles standing out on his neck "You're all going to burn! All of you! You're all going to burn!"

His voice fades as he's dragged into the corridor, dwindling to nothingness. A fresh wave of nausea threatens to bend me double again as I realise what I just escaped. Amira's hand is on my shoulder, worry creasing her face, but I wave her off, pulling it together, and stand. Yao walks by, supported by a medic, and reaches out to squeeze my arm.

Soon we're out, into the tunnels, shot through with torchlight from dozens of stompers. Prakesh is holding my hand, gripping it like he never wants to let it go, and then we're onto the tracks by the platforms. Amira jumps up ahead of me, then reaches out for me. I have to let go of Prakesh to climb up, and when I reach back for him, I see that one of the stompers has pulled him aside to ask him something.

For a moment, I want to be down there with him, but then Amira and Carver are hustling me away, and then he's gone.

21

Riley

I was wrong about the Nest. It can hold plenty of people.

The corridor was already heaving when we arrived, and a huge cheer went up as people caught sight of us. Once in a while, gossip moves faster than the tracers – especially when it concerns someone as feared as Oren Darnell. Seems like everybody wanted to shake my hand or pull me into an embrace. I couldn't help smiling, especially when Carver started making loud hooting noises.

He quickly set up a makeshift ladder into the access hatch, ignoring Amira's protests that we had to keep our home a secret ("It's not as if people don't know where we live already," Carver told her, rolling his eyes, and Amira relented).

Soon, even more people started pouring into the Nest, filling it with music, plates of food, buckets of homebrew. Someone brought some extra tattoo ink, which Yao and a couple of her buddies jumped on immediately, splashing it all over the wall. Despite her head injury, and the skanky bits of dried blood still crusted in her hair, she's made a pretty swift recovery. Kev is still a little groggy: he's been given pride of place on the mattresses in the corner, clutching a cup of homebrew and staring blearily about him, a small smile on his face.

I push through the crowd and find a clear space against the wall, relieved to go unnoticed for a moment. Whatever the medic used on my cut, it's amazing stuff: the wound knitted within minutes, and although there's a dull ache in my palm I can almost make a complete fist. Somebody pushes a mug of homebrew into my good hand, and I take a deep drink. For once, the acrid, salty burn of the alcohol is welcome. I haven't been drunk or even tipsy for quite a while, but I'm enjoying the buzz.

As more people climb the ladder into the Nest, they bring more rumours with them. Someone heard that bodies in Gray's workroom had been identified, and a little while later, someone else arrives with names. Turns out one of them was someone fairly important: a man named Marshall Foster. He used to head up the council, years ago, and moved down to Apogee after his retirement. None of the news coming up through the hatch explains why Gray killed him – or whether he was missing any body parts. In fact, nobody mentions the eyeball at all – it's probably still somewhere in the Air Lab.

Gray might have messed up in a big way when he killed Foster, but he was on a roll. There were two other bodies in lockers. Gray had snatched a sewerage tech and a mess worker using his quicksleep serum, taken them back to his room by the tracks, and done...things to them. Conspiracy theories are already flying around as to what Darnell and Gray were planning together – and whether it had anything to do with Foster's death.

With an effort, I shake off my dark thoughts. Looking over, I see Amira drop onto the mattresses next to Kev. She's sober, despite having knocked back more homebrew than anyone. She leans close to Kev, tilting her head to his ear and whispering something which makes his smile grow wider. She catches my eye, and winks before raising her glass in my direction. I raise it back, and take a slug of the drink – this time, the burn is too much and I cough.

"That's what I always said about you, Riley," says Carver, clapping a hand on my shoulder. "You never could hold your booze."

He's in a good mood. Before we left, he had a chance to raid Gray's place for spare parts, and even managed to grab a few vials of the quicksleep.

"I think I've earned this drink," I say, laughing.

"Oh, hell yes."

He leans in close. He's drunk, his eyes unfocused and floating in their sockets, but it's a good drunk. "They're going to be talking about this for years. The girl who took down the monster of the market."

"Gray?"

"That's what everybody's calling him. And then there's Darnell – he's locked up in the brig with about fifteen guards. I think half the sector wants to break in and beat him to death."

"You do know it wasn't me who killed Gray, right?"

"Doesn't matter. People believe what they want to. One dead murderer, one corrupt Air Lab boss in jail, two rescued tracers. Not bad for a trouble-magnet like you."

"Careful," I say, but there's a smile in my voice. "Anyway," I continue, "nice work on the party. Who brought the booze? Or did we trade for this one?"

"Suki had some with her," he says, waving back over his shoulder, indicating a girl in the corner with a shocking crop of bright red hair, chatting with Prakesh. I know her, vaguely.

Carver wanders away, tottering towards Yao, who's still working on the wall with her friends. It's a riot of colour, extending upwards to the ceiling, the wet ink still glistening in the lights.

Your world's going to end.

Prakesh catches my eye and gives a questioning thumbs-up. I nod and smile, but Darnell's words cling to the edges of my mind like dust.

Words like *sleepers*. And *in the days to come*.

Almost without realising it, I'm pushing off from the wall and walking across to Prakesh.

"Hey you," he says. "You know Suki, right?"

The red-haired sprite flicks me a small salute.

"Thanks for the drink," I say.

"No problem. My brother and I make it. Beats going to work."

I turn to Prakesh. "Listen, I'm going to take a walk. I'm feeling a little closed in."

"Are you sure? I can always come with you if..."

"No," I interrupt him, forcing myself to smile. "I'm fine. Just need to clear my head."

I'm worried he's going to insist – concern is written on his face – but then he smiles too. "I guess we know you can take care of yourself," he says.

I feel like I have to say something more. "Listen, I'm really sorry. About before."

His smile flickers, but he brings it back, waving me away. "I'm good, Ry. Promise. Get out of here."

I hold his gaze for a moment, matching his smile, then turn to leave, ducking through the door. Behind me, another massive cheer goes up, and I turn to see Carver kissing Yao. She has her hand clasped around his head, his on her ass, and behind her Kev is looking stunned. Amira is laughing. "Aaron, I told you, no work relationships!" she says.

Unbelievable. I drop through the hatch.

The sector is surprisingly quiet, and I slip unseen

through the corridors of Outer Earth. I'm taking it easy, walking more often than running, my bruised body grateful for the break.

The brig is on the bottom level, and my mind drifts as I head down towards it, the homebrew giving my thoughts some extra colour. I'm trying to piece everything I've been through together – Gray, Darnell, Foster. I'm dropped so deep into my own world that it takes me a few seconds to realise that I'm walking past the Memorial.

The corridor here is wider than most, and the Memorial takes up a whole wall. Proper paint, not just tattoo ink. Janice Okwembu commissioned it – she runs the station council now. Everybody was allowed to draw something – I must have been the only one in the whole sector who refused – and right in the middle, they let one of the more talented artists paint the ship itself.

I look at it before I can tell myself not to, pulling my jacket closer around me. The painting has faded over the years, but is still recognisable. The huge, tapered body, the swept-back fins, the bulging sections near the back which would have held supplies. And underneath it, in black lettering: Earth Return.

There are religious icons too: dozens of them, stacked on top each other. Candles, crosses, metal bent into strange shapes. Tributes to Allah, Yahweh, Buddha, Kali, Vishnu, to gods I can't even name.

I try to stay away from the Memorial as much as I can, taking the upper levels when I need to leave Apogee. I've spent too long staring at it in the past, and it brings back too many memories I'd rather leave behind. I walk on, my gaze locked on a point further down the corridor. Before long, I reach the brig. It's small – just a few cells, located near the Chengshi border. As I approach, I can see four stompers standing outside, clad in the usual grey uniforms. They look cold and lonely.

Two of them see me coming, and their hands drop to the holsters on their waists, fingers close around the butts of their stingers. But then one seems to recognise me, and motions his buddies to back off.

"You're the one who found him, aren't you?" he says.

I nod. "That's me."

"I got to admit, that takes spine," says one of the others. "I'm impressed. Have to say though, it's a good thing we got there when we did."

They're more relaxed now – apparently a single tracer isn't a threat. I take a deep breath. "So this sounds weird, but I need to get in to see him. There's something I need to know."

A swift shake of the head from the first guard. "Not a chance."

"Seriously, I'll be two minutes. In and out."

But he stares impassively back at me. His colleague steps forward. He's a man almost as big as Darnell, and his jumpsuit seems ready to burst off him. "You heard what the man said. No one gets in. You did well today, but go home."

The thought of trying to flirt with them crosses my mind, but I push it away, irritated with myself. Bribery might work, and I'm on the verge of offering them a job or two for free when I see Royo walk up to the barred entrance behind them. I shout his name, and he looks up, his face clouding with concern.

There's a metallic buzz. The gate slides open, and he strides towards me. He looks tired, more human somehow. "You shouldn't be here," he says.

I hurriedly explain to him what I want to do. His eyes narrow. "Do you think we haven't talked to him already? You don't just hire someone to kill a council member for fun. But he hasn't said a damn thing."

"He's known me for a long time. I used to run jobs for him, remember? He might let something slip."

"He nearly killed you."

I don't have an answer to that one. But after glowering for a moment, Royo relents. "Fine," he says. "You come in with me, you stay two minutes, then you leave. And if I even get a hint that you're going to do something stupid, I'll have you in a cell of your own so fast your words will still be hanging in the air."

The other guards, bored with the conversation, have gone back to chatting among themselves. We step through into the entranceway – there are two doors, and the inner one doesn't open until the outer one is locked shut. Another ear-splitting buzz, and we're through, into a small corridor lit only by a couple of bare fluorescents.

The corridor opens up into a larger one, with the cells on either side. There's no overhead light in this corridor, but the cells are brightly lit. Each tiny room contains a single hard cot and a toilet, and the front of every cell is covered with thick, transparent plastic, nearly unbreakable, with two thin slits cut in it for food trays. Some are occupied, and the people in them are collapsed on their cots, shivering. It's cold here; there's no point diverting heat to the brig, and I pull my jacket closer around me. Walking next to me, Royo has gone silent.

We stop at the last cell on the right. I follow Royo's gaze, and see Oren Darnell. He's seated on his cot, staring at the wall, seemingly unaware of our presence and looking as if he doesn't feel the cold. He's been given a thin, light-grey prison jumpsuit to wear.

"You have two minutes," says Royo, and at his voice, Darnell swings his huge head towards us. His eyes have lost none of their malice, and as he sees me, his face stretches in another awful grin.

"Riley Hale," he says quietly, his voice given an odd tang by the plastic.

I'm careful to keep my expression neutral. "What

did you mean when you said that the world was going to end?"

Darnell points to Royo. "Why don't you speak to him? He's already asked me the exact same thing."

"And what did you say? Why is the world going to end?"

He stands up quickly, his huge bulk rocketing off the bed, at the barrier in an instant. I take a step back.

"Not *the* world," he says. "*Your* world. The world will carry on as it always has."

Royo tries to pull me away. "Same shit. You don't have to listen to this."

I shrug his hand off, and Darnell laughs. The control I worked so hard to keep vanishes. I slam a hand on the plastic. It shudders under my palm. "Tell me!"

"Oh, I don't think so," he says. His voice is innocent, carefree, awful. He looks like a man whose destiny has finally revealed itself. "Why would I? It would spoil the fun. And there is going to be so much fun, you believe that."

"Kind of hard to do from inside the brig, don't you think?"

His eyes are wide, almost beseeching. "We locked ourselves away in this metal box so we could continue to exist, even when everything on the planet was telling us that we'd failed. That's something we're going to fix."

Without wanting to, I think of the tagger, the one Darnell's guard murdered, the one who was spraying up messages for voluntary human extinction. I force the image away. That's not what this is. This is something else entirely.

Without another word, he turns and lies down on his bunk, facing the wall. I bang on the plastic again, yelling at him, but this time Royo's hand on my shoulder is firm.

"I told you you weren't getting anything out of him,"

mutters Royo, and he leads me away, back towards the gate. The other prisoners haven't stirred. A cold dread has settled on my shoulders like a cloak.

As we walk, I half expect to hear something from the cell at the end, perhaps even laughter, but there's just the silence, and the echoing, rumbling movements of Outer Earth.

22

Prakesh

Prakesh has to yell out Riley's name a few times before the Nest trapdoor slides back and her face appears.

"You wanna keep it down out there?" she says.

He shrugs. "Wasn't even sure you'd be home."

"Amira says I need to rest."

"How's that working out for you?"

Her face vanishes, then a ladder drops through the gap, hitting the floor with a clunk. Prakesh climbs up, clambering into the Nest entrance. The door to the Devil Dancers' home is open, and Prakesh can see that Riley's alone. Detritus from the party is still scattered across the floor, and he's amused to see that some of it has found its way onto Carver's workbench, as if ready to be turned into some new toy.

"How's it working out?" Riley says, striding back into the Nest. "How do you think? Amira told me no jobs, no running, no anything."

"She's right," Prakesh says. Under the Nest lights, he can still see the bruised halo around Riley's eye. She's tried to hide it with her hair, pulling some of her fringe across, but it's not quite enough to cover the bruise. It gives her a faintly lopsided look.

"Doesn't matter if she's *right*," Riley says, turning away. "I'm bored out of my mind."

She sits on the floor and folds her legs under her. Taking a pack of frayed cards out of her jacket pocket, she spreads them across the metal plating.

Prakesh sits down opposite her. "What are we playing?"

"Acey-deucy?"

"Sure."

They play in silence for a while. Prakesh is good at the game – something that Riley always forgets. His family grew up playing it, and he was throwing down twos from an early age. He wins the first few sets easily. Riley is reckless, too quick to throw down a challenge. Her eyes are fixed intently on the cards in front of her.

For once, Prakesh is relieved to be away from the Air Lab. Oren Darnell might have been corrupt, but at least he kept some sort of control. Now that he's gone, some of the techs have already begun pushing for the top spot. Prakesh isn't one of them, but it's made getting things done difficult. He'd never dare mention this to Riley – she's been through enough.

After she loses the third set, Riley throws down her cards in disgust. "Cheater."

"I don't cheat. I'm just that good." Prakesh fans his cards.

She lifts up a king of hearts. "See this card? I will stuff it down your throat, Prakesh Kumar."

"Only you would treat a playing card like a weapon."

"It is when I'm holding it," she says.

He can't help but smile. "Death by card."

She lifts the card like she's about to throw it. "Right between the eyes."

"You could roll one up. Turn it into a blowgun."

"Sharpen up the edges."

Now they're both laughing – the kind of laughter you

try to hold in but which sneaks out anyway. Riley clears her throat, still grinning, and looks away.

The words are out of Prakesh before he can stop them. "You should come stay with me, up in Gardens. It'd be a break from—"

"From what?"

Riley is looking at him expectantly, and suddenly Prakesh isn't sure what he was going to say.

He shuffles his cards absently. "From everything."

They're silent for a moment. Then Riley says, "Did you ever hear about Amira's girlfriend?"

He looks up, confused. "What?"

"Amira's girlfriend."

"Amira the ice-queen has a girlfriend?"

"Had. Shut up and listen. She worked in a hospital up in New Germany. Even came by the Nest a couple of times. She was all right."

"What was her name?"

"Doesn't matter. Amira went to visit her a lot, too, but she wasn't there often enough. She'd be on a job, or back here, or doing gods know what. And after a while, her girlfriend asks Amira to choose. Her or us."

"I would never."

"You'd never what?"

He sighs. "Nothing. Don't worry about it."

For a moment, Riley seems about to pursue it. Instead, she quietly deals out another round.

Prakesh wants to rage at her for being so cruel, for being so short-sighted. The business with Darnell was horrendous, but the one good thing he'd thought might come out of it would be he and Riley becoming closer. He still remembers when she hugged him, right after he woke up in Gray's room, when there was light and noise everywhere and she was the only thing he recognised.

He catches the anger before it can really take hold,

consciously neutralising it. For a moment, he briefly wonders if he might not be suffering some sort of post-traumatic stress. It's certainly possible, and he fixes on the idea, keeping it in the front of his mind. It helps. He can feel the anger settling, like ripples in a cup of water, finally fading away.

But the effort has rattled him; he loses the next two games, his usual strategies falling apart. Riley is smirking. She's got the cards up to her face, hiding her mouth, flashing eyes peeking over them. "You might be good, 'Kesh, but I'm better," she says.

Something about the way she says it brings the anger back. Very carefully, he puts his cards down on the floor, face-up, then gets to his feet. "I gotta go."

Riley looks at the cards. "You had double deuce. You don't want to finish the hand, at least?"

"I gotta go," he says again. It's about all he can say, like any other words will mutate into something he'll regret.

Riley jumps up too. " 'Kesh, come on, I was just playing. I didn't mean anything by it."

She reaches out to him, and for the first time, he doesn't want her anywhere near him. He pushes his way out, sits with his legs dangling out the trapdoor. The ladder is there, but he feels the need to drop. To let the shockwave from the landing travel through him.

"Don't be like this," Riley says. She's standing in the doorway, arms folded. The look of contrition has left her face. Now she just looks resigned. Like this fight was inevitable.

A burst of air pretending to be a laugh escapes Prakesh. He could say a million things right now, about choice, about him, about her. But he doesn't. He just pushes himself off the edge, and then he's gone.

23

Darnell

Darnell's clothes have been taken away from him. So has his knife, and his remaining vials of quicksleep. By now, his office will have been searched, the eyeball found, logged, then incinerated. The thought of stompers moving around his beloved bonsai, *touching it*, is enough to bring the rage back.

His hands clench involuntarily, knotting the blankets on the thin cot. The standard-issue prison jumpsuit is too short for him, barely reaching his wrists.

He looks around the cell. Bare walls, a single bright light set deep into the ceiling. The fisheye lens of a camera, socketed next to it. The light is reflected in the plastic barrier at the front of the cell. The place smells the same as his family's hab did, back in New Germany: antiseptic mingled with the sour tang of sweat.

He remembers the hab well. His mother never left her bed. When she smiled, spit would leak out of the drooping, immobile side of her face.

His father worked in the mining facilities, and most of his time at home was spent caring for his wife. He and Darnell cleaned her body, tried to feed her. Darnell hated both of them. There was never enough food, never enough water. And *she* got most of it.

He doesn't know where the bean plant came from, but he remembers it clearly: the plastic pot, the thick smell, the dark soil. He loved how its leaves hunted for the light, how its only purpose was to survive. It took so little, and gave so much back.

Darnell was nine years old when his father died. An accident in the refinery. He was angry at first, angry at being left alone, but also strangely happy. It meant space for more plants. His garden grew, every spare inch of hab space stacked with pots and grow-boxes.

Nobody came to check in on Darnell and his mother. Nobody needed to. Darnell did well in school – enjoyed it, even. Sometimes, the teachers would show them pictures of things that used to exist on Earth, like rainforests and botanical gardens. With fierce pride, he'd realised that he was growing some of the same plants: the flowers and vines and fruit. And with the pride came something else: anger. These plants sustained the whole planet. But the teachers kept saying that everything on Earth was gone, and Darnell couldn't understand why.

And no matter how many plants he filled the hab with, he could never get rid of the stench of his mother.

He would bring home food for her from the mess. Instead of wasting away, her body had ballooned, spreading out across the surface of the cot. One night, he found himself staring at her, at the wobbling fat on her legs where the blanket had rucked up. The pale skin, the patch of drool on the pillow. He suddenly couldn't believe how fat she'd become, how useless.

"You're too fat already," Darnell says, the sound echoing around the cell. He hardly realises he's speaking. "You don't need any more food."

Darnell shakes his head, angry with himself for letting

his memories get the better of him. It's been happening more and more lately – they'll come at odd times, and he finds himself lost in them before he even realises it's happening.

He tries to tell himself that his being locked in the cell doesn't matter. That Outer Earth is finished no matter what he does. It doesn't help. Instead, it just makes it worse. He wanted to spend the final days tearing the station apart, piece by rotten piece.

It won't make a single bit of difference to the outcome. That was set in play ages ago. But it isn't fair. He can rant and rage all he wants, but no one will listen to him. Not from in here. And if he is tried before it happens, if he is found guilty and executed…

"Prisoner Darnell."

Darnell looks up to see one of the brig guards standing behind the plastic barrier. He's got a tray of food with him – Darnell's lip curls as he remembers the fruit that he'd be eating if he was still in the Air Lab. He gestures to the guard to leave it. If there was no plastic barrier between them, he'd break the tray in half and jam the jagged edge into the guard's face.

"Got a message for you, Sir."

It's the "Sir" that makes Darnell look again. The guard's face is familiar, somehow, but he can't quite place it.

Darnell stands and walks to the barrier, resting his forehead on it. The guard meets his eyes, doesn't look away.

"Prisoner Darnell, your trial has been scheduled for three days' time," the guard says, speaking loudly and slowly. "Your case is to be heard by the full council in a public hearing. If you wish to call witnesses in your defence, you must inform me of their names now. Do you have any questions?"

As it happens, Darnell has plenty of questions, but he

doesn't get to ask them, because suddenly the guard says quietly, "Reach through and grab me."

Darnell stares at him.

The guard flicks his eyes down towards the slot in the plastic, the slot holding the food tray with its load of grey slop. Darnell knocks the food tray aside, reaches through, snags the front of the guard's jumpsuit. He yanks him forwards, slamming against the plastic with a dull bang. Somewhere, an alarm begins blaring, but the guard's eyes show no fear. He speaks quickly and calmly.

"I'll be standing next to you during the trial," the guard says. "When the time comes, follow me. Don't ask questions, don't hesitate. Everything is going as planned, Sir."

Darnell smiles, and the guard nods. Then he's being pulled away by the other stompers, and the plastic barrier is whooshing open, and Darnell is being forced to the floor and stomper boots are being driven into his side and his stomach. But even through the pain, even though every kick feels like a red-hot rod being driven into him, Oren Darnell manages to keep smiling.

24

Riley

It's not long before Amira puts me back on the job. Not that I mind. The faster I run, the further I seem to leave the last few days behind. The pain in my collarbone and chest and eye socket dwindle and vanish, replaced by the everyday muscle aches of a tracer.

They've scheduled Darnell's trial for a few days' time. That's no surprise – with space at a premium, people don't usually spend all that much time in the brig. They get them up in front of the sector leaders fast – if they're guilty, it's usually a harsh spell of hard labour, working to clean the corridors or helping to maintain the machinery inside the freezing path that leads to the Core. If what they've done is too serious for that, it's the firing squad.

His words keep coming back to me, and more than once I find myself brooding on what he said.

The trial – and the likely outcome – give me chills. They shouldn't, but they do. They used to hold the trials in private, but after a while the clamour to hold them in public got too loud to ignore. Now, they're a form of entertainment, something to keep people happy. Of course, there are plenty of people who don't want it that way, but it's not like anyone listens to them.

When I wake on the day of the trial, the Nest is cold, resonating with the distant hum of the station. Kev is passed out at the workbench, sleeping on his arms, snoring delicately. Carver and Yao are nowhere to be seen. I pulled a blanket around me when I lay down, but I kicked it off during the night. It lies bundled and twisted at my feet, and cold shivers slither up my body.

There's a noise to my right, and I lift my head, eyes blurry with sleep. Amira is there, stretching, her back to me.

I sit up, rubbing my eyes, and as I reach for a nearby canteen she speaks without turning around. "Got a job for you," she says.

"Another one?" I give off a yawn, so big that my jaw clicks.

"That's right," says Amira. "I went down to the market to get us some work. Two jobs. I'll take one, and since you're up first, you can take the other."

"Sure."

"I need you to go to the sector hospital. Nurse at the market was looking for a tracer. Apparently they need something delivered to the hospital in New Germany. Catch and release job."

I nod, and move on to stretching my thighs, bending down into a lunge position. Amira reaches in her pack and tosses me something small and green – I catch it without fumbling, sleep failing to dull my reflexes. It's an apple, smooth and perfect. I flash her a grateful smile. The apple is crisp, and so juicy I have to wipe my chin after I'm done.

It's right then that I remember something. "I used your move," I say to Amira.

She looks over her shoulder. "What?"

"Your move. The pressure point." I quickly tell her about how I took down one of the Lieren using the strike she taught me. As I tell the story, her face breaks into a huge smile.

"Nice," she says when I've finished, turning back to her stretching.

How long has it been since I've seen a smile from Amira? That, too, seems like years. In the time I've known her, I can only think of a few times when I've genuinely pleased her.

We met a year after my dad died. I was thirteen. For a year, my mum struggled on. I had to watch her getting sadder and sadder. And then one day, she just gave up, and I was alone.

That was when I left school. I dropped out for a few months, scavenging food, doing odd jobs, sleeping in storage rooms or under tables in the cold passages.

They came when I was sleeping in a passage on the bottom level of Chengshi, curled up with my head tucked into the crook of my arm. There were at least four of them, hard men with worn faces. I recognised them as soon as they pulled me into the middle of the corridor: merchants. I'd managed to steal some food that day – it was one of the few times I didn't go to sleep on an empty stomach.

I screamed and shouted and cried, but nobody came. And they were silent: lips tight, faces hard, as if I was nothing more than a piece of machinery which had broken down once too often and needed to be fixed with anger and a firm hand. The only sound was my screams as they dragged me down the corridor. I lashed out at them with my feet, but they batted them away, like they were nothing.

And then Amira was there, a whirlwind of fists and elbows and blades, smashing and cutting and breaking.

I remember being amazed at how fast she was. The man holding my right arm went down first, a red slash exploding at his throat as Amira whipped her blade across it. The others ran at her, shouting, but in moments they were down, with arms twisted the wrong way and deep cuts already turning the floor a dark red.

When it was over, Amira paused for a moment, silhouetted in the lights above, breathing hard. She tucked the blade back into her pocket, then reached out a hand to me.

We lived together, we trained together, we got hurt together. I was her first Dancer, and she taught me everything: how to run, how to move through crowds, how to land. How to fight. How to find jobs, which ones to take and which ones to refuse. And how to never get caught again. By anyone.

"Get going," she says, gesturing to the door. "Jobs don't wait, you know."

Usually, if I have to take a job right after I wake up, my body feels slow and clumsy. But not today. I'm pulling off flawless moves and hitting the mark on every jump I make, even putting a little flair on a couple of wall passes. At one point, I jump down an entire set of stairs, taking a running leap off the top step and grabbing a roof strut before swinging into space, my head up and my arms thrown above and behind me, and landing so perfectly I don't even have to roll. The move feels so good I burst out laughing, and a man sitting on the steps behind me applauds. I wave and take off again, losing myself in the movement.

The hospital's not too far from the Nest. They're regular clients; while most sectors keep to themselves, hospitals across the entire station tend to share equipment, sending supplies wherever they're needed. A lot of our work comes from them – if we're not ferrying the supplies themselves, then we're delivering requests for them, going back and forth between the sectors.

When I arrive, a doctor is deep in conversation with one of the nurses. They're wearing scrubs that used to be white, and like every doctor I've ever seen, they look barely alive. He looks up and sees me; his black hair, like his tunic, has turned silvery grey, and his face is lined with worry. But he smiles, and beckons me over.

"I'm Doctor Arroway," he says and holds out his hand. I give it a quick shake; the palm of his hand is rough, like old rust.

"You had some cargo you needed delivering?" I say.

The doctor reaches behind him, picking up a squat white box from the table. "That's right. We've got a box of—"

I clear my throat, and he looks up, puzzled. Then he nods. "Of course, sorry – I forget that you prefer not to know. But really, it's nothing bad. Are you sure?"

"Positive."

He sighs. "OK. Just get it there in one piece. There's a doctor at the hospital in New Germany, name of Singh. It's got to get to him fast. He's got some people in the isolation rooms who need it ASAP."

"You're talking to the right person," I say, taking the box and dropping it into my pack. "So. What's in it for us?"

He looks at me, his arms folded. "You know, what you're carrying is going to save lives. Maybe a lot of lives. This doesn't have to be difficult."

I return his stare. "Actually, it does. No fee, no delivery, so make me an offer." I hate negotiating. I'm much more comfortable when the price is set beforehand. But it'd be worse to bring back nothing, or something that wasn't worth the trip.

He sighs irritably. "Fine. I'll give you a box of

painkillers. Not the good stuff, by any means, but with your job, they'll probably come in handy."

"Make it the good stuff. It's a long run."

He rolls his eyes. After rummaging in a wall unit behind him, he hands me a small white box. I shake it. It gives a reassuring rattle, and I stuff it into the inside pocket of my jacket.

On the way out, a man seated in a battered chair, who up until now looked like he was unconscious, calls out my name. His beard reaches to his chest like a grey river, and he has a nasty-looking bloody bandage wrapped around his left hand. "Go get 'em," he says, shaking his hand in the air; a couple of blood drops spatter the floor. I dodge back, laughing.

From the chatter I hear in the stairwells, Darnell's trial is in a couple of hours' time, in the Apogee gallery. Better there than in Gardens, where things might get hairy. The gangs Darnell was in with might be reeling a little, like Royo said, but it's not unheard of for people to disrupt trials – sometimes violently. I make a mental note to be as far away as possible. By now, the eyeball is common knowledge, too. It was found in Darnell's office, and was logged and incinerated by the stompers. Apparently, it was already beginning to decay.

By the time I hit the New Germany border, the corridors have become even more crowded. People mill in large groups, leaning up against walls thick with rust and dirt. There's no sign here like there is at the Gardens border – just the supports where one used to hang, jutting down from the ceiling.

Despite the crowds, I make it to the hospital in good time. The doctor, Singh, gives me a brief nod, nothing more, and locks the package away in a heavy steel cabinet. He looks distracted, glancing back towards the exam rooms. His hospital is much busier than the one I was in before, and the low groans of patients fill the air, slipping out of the darkened wards like oil from a worn seal. My good mood feels dampened here, smothered.

As I turn to go, there's a hand on my arm, and I turn to see the grey bulk of a stomper. His face is a perfect blank. Surprised, I try to jerk my arm away, but his grip holds.

"What?" I say. "Did I do something wrong? You got any problems, you can take it up with my crew leader…"

His expression hasn't changed; he looks like he could stand there all day if he had to. It's then that I notice the red patch near his shoulder, in the shape of the station's silhouette, and a little worm of fear coils in my stomach. He's no stomper. Red patches belong to the elite units who guard the council.

His grip gets firmer. "Ms Hale. Janice Okwembu would like a word." His voice is monotone, as immovable as the walls around us.

The head of the council? I'm too shocked to resist, and he starts to walk me towards the wards. I find my voice: "Then why aren't we going to Apex?" But he ignores me, pulling me down the central corridor between the curtained-off wards.

25

Riley

There are more guards here, not lounging against the walls like a regular stomper might, but standing bolt upright, eyes scanning the corridor.

One of them turns to us: "Is this her?" he says. The other guard nods, and releases me.

By now, the anger I first felt has been replaced by curiosity: what is Janice Okwembu doing here? And why does she want to see me? I've never even seen her in person. She occasionally comes down to the lower sectors, but not when I've been there. And I've never been up to Apex – not once, not even to do a delivery. They keep it pretty secure; when you've got the council chamber and the main station control room there, you try to keep most people out if you can.

The guard beckons me towards one of the curtains, and pulls it aside. In the dim light, I can just make out Janice Okwembu. She's leaning over a bed, whispering to an old man. He's heavily bandaged, with a thick gauze patch over his left eye. He doesn't appear to be conscious, but Okwembu is whispering something to him. I can't make out the words, and the guard motions me to wait, gesturing me back.

After a moment, Okwembu bends down, and plants a kiss on the man's cheek. She turns, and sees us standing in the entrance. "I knew him from long ago," she says, gesturing to the old man in the bed. She moves with a controlled, gentle grace. "I shouldn't really show favouritism to anybody, but I like to know that he's being looked after."

I find my voice. "How did you know I was coming here?"

She just smiles. Glancing at the guard, she says, "I believe the room next door is free. Could you please ask Dr Singh to turn up the lights there?" He nods, and turns smartly on his heels.

Okwembu comes closer. The grey in her hair is more pronounced than it looks when I see her on the comms screen; she occasionally broadcasts messages, speaking on behalf of the council. It's her eyes, however, that are the most striking: a pale green, almost white, and ringed with a feathered blue on the outer edge.

She's short, perhaps the same height as me, but even a cursory glance shows toned arms under the white jumpsuit. She catches my eye and laughs, an unexpectedly girly sound. "I try to keep in shape," she says, placing a hand on the small of my back and guiding me out of the ward. "I was a computer technician once, and I realised I didn't want to end up like my colleagues – fat and lazy."

She pulls open the curtains on the ward next door. The lights are up, and she gestures to two chairs in the corner, caked with a layer of dust. I take a seat – I half expect her to wipe down the chair, but she simply pauses for a moment before perching on the edge of it, hands clasped in her lap. Above us, the light flickers silently. With a start, I realise how unkempt I must look, with my scarred jacket and greasy hair. I have to force myself not to run a hand through it.

"I wanted to congratulate you personally," she says. I open my mouth to reply, but she raises a hand. "You did a very brave thing. I was horrified when I heard about Marshall Foster."

"Did you know him?"

"Yes," she says. "I joined the council while he was its leader. He was..." She pauses for a moment. "A friend."

"I'm sorry."

"You have nothing to apologise for," she says. "I've been aware of your crew for some time, and of course we've always been grateful to Amira Al-Hassan for what she did." I think of Amira's missing fingers, her run through the Core all those years ago, and a little dark cloud settles on my heart.

"Thanks, I guess," is all I can come out with.

She sits back, her lips pursed, as if deep in thought. "You could have gone to get help instead of going in. Most people would have. But not you."

"I wasn't going to wait. If I'd gone to get help, Prakesh and Yao and Kevin would be dead too." I trip over my words, realising she might not know who they are, but she just nods.

"They're lucky to know you," she says, but there's no warmth in her voice: it's cool, calculating. "But then, you know what it's like to lose someone."

It takes me a moment to form the words. "That was a very long time ago."

"Indeed. Seven years now. But what your father did – what he died doing – was nothing short of remarkable."

I can't look at her. I was hoping that this year I was going to get away with not thinking about Earth Return. But with this, plus my unexpected visit to the Memorial, it doesn't look like that's going to happen.

If she sees my distress, she ignores it. "After your father... after the *Akua Maru* was lost, we struggled for a long time. This station was designed to support a fleet of ships, but the *Akua* was one of our best, and we took a hit when it was destroyed. Keeping morale up has been difficult."

"I know."

Okwembu raises a palm. "Please. Let me finish. People need something to gather around, and as the daughter of someone like John Hale, you might be just what they're looking for. We were hoping you might testify at Darnell's trial today."

"I'm not a political tool," I say, surprising myself with the note of anger in my voice.

She dips her head. "Of course. I wasn't suggesting that."

"You want to make peace with the gangs and keep people happy, find someone else. Patch up the graffiti. Put plants back in the galleries. Do something about the mess food. Don't use me."

Okwembu raises an eyebrow, and I tail off, but she doesn't interrupt me, and doesn't appear angry.

"Well, I hope you'll think about it," she says after a long moment, her voice so soft I have to strain to hear her.

We fall silent. After a few moments, I meet her gaze. "That's not all, is it? You didn't come down here just to ask me to testify."

"Actually, I came down here to visit a friend," she says. "But since you mention it, there is something else."

She leans forward. "I need to know that you told the protection officers everything. If there's something you held back, you need to let me know, and you need to do it now. Nothing will happen to you, but you must tell me. I can't stress how important it is."

I shrug. "We did a job for him, and it didn't feel right. He took my…Prakesh, and two of my crew. We tailed him, we got lucky. That's all."

But she doesn't sit back. "When we found Marshall's body, one of his eyes was missing. We think it has something to do with why he wanted Foster out of the way, and whatever Oren Darnell was planning. I think you know about it too, Riley. And I think you haven't been honest with us." Her voice is still deathly quiet.

I plaster disgust on my face, hoping that I'm not overdoing it. "I didn't know that. His eye, I mean. Why? Why would Gray do that?"

I can feel her pale gaze trying to reach in, as if she wants to dig around in my mind. Eventually, she sits back, her eyes still on me. "I know you and your friends sometimes take on jobs that involve carrying things that..." She pauses, choosing her words. "Well, let's just say that sometimes what you do is not in the best interests of Outer Earth. We let the tracers exist because you perform a valuable service, and we know that by doing that, we risk that you might transport something dangerous. Something which we should perhaps know about."

The sweat on my face has dried to a thin crust, itching gently. I force myself to keep my hands in my lap. Her words aren't a threat, not really, but there's no mistaking the cold intent behind them.

She continues. "I will be watching you, Ms Hale. You would do well to remember that nothing lasts forever."

Abruptly, she stands up, and gives me a curt nod before drawing the curtain aside. I rise to my feet, and I'm about to follow when she turns back. Her voice is cool, but business-like. "I'd like you to think some more about appearing at the trial."

I want more than anything for her to go, and I nod, which seems to satisfy her. She turns away, motioning for her guard to follow. The sound of their footsteps echoes in the wards as they march off, and I hear her exchanging a few words with Dr Singh. The warmth in her voice is back, as if she flicked a switch. I remain where I am, unable, for a moment, to move.

I pull my jacket around myself, but the cold that I felt earlier refuses to vanish, running icy fingers up the back of my neck. I can't help but think back to when the man from the council came to see my mother and me in our little room in Apogee. I remember his uniform, a heavy grey tunic with red highlights, tight around the throat. The look of sorrow on his face as he told us about the massive explosion on atmosphere entry, the catastrophic reactor failure. That there would be no new colony on Earth, no terraforming, no resources to send home. That John Hale and his crew would not be coming back.

26

Darnell

His hands are cuffed first, the thick metal bands ratcheting around his wrists in front of him. He has to put his hands through the slot in the plastic, then step back once he's restrained. Two stompers hold his legs at the knees, a third holds his arms, and a fourth snaps ankle cuffs on. The chain between his wrists and ankles is too long, clattering the floor whenever he moves.

They march Darnell out of his cell, one on each side. The stompers walk fast, and he struggles to match their long strides with his cuffed feet. He keeps his eyes focused on the floor in front of him, careful not to betray his excitement. He doesn't even know which stomper is the guard who promised to free him. They wear full body armour, their faces covered by dark visors and thick, angular helmets.

He can't help grinning when they walk out into the corridors, past the crowds assembled outside the brig. There are dozens of them, and they're all booing and jeering, shouting his name and laughing. Darnell scans the crowd. He's looking for those who aren't booing. Those who are watching intently.

Darnell has been seeding sleepers in Outer Earth for over a year, tapping into the creeping network of the voluntary human extinction movement. The movement itself was a joke, something that was never going to be taken seriously, so it wasn't difficult to find those who had become disillusioned with it.

It was easier than Darnell would have imagined. These people were emotionally vulnerable, sick of waiting, sick of asking nicely. Even the ones who hadn't considered doing what Darnell asked them to do were easily led in that direction. All he had to do was give them a little push.

And the best part? The beliefs, ideas, whatever you called them, were like viruses. Give them the right conditions, and they thrive. They multiply. They make copies of themselves. And the more revolutionary the idea – the more potent the virus – the harder it would be to eradicate. Soon there was a new network, reaching across Outer Earth: a network of people fuelled by the ideas they carried.

Unless…

It's possible – just possible – that the stompers are messing with him. That they found out about his sleepers, and decided to have a little fun, holding out hope and intending to snatch it away. There'll be no signal, no rogue guard leading him to safety.

For the first time, Darnell feels a twinge of fear. If he is found guilty – and he will be – they'll stand him up against a wall right there, in front of everyone.

Oren Darnell isn't afraid of dying. But he is afraid of dying without his revenge.

"Move it," mutters one of the guards. Darnell, lost in his thoughts, has slowed down, and the stompers holding him nearly yank him off his feet. He stumbles, keeping himself going with the thought of the stompers' faces melting off in screaming agony.

And just then, just as he regains his balance, the stomper on his left looks at him and nods. Ever so slightly. His black faceplate reveals nothing, reflecting Darnell's own face back at him. The moment is brief, and then the stomper is eyes front again, dragging Darnell onwards.

He can hear the gallery ahead. The noise is intense, pushed into a concentrated roar by the corridors surrounding the open space. Darnell smiles to himself, and somehow manages to stand a little straighter, his body dwarfing the stompers around him.

Darnell doesn't know what the signal will be, but he'll be ready.

27

Riley

I don't want to go to Darnell's trial, but after a while I find myself heading there anyway. Maybe Okwembu's more persuasive than even she realises. I'm not testifying though, whatever she thinks.

When I left the hospital in New Germany, I toyed with going up to Gardens to see Prakesh – now that Darnell's gone, the water in his sector is probably running freely again, so he'll be in a good mood – but I decided I couldn't face the crush. I began running back towards the market in Apogee, thinking I could maybe go and see Madala and pick up that job he was talking about.

But the joy I'd felt earlier is gone, replaced by a growing unease. My movements feel stilted and slow, and I can't get Okwembu's words out of my head. You have to be pretty ruthless to stay in the council's top spot for ten years, but it's unsettling to see it up close.

I'm wearing an old hoodie under my jacket, and as I hit the Apogee border I pull the hood up. The corridors have become even more crowded, the crush building inside them as people hustle to the gallery for the best spots. Instead, I force my way up the stairwells, eventually emerging onto the Level 3 catwalk. It's only just filling up with people, and is a lot quieter than the chaos down below. The noise is insane: a roaring mix of laughter, shouts, and calls from merchants taking advantage of a captive audience. They've set up stalls along the walls – one of them has even managed to score a prime spot in the centre. He's a blur behind his table, dishing out what look like cooked beetles, the crates behind him overflowing with traded objects. The smell of frying food drifts up from below in thick clouds. The atmosphere is buoyant, almost like a festival.

The sea of people spread out on the gallery floor stops dead by the far wall, brought up short by a line of waist-high barricades. There are stompers behind it, facing the crowd. They wear black full-face masks, and thick helmets squashed onto their heads. Every one of them is holding a stinger. Behind them, two people are putting the finishing touches on a platform – a dais of some kind, made of steel plates and welded pipes.

A little way down the catwalk, I see Amira and Carver, leaning over the railing. Amira waves me over.

"Didn't expect to see you here," she says, having to raise her voice above the noise. "Everything OK with the job?"

I pull the painkillers out and give them a shake. "Smooth as."

"Good. We've been getting a lot of new work offers after yesterday, so we need to stay focused."

"Relax, boss," says Carver, leaning with his back to the railing and stretching his neck out, gazing up at the ceiling. "We're golden. Or at least, Riley's golden," he adds, jerking a thumb in my direction. "I've never had so many people request a tracer personally."

"Where are the Twins?" I ask.

"Back at the Nest," says Amira. "Although Kevin

still isn't too happy about last night." She gives Carver a pointed look. He's suddenly gone very quiet.

There's movement off to one side of the gallery. A roar goes up from the crowd and, at first, I think Darnell is being brought out, but then I see that it's the council, led by Okwembu, walking towards the dais. There are six of them, grey men and women who look nervous facing the people, as if it's them being judged. Only Okwembu, standing out front, looks confident and proud, her chin up, raising a hand to greet the crowd. Her eyes sweep the catwalks above her. It might be my imagination, but I swear that when she looks at the area I'm standing in, she smiles.

"Okwembu came to see me," I mutter, then wish I hadn't.

"What?" Amira yells – the noise has rocketed, a thundering boom in the enclosed space that has my stomach rumbling with its sheer force.

I reluctantly raise my voice a notch, leaning in closer. "Okwembu. When I was at the hospital in New Germany, she was there. She asked to see me."

I see Amira's eyes widen in astonishment, and she's about to say something when Darnell is hustled out of one of the corridors, and the crowd explodes.

He wears the same grey prison jumpsuit, his hands cuffed in front of him, his ankles shackled. His arms are gripped on each side by stompers in full body armour. Darnell dwarfs his escort, and they have to march in double time simply to keep up with his huge strides. The leering grin is back on his face.

I'm half expecting people to throw things, but nothing comes – they don't want to waste anything, I guess. It doesn't stop them from jeering, and loud boos and catcalls are hurled out from all around me.

Amira leans into my field of view, but I can't hear what she's saying, and after a moment of fruitless shouting she gives up. Her eyes hold plenty of unanswered questions, and it's clear we're not done just yet.

Darnell is led to the area in front of the council platform. The stompers don't raise their stingers, but even from the catwalk, I can see them tense.

On the platform, one of the men steps forward, and the crowd noise ebbs slightly. He's surprisingly young – his forties, maybe, which is unusual for a council member. Most of them make their way up the political ranks over time: level chief to deputy sector chief and then representing their home sector on the council. That can take years – spots on the council don't open often.

The man is holding some sort of device to his mouth, which allows him to transmit through the comms.

"Oren Darnell," his voice booms, echoing off the walls. "You are accused by this council of the following crimes..."

As he begins to list the charges, someone grips my shoulder and pulls me backwards.

For a terrible moment, I'm certain it's one of the Lieren, and I'm about to have a blade rammed into the small of my back. I spin around, ready to attack, and find myself staring into the face of an old woman. She's wearing a blue headscarf, and it takes a second for me to place her.

The market. The strange woman in the crowd.

She embraces me, placing her mouth by my right ear. "I can't believe I found you again," she says, her high voice cutting through the noise. I try to say something, to ask who she is, but she cuts me off, squeezing me tighter, her voice urgent and husky in my ear. "My name is Grace Garner. I was Marshall Foster's assistant. I have to talk to you – there's something you need to know."

"Tell me," I say.

Garner pulls back, looks me in the eyes. "Not here. We need to talk in private."

A million questions fly around my head. Why is she

telling me? And how does she know who I am? The fear is back, the cold fingers tracing the curve of my neck. Behind me, I can feel Amira and Carver tensing, not knowing who the woman is, or whether I'm in any danger. The people around me are starting to take an interest; I can see a couple straining to hear our conversation, desperate to catch what might be a new piece of gossip. In the background, I can still hear the man from the council rattling off a list of crimes.

I'm about to tell her to go and wait in the Nest, or the market, but an idea suddenly hits.

"Go to Gardens," I say. "The Air Lab. Ask for a man named Prakesh Kumar – *Prakesh Kumar*," I repeat, raising my voice. "Tell him I sent you, and tell him that you're to wait for me there. I'll come and find you."

It's then that I notice how terrified Garner looks, how worn. But she nods again, gives me a final squeeze, and vanishes into the crowd.

Carver leans in. "What was that all about?" he shouts, but before I can answer, I hear the announcer ask Darnell to respond to the charges.

Darnell stands proud, his grin wider than ever, staring around the galleries expectantly. One of the stompers, his stinger up, steps forward and holds one of the speaker devices to Darnell's mouth. He keeps it a fair distance away, as if he's worried Darnell might lunge forwards and bite him.

Looking directly at the council, Darnell says, very clearly, "Guilty as charged."

The roar from the crowd is the loudest yet, a shocked eruption of sound. Amira places her hands over her ears; mine are already gently aching from the noise, and I follow suit.

At that moment, with a sickening click, every fluorescent light in the room dies, plunging us into the darkness.

There's a split second of stunned silence, then the shouting starts again. This time, the noise is fearful, with screams starting to slip into the noise, like daggers through a ribcage. Behind me, I can feel the crowd on the catwalk spinning in place, hands frantically reaching out to try and grab friends, family.

The noise builds to a crescendo, and with a huge flare of light from below, a massive explosion rocks the gallery.

28

Prakesh

Prakesh's footsteps reverberate on the metal as he walks across the labs. There are a few other techs tending to the trees; one of them is suspended from a pulley system, legs akimbo over a branch. He glances down as Prakesh walks underneath him, his face expressionless.

Prakesh ignores him. Truth be told, he hasn't had a lot of time to talk to the other techs. Not since Oren Darnell got caught. All those people hunting for the top spot has left a lot of work unfinished, a lot of soil untended. Prakesh doesn't mind. The extra work means he doesn't have to think. He can take Riley and Mr Darnell and just ignore them for a while, letting his hands get good and filthy.

He needs a fresh pH monitor – the one he and Suki were using is dead, its batteries drained. The Air Lab and the Food Lab share a single tool-storage unit, which is just inside the Food Lab. Prakesh slips through the door connecting the two. The air changes. It's darker in here, more humid, and he can feel the heat baking off the greenhouses. The bass rumble from the buzz box rattles the back of his skull.

Prakesh stops. He takes a deep breath, inhaling wet air, picking up a dozen different scents. He can smell strawberries, and pumpkins, and the earthy musk of the potatoes in the far corner, hidden under dark covers. He can smell the refrigerant from the air conditioning, sharp and unpleasant.

And there's something else. Something he can't place.

He shakes his head, and keeps walking.

The tool storage is just ahead, a long, thin structure lit from within by glaring lights. It looks as if the building is on fire, like it's containing something white hot. Prakesh pays it no attention, striding up to the counter. He'll talk to Deakin, the guy in charge of storage. Mention the weird smell. Odds are, it's just a new fertiliser someone's using.

But Deakin isn't at the desk. Prakesh leans over it, twisting his head to take in the stores. There's no one there – just the tools, hanging from hooks and balanced precariously on rusted shelves. The seed bank is at the back, a huge walk-in freezer, its door shut tight and sealed with a keypad.

"Deakin?" Prakesh says. Then, louder: "You there?"

No answer. Just the insects in the buzz box, humming away.

Prakesh decides to vault the counter and pick out what he needs. He can see a tab screen off to one side, which means he can leave Deakin a note. But just as he puts his hands on the countertop, he registers movement behind him.

He whirls, thinking only of Darnell, of how close he was before, but there's no one there.

He takes another deep breath, turns back, and that's when he catches sight of Deakin.

The store controller is standing by one of the greenhouses, his back to Prakesh. He's looking up at the ceiling, his arms hanging by his sides. He appears to be taking deep breaths, his shoulders rising and falling.

"Deak," says Prakesh, not understanding the prickles of fear scurrying across his shoulder blades and along the back of his neck. "Need to take out a pH monitor, man. Could you—"

"I never got to see her," Deakin says.

Prakesh freezes. There is something in Deak's voice he doesn't like at all. He takes a step closer.

Deak turns. He's an older man, over fifty, but in the blazing light from the stores he looks thirty years younger. His eyes are wet with tears.

And in that instant, Prakesh realises what the strange smell is. It's the burned-plastic stench of ammonia. Specifically, ammonium nitrate, a compound created from fertiliser.

Deakin's shirt is open. Underneath it, he's wearing a vest of some kind, a mess of plastic and metal and cotton pouches. His fingers are wrapped around a thin cord, leading right to the centre of his chest.

"I never got to see the Earth," Deakin says, and pulls the cord.

29

Riley

The shockwave rips through the catwalk, and I feel the metal buckle as the rivets struggle to hold it in place. The world is filled with a horrible orange light. My hands over my ears saved me from the worst of it, but it's still loud enough to shake my bones.

Someone collides with me, and I'm thrown to the right. I land on someone else, with only a moment to gasp for breath before another body collapses right on top of me. My hands are wrenched from my ears, and the noise swells back into a dying bass note and the terrified roar of the crowd. Underneath us, the catwalk gives another sickening lurch. The overhead lights flash back on. The people around me are on the floor, bodies piling on top of each other, thrashing, yelling, scrambling for grip.

Whoever landed on top of me is heavy, his elbow pushing painfully into my chest. Over my shoulder, I see Amira grab the railing and leap into space.

For a moment, I'm convinced she's been thrown to her death by the twisting catwalk. I push the man off me with strength I didn't know I had, and scramble to the railing. Then I see her hands gripped onto it, and I realise what both she and Carver have done. To escape the crowd, they flipped themselves onto the outside edge of the railing. Bending their legs and arms, they flexed with the catwalk and held on, away from the crush of bodies. If I hadn't been hit, I'd have done the same thing.

Amira grabs my hand, and starts to pull herself over. As she does so, I see what's below us, and for a moment, I just stop breathing.

The bomb detonated right in the middle of the crowd. The black, burned ring around the centre of the blast is scattered with blood and torn clothing. Darnell is gone, the barricades knocked over, the stompers scattered and shouting. Okwembu and the rest of the council are nowhere to be seen. The Level 1 catwalk has been sheared in half, with the broken edges twisted upwards. The Level 2 catwalk just below us is intact, but only just: the metal plates are bulging in the middle, as if a giant hand had pushed them from beneath. People lie sprawled along it; knocked senseless by the blast.

Far below, a man tries to crawl away, pulling himself along the ground with one arm. His other is gone at the shoulder, leaving nothing more than a nub of bone surrounded by pulpy wetness. Dark blood stains his side. As I watch, he reaches out his remaining arm, as if hunting for something he can no longer see. Then he falls still. Around him lie charred bodies. Some are still smoking.

The scene before me seems too vivid. I can feel it fixing in my mind, its awful roots digging deep and refusing to let go.

I shut my eyes tight and pull, hauling Amira over the railing.

Carver flips himself over too, landing squarely on someone's back. He hops off, a horrified expression on his face, and turns to us. His mouth is moving, but I can't make out the words, and it's only then that I notice the siren blaring from the comms. I'm shaking, and I reach up to block my ears again, but then the siren cuts off abruptly. It's replaced by a voice, female, automated. And far too calm.

"Warning. Fire detected in Apogee sector. Fire detected in Gardens sector. Please move calmly to your nearest evacuation point. Warning…"

And as the message repeats itself, Amira meets my eye, and the same horrifying realisation seems to dawn.

Prakesh. The Air Lab.

He always hated the trials. He's never been to one, always refused, said they were barbaric. He'll still be there, in the Air Lab. And if someone let off a bomb there…

The catwalk under us groans. The left side sags, then jerks downwards, sending shockwaves up through our feet. The shockwave from the bomb has weakened it – all that old metal, some of it a hundred years old. Around us, more panic starts to spread through the crowd: their senses heightened by fear and adrenaline, they begin to push, crushing up against the entrances on either side, a seething mass of flesh.

The man who fell on me barrels past, his face twisted in a rictus of terror. The catwalk gives another terrible noise, and this time I swear I hear the sound of shearing metal. The panic rises, boils over: the crowd is screaming now, forcing up against each other, people clawing others out of the way, desperate to escape. Below us, the floor has completely emptied, the crowd streaming into the corridors surrounding the gallery.

30

Darnell

Free.

Darnell's body is stained with sweat and smoke. His ears are ringing, and he managed to twist his ankle when the explosion knocked him off his feet. It's throbbing painfully, but he doesn't care. He's free.

He doesn't know how they got out of the gallery. He doesn't even know where they are. He's been following the guard, ducking under pipes and threading through deserted rooms and clambering across the monorail tracks. There's a part of him that doesn't want to trust the guard, that doesn't want to trust anyone. But he keeps thinking back to the bomb, how the explosion tore the crowd apart like their bodies were made of paper. He keeps thinking back to how the guard worked quickly, undoing his restraints, pulling him along. No, he can trust his sleepers.

They stop near a ganglia of gurgling pipes. The only light comes from two slits in the wall, no bigger than a man's finger. They must be near one of the corridors; Darnell can hear thundering feet, the sweet sound of panicked shouting.

He collapses against the wall, amazed at how thirsty he is. The guard stays on his feet. He digs behind one of the pipes, and tosses Darnell a canteen. Darnell flips the top off, drinking greedily.

"We did it, Sir," says the guard. Darnell looks at him. He's younger than he thought he was, with a mess of dirty blond hair and a face flushed with excitement. Briefly, Darnell wonders what happened in his past. Why he's so eager. He's not someone Darnell recruited – he's just another node on the network, another flare point on the fuse.

Darnell gets to his feet. "I need to get back to my office. There's a—"

"Way ahead of you, Sir."

The guard produces a tab screen from inside his jacket, and hands it over. Darnell has to hide his surprise; it's the one that he had specially modified. The stubby antenna on the side gives him wireless access to Outer Earth's comms system – with it, he can broadcast at any time. But there's no way the guard could have known about it.

Darnell glances at the man, then back to the screen. "You went into my office?"

"Yeah," the guard says. "I was one of the stompers who got told to search it. Thought a tab screen might come in handy. Got this for you, too." He passes Darnell his knife – the thick-handled wedge of steel that Darnell had previously asked the poor tech to sharpen up for him.

"Nice blade," the guard says.

Darnell stares at him. "You've been busy."

The guard returns his stare. "I'm just trying to help, Sir. We're doing a good thing. Without human beings, the biosphere can recover. You're saving the world, and...and I'm behind you, Sir, you know what I mean? Hundred per cent."

Darnell ignores the rhetoric. But as the man speaks, he glances towards the corridor, to the slits that lead to the outside world. He doesn't see Darnell reach up, doesn't see the hand until it's wrapped around his head.

Darnell slams the guard's head into the wall, again, again. With each hit, the guard's struggles grow weaker, and the red patch on the wall grows bigger and bigger. Blood splatters Darnell's thin prison jumpsuit.

It's over inside ten seconds.

Darnell lets go. He waits a few moments, looking for any sign of life. Nothing.

There, he thinks. Now the only one who knows where he is, is him.

Working quickly, he strips the guard of his hard body armour, then his shirt, jacket and pants. The shirt is long-sleeved, made of a stretchy, artificial fabric, slightly loose on the guard's body but fitting tightly across Darnell's chest and shoulders. The jacket is too small for him, unable to zip closed, and the pants don't quite reach his ankles, but they'll be warmer than a prison jumpsuit. He'll need that where he's going. He tucks the knife in his waistband, behind his back.

He looks down at the tab screen. In a moment, he'll turn it on, accessing the comms. And then he can talk to everyone on Outer Earth, and tell them what's coming next.

31

Riley

Amira grabs me. She's outwardly calm, but her eyes burn with adrenaline. She jerks her head in the direction of the railing, and I realise what she wants us to do. She, Carver and I grab the railing, and in one synchronised movement, hurl ourselves up and over.

For a moment, I flashback to the job where I transported the eye to Darnell, when I threw myself off the Level 5 catwalk to escape the Lieren, and time seemed to stop. It seems like years ago. Decades. This time, there's no silence, no peaceful floating sensation. Just the air rushing in my ears and the screams from the catwalk above.

The Level 2 catwalk is directly below, flying up towards me. There's a body sprawled on the catwalk, someone – man, woman, I don't know – with a long grey coat, their right leg twisted at an impossible angle.

This time, there's no avoiding it. There's no space, nowhere to get a clean landing. Nothing I can do. I bend my knees, throw my arms above my head and make contact, smashing right into the back of the prone body. I feel it spasm under my feet. Whoever it is cries out, and then I'm bouncing forwards, rolling, colliding with the railing and collapsing in an ugly heap of limbs.

Amira has landed a little way along, managing – somehow – to avoid landing on anyone. Carver is nowhere to be seen, and my heart leaps into my throat. Where is he? Did he miss the catwalk completely? But then there's a yell of pain, and I see a hand clenched onto the railing. Carver overshot the catwalk, and somehow managed to grab the rail and check his fall.

Amira reaches down, grabbing Carver under both arms and hauling him over the railing. Carver falls to the ground. His breathing is too regular, as if he's having to will each breath out of his lungs, and he's clutching his arm. His face is deathly white. Amira crouches down. "Dislocated," he says, spitting the word out through gritted teeth.

At that moment, the Level 3 catwalk that we just jumped from gives one last deep, rending screech, and the side furthest from us sheers off from the wall.

"Oh shit," says Carver.

The far edge of the falling catwalk smashes into ours with a dull boom, throwing us off our feet again. The catwalk collides with the railing, crushing it. It's still attached to the wall at the far side, and people are sliding down it, falling off the sides, screaming, smashing on the burned ground below. Above and behind me, I can see the side still connected to the wall beginning to come away, the rivets beginning to twist and turn, jiggling loose.

Fear surges through me, and I leap to my feet, reaching out and grabbing both Carver and Amira and pulling them forwards. "Move!" I yell. The siren is screaming again. We run.

Carver is swearing in pain. Around us, the gallery destroys itself in a whirlwind of screaming, shredded metal. We're barely feet from the corridor entrance ahead when the near side of the Level 3 catwalk rips free, separating from the wall with one final ear-splitting screech. I grab Carver and Amira, and throw us all forwards into the corridor ahead. I get a split-second glimpse of the people still on the catwalk before the falling slab of metal collapses onto them. It bounces upwards, falls back down with another bone-shattering boom, then slides off and crashes to the floor below.

We tumble to the floor, our chests heaving. I'm soaked in sweat, my mouth too dry, the blood in my ears pumping almost as loud as the siren. Carver has gone silent, his eyes tightly shut, his fingers twisted into half-fists. The lights in the corridor are flickering madly, casting dancing shadows across the wall. The sirens pause, and the emergency message repeats itself. Fire in Gardens sector.

Amira is kneeling next to Carver, gingerly testing his shoulder. I open my mouth to say something, but she cuts me off, pointing down the corridor in the direction of Gardens. "Go!" she screams. I force myself to my feet, and take off, at full speed almost at once, not looking back.

It's the most terrifying run of my life. The panic has become a living thing, coursing through the corridors and catwalks like poison through veins. Stompers are everywhere, shouting over the sirens, yelling at people to keep calm. There's stinger fire, both in the distance and, once, shockingly close, where I come up a level to see a stomper draw a bead on a man in a dirty white vest. I'm just in time to see the man raise his arms, the look of surprise on his face, before the stinger goes off and blood blooms on his chest. The stomper senses movement behind him and swings around, but I'm gone, barely pausing, my arms pumping and that sour taste of fear flooding my mouth. I can't lose Prakesh again.

Several times, I nearly fall, barrelling round a corner too fast or not spotting a group of people until it's almost too late. I manage to keep my balance, flying through Apogee and then through Chengshi, my chest burning, a stitch ripping at my side. Halfway there, it occurs to me that I sent Grace Garner to the Air Lab to meet Prakesh, and I'm speared by a realisation that I may have sent her to her death.

No. She wouldn't have had time to even get out of the sector before the bomb went off, let alone make it to Gardens. She could be anywhere.

Not far now, barely five minutes away, up through the stairwells, cut through the Chengshi mess hall and the schoolrooms, take that shortcut down into the service passage by the Level 2 corridor…

And then I turn the corner, and ahead of me is the Lieren with a red wolf tattooed on his neck.

32

Prakesh

The fire consumes Deakin instantly.

There's no explosion, no concussive blast, but the wave of bitter heat is enough to knock Prakesh backwards. Deakin's entire body lights up, and for a second, Prakesh can see his face, staring out of a corona of flame. The tear-tracks on Deakin's cheeks boil away.

Then he's gone, his body writhing, and the fire is reaching out, sucking up every molecule of oxygen, becoming its own fuel source as it spreads. It moves faster than anything Prakesh has ever seen. Liquid waves of it curl up and over the greenhouses, puddle across the floor.

Prakesh runs.

The greenhouses explode behind him, popping with a sound that echoes around the hangar. The air is filling with smoke – hot, sickening, thick, burning his throat and scratching at his eyes. All he can think of is what they were taught in school: the worst thing that can happen in a space-borne module is fire. In an enclosed area like Outer Earth, it can destroy everything. A little one can be contained, controlled. This is not a little one.

The suppressors activate. He can hear their metallic

whine above the roaring fire and screaming techs. The foam is meant to retard the fire and cut off its oxygen, but the burning chemicals slice right through the slick white foam, fizzling it out of existence.

Heat licks at the back of his neck. Techs are streaming past him, running for the main doors. One of them trips ahead of him, sliding across the plate flooring, her hands scrabbling at it. Prakesh reaches down and grabs her under the arm, hauls her to her feet an instant before she gets trampled.

And as he does so, he gets a look at the door between the Air Lab and the Food Lab.

It's supposed to shut if there's a fire. The sensors are meant to seal it automatically. But it's wide open. Maybe Deakin sabotaged the sensors, or maybe they broke down years ago. Prakesh doesn't know, and right then, he doesn't care. He can see the trees through the opening, the air processors arranged in tiered banks on the far wall of the Air Lab. If the fire reaches them...

Prakesh pushes the tech towards the doors. She tries to pull him with her, pleading wordlessly, but he's already moving. He bolts sideways down the greenhouses, the stores to his left – the entire structure nothing more than a burning shell. His throat is stripped raw, slashed to ribbons by the smoke.

There are Air Lab techs running for the doors – they've seen what he's seen, but they're too far away. A jet of fire appears around the edge of a greenhouse, questing like a snake, spitting black smoke. Prakesh dodges to the side, nearly loses his balance, holds it. He can feel his hair singeing, the smell scorching the inside of his skull.

The controls to shut the doors are on a large panel on the right of them. Prakesh slams into it at full speed, hammers on it like he's trying to bust through the wall.

Liquid fire is spreading across the floor, heading right for the gap, seeking fresh air.

This isn't just ammonium nitrate, Prakesh thinks. On some level, he's stunned at how rational the thought is. As if the fire were nothing more than an experiment, something that could be quantified by a DNA thermocycler or a pH monitor.

With a groan, the doors judder closed, seconds before the fire reaches them. Prakesh has no way to tell if they'll hold. He's got to get out of here, got to reach the main doors before—

With a giant bang, one of the greenhouses behind him pops open. The shockwave knocks him off his feet, slamming into the wall and peppering him with shards of molten plastic. He's surrounded on all sides by the fire, its tendrils reaching out for him.

The doors, he thinks. *I closed the doors; that's all that—*

33

Riley

There are three Lieren – Tattoo, the lanky one who looked into my pack, and someone else I don't know, a kid so short he's practically a dwarf. They're standing in the middle of the cramped corridor, hands on hips, breathing hard. I catch sight of the white hospital-issue box under the dwarf's arm. They've been busy.

I see a look of startled recognition on Tattoo's face. But I'm not stopping, or even slowing down. Instead, I push my body into a sprint. I jump, taccing off the wall for height, springing right towards them. Tattoo gets out a "Hey—" before my outstretched foot crashes into his face.

His nose shatters. His head snaps backwards, throwing up blood in a fine spray. The other two Lieren are reaching for me, but I'm moving too fast, my momentum carrying me through. As I tuck for landing, Tattoo gives off a strangled, squawking cry, flailing his arms. I land, roll, spring up and run without looking back.

I can hear a thin mewl of pain from Tattoo as he clutches his destroyed nose, and above it, pounding footsteps and angry cries behind me as the others give chase.

But they're going from a standing start. I'm already back at full speed, vanishing into the corridors, and after a moment their cries fade into the background.

I tilt my head forwards, and force my screaming muscles to go faster. Scared and exhausted as I am, I feel myself smiling. *Gods*, that felt good.

It doesn't take me much longer to get there. I've come into the gallery on the Level 1 catwalk. It's chaos down below. Dumar, Chang and about ten stompers are trying to hold back a rapidly growing crowd. The huge doors are open – both the main one, and the smaller one inside the decontamination chamber – and what's beyond them is hell: a black, smoking, burning wilderness, scattered with flecks of fire and foam. I can hear a man shouting, yelling about salvaging food. Techs are stumbling out of the doors; Prakesh isn't among them.

I have to get inside. I have to find him. I force myself to calm down, to breathe, sucking in huge gulps of air.

And then I see her: a woman with fiery red hair, bent double with hacking coughs. She's come out of the main doors and is standing off to one side, away from the stompers. Her once-white lab coat is now black and streaky with soot, and her hair is matted and dark. I know her. She's one of Prakesh's colleagues, and she was at the party we had in the Nest. What's her name? I know it... Suki. It's Suki.

The idea is fully formed before I realise it's there. I ignore the stairs at the far end, jumping the rail and dropping to the floor below. The catwalk is no more than a few feet up, and with a quick roll, I'm on my feet again. I can feel my back aching in protest against the rolls I've been forcing it to do, but I ignore it. I can worry about that later.

I skirt the crowd, working my way towards Suki. I can hear Chang shouting in his nasal voice: "Please! We can't let anybody in!"

Nobody notices me. They're all focused on the entrance, which is now billowing thick white smoke. I glance up; the top of the gallery is gone, invisible in a white fog. Suki is still bent double when I reach her, shivering, her arms crossed in front of her. Her face under the streaks of soot is deathly pale.

"Suki," I say, skidding to a halt. She looks up, but shock has wiped her eyes clean. I repeat her name, and after a moment she nods slowly, as if only just realising that I'm talking to her.

"Suki, where is Prakesh?" I say slowly, emphasising every word. When she doesn't respond, I grab her shoulders, arresting her panicked gaze. "Suki, look at me. Where is Prakesh? Did he come out with you? Is he here?

"Prakesh, he..." She trails off. Her voice is roughly ringed with smoke. I stay silent, looking her in the eyes. Frustration is boiling through me, and it's all I can do not to start shaking her back and forth, screaming in her face.

Her eyes focus, snapping back to life. "Prakesh! He's in there. He's still in there!" She pulls away and begins running towards the doors, but I reach out and snag her back. She gives an incoherent yell, trying to shake me off, but I hold firm.

"Listen to me, Suki," I say. I'm hissing now, holding the terror back at knifepoint. "You need to get me inside."

She doesn't seem to hear me. "But we've got to get Prakesh!" She's screaming now, fear coursing through her voice. "Someone's got to go back in and get Prakesh!" she repeats, as if saying his name will cause him magically to pop into existence.

"I'll go," I say. Maybe it's something in my voice, because she stops yelling and stares at me. Seizing the advantage, I tell her to give me her lab coat. She hesitates for a moment, her pleading eyes now gushing large tears, and then rips her coat off and hands it to me. It's heavy, the rough fabric damp and slimy with soot. But by now there are more techs falling out the doors, and one more white coat won't be noticed.

"They're going to seal it off," says Suki, the manic edge returning to her voice. "It's the only way to fight the fire."

"What about the foam?"

There are no sprinklers or fire hoses on the station – nobody would waste water like that – but there are systems that spray chemical foam if a fire breaks out. They should be suppressing the fire, but Suki shakes her head, flicking it from side to side for a lot longer than normal. "It didn't work. The fire just burned right through it, like it wasn't even there. You have to be quick, or they'll trap you inside."

I'm already running. Leaving behind a babbling Suki, I head towards the doors, hoping that nobody picks out my face. Not one tech or stomper looks in my direction.

I can feel the darting tongues of heat from the fire. They lick at my skin, and I have to force my eyes shut as one sickeningly hot blast washes over me. Beyond me, the Food Lab is a mess of smoke and flame, lit with showers of sparks and the red glow of emergency lights. I can see a few greenhouses still standing, glowing from within like lanterns.

I should be scared. I should be running, away, far away. But I feel none of that. Instead, I'm gripped by a deathly calm, and there's only a single thought in my mind.

Prakesh. I'm coming.

There's an angry shout from behind me. Someone grabs at my arm, yelling for me to stop. In one movement, I shrug off Suki's lab coat, and start running. Straight into hell.

The heat envelops me, so intense that nausea begins to boil in my stomach. The smoke is thick, and I blink rapidly as I run down the rows of greenhouses. Ahead of me, two of them pop, exploding outwards with a bang, showering the ground with flecks of molten plastic. There's too much fire. It's everywhere, blanketing the floor, the walls.

I don't know how long I've got. I scream Prakesh's name, and get a mouthful of hot, stinging smoke. A series of coughs explode out of me, hard enough to bring me crashing to my knees, each one like something ripping its way out of my throat with ragged nails. I haul myself up, and keep running, pushing towards the Air Lab. The white smoke and dull red fire turns the gardens into a swirling wilderness, and I'm not even sure I'm heading in the right direction.

I turn a corner, and reach out a hand to steady myself, then pull it back with a yelp. A thin line of shiny molten plastic has splattered across the back of my hand, and I frantically wipe it on my sleeve. The plastic peels off my hand, taking a thin layer of skin with it. The pain is so sharp and bright that I actually gasp. By now, my eyes are streaming, stinging from the smoke and the heat.

I stagger on, forcing myself forwards, trying to dodge the pools of fire even as my legs threaten to give way. *I have to find him. I have to.*

But even as the thought forms, I know it's hopeless. The entire hangar is a burning coffin, and I'm trapped inside. I haven't come across a single person since I dived in, but with the smoke they could have passed within feet of me and I wouldn't have known. Even if I somehow find Prakesh, there's no way we'll get to the main doors before they seal us in. And they *will* seal us in: the need to starve the fire of oxygen is going to outweigh the lives of a tracer and a lab tech.

I sink to the ground, collapsing onto my side. The air is clearer down here, and I suck in great lungfuls of it, bringing on another bout of coughing. My chest is a taut drum. There's a hum in the air, rumbling under the crackling of the fire, and it takes me a moment to realise that it's coming from the buzz box. The insects. Millions of them must be dying, their enclosure turned into a furnace.

The smoke is heavy now, starting to rest on the floor, and the searing heat scorches my back through my jacket. I should be scared, but the calm has returned, washing over me. I picture Prakesh's face, holding it in the front of my mind, trying to recall every detail. I see him smiling, laughing at a stupid joke, the concern on his face when he saw I'd been ambushed, the relief when he hugged me in Gray's chamber. The look in his eyes when we were alone.

And then, unbidden, the others come to mind: Carver, Amira, the Twins. My mother and father.

Survived an ambush, caught a killer, went through a bombing, then died in a fire trying to save your best friend, I think, closing my eyes. *At least they'll be able to tell one hell of a story.*

This last thought is like something glimpsed only in passing before it vanishes into the distance.

And then strong hands grab me and haul me bodily off the floor. Prakesh's face is streaked with dirt and soot, ringed with the white smoke. For a moment, I'm paralysed, not sure if he's real or the first thing I see in the next world, but then he wraps an arm around me and starts pulling me with him. I force myself to walk, matching his pace.

My voice takes a moment to kick in. "They're sealing it off. All of it!" I shout.

"I know!" he yells back.

Ahead of us, I can see the doors to the labs: the panes of glass in each glow red with the reflected fire, like malevolent eyes. For a second, I'm seized with the idea that we need to get inside there, that they will provide shelter. But Prakesh seems to sense what I'm thinking and shakes his head, pulling us to the right along the wall. We're both coughing again, trying to find tiny pockets of air in the smoke.

A tongue of fire explodes across the passage. The heat jabs out at us, and we both collapse backwards, turning away from it as we crash to the ground. I feel as if I'm being baked alive, but Prakesh hauls me up again. "Don't you *dare* die on me," he says.

And suddenly, ahead of us, the entrance looms. A figure, silhouetted in the spotlights, is running towards us. More hands pulling us out into the dazzling light. And there is no smoke, only clean air, and Prakesh and I collapse onto each other, crashing to the floor. I never knew how delicious air could be, how cool and sweet. I want to bathe in it, roll around in it, stuff great handfuls of it into my mouth.

Behind us, the doors shut with a boom, and the rumble and crackle of the fire vanishes, replaced by the noise of the crowd.

Prakesh rolls away from me. His face is covered in soot. I turn my head to the side to look at him. He sees me, and half smiles. "Don't worry. Your face is as dirty as mine, I promise," he says, his voice edged with smoke, and despite myself, I laugh. It hurts my chest, and soon turns into another coughing fit. Prakesh reaches out his arm across the floor, and grips my hand. I squeeze back.

There's a shadow over Prakesh, and then the worried face of Dumar comes into view. He glances angrily at me, and grabs Prakesh by the shoulder.

"Please tell me you two were the last ones out?" he asks. "Tell me there's no one in there."

Prakesh shakes his head. "No. Just us. We managed

to get everyone else out, I think." Anxiety flits across his face. "Did someone get the gene banks out?"

"We did," says a voice behind Dumar. It's Suki, who looks as if she wants to hug Prakesh, or punch him, or faint, all at once.

Prakesh sits up, holds his head. I suck in more crisp, clean air – and suddenly, worry surges through me.

"Prakesh," I say. "Please tell me the fire didn't reach the Air Lab. Tell me the trees didn't catch."

He's silent, and for a moment I'm almost certain that our air is about to be snatched away, but then he turns to me and I can see relief in his eyes. "They're OK. I sealed the Air Lab off." His expression turns grave. "But the Food Lab. The insects..." We all turn to stare at the huge doors that now seal the lab away.

We now have no food.

I hear Darnell's words again. *There is going to be so much fun, you believe that.*

34

Riley

The crowd around is still cut through with panic. Several people have begun to bang on the doors to the Food Lab, demanding that they be opened. Dumar hauls Prakesh to his feet, and then reaches out a hand to me. He seems about to hug me, like he did back in Gray's room, but he stops halfway through the motion, looking me up and down instead.

"You all right?" he says. I can't read his eyes.

"I'm fine," I say. I mean it, too: the tightness in my chest is fading, and every breath still tastes as sweet as ice-cold water. I glance at my hand. The red strip across the back where the molten plastic kissed it is painful, but looks superficial. I won't have to get another blast of that white foam from the medics.

Prakesh chances a smile. "Maybe we shouldn't fight any more," he says.

"You think?"

"I'm just saying. Fires, kidnapping, bombs...maybe the universe is trying to tell us something." He gives a nervous laugh.

"What now?" says Suki. She and Dumar look lost.

Prakesh thinks for a moment. "Suki, we should still have some soil in the upper labs," he says. "We need to get an emergency food op going, and we need to do it now. Tell the guys to start bringing it over, along with the spare UVs – do it right in the Air Lab. The GM plants aren't even close to ready, but we can use those new carbide seeds the lab rats were working on. And while you're at it, we're going to need some sort of hydroponic system. Tell Yoshiro to use whatever he needs, and tell him he'll have to do it double-time."

Suki stares at him, taken aback for a moment, but then nods and runs off, shouting for the techs to follow her.

Prakesh turns to me. "The others? Amira?"

"Safe. Carver hurt his shoulder, but they're OK. The Twins were in the Nest the last I heard."

"The message over the comms said there was a fire in your sector. Was there another bomb?"

I quickly fill him in on what happened back at Darnell's trial in Apogee.

"How many were hurt?"

I avoid his eyes, and his shoulders sag. He wraps an arm around me; his grip is strong, comforting. "Let's get you back," he says.

"I can walk myself," I reply, irritated.

"Walk? Ry, you can barely stand. Come on. Suki has things under control here."

I look at the growing crowd hammering on the doors, calling out in terror to the others. "I doubt that."

"They aren't getting in. Not through those doors, anyway. Let's go."

We move towards the stairwell at the far end of the gallery. The lights far above us have dimmed, as if in sympathy with the chaos below.

The world might not have ended, but it can't be far

off. The chaos gets worse as we cross the border into Chengshi. Several times, we pass people fighting over food: men hurling insults at each other over caches of vegetables, held back by their friends. Someone being robbed on the ground as we cross the catwalk above, a knife waved in his face for a box of protein bars. I want to help, but Prakesh pulls me onward. We enter the maze of corridors again, and pass the mess. The door is shut, and two stompers in full armour guard the entrance. I swear I see them tighten their grip on their stingers as we walk past. Prakesh nods to them, but they just stare back.

We're nearing the Apogee border when there's a crackle from a nearby comms screen, set into the corridor wall. The station logo flashes briefly, and then Janice Okwembu is standing there. She's back in the board room, standing alone behind a lectern. We stop to watch; even on the crackly monitor, I can see her lips set tight, the steel in her eyes.

She doesn't bother with a greeting. "Today, we suffered two coordinated attacks," she begins. I hear her words echoing down the corridor, repeating themselves through a dozen different speakers. "The first bomb was set off at a criminal trial in Apogee, and a remote device was triggered in our Food Lab. The first explosion claimed the lives of nearly fifty people, and the second, while less deadly, contained an incendiary chemical agent.

"We don't know how they were set, or what their composition was. The damage was great, both human and otherwise. Fortunately, the structural integrity of the station has not been compromised, and the engineers have told me that our orbit has not been disrupted. I would urge everybody to remain calm, to share what food you have, to help each other through this crisis."

"Like that's going to happen," Prakesh says.

Okwembu continues, leaning forward on the lectern, staring straight into the camera. "There is much to be done before..." The picture crackles, then vanishes entirely. Okwembu's voice cuts off abruptly, replaced by a loud burst of static.

And then Darnell is on the screen and my heart freezes solid in my chest.

It's impossible to tell where he is. Whatever is behind him is cloaked in shadow. Prakesh is squeezing my hand tight, and around me I hear people gasp.

"Sorry to interrupt," Darnell says. "I wanted to take this opportunity to thank everyone for coming to my trial. And if you missed it, don't worry – there's plenty more still to come."

The feed glitches, the static ripping Darnell's face in two. The audio cuts out, and when he comes back a moment later, it's horribly distorted, as if he's put the microphone right up to his face.

"...forty-eight hours. That's the time you have left to live. That's all the time we're giving you."

The last word is caught somewhere in the feed and stretches out, mutating into a metallic buzz that seems to take an age to fade.

I've stopped breathing. I have to force myself to suck air into my lungs, and every word of our conversation in the brig is surfacing in my mind.

"Humans don't deserve Outer Earth," Darnell says, his grin glitching in and out as the feed struggles to keep up. "Not after what we did to our planet. We bombed and killed and—"

This time, the screen goes completely black, the audio vanishing. When it comes back, Darnell is walking with the camera. The lights on the ceiling turn his face into a dark silhouette. He laughs, that childish voice becoming a shrieking cackle, which in turn morphs into a horrendous coughing fit.

"We need to go. Now," I say to Prakesh.

But even as we move down the corridor, Darnell's words follow us, turning into a monstrous echo. Wherever he is, he's hacked the entire system.

"And there are more than enough of us," he's saying. "We're living among you, right now. Your best friend. The person across from you in the mess. Your sister. And all of us together? We're the Sons of Earth."

We're at the sector border. Around us, people are staring at the screens in disbelief. Darnell's words are everywhere.

"And when we're gone? Our planet will restore itself. It'll take millennia. But after a while, it'll be as clean and fresh as it was when we first crawled out of the muck. And do you know why? Because we won't be there."

He stops. For a second, I think the audio has cut out again, hope it has, but he's just pausing. He leans close to the microphone – close enough for us to hear his breathing.

"The next two days are going to be so much fun. We—"

Another burst of static rattles through "...cut the signal! Cut it!"

Janice Okwembu's voice is urgent. I catch a glimpse of a screen as we cut through one of the lower corridors. She looks flustered, her veneer of control cracked. But she nods to someone off camera, and stares at the screen. Her eyes are made of steel.

"I heard what you all just heard," she says, and her voice is strong. "Let me make this clear. We will find Oren Darnell. We will bring him down. You have my word on that. For now, please try to stay calm. We will all get through this." She pauses, and the screen reverts to the station logo.

As the broadcast ends, I can hear shouts from behind us. Fear becomes panic in seconds, washing across the crowd. Prakesh and I keep moving. What else is there to do?

Suddenly, I remember the woman on the catwalk. Grace Garner. Whatever she had to tell me looks more important by the second – a possible piece in the puzzle of Gray, Darnell and the Sons of Earth. I should have listened to her then. I should have made her tell me.

I turn to Prakesh, quickly explaining what happened and what Garner looks like, but his expression is puzzled. "A woman? No, sorry, Ry, she didn't show up. Just as well, right?" He barks a laugh and looks away, and it suddenly occurs to me just how much the loss of the Food Lab must hurt him. There are dark circles under his eyes, and it's not just the smoke and the exertion that's made him look so drawn, so tired.

He shakes his head, as if trying to bring himself back. "If she had something to tell you about Darnell, then we need to find her," he says.

I nod. "We should get cleaned up first. Get some water. And we've got some food back at the Nest."

I start down the corridor, but Prakesh shakes his head. "You go. I need to check on my parents."

"Are you—"

"I'll be fine. Go link up with the rest of the Dancers. When you're together, come and find me."

I give his hand a squeeze, and he turns, jogging off down the corridor.

Without his support, my legs feel numb, soft as a wedge of tofu, and I nearly collapse to the ground. My mouth is coated with thick saliva. I realise I'm still wearing my pack, and I reach back for the water tube, but it's dry, without even a single drop left. I shoulder the pack into a more comfortable position, and head down the corridor, distant shouts from the galleries chasing me.

The Dancers are there when I reach the Nest, and as I haul myself up through the trapdoor, Kev sticks his head out the door. There's uncharacteristic anger on his face. "Where you been?"

I cut him off. "I'm OK. The others?"

"Here." He throws open the door, revealing the rest of the crew. Carver is leaning against the wall, flexing his arm, his hand clasped on his shoulder. Yao is at the workbench, rummaging through the drawers. And in the centre of the room stands Amira, hands on hips, anger on her face.

"Tell me you've got some food in that pack," she says. I shake my head, and she grimaces.

It's then that I see the pile of food on the table; they must have raided every corner of the Nest to see what we had left. It's shockingly little, barely enough to last us three days. Some ancient potatoes, tinged with green and already sprouting little nubbly shoots. A few protein bars. Two withered carrots. A small pile of hoarded sugar shots, little jellies in thin cups. Behind the pile, a dirty bottle of homebrew. Yao reaches up, and dumps a small pile of dried fruit on the bench – apples, it looks like.

Carver says, "Well, at least we won't die hungry."

"Oh come on," Yao says. "You don't believe he can actually pull it off?"

We all stare at her. "What?" she says. "He's a guy with a camera, and now everyone on Outer Earth thinks he's a god or something. I ain't scared of him."

"Save it, Yao," snaps Amira. Her patience seems to be exhausted. I want to tell her about Garner, about Prakesh, but before I can say anything she passes me a cup of water. "Have a drink, then I need you back out there. I want you working the market: that goodwill you stored up after we caught Darnell? Time to use it. Yao,

Kevin, I want you on the gallery floor. There's got to be some people there who need something transported."

I take a slug of the water; it's warm, but soothes my throat, and I have to force myself not to gulp, to take slow sips.

"Are you going to be OK? Your arm isn't going to fall off, is it?" Yao asks Carver.

"Oh, I thought I'd chill out here for a while, sweetie," Carver replies, flashing a smile which turns into a grimace. "Let you do some work for a change."

Amira glares at him, then turns back to us. "We don't know how long this situation is going to last. Even if the stompers find Darnell, food's going to be hard to come by for a while. So we carry on as normal. Trade runs for food – *only* food. It'll be tough out there, but take whatever you can get."

Nobody says anything, but the glances we share speak volumes. Amira's right. With the Food Lab down, it'll be hard enough even for those who have access to mess food. For tracers like us, who have to our find our own food?

I'm about to tell Amira what happened back on the catwalk, but as she glances at me I pause. That can wait. Right now, survival is more important. Wherever Garner is, Prakesh will take care of her.

"Something you want to say, Riley?" Amira's voice is impatient, testy.

I shake my head. "No. Let's do it."

35

Prakesh

Prakesh's parents live on the edge of Gardens, close to the white lights and clean surfaces of Apex. They have their own hab, a comparatively large unit with a double cot and its own bathroom. Ravi Kumar's long-service awards still hang on the wall, strips of black metal engraved with the dates he spent in the space construction corps. His wife has decorated the hab with pot plants – some given to her by Prakesh, some grown by her alone.

"You – inside, now," Achala Kumar barks when she opens the door to Prakesh. He's momentarily stunned, but no sooner is the door shut than she's hugging him tight, her face buried in his shoulder.

"When they said – and then that man..." she manages, and then she's sobbing, her tears soaking through the fabric of his shirt.

Prakesh's father is seated on the edge of the bed. The left leg of his red pants is knotted tight below the knee, his cane resting easily across his lap.

"It's OK," Prakesh says, lifting his mother's face towards him. "We got out all right."

"No, you didn't. Look at you!" She wipes at his face, smearing the soot.

"Achala, leave the boy alone." Ravi Kumar stands up, rising off the bed with an experienced grace. His cane taps as he limps towards them, his eyes boring into his son's. "How bad is it? The damage?"

"Bad." Prakesh reaches around his mother to one of the shelves, snags a canteen. He's more thirsty than he's ever been in his life, and sinks at least half the water in the bottle.

"You two got enough food?" he says to his father.

"Don't ask him," his mother says, jerking a finger at the older Kumar. "He doesn't even know how to fix the chemical toilet when it goes on the fritz."

"Achala."

"Well, you don't. It's just like the plasma cutter all over again, when you were working on the *Shinso Maru*."

"Again, you bring this up?"

Prakesh can't help smiling. It's easy to forget that his mother was his father's boss, a long time ago. He talks over them, his ravaged throat aching. "Someone tell me what your food stocks are like."

"We're fine," his father says. "We have a little stored away."

"How little?"

"Enough. We're fine, Prakesh, and you need to go."

"No, I need to..." Prakesh stops. He has no idea what he needs to do. By now, the Air Lab will be insane: the temporary growth operations will need all the hands they can get, and Suki and company can only keep them going for so long. But Riley sent someone to him – someone she needed to keep safe. And then there are his parents. He doesn't believe that they've got enough food left. Not even close. He should stay, help them keep going.

He shuts his eyes tight. He opens them when he hears the click of his father's crutch, feels his hand on his shoulder.

"Prakesh," says Ravi Kumar. "We're fine. You need to be back out there."

He sighs. "I know."

"And not just in the laboratory," his mother says. "You should be out in the rest of the sector. Making sure this *kutha sala* Darnell doesn't get inside people's heads."

"What?"

"I always said you should be involved in politics," Achala says, folding her arms. "People trust you."

"Only in the Air Lab," Prakesh says. He can feel his cheeks getting hot. "Only when I'm talking about trees."

"Nonsense. People look up to you. You might prefer to ignore it, but they do. And you can't afford to be afraid. Not now."

"But what if—"

"Go," they both say at once, then glance at each other. Achala Kumar has a strange smile on her face. "We can take care of ourselves," she says.

But as Prakesh looks at his parents, all he can see are the things that hold them back. It's not just his father's leg, which keeps him a virtual prisoner in Gardens, which has kept him away from the spacewalks he loved so much. It's the wrinkles around his mother's eyes, the way her neck and upper back are stooped. They were middle-aged when they had him, and the years since then haven't been kind.

His anger at Riley, his frustration, has found another target. He can almost feel it physically moving in his gut, swinging around to focus on Oren Darnell. He's trying to make everyone on the station suffer, and it's people like his parents who will suffer the most.

His mother is right – he does need to get back. But he's not just thinking about the Air Lab. He's thinking about the woman Riley sent to him. The woman who said she knew something.

The Air Lab can wait. If there's even the slightest chance that she could help stop Darnell, he has to find her.

36

Riley

It's amazing how everybody suddenly knows exactly how long we have left. Of course, it's not forty-eight hours any more. It's forty-four hours and thirteen minutes – at least, according to a man I passed on the way to market. His friend disagreed, said it was eleven minutes, waving a homemade watch around like a holy book.

The nervous energy has built up, kettling in the corridors and pushing at the walls of the galleries, thrumming with awful power. Rumours are everywhere, changing and mutating in the space of minutes, stories of possible sightings and citizen watch groups and computer hacks. I've never felt the station like this.

As I approach the market, winding my way through the bottom-level corridors of Apogee, I hear two people talking. They're husband and wife by the look of it, and she's cradling a baby, wrapped in tatty blankets, fast asleep.

"If they've hacked the Apex comms feed, then it won't be long before they take the control room," says the woman. "And when they do..."

The man interrupts her. "I refuse to believe that every single escape pod is gone."

"They are. You know that. But we could always take one of the tugs," the woman replies. There are dark circles under her eyes. "If there are enough of us, we could..."

Her words fade as I slip past. I almost want to go back, tell her not to bother. The tugs, which we use for shipping asteroid slag into the station when the catcher ships come into our orbit, don't have nearly enough range. You'd run out of fuel long before you reached Earth. And it's not as if we can call the asteroid catcher ships for help.

There are only two of them left now: enormous vessels which track the rocks through space, pull them in, drag them back to be processed down into slag. We depend on that slag for our minerals, our building materials. Their missions take years, and right now, both of them are in deep space. If this had happened ten or twenty years ago, they might have been closer, on the moon or on Mars. But the resources that were being brought back weren't good enough, so the catchers were retrofitted to snag asteroids. Even if we sent a distress signal, and they came back for us, they'd never get here in time.

I expect the market to be insane, even to see looters wrecking the stalls, but it's the same as it was yesterday, and the merchants are doing a roaring trade. Food is going for a premium, and several stalls have crowds around them, with impromptu auctions breaking out for mouldy onions or a single protein bar. I cut through a narrow gap between two stalls, earning an angry shout from the merchant. I raise a hand in apology, and as I glance behind me I notice two people in the crowd staring angrily at me, as if memorising my face. Strange.

I find Old Madala near the bar. He's at one of the tables outside, nursing a cup of homebrew. The cup sits on the table in front of him, his hands resting either side of it. I grab a chair, and sit down opposite him. He looks up, surprised.

"Now, about that job you mentioned..." I begin, but he jumps to his feet, knocking over his chair. It clatters on the metal plating as he quickly walks away. I stop, confused, before pushing my chair back and following, cutting in ahead of him.

"Madala, what is it?" I say, but as he turns to me I see fear in his eyes, and it stops me cold.

"Go away. You can't be here," he mutters, and turns away again. Worry coils in the pit of my stomach, and I reach out for him, but he jerks away, the fear turning to anger in his eyes. "Go!" he shouts. "I not talk to you." He moves away into the market, his shoulders hunched, not looking back.

All at once, it feels like the noise of the market intensifies, crowding out my thoughts.

A job from Madala would have scored us some food, some more dried fruit or some green beans. Now, I'm going to have to find someone else, someone who might not be so inclined to trade for something good. I push through a crowd yelling out for what looks like a block of tofu, set on a counter behind a heavily tattooed seller, facing them with his arms folded.

The next three people I speak to act the same as Madala. In one case a merchant I've had a good relationship with in the past tells me angrily to never speak to him again. Nobody tells me why. At first, I think it's just because they don't want to trade away food or don't have anything they need transported, but after a while confusion gives way to fear, and then to a sickening dread.

Darnell said he'd recruited people. What if they think I'm one of them?

I have to get out of here, now. I slip between a pile of crates and a stall piled high with battery cases, heading towards the exit. I'm hoping that something will work out, that I won't have to come back to the Nest empty-handed, but I'm getting more and more glares as I pass by. I keep my head down, and keep walking.

Someone steps into my path, blocking out the light. A bald man, with a nasty, thickened scar on his neck, wearing a soiled T-shirt and old denim pants. His arrival is so sudden that I almost crash into him.

"You," he says, and his voice is tinged with malice. "We know what you're doing."

I stare at him blankly, his words not registering.

He spits angrily, a thick gob of saliva spattering a nearby crate. "You killed a lot of people today. And you walk in here like we wouldn't notice."

"Hey," I raise my hands, startled. "I don't know what you think I did, but I didn't kill anybody."

"You're one of them," he says. "The Sons of Earth. I heard you got Darnell caught just to keep people occupied while you planted the bombs. That's what I heard." His voice has become a low growl.

"I didn't. I'm not!" I say. "I'm just a tracer. I carry cargo."

His eyes narrow again, and he steps towards me. I move back, and bump into something solid and unyielding. The crowd has closed in around me, trapping me in a narrowing circle.

The man behind me places a hand on my shoulder, and I whirl around, throwing a punch in his direction. He swings his head to the side, and my fist glances off his ear. Then the crowd is on me, hands everywhere, grabbing and pulling and yanking at my pack and screaming obscenities in my face.

I lash out, but it's like fighting air. The crowd is a single being, a hive-mind, a monster with many hands and thousands of fingers. I've seen what happens to people who get taken by a mob. I swing my arms even more wildly, desperately trying to punch my way out, shouting for someone, anyone. But there is no help, and I'm lifted above the crowd, hands gripping my arms and legs. I'm propelled towards the back of the market, and at one point my left leg is pulled down, twisted by a dozen hands. I cry out in agony, and throw my foot out.

The movement causes the crowd ahead of me to sway. They're tightly packed, pushing against each other to try and get a hand on me, and they collapse in a heap of tangled limbs. The bodies carrying me shudder. The hands lose their grip and I'm thrown forwards onto the pile of people. I push frantically against them, trying to force my way up, but then more hands grip me from behind, more people bellow in anger.

Someone grabs me. It's Madala, his face a mask of fear. I'm certain he's with them, that he's trying to hurt me too, but then I see the urgency in his eyes, and then he's hurling me forwards, away from the angry crowd.

"Run!" he yells, and then the monster grabs him, hands pulling him inwards. I bolt, terror pricking at my sides as I jump across a nearby table and smash through a pile of discarded boxes. Behind me, Madala cries out, a horrifying wail which nearly brings me to a halt. I'm desperate to go back for him, but I keep running, and his wails follow me, growing steadily fainter.

Somehow, I come out of the crowd facing the front of the market, and I sprint towards the doors. Behind me, I can hear parts of the beast detaching, giving chase. There are no cries from Madala now. My pack is gone, my jacket hanging on by a single sleeve. I pull my arm into the other as I run, then drop into a roll under a table, coming out the other side as my pursuers crash into it, swearing and screaming. My lungs are burning, and a stitch grips my side in a ring of iron. But I keep sprinting, and then suddenly I'm out of the market, the cries of the monster growing fainter behind me.

How can they possibly believe that I'm a part of it? Someone must have told them. Someone said something, and the people on Outer Earth, desperate for justice, jumped on it.

No time to think about that now. If the people in the market think I'm one of the Sons of Earth, then chances are others will too. I have to get out of the corridors, get somewhere safe. And people know where the Nest is, so I can't go there. I've got to find somewhere else. I look back down the corridor, swearing under my breath.

Movement. I swing round, my fists clenched, ready to fight. Yao steps forward out of the shadows, her hands up. "Easy, Riley. Simmer down a little."

Kev steps in behind her, his face grave.

"Listen, you have to believe me," I say. "I'm not one of them."

"We know," says Kev, his eyes calm.

"Come on," says Yao. "It can't be that bad. How many are we talking here?"

"Everyone. All of them. They all..." I'm breathing too hard, and one of the breaths becomes a half-sob.

Without a word, Kev hands me his pack; his water bag is full, and I suck in the water as fast as I can, slaking the ever-present thirst. "I have to get somewhere safe," I say, wiping my mouth. "Any ideas?"

Kev shakes his head, but then his eyes light up. "Near the Chengshi border."

Yao whirls to face him. "Kev! We were keeping that for emergencies."

"It's an emergency."

She huffs. "Fine. One of the Level 3 corridors, near the habs. The conduits in the floor should be OK, and we stashed some water there a while ago. You should be able to hide out for a while."

"How do I get there?"

"Head down on that level until you come to a power box on the wall. It's the closest to the start of the corridor. A few steps on from that, you'll see a trapdoor in the floor. It's easy to miss, but it's there."

I'm about to thank them, but then something bounces off the floor nearby. It's a chunk of twisted scrap metal, and the man who threw it is at the end of the corridor, yelling behind him: "Found her! She's here!"

"If you want to fight them, we'll stay with you," says Yao quietly, without looking at me. Her eyes are fixed on a point in the distance, her fists clenched.

I want to say yes. More than anything, I don't want to be alone right now. And I'm not just scared. I'm angry. I want fists to meet flesh and nails to tear and scratch, and to show these people that I am *not* who they think I am.

But I can't. Even with three of us, we won't be able to fight them all off. And I can't let the Twins get hurt. Not because of me. Not again.

Almost imperceptibly, I shake my head. Yao catches the gesture, glances in Kev's direction, and dives to the side. Kev grabs me, and he too starts yelling. "Got her! She's over here!" I'm too startled to respond, but then he theatrically hurls himself backwards, as if pushed off. A performance like that from someone like Kev almost makes me laugh out loud, but the laugh dies on my lips when I see his expression. It's the same one that Madala had before he was swallowed up. Kev remains silent, his eyes implore me to do only one thing:

Run.

There are more people at the far end now, running towards me, screaming with mad hatred. With one lingering look back at Kev, I take off, bolting down the corridor, away from the monster.

37

Riley

I don't know how long I run for. The corridors are endless, stretching off into the distance, punctuated by galleries filled with noise and anger. I run, and run, and run.

It's not long before I manage to lose my pursuers. But I can't lose the rumour about me being involved. It's spread through the station like a virus, infecting everyone. Every time I think I've got ahead of it, that I've reached a level or a corridor where people don't know who I am, there's an angry shout from behind me. More people chasing me, more crowds wanting me dead. When I do eventually slow to a halt, my chest heaving, it takes me a moment to figure out where I am.

I've overshot the border somewhere. After a while, the corridors blur into one another, an endlessly unspooling road of black metal and flickering lights. I come to a stop, resting my hands on my hips, head down, sucking in great gasps of air. The run has pushed my body to the limit. Thirst and hunger tear at me. If I don't find Kev's stash soon, I'm finished. I need to get my bearings. Work out which level I'm on.

I force myself to move, pleading with my exhausted body to hold on just a little bit longer. Heading back the way I came, I hit the stairwell; it's crowded, filled with nervous energy, but I keep my head down and this time nobody stops me. It occurs to me that there are other tracer crews who might help me – or at least, who won't attack me on sight. People like the Cossacks or the Area Boys probably won't be too pleased to see me – they're no fans of the Devil Dancers – but maybe I can find someone from D-Company. They've never really given a damn about anything that didn't have something in it for them, but they know me, and might give me shelter.

I can't waste time hunting for them, though, and it doesn't take long to find the Twins' trapdoor. It's exactly where Yao said it would be, and mercifully, there's nobody around to watch me open it. It's heavy, rusted with age, and it takes some time and a lot of noise to pull upwards. I'm worried that the screeching is going to bring curious onlookers, but in the end nobody comes, and I manage to slip through into the conduit below the passage.

It's tiny, barely big enough for me to crouch in. I can feel thick dust underneath my feet. Spaces below the floor tend to be dirtier and nastier than ones you reach through the ceiling. Darker, too; I have to sit for some time before my eyes become accustomed to the gloom. There are thick electrical cables running along the corners, and one digs uncomfortably into my ass. But I'm not moving. I'm still. My quaking body sends up waves of relief.

I hear footsteps on the floor above me, booming through the tight conduit, but they don't stop, vanishing into the distance. I realise I've been holding my breath, and let it out in a long, slow exhale. The breath causes a puff of dust to burst up. I have to force myself not to cough. But I can see now, and almost immediately I spot the steel canteen propped against the wall. Not for the first time, I send a silent thank-you winging in the Twins' direction.

Trying to be as quiet as possible, I drink deeply from the canteen. The water is warm and slightly stale, but it soothes my parched throat. I have to force myself not to drink it all in one go, reminding myself that I might have to be here for a little while.

Amira must be looking for me by now. She would have found out what happened in the market, and hopefully the Twins managed to escape and tell her where I was headed. But she might as well be a million miles away. Her last words to me, the irritation on her face, come hurtling back. What if I never see her again? Or Prakesh? The Twins? I'd probably even be grateful to see Aaron Carver.

For the first time in years, I feel truly alone.

I set the water down slowly, trying to lessen the loud tang of metal on metal. I lean my head back against the side of the conduit, my eyes closed. I have to think. Work something out. There's got to be some way I can convince people I had nothing to do with any of it.

It's some time before I open my eyes. Almost immediately, I start cursing myself for falling asleep – how long was I out? – but then I realise the pain in my legs and sides is almost gone. I can't stretch my legs out too far in the tunnel, but even an experimental flex feels good.

Above me, the station is quiet. There's a distant rumbling as some machine or other kicks into gear, but otherwise it doesn't sound like there's anybody around. I risk a peek, pushing up the trapdoor above me just a fraction, wincing as the metal squeals.

The corridor is deserted. I drop back below, and take another sip of the brackish water.

There's something I'm not seeing here. Every time I try to get a hold of it in my mind it slips away, falling just out of reach. Grace Garner, Marshall Foster, Arthur Gray, Oren Darnell... they're all connected, to be sure, but how? There's some big element of this puzzle missing, and somehow, I can't shake the feeling that Garner has information that could stop this whole thing in its tracks. I don't know if Darnell is after her – or if he even knows she exists yet. All I can do is get to her.

Finding her means going back into Gardens. And walking into Gardens means going right onto what used to be Darnell's turf. But it's the only way to the Air Lab. There's no other option.

I drain the water – with no pack, there's no real way to carry it if I want my hands free – and hoist myself into the corridor above. Fortunately, it's still deserted, and I manage to get a good head of speed heading towards Gardens. I've already got the route I plan to take in my mind, one which sticks to the upper levels, away from the main public areas. I'll cut through the corridors around the furnaces – since the station was thrown into a total panic, there's less chance that there'll be any people there. I can take the topmost catwalk in the galleries – no people walking above me, which means less chance of being spotted.

I've been running for less than five minutes, having just exited the stairwell up into the Level 6 corridor, when another ferocious thirst kicks in. My throat goes dry and lifeless almost instantly, and when I swallow, a sharp pain rips through it. I slow down, try to get some saliva flowing in my mouth, but it just makes it worse.

Damn it, why now?

I keep my speed down, trying to use as little energy as possible in each stride. But the thirst just increases, a burning desire for liquid that wraps lead weights around my feet. The last time I felt anything like it, I'd just finished a multi-stage cargo run which took me through four sectors and lasted about five hours. There's hardly anybody around the furnaces, and those I do see barely glance at me. I'm running past one of the open doors when I hear it: the distinctive gush and spray of a water point as someone fills a bottle or a cup. With a pack and full water tank on my back I'd hardly notice it, but now it's like someone flicking a torch on and off in a dark room.

The furnace chamber where the noise is coming from is dimly lit, but even in the low light I can see it's almost deserted. It's a mess, strewn with discarded boxes, but at the far end, lit by a single light, is a water point. A man in overalls is bent over it, his back to me.

As I watch, I hear another soothing gurgle of water. The sound is a soft hand which reaches deep down into my body and then grips tight. The pain in my dry throat swells and stirs, and then I'm walking into the furnace, hoping and praying that I can get just a little water. The tiniest sip, just the tiniest.

The man stands up as I approach; I expect him to take a drink immediately, but he just places a small bottle in the pocket of his overalls. I sidle in beside him, giving him a big smile and a nod. Last thing I need is more hostility.

Instead of moving, he blocks the water point from me, staring me down.

"Hi," I say. He doesn't respond. My heart falls slightly, but I keep smiling.

"It's still working right?" I continue. "I've been running all day, and I don't have any with me. I'm really thirsty." I force a laugh, hoping to put him at ease, but he does nothing, his hand holding tight onto his pocket. I hear the water inside his bottle slosh ever so gently, and it takes everything I have not to reach for it.

Instead, I spread my arms, trying to be as friendly as

possible. "If you're in control of this water point, maybe I can trade for it," I say. "I'm a tracer. I'm with a crew called the Devil Dancers. Fastest on Outer Earth. Maybe there's something you need transporting? Some cargo? A message maybe? I'll take it wherever you need, really, even one of the upper sectors..." I'm babbling now, and he still hasn't uttered a word.

I tail off. This isn't working. I'm torn between pushing my way past him, trying to fight him, and going to look for another water point. In the end, the third option wins out. I'm in no state to fight anyone right now.

"Thanks anyway," I sigh.

"Please don't move," he says quietly.

I've turned around already. There are three stompers, standing in the shadows. Their stingers are out, and every one is pointing right at me.

38

Prakesh

"No ID, no entry," says the stomper.

"Come on, man," says Prakesh. "I *work* here. I'm an Air Lab tech."

"Then where's your ID?"

"Lost it."

"Really."

"Yeah, really. I left it behind in the Air Lab, right before the fire. Which, coincidentally, I helped contain, so maybe you should cut me a break, move out of the way, and let me in so I can do my job."

"You don't even have a lab coat."

"Did I mention the fire?"

The guard pauses for a moment, then shakes his head. "Don't know you."

"Of course you don't know me. I don't know you either. I've never seen you in my life." Prakesh makes himself stop. This is getting nowhere. The door to the Air Lab – one of the auxiliary entrances, one that he was sure would be unmanned – remains stubbornly shut. And now the stomper has his stinger out, not pointed at Prakesh but not exactly held at ease, either. He jerks his head. "Go somewhere else."

Prakesh mutters under his breath, walking away. Ordinarily, he'd look for someone he knows, someone who could vouch for him. But there's no one around – not Suki, not Dumar, not even bloody Chang. They're probably all inside already.

It doesn't matter. There are other ways to get into the Air Lab, access points this moronic stomper wouldn't even *think* to look for. He quickens his pace as he strides down the corridor, heading back towards the galleries, searching for the storage room which he just *knows* has a loose panel on its back wall.

He stops. If he couldn't get into the Air Lab through the regular channels, what luck is Grace Garner going to have? If he gets in there, they won't let him leave – he'll be pulled in a dozen different directions, asked to oversee everything from soil quality to the UV emitters. For a moment, he's torn – that's what he *should* be doing. But then he sees his parents' faces again, remembers how helpless he felt when he visited them.

He decides to look for Grace Garner in the galleries, in the endless corridors surrounding the Air Lab. He's on edge, waiting for another crackle of static over the comms system, waiting for Oren Darnell to appear. But the only thing he finds in the corridors is very scared people. Habs are locked down, barred and shut. Lights flicker above clusters of young gang members, talking in hushed voices and casting dirty looks at Prakesh as he walks past.

He walks up to one group, a mix of what look like Area Boys and Black Hole Crew. Some of them have ritual scars on their faces, parallel lines cut into the flesh and made to heal badly. The livid red scars look like war paint.

Prakesh doesn't hesitate. You show fear with these guys, they'll break you. "I'm looking for someone."

They look at him like he's crawled out of the buzz box. He keeps talking anyway. "Old woman, 'bout sixty, blue headscarf. Seen her anywhere?"

Someone yells for them from the other end of the corridor. The gang takes off at a run. One of them looks back and says, "Doesn't matter who you're looking for, man. We're all done. All of us."

He keeps looking. Garner is nowhere. It's maddening – she could be behind any one of the locked doors. She could also be in Apogee, or Chengshi, or in the middle of the Core, for that matter. It's less than an hour before Prakesh gives up, furious with himself. He sits down on one of the benches in the gallery. A dull ache has settled into his limbs, and no matter how much water he drinks, his throat keeps returning to its shredded state. The crowd outside the main doors to the Food Lab has become mad with fear, screaming slogans, arms around each other.

He leans back, closing his eyes, weighing up the options. Option one: sneak into the Air Lab, get to work making food. Option two: go back to Apogee, find Riley, tell her that Garner is gone. For the second time, Prakesh tells himself that he should be in the Air Lab. He should be doing what he's supposed to.

Which is how, hours later, he finds himself crossing the border into Apogee. The further he gets from Gardens, the worse it gets. He avoids the galleries as much as he can – they've become boiling cauldrons of anger, of stompers trying to hold back growing crowds who are demanding to have their sector councillors address them. The Apogee main gallery has been closed off, blocked by lines of stompers. Prakesh can't understand what they're doing there – they're guarding an empty room. And he can smell the aftermath, a sick, sulphurous smell with an edge of burned fat. It's enough to make his gorge rise, and he quickly makes his way upwards, climbing the levels towards the Nest.

He takes the last few steps at a jog, suddenly desperate to find Riley, to know that she's OK. But as he enters the corridor where he can get into the Nest, he sees Aaron Carver and the Twins. They're collapsed against the wall, and the trapdoor above them is wide open.

Carver looks up as he approaches. "P-Man," he says, using Prakesh's least favourite nickname.

The Twins raise their heads towards him. Kev's face is one big, mottled bruise. Yao's shirt is ripped, and there's a grimy crust of blood under her nose.

There's a sick feeling in Prakesh's stomach, made worse by the absence of Riley, or Amira. "What happened?"

"Your friend Riley's pissed a lot of people off," says Carver.

"Riley – why would—"

"They wrecked the Nest."

"I hate 'em," Yao says, her voice small and furious. "All of 'em. Why can't they just leave us alone? What did we do?"

Prakesh takes a deep breath, and asks them to start from the beginning. The Twins fill him in on what happened at the market. When they tell him what happened to Riley, the sick feeling in his stomach swells and rises, threatening to overwhelm him. "Then we got back here, and they were tearing the Nest up," Yao says.

Kev shakes his head. He seems to have gone beyond words.

"Where's Riley?" Prakesh says. His voice is turned into razor blades by his dry throat.

"We don't know," says Carver. "We've lost Amira too."

"We have to go find them."

"Where?" says Kev.

"Where is right," Carver says. He sounds worn out, more tired than Prakesh has ever heard him. It occurs to Prakesh that if the Nest has been destroyed, that means Carver's workbench, and all his experiments, will have been wrecked as well.

"You want to go looking for her, be my guest," Carver goes on. "But right now, Devil Dancers aren't too popular round here. Or anywhere, actually."

He stands, dusts his pants down. "We need to go. Probably best for us to lie low for a while."

"What if Riley and Amira come back?"

"They'll know where to find us," Carver says, glancing at Yao. "Trust me."

39

Riley

The cell I'm in is six paces long, five across. I've counted them out. Twice.

There's a camera in the ceiling, enclosed behind tough plastic. The white light from the thin fluorescent strips on either side of the camera captures and destroys any shadows it finds. Beyond the transparent barrier at the front of the cell, the brig is dark. The sound of the station is muted here, dwindling to almost nothing.

Turns out there were six stompers, not three. I'm still not sure how they knew where I was going to be. I can only guess that I must have been caught on a surveillance cam somewhere: when so many have failed over the years, you forget that there are some that still work.

The moment they grabbed me, I started demanding to know what they wanted, but all I got was an order to shut up, and they marched me right back into Apogee, to the same prison that Darnell was in yesterday. There was a small crowd outside the prison. They started shouting the moment they saw me, but I was hustled straight through and pushed into the cell. When I realised where we were going, I started hoping that Royo might be there, but he was nowhere to be seen.

After I was thrown in here, and after I'd finished banging on the plastic in frustration, screaming at the backs of the retreating guards, I collapsed on the cot, lying back on the thin mattress.

The water point in the cell isn't working, and nobody's given me any food since I landed in here. My stomach is rolling with nausea. I'm back where I started, my crew has no idea where I am, and outside is a mob that wants me dead.

Brilliant.

Sometime later – hours, maybe – I hear a noise from beyond the cell. The main lights in the prison were turned out some time ago, and I can't see anything. I sit up on the bed, squinting, trying to peer into the blackness. There: footsteps. Very faint. Someone approaching from the end of the block.

In an instant, I'm up and banging on the plastic. "Hey," I say, my voice ringing inside the small space of the cell. "Need some more water in here!"

As my voice fades, I hear the footsteps again. If whoever it is heard me, they give no answer, and continue walking steadily towards the cell. I fall silent, waiting, my hand on the plastic, and Janice Okwembu walks out of the darkness.

She wears the same white jumpsuit. Her expression is grave, her lips set in a thin line. She folds her arms, and her luminous eyes lock onto mine. I'm so surprised that I just stand there, staring back at her.

"You'll have to forgive my lateness," she says. Her voice is dulled by the plastic barrier, stripped of its warmth. "I was in Apex when I heard you'd been found, and it took me some time to make my way over."

My voice comes back. "What am I doing here?"

"You're here for your own protection. Or wasn't that

explained to you?" Her voice is even, her expression impossible to read.

"I can take care of myself."

"No, you can't."

I don't have an answer for her. She pauses, then continues: "People seem to believe you are responsible for the bombings today. I can't allow any more vigilante justice. Not now."

"But it's not true. I had nothing to do with it!"

She doesn't say anything.

"You can't think I did?" I stammer, my confidence leaving me. The room seems suddenly smaller, the darkness at the edge of Okwembu's feet becoming thicker.

"All you have to do..." My voice cracks. The thirst is raging worse than ever. I start again. "All you have to do is get on the comms and tell people that I'm not responsible. That way, I could move freely. My crew could protect me. And I saw the people outside – if they get in here, I'll be trapped. Out there, I can run. Please."

I'm regretting the last word the second it leaves my mouth. Okwembu seems to sense the give, the little pressure point, and steps forward, closer to the barrier.

"How much control do you imagine we have, really?" she says. "The only way we keep the peace any more is by letting people do what they want. We have to give them so much room. If the council were to crack down, to try and force people to do things in a certain way, even on the smallest thing, we'd be destroyed in hours. The only thing we can do any more is advise, and protect."

"So you're just going to leave me in here?"

"Until this crisis is over, yes."

Something occurs to me. I stare at her through the plastic. "And you came down here personally to tell me this?" I say, fear lending an edge to my words. "With Darnell about to destroy the station, you come down to

Apogee to tell me that you're going to keep me in jail? I sort of knew that anyway. Why are you *really* here?" I'm slightly out of breath, but I hold her gaze.

Eventually, she says. "I'll be honest with you, even though you haven't been honest with me. When I asked you if there was anything else you wanted to tell me about Oren Darnell, you said no. You lied."

"What?"

"If you'd told me what you knew, we might have been able to stop Darnell's plan before the bombings. But that doesn't matter now. What matters is that you tell me everything, before more people die."

My heart is beating too fast. I turn away from her, my hands on my head. "This is crazy."

There's something else in her voice now, and it takes me a second to pick it up: she sounds almost excited. "Marshall Foster's assistant is missing," she continues. "A woman named Grace Garner. She worked with him for years on the council, and now she's vanished. Nobody's seen her since the bombings."

"So?" I shrug, feigning nonchalance. "What if she was killed in the blast? Or maybe Gray took her. Who knows how many people he was responsible for?"

"Don't treat me like an idiot, Ms Hale." Her voice is soft, controlled, but her eyes are angry. "She was last seen *after* Darnell was caught. Talking with you, up on the catwalks. Oh, don't look so shocked. Do you think we'd be able to operate without informants here?"

I'm silent, and she goes on. "Foster could have been working with Gray and Darnell. If he was one of the Sons of Earth, then Grace Garner would know.

"Riley," she says, and the use of my first name nearly makes me recoil. The word is like a pointed fingernail touching bare flesh. "I have to know what she said to you, and where she was going. Where did you send her?"

"She said she wanted to tell me something. She didn't say what. I told her to meet me in the mess later. But then, there was the explosion, so..."

"You're lying to me again."

She takes a step closer to the glass, and this time a note of anger creeps into that silken voice. "Outer Earth is my charge and I will do everything I can to protect it. If you won't help me, then I won't help you."

"I'm telling you, I don't where she is. But she's probably still in Apogee. Maybe someone saw her in the mess."

There's a long silence. Eventually, Okwembu says, "It would be so easy to torture you. But I've seen people like you before. When you've suffered loss, physical pain means nothing. But what would you do if we were to hurt your friend Amira Al-Hassan? Or cut off Kevin O'Connell's fingers in front of you?"

Anger and fear are swirling together inside me, creating something else, a new emotion, something big and bruised and awful.

"I'm going to let you think about our conversation," Okwembu says. "I'll be back soon. And do try to remember that those prison doors won't hold forever. I can only devote so many officers to guard duty in these troubled times."

She turns and walks away, vanishing into the darkness.

I lose control. I bang hard on the plastic barrier with both fists and scream myself hoarse. The sound is the same as the one I made when I slammed my hand on the outside of Darnell's cell, but in here it's louder, echoing around the space. I shout Okwembu's name over and over, yelling that I'll kill her if she so much as touches one of my friends. I scramble around the edges of the plastic, hunting for a seam or an edge, but there's nothing, and after a while I sink to my knees, my fists sliding down the plastic.

I've never wanted to kill someone before. It's an odd thought, sitting strangely and quietly in my mind like an unwelcome guest. But instead of turning it away, I feed it, nurture it. If Okwembu hurts Amira, or Prakesh or the Twins or anybody else, I will kill her.

I whisper the words to myself, and in the cell they sound closer than they have any right to be.

I sleep in snatches. I don't dream, but I'm restless, tossing and turning on the thin mattress, trying to get comfortable. There's no way to tell time in here, but I lie on that cot for what feels like hours, grinding my teeth. Eventually, when I'm right on the edge of sleep, I hear footsteps, approaching from the far end of the cell block. She's back.

I rise off the bed, my fists clenched, my nails digging into my palms. Defiance courses through me. Whatever she does, I won't tell her a damn thing. I step to the barrier, place a hand on it...

...and have to yank it away quickly when the barrier slides quietly into the wall. Stunned, I step forward, into the tiny circle of light beyond. It's bigger now that the slightly opaque barrier is gone, but the rest of the block is still dark.

An electric charge crackles up my spine; Okwembu wouldn't let me out. That can only mean one thing: the people outside have come for me. They've overpowered the guards and they've busted their way in. I shift into a fighting stance, keeping my centre of gravity low, my arms ready. I can hear the footsteps again now, getting close.

A figure steps out of the gloom, and holds out a hand. Amira.

40

Darnell

Oren Darnell takes a deep breath, and jumps.

For a moment, his body is suspended in space. The gap is eight feet wide, and there's nothing below him but a long fall, all the way down six levels to a very messy stop at the bottom. Just as he thinks he's misjudged it, that his body is too big to get enough power into the leap, his fingers grasp the ledge on the other side.

He slams into the wall, barking his knees on the surface, nearly toppling backwards. The ledge he's holding on to is nothing, a protuberance where two sheets of metal are joined. Hot, noxious air wafts up from below.

He tries to be as still as possible. He can hear his heart beating through his shirt, and it's as if each beat is trying to push him away from the wall. His jacket flares out behind him, and the tab screen, carefully slipped into an inside pocket, comes loose. It bounces off the walls as it tumbles, and it's a full five seconds before Darnell hears the faint smash.

"Doesn't matter," he says to himself. "Won't need that any more." He barely realises he's voiced the thought aloud.

Slowly, he begins to inch his way along, aiming for

an open duct a few feet to his right. Darnell can hear his own breathing, hard and heavy. His jacket has been torn to pieces by the jagged, malformed edges of the back passages and conduits. Doesn't matter. He's here.

This gap, this empty space between the sectors, is the only way into Apex. The main corridors have been sealed off, guarded by stompers with orders to let no one in or out. Hardly surprising, given the precious jewels that Apex holds: the main control room and the council chamber. But it's not as secure as its citizens might think. Darnell traded a lot for the location of this duct, this one little glitch on the station blueprints that nobody remembered to have closed off.

Hauling himself into the opening is hard, but he manages it. For a moment, he's on all fours, and then the duct opens up into a larger space, its walls hidden behind nests of wiring and open fuse boxes. An ordinary person could stand upright, but Darnell has to walk bent over. He doesn't mind. Low lighting illuminates his lower body, leaving his face in darkness.

A few yards on, he has to drop to all fours again, to push his way past a protruding power box in the upper half of the space. This close to the ground, he can see a little light filtering through the cracks between the floor panels. When he stands, his hands are caked with dust and grime.

The access point is a neat white trapdoor, set into the floor. It's fully pneumatic, and when Darnell presses the recessed button beside it, it slides silently away.

White light floods into the space from below. Darnell listens hard, but Apex is uncommonly silent. Darnell's been there before, knows how small the sector is. He should be hearing footsteps, urgent voices, the hiss and buzz and clatter of a very nervous sector. But there's nothing. Just the thin hum of the station.

Darnell drops through the gap. He's momentarily blinded by the harsh white light, blinking as his eyes adjust. He's in what looks like a small waiting area, the walls slightly curved, the lighting coming from fluorescents in the ceiling. One wall is lined with hard plastic chairs, the other with a slim flowerbed. Darnell's gaze lingers on the flowers, on their fragile orange petals. *Nasturtiums.* He wonders where the council managed to get the water to grow them.

He draws his blade, seats it in his hand, and walks down the corridor leading off the waiting area. If he's got it right, he should be on the upper level of Apex, a few minutes from the main control room. Skeins of dust fall from his shoulders and hair as he walks, dirtying the pristine white floor.

"You took your time."

Darnell whirls around, his knife slashing out.

Janice Okwembu steps smartly backwards, and the blade cuts nothing but air. Darnell stares down at her, his shoulders heaving.

"You shouldn't have let them arrest me," he says, after a moment.

"You shouldn't have got arrested," Okwembu says. "In any case, it doesn't matter. Everything else is on schedule."

41

Riley

I pull Amira into a hug, squeezing her tight. She pauses for a moment, then squeezes back.

"How'd you find me?" I ask.

"Don't worry about that," she replies. "Are you hurt?"

I shake my head. "But what about the crowd? The stompers? How did you..."

"The crowd left a while ago. As soon as they realised that they weren't getting in."

"But the stompers..."

She pauses, and it's only then that I see the thin splatters of blood across her shoulders. She shrugs, and says, "They have no idea how to fight. They think stingers make them invincible."

I tell her about my conversation with Okwembu. But before I can finish the story, there are shouts from the other end of the block. More guards, at least four of them. Amira motions me back. "In the cell. Lie down on the bed." I'm puzzled, but I do as she asks. I see her step into the shadows, flattening up against the wall on the far side.

I'm staring at the ceiling, hands folded under my head, when they arrive, stingers out. They crowd the entrance to the cell, their stingers sweeping wildly around the tight space. They look young, almost certainly some kind of trainee unit, nothing more than kids with guns. The one who arrives first seems older than the others, but still doesn't look a minute over eighteen or nineteen. His stinger, at least, stays steady.

"What did you do?" he yells.

He doesn't hear Amira slip in behind him, or see her arms reach around his neck and over his head. She grabs and twists, and I hear his neck snap, a sound that shocks the others into silence.

It's all the opening she needs.

Amira is amazing to watch in battle. She could almost be dancing. Not a single movement is wasted, and each one flows into the next, as if she had practised the entire sequence beforehand. No matter what the stompers try, Amira is three steps ahead, driving elbows into stomachs and open hands into temples.

She knocks the last one flat, striking the heel of her hand into the middle of his face. His nose explodes in a flare of blood, the crack of the bone echoing through the brig. He gives a muffled howl of pain. As he falls, she grabs his stinger, and in one quick movement dismantles it, dropping out the clip and separating the slide from the body. She tosses the pieces aside, and they strike the floor, the noise echoing in the sudden silence.

I hop off the bed. "I could have helped, you know," I say, glancing at the moaning guards. A tiny frisson of fear shoots through me at the sight of the guard who got his neck snapped, but I tamp it down.

She ignores my comment. "Why didn't you just tell Okwembu whatever Garner told you?"

"Because she didn't tell me anything. Not back at the trial, anyway. I said I'd meet her in the Air Lab."

"So why not tell Okwembu that?"

I shake my head. "Amira, there was something... I don't know. Off about her. Like she knows a lot more than she's letting on."

Amira studies me. Her eyes reveal absolutely nothing.

"Well then," she says after a moment. "We need to find Garner. The sooner we hear what she has to say, the sooner we can stop all this."

I think for a moment. "It's too dangerous for me to go all the way up to Gardens. I should lie low. I'll go find the other Dancers, you go find Garner."

"No," Amira says. "She sought you out, not me. I don't want to get all the way there to find that you're the only person she'll talk to. We go together."

"And after we talk to her, what then?"

The oddest look crosses Amira's face. It only lasts for a split second, but it seems filled with sorrow and with anger.

"What? What is it?" I ask.

She looks away. Then says, "It's all gone to hell, Riley. All of it. It's a nightmare out there."

Her words hang in the air, a reminder of what we're up against. Eventually, she says, "We have to go."

"All right," I say. "But I need water, and something to eat. They didn't feed me in here. How much time do we have?"

Another shadow crosses her face at the mention of Darnell's countdown. "I don't know. Thirty hours? Anyway, you're right. There's some food back in the Nest. We go there first, then we head to Gardens."

And then we're running again, out of the cell block and into the main station. The guards Amira took down outside the prison are still lying there. It half occurs to me that she might have killed some of them too, but I push the thought away. Besides, I tell myself, you were ready to kill someone not more than a few hours ago. Amira did what she had to.

She takes point, her scarf billowing out behind her. It's

been a while since the bombings, and the station seems to have calmed down a little. But the people we do see are harried and drawn, talking quietly in worried little groups, barely glancing at us. We're not chased, and as we approach the Nest, Amira slows to a jog, dropping in beside me, her breaths coming quickly. There's a thin sheen of sweat on her face, and she runs a hand across her forehead.

She gestures for me to go first, and I tac off the wall and pull myself up through the trapdoor. The entranceway is dark, and as Amira pulls herself up behind me, I stand and reach for the keypad.

It's only then I notice that the door to the Nest is slightly ajar, a tiny slash of light creeping through the opening. As Amira gets to her feet, I raise a hand, motioning her to be quiet. I feel her tense behind me, and a growing feeling of dread wells in my chest as I push the door open.

Whatever Carver was working on has been torn apart, thrown around the room, a blast of welded metal and chemicals. His workbench is on its side. The mattresses are upside-down, with stuffing pouring out of deep slashes. Carver and the Twins are nowhere to be seen. Yao's mural – her beautiful, beautiful mural – has been sprayed over, defaced with what looks like burn marks, angry, ugly blotches that cover the entire wall. It takes me a moment to see that the blotches form a word: TRAITOR.

Amira steps from behind me, and reaches down to the floor. She straightens up, and in her hand is a small, twisted object, burned and black. She tilts it towards me. I can just make out *Treasure Isl*... on the tattered spine.

There are no words.

We slump against the wall. My stomach aches; the food and water we had have vanished. Whoever did this – almost certainly people trying to find me – would have taken them.

"What do we do now?" I ask.

Amira's silent for a few moments. Her body is still, her eyes staring into the distance. Then she rises, leaping to her feet in one movement, and says, "We stick to the plan. But we find some food and water, because we're not making it to Gardens without."

I nod, and as I do so, something catches my eye. There's another mark on the wall, different from the others. It's as if someone rubbed their finger in the burn marks, then used it to paint a design. I lean closer, my hand resting on the wall next to it. The bottom half of a circle, with three slashes above it, running downwards from left to right. The slashes are uneven, as if drawn in a hurry.

Codes and picture ciphers aren't too common among tracers. Some of the other crews, like D-Company, have dozens of members spread out across the sectors. They use the ciphers as a way to communicate, marking out their territory or their stash locations. Unless you know what to look for, the ciphers are just one graffiti symbol among many. With small, tight-knit crews, you usually don't need them. There are a few we still use though, and I'm sure I've seen this one before. I'm almost certain that it was left by Carver and the Twins.

"Amira, look at this."

She turns, her head tilted to one side, and her eyes widen as she catches sight of the cipher. "That's a Caves symbol."

I stare at it, my brow furrowed. "You sure?"

Amira says, "That's where they'll be: in the Caves. Kev must have drawn it. His family still lives there."

I shudder. "When was the last time you went down there?"

"Must be a year ago now. I don't run to New Germany too often these days."

"Will they have food?"

"They'd better."

42

Darnell

It's not long before Darnell finds out why the sector is so quiet.

The Apex amphitheatre is packed with a hundred people – techs, administrators, council members. Their mouths are open in huge, terrified Os, and their foreheads are shiny with sweat. Darnell can see them through the big transparent doors, but he can't hear them. The doors are completely soundproof, sealed shut.

"How did you do it?" he says to Janice Okwembu. "How did you get them in there?"

Okwembu shrugs. "Called an emergency briefing. Everybody to the amphitheatre. Then all I had to do was seal the doors."

She stands, arms folded, looking at the door. Someone, a tech with thin eyeglasses, is hammering on it, pulling at the handles, screaming unheard curses. Okwembu looks back at him, impassive.

"There must be others," Darnell says. "This can't be everyone in the sector."

"Oh, there'll be a few people. I'm sure you're up to taking care of them."

"What about the control rooms?"

"Everything's automated. The techs left their stations when I asked them to."

Darnell has to admit to himself that he's impressed. When Okwembu came to him, two years ago, he struggled to believe that she really wanted the same thing he did. The end she had planned for the station sounded fascinating. Brilliant even. But even then, he was never quite sure that she'd go through with it.

But when she'd told him about her frustration, her own anger at the people of Outer Earth, how they squabbled and fought and squandered everything they had, he began to see. She was proof that his idea could infect anyone: she was just as susceptible as any other sleeper. Someone sympathetic to the human extinction movement, but who felt betrayed by it, let down, frustrated with the council's inability to get anything done.

Okwembu turns away. Suspicion floods his thoughts, automatic and instant. He puts a huge hand on her shoulder, rests it there. He can feel her bones underneath her jumpsuit, fragile and angular. She stops, but doesn't turn to look at him.

"What's to stop me from killing you too?" he says.

"Because you owe me more than that."

"Oh, do I?"

"I got you out of the brig. You wouldn't be here if it wasn't for me."

He laughs. "And you think that means I owe you something?"

This time, she does turn to face him, and there's a tiny spark of anger in her eyes. "You would have stayed in there until the end. When you screwed up with Foster's eye, and got yourself arrested, you lost any chance of doing something meaningful. But I saw an *opportunity*."

"Opportunity?"

She nods. And when she speaks again, there's a thin, weary contempt running through her voice. "The people of this station need to feel fear," she says. "They need to know what it's like to be truly powerless. It's no less than they deserve. And you do have that effect on people. Being arrested made you even more infamous than you already were."

Despite himself, he smiles.

"So yes, you owe it to me," she says. "I want to be here for the end. I want to see it happen."

"And our friend is on schedule?"

She nods.

"I want to talk to him."

"Perhaps. First, you need to make a broadcast. You can say you've taken Apex, that you've got the council hostage. Make people believe that you'll kill us, one at a time."

As she turns to walk away, Darnell calls after her.

"What about Garner?"

"It was only a matter of time before Hale's friends broke her out. All we have to do is wait and watch. They'll lead us right to her."

"And we can see her?"

Okwembu nods to the camera. "Apex isn't the only place on the station where the cameras still work. I haven't found Garner yet – she's clever, staying out of sight. But if Hale really knows where Garner is, so will we, eventually."

"We should have Hale brought here. Give me five minutes with her, she'll tell us everything we need to know."

"I prefer a more subtle approach," Okwembu says. "For example, take the people in that conference room."

The people behind the doors have stopped hammering. Their eyes are flicking back and forth between

Darnell and Okwembu. Darnell can see the true panic forming, the realisation that they're not just going to be held prisoner. He can see over the shoulders of the people at the front, see those at the back running their hands over the walls, looking for an escape route that isn't there.

Okwembu turns to Darnell, and tells him how they should die.

43

Riley

We leave the Nest, not bothering to latch the door behind us. There's nothing left to take. Amira gestures me to take point, breaking into a full run as soon as I hit the corridor below.

I'm trying very hard not to think about what I'll find in the Caves. When they were building what was to become New Germany, they made some of it smaller. More cramped. Someone messed up the blueprints, or perhaps they just found that they were running out of time. Or money – that was a big thing back then. Whatever it was, what they ended with was a section of the station with only one way in or out: a single, heavy door.

The place is a breeding ground for horror stories. The last one I remember was that the walls were too thin to keep the radiation out, meaning that anybody who lived there would end up riddled with cancer.

You go down to get to there, dropping onto the bottom-level corridor and entering through a stairwell at the far end of the gallery. The door is closed when we reach it, and Amira and I both have to grab it and yank it open; the metal screeches as we pull it back, the heavy door taking what seems like an age to open.

"Riley, look," says Amira.

I'm focused on the door, and don't realise she's spoken until she turns me around and I'm staring right at Oren Darnell.

The comms screen is just above us, suspended from a catwalk. Wherever the camera is, it's looking down at Darnell from above. From where we're standing, it's a disorientating effect, as if the world has twisted on its axis. He's standing in front of a door in a corridor somewhere, and there's movement behind him, fuzzy and out of focus.

His voice, when he speaks, is distant and tinny. "Apex is ours," he says. "We've taken the station council, and we're going to kill them, one by one, for your entertainment."

I find myself wishing for a glitch, hoping that the feed will cut out. No such luck.

"Of course," Darnell continues, "you might wonder what's happened to everyone else in Apex."

He steps to one side. The movement behind him is still out of focus, but impossible to mistake. There are people, dozens of them, trapped behind a door.

Darnell's gaze finds the camera. His hand strays to a control panel on the wall, and works its way across it.

"We've modified the station's life-support systems," he says. "I can control them right from here. It's very useful."

Something begins to happen to the people in the room. They start screaming wordlessly, pushing up against each other, as if they can knock down the walls through sheer numbers.

"I've just vented their oxygen into space," Darnell says. "Let's see what happens."

There's nothing we can do. Not a single thing. It doesn't stop anger and an awful, furious despair from shooting through me. Without another word, Amira turns me around, and pushes me into the Caves.

Inside the door, there's a small entranceway, with multiple corridors branching off it. We take the leftmost one, Amira letting me take the lead. From the minute we enter, it's as if something is gently squeezing my shoulders. Claustrophobia begins to build.

There aren't any main lights in the corridor, and the only illumination comes from the entrances to the dorms, set into the walls at regular intervals. It's quiet, too: the Caves might be one of the most crowded areas on the station, but there's hardly any noise.

Here, nothing has a name – only numbers and letters. We're in 1-B; it's painted onto the wall, sprayed in huge, uniform characters. A few of the doors we pass have faces peering out at us. The women have wrinkles that are too deep and the men are almost all bearded, with dark eyes. Nobody tries to stop us, but as we reach the end of the corridor one of the shadows on the walls stretches and elongates, and a man rises from where he was sitting against the wall. He's wiry, not large, but the space is tight enough that he blocks the corridor, and we have to stop. His greasy, dark hair frames a pitted face; I can't place him, but he looks familiar.

"You," he barks, gesturing angrily. I don't know if he's referring to one or both of us, but before I can reply, he says: "What's your business?"

I hear the soft squeak as Amira shifts her foot backwards, lowering herself ever so subtly into a combat position. I'm about to speak, when she says, "You've got three seconds to get out of our way, starting now."

The man narrows his eyes and takes a step towards us, but I quickly raise my hands. "We're tracers," I say. "One of our crew lives here. Kevin O'Connell."

"Don't know that name."

"Sure you do. You know his family," I say, and then I realise where I've seen him before. I smile, and it disarms him for a moment, doubt crossing his face. "Come on, Syria. It's been a little while but I know you haven't forgotten about me."

He looks blank. "Riley," I add helpfully. His expression doesn't change, and for one heart-stopping moment I'm sure I've got it wrong. But then he relaxes, his shoulders dropping as he glances around the corridor. "Sure, Riley. Sure. I remember you now," he mutters. "You took that message up the ring for my cousin a while back."

I nod. He's still not exactly friendly, but behind me I feel Amira relax. "You're not getting through here without a pat-down, though," he says. "Can't be too careful."

"Is that really necessary?" says Amira. "We're a tracer crew. We're not looking for trouble."

"Says you who was ready to brawl a minute ago," says Syria. Amira sighs in irritation. Before she can say anything else, I hold out my arms as far as the corridor will allow, letting Syria check for weapons.

"So, about Kevin. Know where we can find him?" I ask, as he runs a thumb between my ankles and my shoes, checking for blades.

He grunts noncommittally. "Lotta Kevins down here."

"No, there's not," I say. "There's only three. One of them's a mental case, the other runs with a gang up in Chengshi, and the third is a tracer. Take a wild guess which one we're looking for."

He starts checking Amira – she's visibly irritated, staring pointedly at the ceiling. But as he runs his hands down her sides, he relents. "Yeah, yeah. Down in 3-C. Last door on the right. Come to think of it," he says as he brushes Amira's scarf back into place, "he came through with some other guys earlier. Friends of yours?"

"One of them with an arm in a sling?" Amira asks.

"Yup."

I catch Amira's eye. So she was right about the code on the wall.

"Sorry for the shakedown," says Syria. "Things have been pretty hairy ever since that bomb went off. We've already had some trouble with those idiots from the D-Company tracers, trying to get in here."

"Oh what, Syria, you were going to take them down all by yourself?"

He smiles, displaying blackened stumps where his teeth should be. "Who, me? No. Them, though…"

He gestures behind us. At every door, there are people holding weapons: homemade blades, lengths of pipe, even one or two homemade stingers. Had we tried to fight our way through, we would have been dead in seconds.

Syria stands aside, and we head to the stairs at the far end of the corridor. We're not running, but every so often we have to flatten ourselves against the wall to let someone else squeeze past. Several times, we're looked at with suspicion, but no one else stops us. We're both on edge, and I'm aware of time slipping away. My stomach is a knotted ball of hunger. Around us, Outer Earth rumbles and creaks, the sound getting increasingly louder as we continue deeper into the Caves.

44

Riley

Kev's father is as big as I remember, and seems to open his mouth even less than his son. He greets us at the entrance to the hab, a huge, heavily muscled man, with arms thick from endless shifts lifting containers in the sector kitchens. He doesn't say anything when he sees us, just nods, and gestures behind him. There, lying on a cot and looking poisonous, is Carver. Behind him are the Twins, leaning against the wall by the bed, their arms folded.

And with them: Prakesh.

Yao spots me, then so does Kev, and then everyone is talking at once. The relief at seeing everyone there must show on my face, because Kev flashes me a rare smile.

Kev's family are clustered one bunk down, huddled together: his grandfather is nothing more than a wizened face peeking out of a bundle of blankets. His mother sits on the edge of the bunk, holding Kev's baby brother in her arms. She stands when she sees me, forcing a smile onto her face.

"You're the last, right?" she asks. The swaddled baby is held before her like a shield. She rolls the edge of the blanket between her finger and thumb, worrying the fabric.

We nod, and she shouts to her husband, "Ira, that's it. You can close the door now."

I turn to Kev. "What happened at the market..." I say, and I'm surprised to find my voice catching. "Thank you."

"Tell me you found our stash," says Yao.

"Saved my life. How many of those do you have?"

"A few," Kev says. As he turns his head, his face catches the light, and I notice the bruises there, already turning an ugly purple. I reach up, gently running my hand over his cheek. He doesn't flinch, but he must see the look on my face, because he shrugs and then looks away. "No big deal."

I catch his mother staring at me. Kev told me once that they wanted him to be a ship pilot, training at the academy in Tzevya, and they're still not happy with how he spends his time. Or who he spends it with.

Yao's face is crusted with dried blood, but she looks OK. She smiles as well, and gives me a thumbs-up. Around us, the dorm is quiet, with only a few people sprawled on the beds. They're either straining to hear us or doing their best to ignore us; right now, I don't care. Kev passes around protein bars, some fruit, some water. I'm not proud about digging into his family's food supply, but we can't do anything unless we eat.

"The Air Lab?" I ask Prakesh, as I swallow a bite of protein bar.

"Wouldn't let me in," he says. "Lost my ID in the fire."

"That means Garner could be anywhere," Amira says. "And with Darnell in Apex..."

"The what now?" Carver says. Yao and Kevin stare at us, open-mouthed. Even Kev's family start listening.

"Darnell made it into Apex?" Yao whispers. "And who's Garner?"

"You don't know?" I say, confused. "You didn't see the comms?"

"This is Caves," says Carver. "Nothing works down here."

Kev looks sideways at him. "What?" Carver says. "It's the truth."

Amira and I fill them in, starting with Darnell's latest broadcast. After we're done, nobody says anything for a minute. Carver's face has gone pale.

"How is he doing this?" asks Yao, rubbing her ankle. "You don't just waltz into Apex. They've got security codes, scanners, watchdog programs, killer robots for all I know. Things that do nothing but keep people out."

Nobody answers. It's almost certainly my imagination, but it seems like the room just got a tiny bit hotter, the air a little thicker, as if someone was blowing smoke. A thin film of sweat coats my forehead.

"I think I know," I say quietly, and everybody turns to me. I take a breath. "Or at least, I think I know how to find out."

I tell them about Grace Garner and what Okwembu wanted from her. "I was hoping she'd made it to Gardens and found Prakesh," I say.

"Why does it have to be us?" says Carver.

I look at him. "What do you mean?"

"There's got to be an easier way to find her. Why should we stick our necks out by hightailing it up to Gardens?"

"Because there's no one else. No one we can trust."

"How do you even know she's in there? P-Man said he couldn't find her."

"It's our best shot. We look there first. If she's not there, we can search the rest of the sector."

"Amira, back me up here," says Carver. "You can't think this is a good idea."

Amira's silent for a moment, looking away. When she turns back to us, her face is hard. "Well, let's see, Aaron.

What I think is that I have one tracer with a dislocated shoulder, and two more who look like they tried to punch out a meteorite. My fastest tracer" – her gaze falls on me – "is currently the most wanted person on Outer Earth. And I just took down eight stompers getting Riley out of the brig."

"Amira..." says Carver, but she cuts him off. "And that's not even taking into account the rioting, the looting, or the fact that every one of us is apparently going to die in a matter of hours – and we still don't know how. Do I think going up to Gardens is a good idea? I think it's a terrible idea. But we're going to do it anyway."

Her voice hasn't risen; it's softer now, as quiet as a blade slipping out of a sheath. "We are not," she says, and her voice is a husky whisper. She clears her throat. "We are not going to rely on anyone else. If Riley thinks this Garner person has information that could stop Darnell, then she and I are going to find her. We're going to do it fast, and we're going to do it now."

There's silence. "What do you mean, 'she and I'?" I ask.

"Yeah," echoes Yao. "You can't be thinking about going by yourselves?"

"That's exactly what we're doing," says Amira.

"Come on," says Carver. "My arm's busted, but my legs still work fine, promise."

"You stay here. That's an order."

"Sorry, Amira," says Yao quietly. "But Carver's right. If you want to go to Gardens, fine. But you're not leaving us here. Not on something like this."

Amira takes a long, deep breath, fighting back her anger. "All right," she says, through gritted teeth.

"I'm coming too," says Prakesh. He's been quiet for a while, and all eyes turn towards him.

"No," says Amira, exasperated. "They're tracers. They can run. You can't. We don't have time to baby-sit."

"You're going to Gardens," says Prakesh, his voice hard. "How were you planning on getting in there?"

"We'll figure something out."

"Not very smart. Riley always told me you were better than that."

Behind us, Kev's family has drawn tighter together on the bed. His dad, Ira, is there now, his arms around his wife. Kev's grandfather is still staring at the ceiling, his lips moving silently.

Prakesh steps forward, squaring up to Amira. She doesn't move, her dark eyes locked on his. "I can't get to Gardens on my own," says Prakesh. "It's getting dangerous out there. I don't know the best routes, the ones that'll be quiet. But you do. And you won't get into the labs without me. We need each other."

For a minute, Amira just stares at Prakesh. I'm expecting her to refuse, but eventually she gives a curt nod. Prakesh is about to say something, but she raises a finger to silence him. "We won't wait for you. You run at our speed, and if you get into trouble, you're on your own."

Prakesh half smiles, and turns to me. "Ready to give me a crash course, Riley?"

But Amira isn't finished. "We take the monorail tracks. Get to the top of the sector, then cut around all the way towards Gardens. They won't be running the monorail right now, not when there's no food to ship."

"The tracks?" I ask. "You think we can make it?"

"It'll be safer than running out in the open. Quicker too, if we watch our step."

I'm about to protest further, but then I realise she's right. It's dangerous, but better than risking the catwalks.

It doesn't take us long to get ready. We leave the Caves, walking single file down the tight corridors, and this time nobody stops us. As soon as we enter the ground-floor corridor, we start running. Amira takes point, leading us up the station levels to the tracks; behind her are Yao, Kev and Carver, with Prakesh and me bringing up the rear. I'm not used to being in the back, and I'm nervous that he'll fall behind or get hurt. But although he's no tracer, and has to pull himself over jumps and walls that we take in a single leap, he stays with us. Somehow. I can hear his breathing behind me as I run, heavy and hard.

The comms screens are black mirrors, reflecting us as we sprint past. I half expect them to spring to life, the face of Oren Darnell to appear, but they stay silent.

To get to the tracks, we have to cross through the gallery, and we hear the crowd before we see it. The noise is a huge, angry buzz, as if every insect burned in the Food Lab fire came back for revenge. We're still in one of the ground-floor corridors; the lights have gone, plunging it into near-darkness, with only the distant light from the galleries providing any illumination. The horrible noise fills the space. Before us is the exit to the gallery floor, and even at a distance we can see it's packed with people.

I've already heard from Yao how different groups are reacting to Darnell. The Caves are pulling in tight, letting hardly anyone in. The rest of New Germany is in chaos, with rumours of food riots, and the other sectors aren't much better. Yao says she heard that Tzevya is doing OK – there's a curfew of some kind, and an armed group preparing to find a way into Apex.

Amira raises a fist, bringing us to a halt behind her. We pause, breathing heavily, standing in a loose circle. My hips ache with the effort, and a stitch is gnawing at my side. Prakesh comes in last, his face flushed, but Amira glances at him and his expression hardens. She turns away from him, beckoning us closer.

"No running," she says, her voice rough with exertion. "Single file through the crowd, and don't talk to anyone.

Go for the corridor at the far end, and wait. We'll keep going when everyone's through." With that, she plunges into the crowd.

I pull my hood up, hiding my face, and glance at Prakesh. He gestures me ahead, and I step into the galleries. The noise explodes around me. There's a full-scale protest going on; at the far end, I can see a line of stompers with riot shields, protecting what looks like one of their captains. He has that speaking device, and as I slip through the crowd, he raises it to his mouth. "If everybody could remain calm," he begins, and is drowned out by a fresh roar of protest. Something flies through the air, and he has to leap back as the projectile smashes on the platform.

It's hard to tell what the crowd want – whether they believe their leaders can just bring them Darnell, or if they want new leaders entirely. One of the stompers raises something above his head, but before I can see him bring it down I'm given a rough push to the right. Someone gets into my face, yelling, and I instinctively raise a hand in apology before hurriedly moving on. My heart seems to have climbed from its regular position to my throat, choking me. I've lost track of both the Dancers and Prakesh.

I turn sideways to slip through a narrow gap in the thick crowd, and as I turn my head I see something that causes my heart to leap from my throat right into my mouth.

Zhao Zheng, the man who controls the Lieren, is standing a few feet away.

His back is to me, but there's no mistaking the bald head, lined with thick, jagged tattoos, or the hands, covered with tarnished metal, hanging at the end of unnaturally long arms. He wears a black, sleeveless vest, and is surrounded by four – no, five – Lieren. There's a small space around them, and people seem to be giving them some room. If I'd taken a different route, I might have gone right through the middle of them.

Someone bumps into me from behind, and suddenly I'm being propelled right towards Zhao's back.

In one horrifying instant, I see the chain of events locking into place before me, the knives coming out, the split second before I'm cut to ribbons, the triumphant smile on Zhao's face.

But I pull myself up, almost touching him, regaining my balance even as the noise from the crowd is drowned out by the roaring in my ears. At the edge of the group, one of the Lieren senses movement, starts to turn his head, but I quickly step backwards, vanishing into the crowd.

It's a little while before I breathe again.

As I reach the edge of the gallery, I can see people spilling into the corridor beyond, but I quickly catch sight of the Dancers. It takes me a second to see Prakesh as well, leaning against the wall, his hands on his knees. Amira sees me as I slip through, but then the look of relief on her face is replaced with one of horror. Before I can say anything, there's a hand on my shoulder, and I feel the cold touch of those metal rings.

Zhao Zheng leans in until his face is right up close to my ear. "Going somewhere?" he whispers.

45

Riley

There are at least ten Lieren. They stand on either side of their leader, fingering blades and flexing fists. The light from the gallery makes them into silhouettes, turning their bodies into little more than dark apparitions.

Zhao gives a nasty smile, twisted by a small scar on the right corner of his mouth. The top of the scar meets the tip of one of his tattoos: a huge, slashing black mark, running up his cheek and around his head.

Amira steps in beside me, but I raise a hand, and she stops, puzzled. The people at the edge of the crowd have seen what's happening, and have started to move away.

"Zhao, this really isn't the time," I say, but he just laughs.

"Tell that to Marco," he replies. He indicates one of the Lieren, standing off to the side, glaring at me. It's the one who led the ambush that started all this, the one I kicked in the head on the run to Gardens. His nose is a bulbous black mess. His blade twitches, gripped tight in his hand.

Hello, Tattoo. Apparently you have a name.

I look back at Zhao. "They jumped me, and they tried

to take my cargo. Your boy here" – I gesture at Marco, and his eyes narrow in anger – "wanted to cut my ear off. I was just repaying the favour."

"No, it doesn't work that way," Zhao replies. The smile stays etched on his face, but his eyes are cold. "You kind of – well – you insulted Marco. And that means you insulted me."

His eyes pass over the bruised twins, the crippled Carver. They're standing firm behind me, staring down the Lieren.

"I'll offer you a way out," he continues, leering. "Call it a debt of honour. We'll leave, but we're taking a body part of yours with us. I'll let you pick which one."

Amira steps forward, her teeth bared. "Not going to happen," she says.

"I thought as much," Zhao replies. And then he drives a fist deep into Amira's stomach.

She cries out and collapses backwards, the air leaving her in one huge burst. Time slows to a crawl as she falls. I leap forwards, twisting my left elbow round in the direction of Zhao's throat, and the corridor explodes.

Sometimes, the choice about whether to fight or to run gets made for you.

Every one of the Dancers attacks at once in a wave of fists and feet. My vision blurs at the edges; Zhao dodges out of range, laughing, but it dies on his lips as I bring the elbow round into the face of another Lieren. I feel his cheekbone crack under the strike, hear the howl of pain, but I'm already bringing my right hand up, balled into a fist and swinging at the man behind him. He's short, scrawny, barely out of his teens, and for a bizarre moment I wonder how someone like him ever fell in with the Lieren. Then my fist slams into his side with a noise like a wet jacket thrown into a corner, and he doubles over, retching.

Yao takes a few quick steps back, and then launches herself towards Kev. He's already dropping to one knee, cupping his hands to meet her. With a yell, she plants a foot in them, and Kev hurls her forwards. She explodes across the passage: a screaming, airborne ball of fists and feet, knocking two Lieren to the ground. As she tries to rise, another assailant appears above her – but doesn't even get to plant his feet before Kev hits him with an enormous right hook.

Behind them, Carver is facing off against two others; his arm is useless, but at the same moment that the Twins take down their opponents he launches himself towards the corridor wall, tic-tacs off and delivers a kick to the chest of one of the Lieren, knocking him backwards. Behind me, Prakesh makes a strange groaning sound – I can't tell if he's taking a hit or giving one.

Before I can find out, someone drives an elbow into the small of my back. The pain is so sudden, so startling, that I can't even cry out. It just stops dead in my throat.

I fall forwards onto my own elbows, my vision a starburst of colours. Instinctively, I lash out with a foot, and catch something – a leg – which jerks away, accompanied by a sharp cry. A hand gropes my hair, finds a purchase and yanks upwards, snapping my neck back. I have a split second to try and pull away, but then the fist smashes across my face. I taste blood instantly, salty and metallic.

Whoever owns the fist rears back for another strike, but then vanishes, ripped away. Amira, her left arm clutching her stomach, breathing heavily through her nose, disables my attacker with a jab to the throat.

For a moment, we're apart from the battle. I'm on all fours, staring up at her. A few feet away, Carver, Prakesh and the Twins duck, block, swing, strike, retaliate. Zhao is wielding a knife, a thin blade, long as my forearm. The knife rips into Carver's right shoulder, opening a jagged wound. He grunts in anger, before grabbing Zhao's knife hand and twisting. The blade flies out of his grip, bouncing and skittering down the corridor. I'm dimly aware that the noise from the gallery has got louder, though whether in reaction to the fight or because the crowd has finally broken through the line of stompers, I can't tell.

The Lieren are everywhere. Another runs towards me, his face gleaming with triumph. I'm back on my feet now, and sidestep before whipping my fist into his stomach, sending him crashing to the floor.

And then it all goes wrong.

From somewhere behind Amira, one of the Lieren appears – one I've never seen before. He's tall, thin as a corpse, wearing a jacket of some dark blue fabric. In his hand, already raised over his head, a long blade: Zhao's knife.

It's my imagination, it has to be, but the knife is as black as the deepest space, reflecting no light, and its wielder is fast, much too fast, and before I can do anything he's swinging it down towards Amira's neck.

Every part of me kicks into overdrive, snapping the corridor into sharp, clear focus. But even as my hand is reaching out to block the blade, I already know it won't be quick enough. Amira's eyes widen when she sees me, and she begins to turn, but the knife is almost there, its point finally picking up a flash of yellow light.

And then something – no, someone – appears between Amira and the blade.

There's a horrible sound, a kind of wet thud, like something plunging into a bucket of rotten food. The attacker's knife is ripped from his hand, and he staggers backwards.

Yao falls to the ground, the thin blade buried up to the hilt in the side of her neck.

For one terrible moment, her eyes meet mine, and it's as if someone has driven a blade through me instead. The corridor has fallen silent, Lieren and Dancer pausing their attack, everyone fixated on the dark blood that suddenly begins to spurt from Yao's neck, coming in thick, gushing bursts, collecting on the corridor floor. She sighs – a soft, calm sound – and then her eyes go dark.

46

Darnell

Councillor Morton holds out the longest.

He was one of the dozen people who ignored Janice Okwembu's summons to the amphitheatre. He was in the council chamber, diagramming plans for diverting more resources to the Air Lab, when he heard Oren Darnell's voice from one of the comms screens. He looked up just in time to see everybody he ever worked with asphyxiate, clawing at the walls.

Now he's barricaded the doors to the chambers. Unlike most of the sliding doors on Outer Earth, these ones swing inwards, and he's pushed every chair in the room up against them, jamming the handles shut. It's enough to hold Oren Darnell back for a good two minutes.

Morton shrinks down behind the table, mad with fear. Darnell is using a plasma cutter, burning a hole through the steel door. The air is hot with the stench of ozone. In seconds, he's cut a hole large enough to thrust his arm through – Morton sees the molten edge burn through the sleeve of his jacket, sizzle at the flesh beneath. Darnell doesn't seem to feel it. He knocks the chairs away, then withdraws his arm and kicks the door open.

Darnell crosses the room in seconds, a black hulk silhouetted by the ceiling lights. Morton is pulled from the chamber, Darnell's hands on his shoulders. He tries to fight back, hammering on the giant's arms, but he may as well try and bend a steel bar with his mind.

Darnell drags him into the passage, spins him around, hurls him to the floor.

"Whatever you want," Morton says, and that's when he sees Janice Okwembu. She's standing behind Darnell. As his eyes fall on her, Darnell can see the pitiful hope in them, as if he thinks she's arrived unnoticed, that she can knock Darnell out and save him. When she doesn't move, he says, "Janice, help me."

Okwembu steps past Darnell, and crouches down, so that she's level with Morton. He's shaking his head now, not understanding, not wanting to understand.

"Janice, please," he says. "What you're doing... this is insane."

"No, it's not," she says quietly, her eyes never leaving him. "You know what's insane, Charles? You. Sitting in that chamber for years, trying to legislate for this station, like it could make a single bit of difference."

"But Outer Earth—"

"Isn't worth keeping alive any more."

Morton's fear is starting to be replaced by anger, furious and disbelieving. "So you kill your colleagues? Torture them? It's monstrous."

"Yes," she says, standing, glancing at Darnell. "But necessary."

She walks away, not looking back. Morton tries to rise, pushing himself up to one knee. Darnell reaches down and draws the knife across his throat.

Morton takes a whole minute to die.

As Darnell turns away, he finally registers the burn on his arm, the one he got from the plasma cutter. He runs a finger along it, registering the pain but not responding to it. His stomach turns over, not from revulsion, but from hunger. When did he last eat? Or sleep? He doesn't remember, and at that moment it doesn't seem important.

He takes a step, then stops. The corridor swims in front of him, and he has to put a hand on the wall to steady himself. The memory comes, arriving to replace the pain, and he's halfway through it before he even knows it's there. The memory of his family's hab.

Darnell had given up keeping track of the number of species he'd managed to cultivate – they all blended into each other, sprouting flowers and swollen fruit and questing tendrils. He had to be careful not to step on the plants or trip over their roots. He didn't mind.

Nobody asked after his mother. At first, he'd been worried that they would, but nobody wanted to get involved. He kept collecting food packages from the mess, and would eat them standing up, alone in the hab.

On one particular day, he was just leaving for school, closing the hab door behind him. He was thinking about a new cultivar he was trying, one which wouldn't...

"Son?"

The man's eyes were bright over thin-rimmed glasses. He wore brown overalls, and carried a tab screen in one hand. He looked down at the screen, squinting. "Hab 6-21-E... Darnell family. Your parents' home?"

Darnell shook his head. "Dad's dead. And my mom's not at home."

"Ten-year maintenance inspection, son. Gotta make sure the chemical toilet doesn't need repair. Look here, see? My ID."

He held up the tab screen, showing the Outer Earth logo along with the words *Maintenance Corps.* Underneath the words, there was a pixelated photograph, and the name *Mosely, Lewis J., Inspection Officer.*

Darnell shrugged. "I'll tell my mom you came by."

Mosely smiled. "I don't think we need to trouble her, do you?"

"I gotta go to school," Darnell said, turning to lock the door behind him.

He didn't get the chance. Mosely reached over and pushed it open, and before Darnell could stop him, stepped inside. Darnell didn't move. Didn't breathe.

"Won't be a second, son," Mosely said. "Then we can—"

His words choked off as he saw the inside of the hab. Mosely turned, his hand over his mouth. Darnell remembers stepping backwards as Mosely let go, vomiting all over the door.

"Are you coming?" Okwembu says from the far end of the corridor.

Darnell looks up, the memory vanishing like smoke. He takes off after Okwembu, stepping over Morton's body. There's a distant stinging from his arm, the smell of burned fabric, but he's barely aware of them now.

"I want to talk to our friend," he says, as he catches up with Okwembu. She's at the bottom of a flight of steps, walking down a long passage towards a door. "I want to know where he is."

"You will," she says. "Once Hale has found Garner, and we've got what we needed."

At the mention of Hale, a comfortable rage flares inside him. All the same, he's about to tell Okwembu to do what he says when she opens the door, and then every thought he has falls away.

He's looking at the main control room of Outer Earth.

The room is as long and narrow as the corridor, with screens arrayed across each wall. Darnell touches the nearest one, and it responds smoothly at his touch, menu options appearing under his fingertips. *Orientation. Lighting Circuits. Core Operations.*

"I'll leave you to it," Okwembu says. "When you're ready, come back to the main council chamber. We'll do another broadcast from there."

Darnell barely hears her. He's moving down the room, hardly knowing where to look next, a giant grin on his face. Then his eyes fall on one particular display, and his grin gets even wider.

"I'll be along in a minute," he says, taking a seat at the screen.

47

Riley

Zhao breaks the silence. He gives an inhuman yell as he flies towards a startled Carver, his hands twisted into claws. But then Amira is there, darting across the room and slamming into him, pushing him into the wall, past a startled Kev, still frozen in shock.

"Run!" she shouts.

Prakesh grabs my arm. The Lieren are stunned, but only for a moment. Then they're giving chase, filling the corridor behind us with angry shouts. There are people further down the corridor, but they shrink against the wall with expressions of terror.

I run on automatic, my feet pulling me forwards all on their own. But my mind is lingering, staring into Yao's eyes, hearing that last whisper of her breath. Alongside me, I can hear Prakesh's breathing, heavy and ragged. There's someone else alongside us – Carver, I think. I don't know where Kev and Amira are.

Slowly, the cries of the Lieren vanish behind us. For a while, I lose track of where we're going. Prakesh is leading the way; he must be taking us towards Gardens. My chest is burning with the effort, and my calves are nothing more than twin slabs of aching flesh.

The guilt comes, blossoming in my mind like a diseased flower. If I hadn't attacked Marco, if I'd stayed down after that ambush, then Yao would still be alive. The realisation nearly doubles me over. I stumble to a halt, retching helplessly, desperately wanting to throw up, to force the feeling out of me, but nothing comes. I'm too shocked to cry; all I can do is hold my stomach as a creeping numbness spreads up my limbs.

Prakesh has run ahead, but he turns back when he realises I'm no longer with him. "What are you doing?" he rasps, his voice ragged with effort. "We have to keep moving. Come on."

There's a hand on my back. Carver is crouching down, looking up at me. His arm is crusted with jagged strips of blood.

"Ry," he says quietly. The kindness in his eyes takes a second to register. "We can't worry about it now. We have to finish this. For Yao."

Slowly, I nod.

The lights go out with a soft buzz, leaving us standing in pitch darkness. "What the hell?" Prakesh says, and then gets control of himself. "I know where this goes. Hopefully we can get to the tracks."

The further we run, the more chaotic the station seems to become. Now it's not just angry crowds hurling threats – it's full-on running battles, stompers with stingers and stun-sticks raised, plunging into huge brawls in the corridors and galleries. The fate of my crew, the death of Yao, all of it digs into my mind, and every fibre of my body tells me to turn back and find them. But I push forwards, because deep down I know Carver is right. I've got a job to do, and this whole situation is getting worse by the second. Darnell and the Sons of Earth are still in control. They could do anything: more fires, more bombs, even open one of the other airlocks and shoot all our air into space, suffocating us where we stand.

Every moment of my life – every moment of almost everyone's life – has been lived on Outer Earth. This station is my home, as familiar and comforting as an embrace. But in the hands of Darnell, it feels like it's been turned against me. Like every floor plate has become a trapdoor, and every pipe has a tripwire tied tightly around it.

We hit the stairs. They're almost silent around us; there's shouting in the distance, but I can't tell if it's another crowd or the Lieren coming after us. Little by little, we adjust to the darkness, and I find I can make out the floor ahead of us.

My thoughts drift to the asteroid catcher ships. There are only two left – big, hulking vessels with skeleton crews. What if the Sons succeed, and kill everyone on the station? The ships will return to find that they're the last humans in the universe. Where would they go? Would they try to return to Earth? Would they contact each other? Or just continue into deep space, drifting until their supplies run out and their engines sputter and die?

We've been climbing in silence, and every so often Prakesh will reach a hand back – I squeeze it, hoping that it's enough. But I'm deep in thought when I realise that the stairwell is getting lighter: whatever killed the lights isn't affecting areas above us. Before long, we hit the top level of the sector, and then we're climbing the stairs to the monorail platform.

And then, a triumphant shout from behind us: "Found you!"

Lieren: two of them, both carrying knives, their features hidden in the shadows. Can we risk running in the tunnels? Should we double back? I'm frantically running through places where we could lose them.

It's then that I realise Carver isn't with us. I turn back mid-stride, and see him standing with his back to us, his shoulders squared, facing down the oncoming Lieren. I can't see his face, but I see his fists in the low light, clenched at his sides.

"Get out of here, Ry," he says. "I'll buy you guys some time."

"Carver, come on!"

But he raises a hand, waving me away – it's his left hand, and I see his face tense as he does it; it must be screaming at him, racking his body in pain. He's in no condition to fight. I start towards him, but he senses me coming, and turns, his expression angry.

"Why can't you just do what you're told, for once?" he growls, but behind the anger I hear a note of pleading that brings me up short. The Lieren are almost on him, their blades dancing, and he turns back to them, bending his knees slightly.

Prakesh is behind me: "We have to go. Now."

I wheel around, furious. "We can't leave him!"

"Yes, you can," says Carver, and swings his good arm in a huge, pistoning strike that takes one of his attackers in the side of the head and sends him sprawling back down the corridor. The other Lieren pauses, surprised, and then Carver is on him. Prakesh grabs my arm, and then my reserve breaks and we're running into the darkness, leaving Carver fighting to the death behind us.

48

Riley

It takes a long time for us to adjust to the darkness in the tunnel. Right now, the only thing we can be sure of is that we're heading in the direction of Gardens. We have to move slowly; the ground under our feet is twisted and uneven, and the tracks are nothing more than thin black lines. Our footsteps echo into the gloom.

"Do you think they'll follow us in here?" Prakesh asks quietly.

"Probably. But they won't see us right away. And we have a head start."

"Thanks to Carver."

I don't reply.

Eventually, after what seems like hours, we reach Gardens. The platform is deserted, lit by that ghostly orange light. Soon, we're on a catwalk high above the main entrance to the Food Lab, which is still spouting puffs of acrid smoke. I can't see the floor below, but I can hear people down there: it doesn't sound like a fight, but every so often angry voices are raised: people pleading for food, demanding to be let in.

Right then, there's the crackle of the comms systems.

There's an enormous screen at the far end of the gallery, and as it flashes up the station logo, a cold chill settles over me. I know exactly what's coming.

Darnell appears on the screen. He's seated at the main table in the Apex council chamber, his hands folded in front of him. His frame is too large for the chair he's sitting in, and he towers over the table. He's smiling.

"It's time to make things a little more..." He pauses, as if searching for the right word, then his smile gets wider. "Uncomfortable."

Now that he's in the council chamber, there's no need for him to hack the feed, and the lack of glitches somehow makes it even worse. "We can control the thrusters from here, turn off all the oxygen, even send a little signal down the lines that'll boil every drop of water on the station into nothingness."

Prakesh has gone very still. His hand finds mine, and grips it tight. I can't take my eyes off the screen. Darnell leans back in his chair, his huge hands laced over his stomach. "But none of that seemed to be enough. Not for the people on this station. So we've told Outer Earth's convection systems to cease functioning. It's not quite as efficient as fire, but it's so much more fun to watch." The screen cuts to black.

There's perhaps half a second of silence before the crowd below us starts screaming. I turn to Prakesh, my eyes wide. I'm no scientist, but I know how this place works. And I know that we're in serious trouble.

You can heat Outer Earth without too many problems. But cooling it? Keeping the temperature down with a million people, a bunch of power sources and the regular blasts of direct sunlight when the station swings round in its orbit? That takes a lot of work. There are big fins on the station hull, convectors which let the heat just radiate off into space. They rely on coolant, circulating through pipes around the station, an enormous nerve system of liquid which keeps the temperature stable. If they shut down, if the liquid stops flowing...

"How long do we have?" I ask, my voice high and thin.

Prakesh looks away, and for a second I think he hasn't heard, but then he says, "Probably as long as Darnell's deadline. A day. Maybe less."

"Could someone get into the main systems and turn the coolers back on?"

He shakes his head. "No way. Maybe. I don't know."

We stand, listening to the chaos unfold below us. Eventually, Prakesh takes his hands off the railing. "This way," he mutters, straightening up, but instead of moving, he just stands there, hands on his thighs. His face is slick with sweat, his breath coming in huge, ragged gasps. The signs are hard to miss: the quivering calves, the slumped shoulders. Every rookie tracer goes through them. Prakesh is muscled from constant work in the Air Lab, but he's nowhere near tracer-fit. Not even close.

I crouch down, looking up at him. He tries to force a smile, and doesn't succeed.

"Will there be food and water? In this little entrance of yours?" I ask. He nods. "Good. And it had better be all natural. I don't want to be eating any genetic stuff."

He laughs, forces himself up. I rise with him. "Come on," I say. "We're almost there. Let's get into the Air Lab, and then we can rest. Promise."

Prakesh takes the lead at a slow jog; I desperately want him to move faster, but bite my tongue, letting him go at his own pace. He leads us off the catwalk and down through a maze of corridors and stairwells, taking us through a couple of keypad-protected doors. The corridors change slightly, the sparse metal plates and recessed lights giving way to banks of computers, some of which look like they haven't been used in decades. The glaring white lights from the ceiling reflect off the dark screens.

I'm uneasy. We're so close, and the thought that we might not find Garner – or worse, that the information she has might turn out to be useless – continues to gnaw at me.

"We're here," calls Prakesh. He's gone a little way ahead, to a low door set into the left side of the corridor. He leads me through, and as I come into the room I see him twisting a panel off the wall. I help out, both of us pulling hard, and it comes off in a screech of metal. The space beyond is dusty and dirty, but I can see light leaking through from further along.

Without a word, Prakesh slips inside. I follow, and soon we're in the Air Lab.

We've come out onto one of the paths between the algae pools. The huge trees lie silhouetted against the lights. I see a couple of technicians in the distance, off to the right, doing something to the base of one of them.

Whatever carnage the fire wreaked in the Food Lab, it looks as if Prakesh really did stop it reaching the Air Lab. The air, after the stale smokiness of the gallery and the corridors, is refreshingly cool. I'm expecting the lab to be packed with techs, but there are only a few, dotted here and there among the trees. There are voices and loud banging coming from one of the smaller buildings on the other side of the lab – the structures I've heard Prakesh calling mobile labs. Must be where they've set up food production.

"Let's look in the control room," says Prakesh. He points to the huge structure jutting out of the wall, visible through the trees. It's where I handed the eyeball to Darnell. "If she isn't there, we can fan out across the lab."

We head towards the control room, jogging between the algae ponds. Their surfaces are smooth, calm, with only the odd tiny shudder floating through them, as if wind had touched the water. After the insanity of the battle with the Lieren and the run through the station, the ponds are calming.

The control room looms above us, staircases and power lines underneath it. The upper part is level with the tree canopies, and holds a massive window. I can just see inside from where we are, and I scan the rooms for any sign of life, but there's nothing: just more computers, blinking softly through the glass.

Prakesh points, indicating a narrow staircase off to one side, which leads to the metal gantry that curves around the structure. "What are you going to do after we've talked to her?" he says.

"I don't know," I reply. "Depends on what she has to say. Maybe she knows what Darnell was trying to get out of Foster."

"It's just..." He shakes his head. "We've come a long way on faith, Riley."

"Don't," I say. My voice, drained and weary, doesn't communicate the anger I feel.

He continues, unfazed. "What happens if she can't help us? What then?"

"I don't know," I say through gritted teeth. It sounds helpless, pathetic. And he's right: if she can't help us, then Yao – and Carver, possibly – died for nothing. Not to mention Amira, who could be anywhere.

We try to minimise the noise we make, but with every step the metal clangs and booms, sounding too loud in the quiet of the Air Lab. We're just at the top of the stairs, stepping onto the bottom part of the gantry, when a voice booms out from far below, somewhere under the trees.

"My offer's still open. Better take it – unless, of course, you want your friend to contribute some flesh in your place."

Zhao.

Prakesh and I crouch quickly, ducking behind the metal barriers on the gantry. And then I see them, through a gap in the metal. Five of them, scratched and bleeding, but very much alive. Zhao standing at the back, his arms folded, death on his face. And lying at his feet, her hands bound behind her, her eyes closed: Amira.

All at once, there's too much saliva in my mouth, like the feeling you get before you vomit. There's no sign of Kev or Carver. Zhao continues, raising his voice, and this time the anger in his voice is palpable. "You think this is a joke? I know you're up there somewhere – you and your scientist friend."

I know you're up there somewhere. We're off to one side, partially hidden by the curve of the control room wall. He's seen us go up, but he doesn't know where we are. I meet Prakesh's eyes, and I can see he's realised it too.

He leans forward, bringing his mouth to my ear. "I'm going to make a dash for the control room. Wait for my signal."

"Signal?" I hiss back, but he's up, running along the catwalk to one of the doors. I hear a shout of triumph from below as Zhao spots him, and I have to force myself not to leap to my feet.

"Hiding in there won't help you," shouts Zhao. "Hey, Riley," he continues, and the laughter in his voice chills me to the bone. "Do you think your friend here will notice when we start? Marco hit her over the head pretty hard, but I'm hoping she's awake enough to know what's happening."

I'm clenching my fists so hard that my hands have gone white. Every cell in my body is screaming at me to help Amira. There's nothing Prakesh can do: what weapons is he planning on finding in the control room? Bags of fertiliser?

49

Prakesh

As it happens, fertiliser is exactly what Prakesh is thinking. More specifically, he's thinking about ammonium nitrate.

He sprints through the door to the Air Lab control room, ignoring the shouts from the Lieren below. He's expecting to find some techs there, but they're all in the mobile labs, and the room is mercifully empty. Oren Darnell's barrels of water squat at the back of the room, their surfaces rippling.

The only internal light comes from the computer screens. Prakesh is still sprinting, and doesn't see the knocked-over chair until his feet are tangled in it. He goes down, bloodying his nose on the floor, fists pounding the metal in frustration even as he gets to his feet.

Blood gushes down his chin, and he can feel his bottom lip swelling too. He ignores it, stumbling to the screens and hunting through them for the right menu.

Prakesh knows how fire works. Every single tech on the station goes through a fire prevention course, where they learn about things like backdraught, and chain reactions, and oxidizers. Even fire which spreads like liquid and bites through chemical foam has to behave, in some ways, like fire. You can starve it of air to put it out, but it'll just lie dormant, smouldering. If you add the right mix of air back into the environment, and come up with a suitable ignition source, then you can restart that fire.

Prakesh begins to pump air from the Air Lab to the Food Lab, sucking it through the vents. He's going to have to control the flow precisely, reversing it and cutting it off at just the right moments. If he screws this up, he'll bathe the Air Lab in fire.

In seconds, the oxygen levels in the Food Lab have risen. Prakesh has already picked an ignition source. The main fuse array in the Food Lab will have been destroyed by the fire, but Prakesh doesn't need it to power anything. He *needs* it to be broken, because he needs the spark. Even a single wire, its insulation burned away, will do it.

He grits his teeth, and activates the fuse array.

Nothing. The power indicators on screen remain stubbornly blank.

Blood drips onto the screen from his damaged nose. He hits the option again, then a third time, willing the fuse array to work.

50

Riley

I risk another peek over the railing, and the sight brings my heart to my mouth.

One of the Lieren, his back to me, is crouching over Amira, dragging a knife delicately over her forehead. She shifts, groans, as the point of the blade touches her skin.

"You've got about ten seconds before we start," says Zhao. "And I should warn you: I never like telling my boys to stop once they get going."

Something tickles my throat. I ignore it, but it comes back, demanding attention.

I look up, and my eyes widen: the entire top half of the hangar is wreathed in grey and white smoke. The air-conditioning vents have been activated, and smoke from the Food Lab fire is pumping in, drifting down onto the Air Lab below.

Prakesh, you genius.

"Have it your way then," says Zhao, but then I hear a puzzled shout from one of the others. The smoke is thicker now; I drop my head to the floor, where the air is still just clean.

I take a deep breath, and hold it.

Zhao's voice drifts up from below: "Where's it coming from? Marco, I thought you said the fire was only in the Food Lab."

"It was!" says Marco, his voice muffled by his smashed nose. "Zhao, I'm telling you, I don't know what this is."

The smoke has reached the floor level, shrouding the Lieren in a white fog. And at that instant, I stand up, anger burning in my veins like a hot, bright filament, and hurl myself off the gantry.

I can't see the ground below me – the smoke has got so thick that the ground has vanished. I pull my legs up, bending my knees and tucking my arms, ready for the roll, hoping that I've done it in time. When I do hit the ground, a second later, my ankles explode with a pain that shoots rapidly up my legs and into the base of my spine.

But I was ready for it, prepared for the impact, and even before I register the pain, I'm rolling forwards. The landing forces me to exhale, and as I spring upwards from the roll, already scanning for the Lieren, I have to suck in another breath. The smoke sinks in, clawing at my throat, but there's just enough clear air left to breathe.

One of the Lieren appears out of the smoke. This time, I don't bother lashing out; I go low, channelling all the energy from the roll into a shoulder-charge which takes him at the knees.

He's a lot bigger than I am, but the rage I'm feeling gives me strength and the hit sends him flying, filling the space above with flailing arms and legs. I catch an expression of total surprise on his face, and then he's gone, hitting the ground so hard that I hear his skull crack.

No time to congratulate myself. Even before I'm up, another Lieren has materialised out of the smoke, waving a knife before him. He slashes out, his eyes wide, but I dodge to the left, grabbing his wrist and yanking it upwards. He screams in pain, a sound cut off a second later when I plant my elbow in his mouth. I feel one of his teeth break through the sleeve of my jacket, but I'm already pushing him aside.

This is different from when I'm running. Then, I'm on autopilot, my body responding to muscle memory, the focus so effortless it's like a second skin. This? This feels like someone just plugged me into the station's fusion reactor and flipped the switch. My muscles are rods of iron, my teeth clenched, my vision razor-sharp, even as the smoke gets thicker. Everything Amira taught me about fighting is right in the front of my mind, like I've opened a book. In the background, somewhere unimportant, lies the dull ache in my lungs, burned raw with smoke.

Two more Lieren fly out of the gloom; I gut-punch one, throwing every atom of energy I can find into it. He goes down, but a split second later a line of fire burns on my shoulder; the other Lieren has cut me, slashing downwards through my jacket. My arm is instantly soaked in hot blood. But the pain just focuses me further, and I swing round, ducking under his next slash, before driving the heel of my hand upwards into his face.

He tries to knock the blow aside, but he's too slow, and his chin cracks under my hit. He falls, his eyes rolling back in his skull. The smoke is almost impenetrable now. What little fresh air I was getting is gone, and the slight pause in the fight causes the ache in my lungs to rocket up into my skull, clanging with pain. I'm bent double by hacking coughs, dimly aware that my right arm is wet and sticky with blood.

As I reach up to touch the wound, Zhao Zheng lunges out of the fog, whirling two more knives in front of him, murder on his face.

I have a moment to wonder where he got the knives, whether he had more on him or took them from the fallen Lieren, before I hurl myself backwards, tucking into a clumsy roll as I feel one of the knives slash so close that the air moves across my forehead. The adrenaline that focused me, that let me take down the Lieren so easily, has drained away, replaced by a leaden exhaustion. I spring out of the roll, my chest on fire and my vision blurred, as Zhao leaps forward again.

You don't survive as a gang leader on Outer Earth without some serious moves. I dodge once, twice, desperately looking for an opening, but Zhao lets nothing through. Another slash tags my forehead, singing with pain. Blood drips into my eyes as I try to circle round him. He jabs to the right, but as I dodge away I realise it was a feint – only a nanosecond of reaction saves me from being skewered in the stomach. He dives forward, leading this time with both blades, sure of his aim.

A black form explodes out of the fog, tackling him round the waist and sending him flying through the air. Zhao and Prakesh crash to the ground, a tangle of limbs. Prakesh rolls away, and then I'm on top of my enemy, my knee in his throat. Zhao's lost one of his blades, but still has the other in a tight grip. He tries to raise it, but I grab his hand and twist.

Zhao yells in fury, dropping the blade. He tries to rise, but I slam my knee back into his throat with every ounce of venom I can put behind it. He gags, fights for breath, tries again to force me off him, but the strength has gone out of him. His arms flail against me, but I barely feel them.

I start punching him. And I don't stop.

My knuckles rip and tear and shred as his face explodes with blood and bruises. I'm yelling something, words maybe, I don't know. Everything is just white; I can't tell where the smoke ends and my vision begins. My hands go numb, and it's only when his face is a jagged mash of blood and broken teeth that Prakesh pulls me off him.

"Riley, that's enough," he says. My first instinct is to rip out of his grasp, to attack Zhao again, but I don't. Horror and elation cascade through me, colliding together.

We stand, our shoulders heaving, and it comes to me that I'm breathing actual air. I look around, startled; the smoke seems to have cleared somewhat, drifting away into the Air Lab. Prakesh must have killed the vents. Zhao lies before us, breathing in wet gasps, his face a ruin.

And then, from the trees: "Is it over?"

Her hands are clutching a blue scarf, which has slipped off her head and lies bunched at her throat. Her face is creased with worry, her shoulders trembling.

Grace Garner.

51

Riley

I have to stop myself from gulping the water in the cup. I take small sips, savouring it.

Amira, Garner and I are in one of the control rooms above the Air Lab. The room is dark, with the only light coming from the screens and control panels on the walls.

The water helps, but there's nothing for my aching knuckles. Prakesh is checking on his trees, making sure the smoke didn't damage the young ones.

I'm seated on a pile of fertiliser bags, my hands throbbing with pain. I've bent them in half-fists, and my knuckles are little more than torn shreds of flesh. The cuts in my arm and forehead aren't deep, but they're still singing with pain. Amira, freed of her bonds, is leaning against one of the control panels, massaging her wrists. An ugly, black bruise is already forming on her cheek.

She's been silent ever since we brought her up here, occasionally rubbing the stumps of her missing fingers. She's lost her scarf somewhere, and the expression on her face is impossible to read.

Beside her, Grace Garner is in the room's lone chair, hunched forwards, hands clasped around another cup of water. Her face has more lines on it than I remember. I want to ask her about Darnell, Gray, Marshall Foster, the Sons of Earth, everything, but something inside tells me to wait.

Several times, Garner opens her mouth, seems about to speak, but then stops, like she too isn't sure of where to start. Eventually, she says, "I thought you'd never come."

I smile, despite myself. "The trains were running late."

She doesn't smile. "I got caught up in the crowds after..." She clears her throat. "After the bombs went off. I didn't even know there'd been one in Gardens until later. It was awful. People screaming, people pushing me."

"How did you get into the Air Lab?"

"It took me a long time to get here, and it got worse. People were trying to break in. To salvage food, I think. There were protection officers here, trying to hold them back. I knew one of them, and asked him to hide me. The look on his face when I first saw him...it was like he didn't recognise me at all." At this, her voice cracks, and silent tears begin to run down her cheeks.

She shakes her head, and seems to be steeling herself to continue. "But he helped me, eventually. Sneaked me through a back way. That man you told me to find, the one who was with you – he wasn't here. There were others, other techs. They chased me, but I got away and I hid. Then the smoke came, and then..."

"You found us," says Amira. Her voice is an impatient croak.

"Grace," I say. "You worked with Marshall Foster. Why did they have him killed?"

Something changes in her eyes – a tiny fragment of old strength that comes creeping back. It's only then that I really notice the high cheekbones, the lips, still full. She was beautiful, once.

"I was his assistant for years," she replies. "I served under him when he was on the council. He was in charge of the Outer Earth digital systems – all the computer codes and subroutines that keep the station running were maintained by him. Marshall asked me to come with him when he retired, so we settled in Apogee. We were close, closer than you can imagine. And then…"

She stops, her head bowed.

"Gray," I say.

Garner nods. "I was reading in our room. Marshall collected books – he hoarded them while he was on the council. Silly habit of his, but I liked them.

"I wasn't really paying attention, and I didn't even hear Marshall come in until he grabbed my hands. I'd never seen him look so terrified. He didn't say anything, just grabbed me out of my chair. He wouldn't tell me what was happening. He lifted up one of the panels on the floor that we used for storage and told me to get in. It was a tiny space, and I could barely scrunch down in it."

"So you just obeyed him?" asks Amira.

"What was I supposed to do?" says Garner, her voice turning into a wail. "I'd taken orders from him *my whole life*. He was everything to me. And I knew he wanted to keep me safe. I wanted to know what was going on, but he still wouldn't tell me. I'd never seen him like that. And still, he… he wouldn't tell me why."

"What did he say?" I ask.

"He said he was sorry. He said that no matter what happened, he… he loved me, and he was sorry for everything he'd done, but I had to hide for as long as possible. I told him I didn't know what he was talking about, that he didn't have anything to be sorry for, but then he said he needed to tell me something else, that there wasn't much time."

The tears are streaming down her cheeks. Her hands

are limp in her lap. I can't even imagine what she's been through, hiding in the trees, waiting for someone who might never show up. Knowing that the entire world was collapsing around her, and that the man she trusted was dead.

After a few moments, I rise off the fertiliser sacks and walk over, crouching in front of her. Her face is red and blotchy, streaked with the shiny tracks of tears. "I know this is hard for you," I say, "but we're running out of time. There are people who want to destroy Outer Earth, and whatever Marshall Foster told you might be able to stop them."

I don't know if this is true or not. But I have to try.

"He told me to find a tracer named Riley Hale in Apogee," she says.

"Why me?"

"I don't know. He told me I had to give you a piece of information . . . but it didn't make any sense. I don't know what it means. I tried to get him to tell me, but he said . . . he said there wasn't any time. The last thing he said to me was that you'd know what to do with it when the time came."

I raise my face to hers, and she says, "He told me to give you a word. Iapetus. That's all."

She must see the look of confusion on my face, because she says, "It's one of Saturn's moons. But I never got a chance to ask what the word meant, or what it was used for." She shrugs helplessly. "He told me that, and then he was gone. I never saw him again." More tears come.

Iapetus.

I rack my brain for any mention of the word before. Nothing comes. Why would Foster say that I'd know what to do with it? I never knew him, I've never heard the word before, and even if I had, I have no clue how it helps us defeat Darnell.

But before any conclusions can form, there's a bang. The sound is enormous, replaced instantly by a ringing in my ears. The chair Garner is in pitches backwards. Her chest flares with blood, staining her blue scarf black.

She seems to fall in slow motion, her arms thrown out to the sides, like she's trying to break her fall. For one horrible moment, I see the surprise on her face, the life already beginning to fade from her eyes. She hits the ground, and then there's just silence. Nothing but the ringing in my ears.

I turn, and see Amira. She's holding a stinger out in front of her. And as I watch, she swings the gun around until it points directly at my chest.

52

Prakesh

The other techs must have cleared out when the smoke came down. Prakesh is alone on the floor of the Air Lab, and he can't remember the last time the place was so silent. The only sound is the distant hum of the ventilation system, sucking the last of the smoke away from the labs. Most of it's gone already, and the few wisps that remain are hanging around at canopy level.

In truth, the smoke was never really going to hurt the trees, or the algae. That was just something Prakesh told Riley to give him a chance to get away. He needed time to think.

He heads for the mobile lab, making a detour around the bloodied patch where Riley beat the crap out of Zhao. He keeps glancing up at the main window of the control room, but it's reflecting some of the light at him, turning it into a shining white beacon which reveals nothing.

He has to think of a way to stay with her.

Prakesh is well aware that he's done what he said he would. He got Riley and Amira into the Air Lab. They've found Garner. Prakesh doesn't know what she'll tell them, or what they'll do next, but he knows that there'll be no good reason for him to stay with them. Riley will tell him to lie low, to stay in the Air Lab, to let her and Amira take care of... whatever the hell they need to take care of.

Riley can handle herself. Prakesh knows that. But it doesn't stop him wanting to stay with her. If he's with her, he can...

He groans in frustration, resting his hands on the edge of an algae tank. His fingertips just touch the water, sending out a ripple which distorts his reflection.

She doesn't want you, he thinks. *Not in the way you want her.*

He pushes off, striding towards the mobile lab. He'll check on the trees anyway. Get some equipment, test soil pH levels, check the temperature of the algae ponds, do something to get his mind off it.

It takes him a few minutes to make his way to the mobile lab. Most of the equipment was in the stores, destroyed in the fire, but there are still a few units scattered across the shelves here. Prakesh looks at them without seeing. Eventually, he grabs a pH monitor, more or less automatically, and turns to leave. Maybe he's overthinking this. Maybe he can...

There's a noise, right at the edge of his hearing, almost inaudible. An echoing bang.

He pauses for a moment, confused, and it takes him a second to identify the sound. Stinger fire. A single shot. He listens hard, but the sound doesn't repeat itself. At first, he thinks it's coming from somewhere in the Air Lab, but it was barely there to begin with, and the echoes smudge the sound. He can't place the source.

Prakesh turns around, meaning to investigate.

And finds another stinger barrel less than an inch from his face.

The barrel is a giant black hole, sucking in light. Prakesh becomes exquisitely aware of every movement, of every twitch in his fingers and every breath he takes. He makes himself focus, makes himself look past the barrel and see the person behind it.

It's a stomper. The underarms of his grey uniform are soaked with sweat, and his dark skin and shorn head gleam with it. Prakesh has seen him before, although it takes him a moment to remember where. He was one of the stompers who busted into Arthur Gray's room by the monorail tracks.

"Show me ID," the stomper says.

Prakesh tries to breathe. "I'm a tech. OK? I work in the Air Lab."

"Show me ID," the stomper says again.

"Seriously, don't shoot me, my name is Prakesh Kumar. I was there when Arthur—"

"*Show me ID, now.*" The stomper's grip on the stinger makes it pretty clear that he won't ask again, and he doesn't show the slightest hint of recognition when he hears Prakesh's name.

Prakesh's hand moves to where the pocket of his lab coat would be if he were still wearing one, then stops. "I lost it."

He doesn't have time to berate himself for how stupid that sounds, because he sees the stomper's trigger finger move ever so slightly. "Wrong answer," the stomper says. "I've got techs evacuating, talking about more smoke, and now I find you. Move."

Prakesh starts to walk, painfully aware of the stinger. He doesn't know what to do with his hands.

There's another bang, distant and echoing. Both Prakesh and the stomper are facing the control room when it comes, and it's impossible to miss the flash, the tiny white-yellow burst of stinger fire, from the control room windows.

"Riley," Prakesh breathes.

And before the stomper can stop him, he's running.

53

Riley

Time stops.

Amira has the stinger clasped in both hands, her finger inside the trigger guard. A tiny wisp of smoke is curling from the barrel, catching light from a nearby screen. For one weird instant, I wonder how she managed to keep the gun on her when she was captured by Zhao.

Above it, her eyes are cold. She has the same expression she had back at the brig, when she broke me out. Sorrow and anger, fighting for control.

I slowly find the words, my voice shaking. "Amira, what are you doing?"

"Don't," she says.

Her voice cracks a little. Does she have to reload? Can she fire again straightaway? Impossible to tell.

My eyes fall on Garner's body. Her legs have tilted to the side as her chair toppled over, and she lies sprawled across the floor. As I watch, her hand, splayed out above her head, twitches ever so slightly. "She's still alive." I look at Amira, trying to hide the desperation in my voice. "We have to help her."

"I said, don't."

She takes a step forward, the gun still pointed right at my chest. "Turn around."

I do as she says, trembling. I'm running over the last few hours in my mind, trying to find out why she's doing this. I see her breaking me out of the brig. Back in the Caves, trying to get us to go to find Garner without the rest of the crew. Telling the Dancers to split up when we were attacked by Zhao. And now, her and me, alone with Garner.

"It wasn't real, was it?" I mutter, and I'm surprised to hear a tiny core of steel in my own voice. "None of it. You planned it all."

The gun lightly touches the back of my head.

"I'm sorry, Riley," she says. "I wish it didn't have to happen this way, but it does."

My gaze is drawn back to Garner, and this time the hand is still. Something inside me says to keep her talking. *Buy time. Prakesh might come back.*

"Tell me why. You owe me that much," I say.

"You're the only one Garner would have spoken to. You were the one who had to find her. But once we'd got the information, that word, whatever it is, there was no reason for her to live. And no reason for you to, either."

The realisation settles over me, heavy, like a thick blanket. "You're one of Darnell's sleepers. One of the Sons of Earth."

"Yes." She says it in a whisper.

Call it instinct. Call it whatever the hell you want, but I know that she's about to squeeze the trigger. Right now. Right this second.

I whip my head to the side. She fires. The bullet is so close that I feel it whip-crack past my ear. She screams in fury, swinging the gun around. But my instinct is still in control. I'm just along for the ride.

I snap my left arm upwards, grabbing her wrist and

twisting. She snarls, but doesn't let go of the gun, leaning into the move. I can feel her shifting stance, trying to pull me off balance. Her free hand swings round, and claps me on the ear, which explodes in ringing pain. I'm immediately nauseous, and she tries to throw me off, but somehow I hold on.

It can't be her. This twisting, slashing thing on top of me can't be Amira. It's someone else, something else, some *thing* that's taken over her body. This can't be the same person who saved me, all those years ago.

But a part of me – the instinct, the part that kept me alive when Amira pulled the trigger – knows different.

Amira is the best fighter I've ever seen, anywhere. The only hope in hell I have of beating her is to get to that gun.

And then I remember something else.

She was also one of the best teachers.

We fall to the floor. She gets on top of me, her nails scratching across my forehead, reopening the cut I got from the Lieren. She jerks against my grip on her wrist, trying to bring the gun round, trying to push it into my face.

I reach up and pull, swinging the gun past my face and to the side. My breath catches in my throat – Amira is so quick that she might just have pulled the trigger right then – but she doesn't, and then the gun is on my right, and she's off balance.

I swing it back the other way in one sudden movement. The stinger flicks out of her grip, skittering across the floor. She howls in frustration, torn between fighting me and going for it. I seize the opportunity, hitting her sideways across the cheek. She tumbles off me, and I scramble for the gun, hunting for it in the half-light.

My fingers close on the barrel just as Amira lunges forward and drops a knee into my back. The agony flares upwards along my spine. I smash into the ground, and it takes every ounce of control I have not to let go of the gun. My fist is closed so tight around it that I can feel every tendon in my hand.

I buck my body upwards. Amira crashes off me, coming to rest on her knees. With a gasping cry, I swing the gun round, the metal slipping under my fingers, fumbling with the trigger guard.

I'm lying on my side, the gun in both hands, pointed right at her. The only sound is our breathing, heavy and ragged.

She slowly raises her hands. "You don't understand, Riley. What we're doing? All of this? It's for the greater good. Humanity nearly destroyed the planet. If we continue to exist, then we'll return, and we'll do it again. The only way to make sure the Earth survives is for us not to."

My thumb touches the stinger's safety catch – it's off, and I keep it that way. But there's no way of telling how many bullets are still inside. My body is humming with adrenaline and pain, and the gun shakes in my grip.

"You don't believe that. You can't."

Unbelievably, she smiles. "You forget," she whispers. "I saved Outer Earth. I saved it. I ran the Core."

My eyes flick to her hand, her missing fingers.

"I believed in it back then," she continues. "Believed it was worth fighting for. But nothing changed. We still kill and rape and steal and destroy. We don't deserve to live. We never did. And without us, the Earth can recover."

"Shut up!" I scream. Tears prick the sides of my eyes. This can't be happening. It's as if the insane Darnell is there, speaking through Amira, using her like a puppet. "What about the Dancers? What about us? Do we deserve to die?"

Regret floods her face. "I knew none of you would understand. I wanted to make you see, but I didn't know how. You would have stopped me. You would have stopped us. I always knew I'd have to choose between the Dancers and doing the right thing. I just made my choice. That's all."

The betrayal gives way to anger, bright and hot. "The bombing, the fire, the heat convectors... is that what you want? For everyone to suffer?"

There's a flicker of doubt. Just for a moment. "No. I just did what Janice Okwembu asked me to. I had to find you, bring you to Garner, and get the code."

"But Darnell has Okwembu. He said he's going to kill her."

Now she laughs, getting to her feet. "I work for her. So does Darnell – he's just the face. She came to me two years ago and asked me to join them."

"That's impossible. Back up!"

Amira has taken a few steps towards me, and stops, her hands raised. "How do you think that idiot Darnell got into Apex?"

Iapetus. "The word Garner gave me. What's it for? What does it do?"

"If you think you can get something out of me, then I'm sorry to disappoint you. I don't know what it's for. It's something Okwembu needs, that's all."

"Some kind of destruct code, is that it? She going to blow up the station?"

"Maybe."

The ringing in my ears has gone, replaced by a dull roar. I don't know whether it's the blood rushing through my veins, or something else entirely.

"I don't know what made you think this way," I say, "but they've brainwashed you. Even if we don't deserve to live on Earth, we deserve a chance. The people here aren't monsters. They didn't kill the planet. Amira, these are *innocent people*."

"They aren't innocent. No one here is. Everyone deserves what's coming."

I cut her off. "What about me?"

She falls silent. I keep talking: "You saved me once, Amira. If you believed we all deserved to suffer, you would have left me with the men in that corridor. But you didn't, did you? And after all we've been through, all we've done together, you want to throw it away?"

Prakesh has been gone too long. He should have come back by now. But even as the thought occurs, I realise a part of me wants him to stay away. I don't want anyone to see this. Any of it.

Right then, I see that Amira has shifted ever so subtly, rocking back on her heels.

To anybody else, it would be something almost imperceptible. But I've been running with Amira for long enough, and in one horrible moment I understand what she's about to do.

"No," I whisper. With a cry of triumph, she launches herself towards me.

I pull the trigger.

54

Riley

The sound of the gunshot fills the room. The whole world.

The bullet takes Amira in the stomach. She makes the oddest sound – a kind of *phuh*. Her grace and agility vanishes, sucked out of her, her body becoming a flying rag-doll, crashing to the ground. The fabric of her tank top is soaked with blood.

As she rolls to a stop at my feet, she begins screaming. She clutches her ruined stomach, sweat beading her forehead.

I drop to my knees, pressing down on her stomach, causing her to howl in pain again. I've gut-shot her. I didn't even aim. My hands are drenched in seconds, slick and hot with her blood.

"I have to stop the bleeding," I say. "We can get you to a hospital. I think there's one near here. If we just..."

She reaches up and grips my hand. For an absurd moment, I think she's going to continue attacking me, but she doesn't. The pain is written on her face, rippling under the surface, but it's been shrouded by a kind of calm.

"You don't have to do that," she says. A tiny sliver of blood trickles from the corner of her mouth.

After a moment, she says, "I was told to kill you first, then Garner. Not to wait, not to talk, just to do it. But I couldn't. I couldn't."

"Amira..."

Her voice, husky now, coming in bubbling gasps. "You mustn't stop Okwembu. This has to happen. It needs to happen."

The anger is back, all at once, like a light turning on. Blinding, white-hot fury erupts and I slam my fist on the ground next to her head. She barely flinches.

"Why do you keep saying that?" I scream. "There are *people* on this station. People with lives, with families. Who the hell are you to say that they should die?"

She doesn't reply. I'm crying openly now, the tears dropping off my cheeks onto Amira's chest.

I should let her die. In pain.

The thought shocks me, but I can't shake it. She lied to me, to the Dancers. She betrayed us in the worst way possible. She deserves this.

"Everything you taught me," I say. "Was it all a lie too? Was everything leading up to... to this?"

Something changes in her expression. Like a barrier falling away.

"No," she whispers. "When I saved you... that wasn't a lie. And you became everything I hoped you would be."

Blood pools around her. I reach for her hand again, grip it tight. She gasps in pain, a noise which becomes an awful moan. My hatred cracks, then shatters.

Amira closes her eyes. Her face is a pale, ghostly white, and it seems like all her will leaves her at once. "You need to get to Apex."

"I can get there from here. Maybe the code will let me in somehow."

"No," she says. The air whistles out with her voice, obscuring her words. "That's not what the code does, I'm sure of it. You can't get in from the adjoining sectors. It's more secure than here. It has to be. Even if you could somehow find a way to get the doors down, you're running out of time."

She opens her eyes again, and looks at me. For a moment, I'm back in that corridor, seeing her hold out her hand to me, her eyes burning with life, as if daring me to accept. The same fire is in her eyes now, her hand gripping onto mine.

"Riley," she says. "You have to run the Core. It's the only way you'll get there. You have to."

"I can't do it."

"You have to," she says again, the pain adding an edge to her words. "Run fast. Get ready for the gravity change. Don't stop. Whatever you do, don't stop running."

"Amira..."

But what else is there to say? I feel as if I'm in zero gravity already, tumbling out of control.

"There's only one other thing I need to ask you," she says. "You need to finish it."

I shake my head, stunned. "I'm not. I can't."

"You're better with a gun than I thought you'd be. And I've seen people shot in the stomach before. The pain is bad now, but it'll get worse. A lot worse."

Her voice cracks on the last words. Amira – my beautiful, strong Amira – is begging.

I've picked up the gun without realising it. Slowly, I move it to her forehead. I touch it to her skin as delicately as she touched it to mine.

"I'm sorry," she says.

I pull the trigger for the second time.

55

Riley

I've met death in the past. My father, blown to pieces thousands of miles from home. My mother, wasting away to nothing. Gray and Darnell, and the lives they took. Yao. Grace Garner. But I've never felt anything like this. It's as if something has reached into my gut and just torn it away. It's worse than the hottest anger, worse than anything I've ever felt, and as I stare at Amira, see her eyes, glazed over, robbed of their power, I know, deep down, that the feeling will be with me forever. I'll feel it when I awake in the dark, and everyone around me sleeps. I'll feel it when I'm hurt, or when I sense someone standing behind me, ready to strike. I'll feel it in my bones and my flesh and my heart. The tears come. And this time the trickle becomes a river, then a flood.

I'm still there, bending over her body, when Prakesh arrives. He stops in the doorway, his eyes wide. Someone else is with him. A stomper. Royo.

Royo has his stinger up, sweeping from left to right. Prakesh wraps his arms around me, pulling me away. My sobs turn to screams, racked with the worst pain I've ever felt, and I bury my head in his chest. He says nothing. Just holds me close.

"So," says Royo at length. His stinger isn't quite pointed at us, but it's held ready. "I have two dead bodies, and no answers. If I don't get the second, there's going to be a few more of the first."

"What happened, Ry?" asks Prakesh.

Slowly, between sobs, I tell them. About Amira and Garner. And Okwembu.

When I'm finished, Royo looks at me. "Why should I believe you?"

"What?"

"How do I know you didn't just kill them both?"

"You think this is an act?" I scream at him. But Prakesh raises a hand. His voice is calm.

"She's telling the truth. I know she is."

It can't be enough. Surely not. But Royo is silent. He seems to be weighing his words carefully.

"My gut's kept me alive on this wreck of a station my whole life," he says. "It's telling me to trust you, so I will, but that trust can be rescinded if or when you do anything to make me doubt you. If you're telling the truth, then we need to go. I don't know how long we've got until that monster in Apex does whatever he's going to do, but it's not long."

"He's right, Ry," Prakesh whispers to me. He's still holding me tight. "We've got less than twenty hours left. The station's getting worse – the heat's starting to build up already. And there's nothing more we can do here."

I feel dizzy. My nose is clogged, my eyes wet. But I nod, silently, and he releases me. Behind us, Amira's body lies sprawled across the floor.

A thought occurs to me. "Garner. Is she…"

Royo clears his throat. "She's gone. I'm sorry."

Prakesh says, "Maybe I'm misreading things here,

but if Okwembu is behind all this, maybe there's a way we can let people know. Maybe we can stop her without having to go anywhere near Apex."

"Not a chance," replies Royo. "I'm not saying I believe that woman" – he indicates Amira–"but if the head of the council is responsible, we can't get anywhere near her. I've seen the security in Apex. After those riots all those years ago, they weren't taking any chances. You can lock the entire place down. So even if we did somehow get the word out that she's doing it, there's not a lot we could do about it."

I force myself to concentrate. "If we can get to Apex, maybe we can figure out how to use the code Garner gave me. It's the only way to stop this. I'm sure of it."

Prakesh frowns. "You don't think that maybe it's a way for Okwembu and Darnell to finally destroy the station? Something they needed for their endgame? If it is, then why don't we just drop off the radar? Hide out somewhere?"

"No," I say. "She wouldn't have started all this unless she could finish it. Not Okwembu. Iapetus isn't her way to destroy Outer Earth. It's the only way to stop it from happening. This was all about making sure there's nothing to stand in their way."

"Was Amira really serious about going through the Core? There has to be another way round."

Royo laughs, a sound with no humour in it. "Even if we wanted to, there's no way. Chengshi is tearing itself apart right now. Along with Apogee, Tzevya and every other damn sector on this station. It's going to pieces out there."

My eyes stray to Amira's hand. The missing fingers, stolen by frostbite all those years ago.

A thought occurs to me. "How did you get here?" I ask Royo.

"They assigned me to guard the Air Lab entrance. We got an alert from a smoke alarm. I came to check it out." He gestures to Prakesh. "Met your buddy when I came in."

Silence falls over us. I think of the sun. Of wanting to feel its warmth on the back of my neck. I think of what it feels like to run, to lose myself in speed and the air rushing past my face. I think of the Devil Dancers: Carver, Kev, Yao. I think of the Nest. It seems like a million years ago.

I think of my father, of how he died. Fighting. So that the human race could keep going.

And then, finally, I think of Amira. How, at the very end, she once again told me what I had to do.

I turn to Royo. "How do we get to the Core entrance?"

"The monorail. Maybe there's a train near here. We could use it to bypass the worst of the rioting and get back to Apogee."

"You can drive a train?" I ask, incredulous.

"No," replies Royo. "But I'd say now would be a great time to learn, wouldn't you?"

56

Darnell

Darnell slams Okwembu up against the control room screens, their faces inches apart.

"You call that subtle?" he screams at her, his words made metallic by the narrow room. "Now it's even worse. Now she's got a stomper escort."

"It doesn't mean anything," Okwembu says. Darnell's hands move to her throat, but she gets her fingers up just before he grips her neck.

"Oh really?" he says, tightening his hold. "You heard them. They know what's behind that retinal scanner. The whole point was that no one but us and our sleepers would ever know. Now *she* knows, *she's* still alive, and *she's on her way over here*."

He lifts Okwembu up, so her feet are off the ground, then slams her back against the screens. One of them cracks, spitting sparks. A shard of glass scratches a thin line across Okwembu's forehead. Darnell squeezes, his thumbs hunting for her windpipe. Okwembu has her hands up, two fingers the only thing between her and strangulation.

She raises her eyes to meet his, and pulls her fingers away. "So kill me," she says, her voice thin and hoarse.

Her eyes refuse to leave his, and Darnell's fingers pause, just touching the skin above the scooped hollow of her collarbone.

"Go ahead," she says, her voice brimming with venom. "You can do it all yourself. Isn't that right? Set up the comms feed, run the camera, even figure out everything the control room can do. You don't need me. I'm not useful any more, am I?"

In the silence that follows, Darnell can hear his heartbeat, feel the blood pumping in his ears.

There's a tiny ping, an alert from one of the screens. It's a long moment before Darnell glances down at it. He drops Okwembu, and she crumples to the floor, coughing, holding her throat. Darnell kills the pinging, his fingers leaving dark smudges on the surface of the screen.

"Someone's coming in through the Core," he says. "They're opening the Apex-side doors."

Okwembu looks up at him, her face expressionless. After a moment, she rises, and begins swiping through camera feeds, hunting for the Core access in the upper level of Apex.

"It's not Hale," Darnell says. "It's too soon."

"True. Although I'm surprised it's taken the protection officers this long to get here."

The camera viewpoint appears, just in time to catch the vast doors opening. There's no sound, but they can see people slipping through the gap in the ceiling, dropping to the floor. Stompers, dressed in bulky thermal suits, their movements slow and uncoordinated.

Darnell glances at Okwembu, his eyes narrowed. "You told me those doors were sealed."

"Do you think they'd just give up and go home?" Okwembu taps the screen, pointing to the doors, where a wisp of smoke is curling away. "They blew the lock."

Three stompers are already through the gap, starting

to strip off their thermal suits. Three more are clambering through, hanging off the open doors and dropping down.

"Thought they'd send more," Darnell says.

"It's a classic stomper tactic. Sacrificing numbers for speed." Okwembu's voice has been torn to shreds by Darnell's grip, but there's no mistaking the worry in her voice.

Darnell reaches behind his back for his knife. He pulls it out, running a finger across the edge. A wave of dizziness overcomes him, and his gut rolls with a burst of nausea, but it's gone almost as soon as it starts.

"I'll deal with them," he says.

Okwembu doesn't look at him. "No."

He bristles. "You think I can't handle a few stompers?"

"They have stingers. You don't. I'll wait until you get close, then kill the lights. You should have some element of surprise."

She turns, looking Oren Darnell dead in the eye. "You need me. You don't want to admit it, but you do."

Oren Darnell leaves the control room, rolling his thumb across the point of the blade.

57

Darnell

It's just like before, Darnell thinks. *They're going to take everything away from me.*

He's barely aware of what he's doing. He's walking through the top level of Apex, heading for the Core entrance, but his body is moving on autopilot. His mind is somewhere else, twenty years and two sectors away, and this time the memory is so vivid, so overpowering, that he can't fight it off. He sinks into it completely.

At first, it was just him and Mosely outside the hab, but then the corridor filled with dozens of people. He kept telling them that he had to go to school, that he was going to be late, but they didn't listen. They all kept stealing horrified glances into the hab.

The thing that used to be Darnell's mother had melted into the cot. Plants covered her, their tendrils and roots and leaves colonising the spaces between her bones. A glistening, yellow ring of fat surrounded the corpse.

Darnell didn't understand the shocked faces, the horrified looks. She'd been useless before, and now she was helping his plants grow. Didn't they see what he'd made?

The protection officers huddled a short distance away,

exchanging angry words, their hands over their mouths and noses. He tried to talk to them, but they ignored him. That was when he first heard the words "Controlled burn."

Darnell went crazy. He fought, pleaded, begged. But he was still a child, a long way away from the size he would attain later. When the chemicals arrived, he tried to knock them over, but the white-clad operator pushed him away. Darnell can see the look on his face, even now. The stupid, bovine hatred.

The corridor was narrow, unable to contain too many people. But in Darnell's memory, there were dozens, *hundreds* of people there. A tiny flicker of hope sparked inside Darnell. They would help him. They wouldn't let his plants burn.

But no matter how much he pleaded, they wouldn't do anything. *They just watched.*

And when the fire started, they were cheering. More than that: they were *laughing*. Cackling as his plants burned. In his mind, he can still hear some of them jeering at him.

With an effort, Darnell pulls himself out of the memory. He makes himself focus by rolling his thumb down on the point of his knife. A tiny drop of blood wells up, and the dart of pain helps focus him. He comes back just in time to hear a noise from up ahead.

The corridor he's in ends in a T-junction, and as he looks up he sees a stomper peek round the side. The stomper catches sight of him, sucks in an excited breath, and vanishes.

A second later, the corridor is filled with shouting and the sound of running feet. Six voices shout at him to drop the knife, six stingers aim right at his chest. The six become four when two of the stompers turn, covering the corridor behind them.

Darnell stops, lowering the knife. His eyes flick up to

the ceiling where, just behind one of the long recessed light bars, he can make out the eye of a camera. He looks back to the stompers, memorising their positions, fixing them in his mind. It's hard – his memories want to fight him, fuzzing his thoughts – but he manages it.

The lights click off, plunging the corridor into darkness.

Darnell reaches out, grabs the nearest stomper's wrists, and twists. He hears the bone break cleanly, followed an instant later by a scream of pain and the sound of a stinger clattering to the floor.

The other stompers open fire. A bullet grazes Darnell's shoulder, digging a furrow in his flesh. He barely feels it. He's already moving, staying low, using the flashes from the stinger fire to pick his targets.

The stompers' training takes over, and they react just like Darnell hoped they would: feet planted, not moving, aiming with two hands. They're static, slow, and Darnell is a whirlwind, smashing and crushing and slicing. His body is soaked with blood, both his and the stompers'. Somewhere very distant, his shoulder is on fire, and it's joined by a screaming pain from the side of his head as a bullet rips off the top of his left ear.

The lights come back on.

Three stompers are dead, their bodies ragged with stab wounds. Two more are down: one is unconscious, the other cradling her broken arm, moaning in pain. Only the final stomper is still standing. He points his stinger at Darnell, his hands shaking, and pulls the trigger.

Click.

The stomper tries again, and again, shaking his head furiously. Darnell towers over him. He reaches down, and plucks the useless stinger out of the man's hands. In that instant, the look in the stomper's eyes is exactly the same one Mosely had, all those years ago.

Darnell smiles.

58

Riley

There's no choice but to leave Amira and Grace Garner behind. We can't carry them, not with time against us, but I promise myself that I'll come back for them. *If I come back at all.*

I follow Prakesh as we leave the control room from the back. Deeper inside the complex, the corridors are wider, designed to let heavy equipment pass through. I've never been this way, and I'm surprised to see just how clean it is, with soft lighting and spotless floors. At one point, we cross through another hangar, smaller than the Food Lab but still enormous, criss-crossed with conveyor belts and littered with processing equipment. There's nobody around, and the black conveyors lie silent.

"Monorail's this way," says Prakesh. He's sure-footed, taking the stairs two at a time. More than that: he seems upbeat, confident even. I want to scream at him. Instead, I force myself to match his pace, pushing away the anger, trying to focus on the movement. Stride, land, cushion, spring, repeat. Behind us, Royo puffs as he tries to keep up. He's fit, but heavy with muscle, and his bulky frame – made heavier with his combat armour and equipment – isn't built for speed. He keeps snagging his gear, muttering under his breath.

What Amira did is like a splinter, lodged deep in my mind. We were hers. Her crew. Her Dancers. She was the calm, controlled centre of everything we did. We would have died for her. Yao did die for her. It wasn't just that it was unquestioned loyalty; it was loyalty that never needed to be questioned.

But it meant nothing. She betrayed us. And worse, she betrayed us over something so stupid, so pointless. She must have felt like that for years, locking the thought away in some deep, dark part of her being, nurturing it. And then one day, Janice Okwembu found her, and pulled that poisonous little thought into the light.

In the end, the Devil Dancers were just in the way.

But I can't let what she did be the end. I won't. Okwembu and Darnell betrayed the station, and Amira betrayed her crew, but it doesn't matter. Because I'm not just loyal to the people who are supposed to lead me. I'm loyal to things no one can ever change or touch or hurt. Like the memory of my dad. Like the hope that one day I might run in the sunlight.

I won't let what Amira did stop me.

My stomach growls as we walk through the processing hangar, but I ignore it. I'm hungry, and thirsty, and more exhausted than I've ever been in my life, but I can't focus on that now.

The hangar leads to a loading dock, brightly lit, and two huge rolling doors which lead onto the monorail tracks. I'm worried that there won't be a train there, that we'll have to walk the tunnels, but there's one sitting by the platform, ready to receive cargo. Most of the cars are flatbeds, lined with heavy-duty locking mechanisms designed to hold large containers. Several of these are stacked along one wall of the loading dock: huge, misshapen things, tall as two men, made of bent metal. Above the main doors, two large screens display destinations and shipment details in that orange text.

The heat hits us as soon as we walk out onto the dock. The air is muggy, cloying and thick with warmth, and beads of condensation run down the walls. At this rate, it won't be long before people start dying from heatstroke. Any longer than that, and we really will be roasted alive.

"Where's the driver's seat?" I ask Prakesh. He points to a few cars up. It's little more than a raised platform, a small space with waist-high railings and a bank of controls. Beyond it, the darkness of the tunnel. Royo climbs up, and Prakesh and I follow, jumping in behind him.

He thumbs a switch on the far left of the panel. Nothing happens.

Royo stands, brow furrowed, staring at the controls. After a full minute, Prakesh leans forward. "Ah, Royo, maybe you should try some of the other buttons?"

Royo turns slowly and stares at him. Prakesh raises his hands in apology. "OK, then. Sorry," he mutters, then glances at me as if to say, *what's with this guy*?

Eventually, Royo stabs a few more buttons, and the engine below us hums to life. The rest of the control panel lights up, clicking gently. Royo exhales, turning to us to say something, but as he does so we hear the crackle of the comms system. We all spin round at once, to see a large screen above the loading doors – unnoticed until now – briefly flash up the Outer Earth logo. This time, there's no trickle of fear down my spine. Just cold intent. Whatever Darnell's doing, I know we can stop it.

He's no longer in the council chamber. Instead, he's somewhere in Apex, and the feed is almost too glitchy to make out. His words mutate, twisting themselves into new and hideous sounds, and his face is a mess of damaged pixels. Blood soaks the top half of his body.

"It's time to talk about those sleepers," he says. "Actually, it's time to talk about one in particular."

I know what he's going to say. I squeeze Prakesh's hand tight.

"She's a tracer, and she's been planting bombs all around the station. Her name is Riley Hale. Kill her and bring her body to the gallery in Apogee, where we can see it, and you get to live. Everyone else gets to die."

He leers. "In fact, you don't have to kill her right away. If you bring her to the gallery and set her on fire" – he lingers on the words, tasting each one – "then we'll make sure that some food gets left somewhere for you.

"Until then, I'd like to show you what happens to people who think they can stop us."

The camera pulls back. He's in front of an escape pod access point. Inside the pod, hammering on the doors, are three stompers. The pod isn't big enough for all of them; I can see their bodies squashed up against one another.

Without another word, Darnell launches the pod.

59

Riley

The feed ends.

I can feel Prakesh and Royo staring at me. Below us, the train idles. Darnell kills the feed.

I turn to them. "Well, it wouldn't be much fun if it wasn't a challenge, right?" I say, but their faces are grave.

Without a word, Royo pushes a large lever forwards, and the monorail begins to slide slowly out of the station. For a moment, we're swallowed by the blackness of the tunnel, but then the massive lamp on the front of the train flickers to life, bathing the track ahead in a soft, yellow light. Royo pushes the lever forwards a little more, and we begin to pick up speed, the struts on the side of the tunnel starting to pass more quickly.

Not quick enough.

"How far to Apogee?" I say. I have to raise my voice to be heard over the train.

He shrugs, his eyes on the tunnel ahead. "Twenty minutes, maybe? Half an hour?"

"Can we go any faster?"

"We're at full acceleration already," he says.

I look over my shoulder. Behind the cabin, the empty

pallet cars rumble and shudder over the track, bumping together. I turn back to Royo: "What if we got rid of the other cars? Would that make a difference?"

"Good thinking," says Prakesh, and before Royo can say anything, he hops down onto the back of the car and begins to walk his way to the end. Kneeling down, he begins pulling at the coupling. After a few seconds, he looks back to us, yells something, but in the noise of the tunnel I can't make it out.

"What?" I shout, barely able to hear myself. He jabs his finger downwards.

Realisation dawns. "Is there a control for the coupling?" I yell to Royo.

"I don't know," he says, looking around the console. "But if every car unhooks at once, this entire damn train could derail. We have to make sure that we only unhook *our* car."

Visions of tumbling train cars bearing down on our little cockpit fill my head. I glance around the console, appalled by the number of buttons and levers and switches. How many controls do you need to make a train go forwards and backwards? It's not as if this thing's going out to catch asteroids.

"Got it," says Royo, and his hand flies out, turning a raised switch one click to the right. Behind us, I hear a loud clunk over the roar of the train. The car gives a huge lurch forwards as it disconnects from the others, and as I turn I hear a cry of surprise. It's Prakesh; the car disconnecting has hurled him backwards, and his feet are hanging off the edge, his fingers frantically scrambling for purchase.

I throw myself at the back of the car, reaching down to grab his arm. He grips my wrist tight, and with strength I didn't know I had, I haul him over the side.

We lie on our backs, breathing hard. And then, to my surprise, Prakesh begins to laugh.

I stare at him like he's gone mad, but soon I'm laughing too, falling into full-blown hysterics, the sound flowing out of us like water.

"What the hell are you two doing?" yells our driver. I tilt my head, expecting to find him furious, but instead his expression is one of bemusement.

"Wow," says Prakesh, sitting up. "I think I've lost count of the number of times we've saved each other."

"Maybe you should stop getting into trouble then."

"Speak for yourself."

I shake my head. "How did none of us realise that was going to happen?"

"Oh, I knew it was coming."

"So you didn't need my help at all, then? You had it all under control?"

He nods. "Of course I did. I just thought that after running through the entire station, suffocating on smoke and then fighting off every Lieren on Outer Earth, I'd cap the day off by falling under a train."

We sit against the control platform. My feet are pulled up to my chest, my arms wrapped around my knees. Prakesh has his feet stretched out, his arms by his sides. The noise of the train has lessened somewhat; we're passing through what looks like a siding, and I can see the dark shapes of other trains to either side of our track. Prakesh finds my hand, his fingers closing over mine. This time, I don't freeze. I don't pull away.

All at once, I realise just how much is riding on me running the Core. If I can't get through it, if I'm not fast enough, then everyone on this station will die. It's all on me. And I've been wrapped up in this since the beginning. If I hadn't discovered Marshall Foster's eye in my pack, then I'd just be part of a panicked crowd somewhere, fighting for food. Like it or not, I'm in the middle of this.

The train dips into a narrower tunnel, and around us the rumble grows until it shakes my insides. We can't be more than a few minutes from the main station in Apogee.

I turn to Prakesh, trying to keep my voice steady. "If I can get to the main control room in Apex, I'll try to restore the heat convectors. I don't think they've damaged them, just shut them down. It'll buy us some time at least."

He looks worried. "If Okwembu's really responsible, that's where she'll be. How do you know she won't just kill you on sight?"

"I don't. She might. I don't know. Look," I say, trying to marshal my thoughts. "The answer's in Apex. One way or another, someone's gotta get there, and I think I might stand a better chance than a bunch of stompers."

I don't know if that's true or not. But I know that the stompers won't send more people straightaway – not when the last attempt failed so badly. By the time they get going again, it'll be too late.

"You ever been?" Prakesh says. "To Apex?"

I shake my head. Compared to the other sectors, Apex is tiny: a main control room surrounded by living quarters for the council and their families. Since the sector is so self-contained, they've hardly ever needed tracers. Strange that I've lived my entire life inside an eighteen-mile ring, and there's a whole part of it I've just never seen. I have no idea what it looks like, or what kind of security there is.

"How are you planning to access the computers?" Prakesh asks. "You don't just walk into the main control room of Outer Earth and start tweaking the systems. There'll be passwords, fail-safes."

"Well, we've got one password at least," I say, thinking back to Grace Garner. The entire conversation with her seems blurred in my memory, like something out of a dream. I shake it off. "Maybe it'll get me through the system security."

"You'll need to find a way to lock the control room down. How are you..."

"I don't know, 'Kesh!" I say – louder than I intended, and above us I see Royo look round, puzzled. I lower my voice slightly. "I don't know. But if you've got another way for us to get to Apex, I'm waiting to hear it."

"We could go around—"

"One that doesn't involve running through crowds of people who've just been ordered to kill me."

He opens his mouth, closes it again.

"What can I do?" he says, his voice steady.

"You can get me into the Core. Keep me safe. And from there..." I shrug, try to inject some humour into my words. "Well, I've always wanted to go zero-G."

"We're nearly there," says Royo.

Prakesh stands, strides to the cockpit. "Do you have a first name? Seems kind of strange to be calling you Officer Royo all the time."

Royo glances at him, irritated. "Is this really important?" He turns back to the tunnel, softening a little. "Sam," he says.

Prakesh laughs. "Pleased to meet you, Sam Royo. I'm Prakesh Kumar, and in case you haven't already met the most wanted woman on Outer Earth, this here is Riley Hale."

But I'm not listening to him. I'm looking at the tunnel ahead, into the darkness just out of the spotlight's range, and my heart has started to beat a little too fast.

There's something on the track.

I can see the orange glow of the Apogee loading dock ahead of us. But something is blocking out the light. I squint, trying to make it out, telling myself that it's nothing, a shadow. But I'm not fooling anyone, least of all myself.

"Guys," I say, trying to keep my voice even. "What is that?"

Prakesh peers into the darkness, his hands on his hips and his eyes narrowed. "Yeah, what..."

The light from the train's headlamp washes over the thing on the track. It's a huge pile of cargo containers, like the ones we saw back in the loading dock in Gardens. The rusted metal crates have been piled on the track, right where the tunnel opens up, pulled on top of one another to form a makeshift barrier.

Prakesh has seen it too. He turns to me, his eyes wide. "They can't know it's you on this train. There's no way."

"They don't," says Royo. "Assholes think it's a food train coming from Gardens."

"Can we stop in time?" I ask. Royo shakes his head, even as he yanks back the power lever. A horrible squealing sound fills the tunnel as the brakes kick in, but even as I'm trying to work out if it'll be enough, my mind is racing ahead of me. We're going way too fast, and in about ten seconds we're going to hit the crates.

Royo is hanging on to the power lever, desperately trying to coax everything he can out of the brakes. "Hold on to something!" he shouts. Prakesh grabs me and pulls me down, using the raised cockpit as a shield between us and the barricade. Royo growls in fury and abandons the brake, hurling himself down onto the car's main platform, scrambling for a handhold. The struts on the side of the tunnel are passing way too fast.

A half-second later, the train hits the barricade.

The impact is enormous, a bang that shakes the tunnel and lifts the entire back end of the car clean off the track. Prakesh and I are thrown against the cockpit platform, and I hit it so hard that for a moment the world turns a dull red. Royo crashes into us, squashing us against its surface as the train bucks and screams, and then he's over us, crying out in alarm as the momentum carries him over the cockpit, his arms flailing wildly. The tunnel is filled with tumbling shapes, and I realise we've hit the barricade so hard that we've smashed *through it.*

"Watch out!" yells Prakesh, and yanks my head down just as one of the crates collides with the spot where I was a second ago, hitting with a clang that rattles my teeth.

At that instant, the back of the car, freed from its coupling to the rail, swings out. Prakesh has just enough time to yell out something before the car flips onto its side.

We're hurled forwards, our arms thrown out in front of us. Time does its big slow-down trick again, and the crates, smashed into the air by the train, hang in space around us. I see our shadows, two huge Xs on the track, cast by the light from the platform. The tunnel is quiet suddenly, the roaring and squealing dwindling to nothing.

My muscle memory kicks in, and I tuck for a roll, swinging my body to take the force of the impact. Images of broken bones and shattered shoulder blades have half a second to dance mockingly through my memory, and then I hit the ground.

I hit it shoulder first, tumbling end over end, like someone rolling a barrel down a corridor. My left shoulder has maybe a nanosecond to realise what's happened to it, and then it begins screaming in huge, horrid pain, which rapidly spreads across my back, forcing me to cry out. I lose count of how many times I tumble, but it's punctuated by me cracking my head on the track. Twice.

Eventually, I come to a stop, lying on my back. I'm staring at the roof of the tunnel, now a mess of flickering shapes and orange light. The enormous ache comes to a stop in my shoulder, pulsing like a strobe light. I gingerly move my left arm; it hurts, but it moves freely, and I breathe a tiny sigh of relief. Prakesh would kill me if...

Prakesh. Royo. Before my body even has a chance to react I'm sitting up, causing a wave of pain so fresh and immediate that I nearly throw up. I've landed closest to the platform, a few feet into the tunnel. I spot Royo immediately: a crumpled form a few yards up the tunnel from me, his head turned away, his right arm twisted at an unnatural angle. He's not moving. Prakesh has landed a little way behind me. I see the trickle of blood from the corner of his mouth, and then I realise how glassy his eyes are, and all the blood seems to leave my upper body.

But then he stirs, shakes his head, and the blood comes rushing back, leaving a pounding in my ears and an odd light-headedness. "Riley," he calls out, his voice harsh. Unable to form words, I lift my hand, and a smile cracks my face...

...which dies when someone yells the words, "It's her! It's Hale!"

Standing on the platform are a group of people, holding knives, their eyes greedy with bloodlust.

60

Riley

"Prakesh," I say, shaking his shoulder. "Prakesh, get up."

He groans and holds a hand to his forehead, gazes blearily at me. Concussion. Got to be. But if I don't get him moving in the next ten seconds, we're going to be cut to ribbons.

I shake harder. My voice has become an awkward, hissing whisper, repeating the words like a mantra. "Get up, get up, get up."

The people have started to jump off the platform and head towards us. I recognise the one at the front of the pack. A teacher. I've done jobs for his schoolroom before. But any kindness in his eyes is long gone. "She's on the tracks!" he yells.

"Thanks," says someone from behind him, and shoves him roughly out of the way: a heavily built woman with scraggly hair, holding a metal pole in both hands. I hear her mutter, "You're mine."

I can see the desperation in these people's eyes now, even as they push past the woman. They're scrabbling for a chance at life, trying to kill me in the hope that Darnell will save the one who does.

At my feet, Prakesh groans again, tries to rise, falls back. The crowd is ignoring him, focusing on me. If I can run, draw them away, he might have a chance. I can't risk a look behind me – getting a head start is the only chance I have. But I know the tunnel is clear, and I get ready to run.

And then I pause, confused. The crowd have stopped, their eyes angry. Their weapons are held out in front of them, but almost fearfully now – and the ones at the front are trying to edge away, back into the crowd. I hear a gruff voice from behind me: "I don't know how long I can hold this gun straight. Get Prakesh, and get out of here."

Royo is on his back, between us and the crowd. He's holding his stinger, pointing it right at the attackers. His left arm lies useless, twisted and bent, and the right side of his face is soaked in blood. He catches my eye and jerks his head, gesturing me back down the tunnel. "I said, move," he growls.

"You wanna die along with her, stomper?" someone yells from the crowd. "How many of us can you shoot before we tear that gun out of your hands?"

"I don't know," says Royo, his voice thick with effort. "Thought I might fire a couple of rounds at the ceiling, see if those of you in the middle can dodge the ricochets."

I help Prakesh to his feet, throwing his arm over my shoulder. "Can you walk?" I ask him, terrified that he won't answer, but then he nods and grips my shoulder tight. We start to move down the tunnel, away from the platform, but I linger next to Royo. It seems like everyone around me today has died, and I'm not sure I can lose him too.

"Hale," he says. "If you don't get your ass down that tunnel right now, I'll kill you before they do." He keeps his eyes on the crowd, who are edging closer even as he speaks.

I shoulder Prakesh, and start walking down the

tunnel, into the blackness. I force myself to picture the layout of Apogee in my head: there's got to be another platform somewhere on the line. Then I see a glimmer in the darkness, and my heart leaps. It's far, but I can see it: the light of a second platform, a little further down. I've got no idea where it comes out, but it's our only shot.

" 'Kesh, we don't have much time," I say through gritted teeth. His hand is digging into my shoulder, each step causing it to flare with pain. "Do you think you can run?"

He starts to answer, but is cut off when gunshots echo down the tunnel. I turn to Prakesh, my eyes urgent, and with a supreme effort of will he seems to clear his head, forcing away the after-effects of the crash. The blood at the corner of his mouth is just visible in the gloom. He lets go of my shoulder, and starts to jog, first haltingly, then with more confidence.

We reach the station way ahead of the crowd, stumbling and shouting in the blackness of the tunnel. I hop onto the platform, then reach out and haul Prakesh up. Every cell in my body is screaming at me to keep running, but one look at Prakesh and I know that we have to rest, if only for a minute. He's breathing heavily, almost panting, and his face is contorted with pain. My shoulder is burning. When did I last have a drink? In the control room in the Air Lab, when Garner was telling us her story, right before...

I close my eyes. A moment later, I hear the crowd in the tunnel. They're closer than I thought.

I pull Prakesh towards the station's main door; the platform is smaller than the one at the main station up the track, and I'm hoping it'll bring us out near the gallery. From there, it'll just be a matter of climbing up the levels to the Core entrance. Assuming, of course, that we don't get torn to pieces by a mob on the way.

The first of the attackers arrives at the platform just

as we slide through the door. He manages to get off a strangled "They're up—" before I slam the door shut, cutting him off. I have no idea if it locks, and I don't have time to check. We're in a small open area in one of the corridors – as far as I know, the Core entrance is a few minutes away.

"This way," I say, already picturing the route. We're on the same level as the Core entrance, but there's the gallery between it and us. That means we'll need to cross on one of the catwalks.

We're almost at the gallery when we see it. The entire corridor has been blocked off, this time by a bunch of burning debris. A single sprinkler is sputtering above it, dripping white flecks of chemical foam onto the fire.

I double back. Prakesh groans, but follows, and we hit the stairwell, dropping down onto Level 5. *Please let the way be open this time . . .*

It doesn't take us long to reach the catwalk. The gallery below us is mostly empty, but there's bad noise filtering in from somewhere, shouts and screams and banging. There are still a few people on the catwalk. One of them, a man wearing a tattered pair of overalls, is fighting with a stomper, grappling with him, as if trying to throw him off. It's hard to tell what they're fighting about.

He takes a swing at the stomper, his fist balled up and his face a horrible grimace. The move swings him around, and our eyes meet, just for a second.

The stomper goes down. The man sprints at me, screaming. "Are you watching? I'll kill her for you! Do you see?" He's got no weapon, but the expression on his face is one of such rage and desperation that it leaves me paralysed.

Prakesh steps in front of me and swings a punch so fast it's just a blur. The man drops, out cold. Prakesh swears, clenching and unclenching his hand, but even as he does so I see the other people on the catwalk look our way. I swing around, hoping for anything, a weapon, a way to run, but we're trapped. Behind us, an angry mob, and in front, even more of them. And still, my body refuses to move.

"Riley…" says Prakesh, glancing at me. He's backing up now, his eyes on the people advancing towards us.

There's a noise from above. I look up, startled, and see someone leaning over the railing of the Level 6 catwalk. Someone shouting my name.

Carver. And beside him, hanging off the railing: Kev.

It takes me a second to understand what else Carver is yelling: a single phrase, but I can barely make it out over the shouts. He raises his voice; I hear what he's yelling, and his plan is instantly clear; he and Kev are already leaning off the railing, their arms stretched towards us. On our own, it's way too high to jump and grab.

But what Carver says is: "Tic-tac!"

I grab Prakesh, say through gritted teeth: "Up above. Follow my lead." He stares at me in confusion, but there's no time to explain. I take a couple of steps back, and then take a run at the gallery wall, taccing off it and throwing my body around, reaching up as high as I can with my outstretched hands.

There's a moment when I think I've missed them – when they're passing through my field of vision too fast and I think that I'm going to crash to the floor below – but then Carver's fingers close on my wrist, and grip tight. My momentum keeps me going through the swing, but he leans into it, adding extra weight, propelling me towards Kev, who grabs my other arm. His fingers lace tight around my wrist – and slip.

I see it in horrifying slow motion, the tip of his thumb running up the back of my hand, his fingers scrabbling for a hold. But at the last second he makes a final lunge, grabbing my wrist tight. Without even waiting for me to stop swinging, they haul me upwards, their combined strength easily lifting my slender frame. Before I've even grabbed the catwalk railing, I'm yelling "Prakesh! Get Prakesh!"

Carver yells something I can't quite make out. I grip the metal tight, and throw myself over, aware of the need to get out of the way. I land in a sprawl on the catwalk, and scramble to my feet, running to Kev's side and looking over the railing.

They've got Prakesh. Somehow, he pulled off the move, and Carver and Kev have grabbed him cleanly at the wrists. But as I watch, I see someone else take a running leap at Prakesh. He jerks his foot out of the way just in time, and the man misses, giving a frustrated yell as he crashes to the floor. But the crowd behind him is angry, eager for blood.

Someone hurls a length of metal pipe. It only just misses Prakesh, spinning away and clanging off the wall, but then Carver and Kev haul him bodily up and over, all of them falling in a tangle of limbs on the catwalk. For the first time, I realise that it's deserted, and wonder why. But then Prakesh pokes his head out the top of the pile and grins at me.

"You all right?" I say, trying to keep the worry out of my voice.

"Hanging in there," he replies.

Under him, I hear Carver say, "Maybe chat when you're *not* on top of us?"

I don't feel like laughing, but I do anyway. Carver and Kev get to their feet. "Hell of a way to treat your rescuer," mutters Carver, which is swiftly followed by a surprised, "Whoa..." when I embrace him. I reach out an arm and pull Kev in, squeezing them both tight.

"Watch the arm," says Carver. I pull back, startled,

expecting to see it hanging limp by his side, but it's back in place. The shoulder, however, is purple with bruising.

"Well, that was new," says Carver, his eyebrows raised.

"Don't get used to it," I say, ignoring the angry shouts from below us. "But I don't think I've ever been this happy to see you. When we left you back there with the Lieren..."

"With the knives? I'm surprised you think so little of me, Riley."

"And Kev," I start, turning to him. But then I see him look away, clenching his fists. Yao. His Twin. It can't be more than a few hours since she died, but it feels like weeks. I reach out a hand, but he doesn't take it, just turns away slightly. It's then that I notice his ankle. It's swollen – not badly, but enough to probably hurt like hell when he moves. Where did that happen?

A bullet ricochets off the railing. We all hit the deck. I'm painfully aware of how little protection the catwalk gives us, and I hear Prakesh yell over the noise, "The corridor! Go!"

We don't need telling twice. As one, we break for the corridor. It's no more than a few yards away, but even as we start running I hear another gunshot, this one followed by screams from below.

The far corridor is deserted; Carver, Kev and Prakesh have collapsed against the wall, breathing hard. "Why's there no one here?" asks Prakesh, looking around. "Where is everyone?"

"Glad you asked me that," says Carver. "Kev here came up with the rather brilliant idea of blocking off the stairs." He gestures towards the far end of the catwalk. "Amazing what a localised slow burner can do to encourage people to find another way round."

"A slow..." I stop. Carver's eyes are bright, and it takes me a moment to get my thoughts in order. "I thought you lost all your fire bombs to the stompers after that time in Tzevya?"

"Not all of them."

Prakesh's eyes are urgent. "The other stairs," he asks Carver. "Did you do them too?"

Carver shakes his head. "I only had the one. Those things are hard to make."

We get to our feet, but then Kev says, "Where's Amira?"

The silence that follows goes on just a second too long.

"I don't get it," says Carver. "Wasn't she with you?"

Mercifully, Prakesh comes to my aid. "We'll explain later. Right now, we need to get to the Core."

Carver glances at me. "He's kidding, right?"

"Nope," I say, sounding braver than I feel. "It's the only way into Apex."

"You're going to Apex?"

Kev's shaking his head. "Bad move."

I have to bite back the frustration. "We're running out of time," I say, looking right at Carver. "Are you gonna help us or not?"

"OK, Riley," Carver says. "First off, you look terrible. I'm a little surprised you're still standing upright. Second, you do know that the Core entrance is going to be rammed with stompers, right?"

"Yeah, but—"

"What were you planning on doing, exactly? Because even if you get inside, you've got no thermo-suit. You'll freeze solid in about ten seconds. That's if you think you're going in there alone, which you're not."

I look to Prakesh, but he just shakes his head. He's shattered. It's in his trembling legs and hunched shoulders. I must look the same way.

I turn back to Carver. "If we don't get there soon, Darnell—"

Kev slams his hand into the corridor, his fist balled up. The bang is so loud that we all jump, and when he draws it away, I'm a little surprised that the metal isn't dented.

"Yao's dead," he says quietly. "I'm not letting you die, too."

In the silence that follows, Carver says, "If we go in there now, it's over. If we take a minute, figure out a plan, then maybe we have a shot."

"Where, though?" I ask. "There's nothing left in the Nest."

"D-Company?" Kev says.

I shake my head. "Nowhere near close enough. We'd spend too much time getting there."

Carver thinks for a moment, then his eyes light up. "OK, so you know the guy P-Man laid out?"

Prakesh looks at him. "Huh?"

"The guy you knocked down. Back there, before Kev and I saved the day."

"What about him?" I say.

"I know him. He's local. More importantly, I know where he lives."

"And he's not exactly using his hab right now," Prakesh says. "Clever."

"What if he's gone back there already?" I say.

Kev shrugs. "Prakesh can hit him again. I'll help."

Carver's eyes find mine. "Food, water, some sort of plan. That's all I ask." Before I can protest, he takes off down the corridor. After a moment, the rest of us follow. I'm not wild about busting into someone's home, and there's no telling who or what we'll find there, but Carver's right.

Apogee has been torn apart. The corridors are a mess of bent metal, broken lights and power boxes that have been torn open and scavenged. Frequently, we have to travel in darkness, slowing to a crawl as we negotiate the detritus. Once or twice, we come across groups of people, either cowering in shadows or spoiling for a fight. But there's not a lot of them, and they don't seem keen to take on a large group of us.

I ask Carver if it's like this everywhere. He nods. "Every sector. Ever since that psycho turned off the convectors." He looks at me. "We heard him on the comms talking about you. You must have really pissed him off."

Prakesh slips in beside me. "You OK?" he whispers. I nod, and he wraps his arm around me as me walk. I'm glad he does because, despite the heat, I feel like I'm about to start shaking.

The hab is on Level 3, past the schoolrooms. The door's locked, but Kev gives it a huge kick, and it flies open. The place is a mess, scattered with trash and scummy food containers. The floor and walls are streaked with grime, and the bedclothes on the single cot are rumpled. Kev wrinkles his nose. It looks strange on him, like something a child would do. He closes the door behind him, almost tenderly. Whether the owner is still unconscious or not, he hasn't made it back here.

It's hotter here than outside, the cramped space collecting heat, springing more sweat from my forehead. Carver takes a quick look in the attached washroom. "Nobody here. I'm guessing the guy lives alone. Let's see if he's got a secret stash."

It doesn't take us long to find the water. A single canteen under the cot, pushed right against the back wall. I force myself to take small sips when Carver passes me the bottle, not wanting to upset my stomach. There's just enough for four of us. My thirst is still there, but it's muted now, hovering in the background. Kev disappears for a few minutes; when he returns, he has his pack, and pulls out some apples and a few protein bars.

I've never been so happy to see food. I'm a little worried that the owner of the hab might come back, but even if he did, I tell myself, what is he possibly going to do against four of us?

We eat in silence, collapsed against the wall, the ceiling light above us flickering. I try to eat as fast as I can, but my stomach won't let me. After a while, Carver says, "So are you going to tell us where Amira went? Because we could really use the extra help right now."

He says it with a smile on his face, but I see his eyes, spot the worry in them. Kev, too, is looking apprehensive. I've been dreading this moment, dreading it even before I'd really taken in that Amira was dead.

But I do it. I take a deep breath, and tell them everything. When I finish, my mouth is a desert again, my body already aching for more water.

The hab is silent; even the rumbling from the station around us seems to have ceased. Neither Kev nor Carver have said a word since I told them about Amira's death. Kev is avoiding my eyes, his hands clasped together between his knees, his jaw set. But Carver – Carver is staring at me. His mouth is a tight line, and in his eyes, nothing but raw, barely contained fury. It shocks me more than it should, and it takes me a moment to realise why: I can't remember the last time I saw Carver truly angry.

I have maybe half a second to process this thought before he forces himself off the wall and dives at me, his hands twisted into claws, murder on his face.

61

Riley

The attack is so unexpected that I just don't react. Carver slams into me, forcing me back into the wall. His hands are aimed at my throat, but at the very last second he drops them, gripping my shoulders instead. He winces in pain as the force of his grip travels up his arm into his damaged shoulder.

"You killed her!" he shouts, his mouth inches from my face, his voice cracking.

I try to say something, anything. A million emotions jumble together: disbelief, then anger, then fear, flaring one after the other, like a set of lights on a circuit. Carver's words have dissolved into incoherent yells. Tears stain his cheeks.

Kev and Prakesh wrap their arms around him and yank him back. He finds his voice again, screaming, "Get off me!" He collapses back against the other wall, stumbling, like he's drunk. For a few seconds, he just leans against it, and then sinks down, his fist slamming the floor in anger.

I can't take my eyes off Carver. He senses my gaze, and raises his head to look at me. This time, all he can manage is a whispered, "Why?"

Somehow, nothing I can say seems good enough.

For a long time, none of us do anything. Prakesh keeps a wary eye on Carver, but he just sits, his head down, his body shaking with silent sobs. Eventually, he looks at me. His face is blotchy and red, but his eyes are clear. The anger in them appears to have dimmed, but when he speaks, his voice is harsh. "Why'd she do it?"

I shake my head. It's like trying to describe something on the Earth below. Some animal I've only seen in pictures.

It's Kev who answers him. "Doesn't matter now."

"Yes, it matters!"

Carver's words reverberate within the cramped hab, leaving a cold silence behind. I rest my head against the wall, trying to stop the tears I feel pricking the corners of my eyes, squeezing them shut. Out of nowhere, I see Yao's mural, from before it was destroyed by whoever wrecked the Nest. I see its colours and its swirling shapes, the image so vivid that I can pick out the parts where the ink hadn't dried yet.

"We can't bring her back, or change what she did," I say quietly, turning to face them. The words sound awkward in my mouth, as if I'm reading someone else's writing, but I say them anyway. "She thought we'd lost our right to exist as a species. I say: not without a fight. I'm going to run the Core. I'm going to find Janice Okwembu, and I'm going to end this."

I say it evenly, trying to keep the fear out of my voice. Nearly manage it, too.

"I'll go," says Carver, getting to his feet. He won't look at me. "I can do it."

I stare at him. "You're going to run through the Core with a busted shoulder? Really?"

"I'm fine," he says. I step forward, and lightly tap him on the shoulder. He tries to turn away, but I see him grimace in pain.

"I can do it," he says again, but the fire has gone out of his voice.

From the wall, Kev says, "Why can't I go?"

"With that ankle? We don't have time for this." I shake my head, frustrated. "It's not just that I'm the fastest here, which I am. I was there when she died, OK? I was there. She played me. She *used* me. This is my fight."

"Did you see what Darnell did to those stompers?" says Carver. "The ones who went through the Core? You want that to happen to you?"

I don't have an answer.

"Riley's right," says Prakesh. "I don't like it either, but this is the best shot we have."

"I'm not just going to sit here," says Carver.

"You won't have to. The Core entrance is guarded, right? If we can create a diversion or something, we can get the doors open long enough to get Riley in. What'll you need, Ry? Five seconds? Ten?"

"Three," I say, and walk right over to Carver. He avoids my eyes, but I place a hand on his good shoulder, and after a moment, he puts his on top of it. "I can do this," I whisper.

After a long moment, he nods.

I turn to Kev. "We good?"

"We good."

"Look, I hate to be the one who drops the doom-bomb here," says Carver, "but it's like I said. We're not just talking about one stomper on guard duty. You don't get into the Core with a wink and a smile. How are we going to get past them?"

"There's always stompers," Kev says. "Five. Six."

I think, trying to picture the Core entrance. I've run past it plenty of times too: a big open room, bisected by the Level 6 corridor, with huge blast doors set into the ceiling. Equipment storerooms lead off the main area.

There are control panels at opposite ends of the room – old things, with dusty digital readouts and clunky switches. Presumably, that's how you open it up.

Prakesh reads my mind. "There'll be fail-safes there, too – more than likely two keycards or passcodes that'll need to be used at the same time at opposite ends of the room."

I frown. "Can we get a keycard?"

"I could probably hack it if we had enough time."

"How long?"

He looks helpless. "Ten minutes?"

"Why sure, officer," says Carver. "This little speck on the wall is the most fascinating thing you'll ever see in your life. But you'll need to stare at it for at least ten minutes to fully appreciate all the nuances..."

"Not helping," I say.

"We could lock the place down, maybe," Prakesh says thoughtfully. "Get everyone out somehow and then barricade the entrances. It might buy us enough time."

I shake my head, frustrated.

"Hello?" says Kev. We all look at him, and he spreads his hands wide. "Just break things."

Carver rubs his temple. "Much as I love your enthusiasm Kev, stuff tends to stop working when you smash it to pieces."

"Yes – but not the stuff it's connected to," says Kev slowly, as if talking to a child. His voice is clearer than it was before. "Smash the panels. The blast doors will think there's been a power short. Open right up."

"Any chance it could work?" I ask Prakesh. Of all of us, he's the most familiar with the station tech, especially the parts which give you access to secure areas. He thinks for a minute, his fist raised to his mouth.

Eventually, he says, "It's possible. Doors on Outer Earth *are* configured to open automatically using auxiliary batteries if there's a power cut. Or at least, they're supposed to."

Then he shakes his head. "But we don't know anything about the Core system. It might not work the same way as the other doors on the station. We could spend hours wrecking the access panels, and it'd stay locked tight."

"I don't like it," says Carver. "There's just too much we don't know. We don't get a second run at this."

I choose my words carefully, looking him in the eyes. "If there's even the slightest chance that it'll work, then I'm going to take it."

He returns my stare for a long minute. I'm certain that he's going to argue some more, but then he says, "Well, you're going in there, not me. Although if the doors don't open I am leaving you there and running like hell."

"Fair enough."

Prakesh puts his hands on his hips. "I'm in too."

I take a deep breath. He's not going to like this.

"I need you to stay in Apogee. If it goes wrong in the Core, you'll need to warn people. Tell them what we know."

Even before I've finished, he's opening his mouth to protest, so I talk quickly. "We could be injured, or captured, or . . . anyway, it doesn't matter. We need a backup plan. You're it."

"If this is about speed, I'm not going to slow you down," he says. "I've kept up with you so far, haven't I? Let me help get you in there."

I shake my head. "It's not about that. People trust you. They listen to you. Us?" I gesture to Carver and Kevin. "We're just tracers. People pay us to take their cargo and get out of their sight."

His expression has softened a little, even if he isn't completely convinced. I lower my voice. "You have to trust us, Prakesh. We can do this."

The silence that follows seems to stretch forever, but eventually he gives a curt nod, not looking at me.

"So that's it. We go," I say. But still, nobody moves.

Which is when I realise: this is when Amira would have inclined her head, the tiny gesture indicating that this is how we proceed. She'd be leaning against the wall, just there, her arms folded, staring into the distance, as if holding up every option individually and examining it for flaws.

It's Kev who breaks the silence – and before he does it, he glances at the place where Amira would have been, as if expecting her to reappear. When he speaks, he says, "If it comes to a swinging, swing all, say I."

It takes a moment for his words to make sense. Then understanding dawns: *Treasure Island.*

With a small smile on my face, I nod. "Swing all."

Carver sighs. "Since I've agreed to this insane idea," he says, "does anybody know how we're going to get enough time to destroy these damn panels?"

"Actually, I do," I say. I'm thinking back to something Carver said. Something about running through it.

It takes me less than two minutes to outline my plan. Carver is sceptical at first, but before long he's nodding, thinking hard.

"I'll need to see if I can salvage a few things from the Nest," he says. "I don't have anything to work with here. Kev – you come with me. And you two: for the love of every god there is, stay here."

"What do we do if the man who lives here comes back?" Prakesh says.

Carver winks at him. "Like Kev said. Hit him again."

He points to a big storage locker, over by the wall. "Meantime, drag that in front of the door after we're gone."

They leave, and Prakesh and I haul the locker over to the door. When it's in place, I take a minute to stretch, working my tight leg muscles and rotating my shoulders to work out the stiffness. All the injuries from the past few days seem to make themselves felt at once – the bruised collarbone, the ring around my eye, the marks on my neck and stomach from my fight with Darnell. The gashes in my hands and forehead, healing but still ugly, and the burn on my right hand where I pawed at my jacket sleeve in the fire. And I ache everywhere, my body telling me in every possible way that I'm nearly at breaking point. But I can't stop. Not now. *Please*, I silently say. *Just a few more runs. Then we'll sleep. We'll sleep for weeks.*

I sit down on the cot to stretch out my legs. Prakesh comes over and sits down next to me. He looks worried, more worried than I've ever seen him. "What are you going to do if they come after you into the Core?" he says.

I shrug, try to act like I'm beyond worry, even though there's a band of fear that feels like it's squeezing my chest to bursting point. "What I always do, Prakesh," I say. "I run."

I'm about to say something else, but then Prakesh is kissing me with so much force that it nearly knocks me over backwards. I'm so surprised that for a second his open mouth is locked on my closed one.

I pull away. " 'Kesh, I... we can't."

He's shaking his head. "Why not?"

I laugh, using it to mask the tremor in my voice. "Look at this place. It's a mess. It's not even ours."

I expect him to smile back. To let the moment pass. He doesn't. He just looks me right in the eyes. His hand touches mine, clasps it, then squeezes tight and doesn't let go.

"You remember when you said you'd have to choose?" he says. "That if... that if we were together, you'd eventually have to choose between me and the Dancers?"

He doesn't give me the chance to answer. "I wouldn't care. You hear me? Because even if you chose the Dancers, even if you couldn't be with me, I'd still have a little bit of time with you. And now you're going to Apex – you're off on this *stupid run* – and you're not giving me a choice."

"If I don't—"

"No, *listen*. I know you have to go. I get that. But you don't get to do it without giving me a chance. You don't. That's not a choice you get to make."

His other hand is gripping my forearm now, and he pulls me into another kiss. This time, I kiss him back.

"We don't have enough time," I whisper.

"I don't care," he says.

Neither do I.

His hands, wrapped around my back, slip silently under my top, and begin tracing the curve of my spine. His touch is gentle, hesitant at first, but growing bolder, faster. Little prickles of heat shoot through me.

We fall back on the cot, pushing aside the blankets, my hands pushing under his shirt, lifting it over his head. His mouth moves down to my neck, then my own shirt comes off and he moves lower still, kissing my breasts, skin on skin.

He pushes me too hard, and my head bumps against the wall. I wince, but he's there immediately, kissing my forehead and laughing. I try to tell him it's OK, but I don't get to finish the sentence, because right then he slips inside me.

He holds it for a moment, looking me in the eyes. Then he slides deeper. The aches in my body vanish, melting away. Soon, there's no hesitancy, no holding back: just us thrusting together, and my nails digging deep ridges in his flesh. His mouth, my mouth, his hands, everywhere, all at once. When I come, when Prakesh finally pushes us over the edge, it's as if every scrap of energy I have has concentrated into a single burning point, deep in my own core.

I can't move, I can't breathe. I don't want to. I'd trade everything, every run I've ever been on, every good memory I've ever had, to freeze time at this instant. His hand is on the back of my neck, his skin warm. It feels good.

Like how I imagine sunlight would feel.

Afterwards, we lie together. Our breathing has slowed, quietened. He lifts his left hand and caresses my cheek.

"You come back," he says. "No matter what happens, you come back to me. You find a way."

And I whisper, "I will. I promise."

I hold him for as long as I dare. I want the memory of his touch to be as powerful as possible. If I die, if I can't save my world, then I want this to be the last thing I remember.

I don't know how long we lie together, but by the time Carver and Kev come back, we're clothed again, sitting against the wall quietly, sharing some more water. I thought there was nothing useful left in the Nest, but I guess I don't have Carver's eyes. He's got an armful of tools and spare parts. Kev has managed to find some food: more protein bars, pulled from another of his secret stashes.

We eat while Carver puts everything together. It takes him a little longer than I'd like, but eventually, he straightens up, pulling his goggles off.

Prakesh hugs me tight.

And then we're out into the passage. And we're running. Not in single file, not this time, but in a tight group, Carver and Kev close on my sides. We run at full speed, barrelling through the station, and for a little while, it's almost as if we're not running to any destination. We're just running.

62

Prakesh

Prakesh watches her go. It's the hardest thing he's ever had to do.

He sits for a few moments longer in the hab. The air is cold, but when his hand strays to the blankets that he and Riley were sitting on, he finds they're still warm.

Riley asked him to spread the word if they failed. He tries to think about how he'd do this, but it's too big a task. Outer Earth is chaos, turned feral by Oren Darnell. How do you get people to stop fighting long enough to listen to you?

He hauls himself to his feet. It's more than that. He's a lab tech. He knows about plants, and machines, and chemicals. He can transfer smoke from one room to another. He can't capture people's minds, or change them.

I changed hers.

Whatever he has to do, it won't come from staying in here. Prakesh steps out, closing the door behind him. He can hear the fighting from here. It's a jarring rumble of noise, trapped and funnelled by the corridors, twisted and bent by every corner. The air is thick and cloying, and so hot that Prakesh gasps. It's his imagination, it has to be, but he could swear there's a heat haze rising from the end of the corridor, shimmering in the lights. Somewhere, an alarm is blaring, an electronic voice spouting unheard warnings.

The noise changes. Shouting. It's closer – close enough for him to pick out individual voices.

Prakesh wipes sweat from his eyes, and jogs down the corridor. When he comes round the corner, he sees a group of people standing in the middle of the next section. Three of them wear gang colours, blue shirts and armbands with black pants. They've surrounded two others, an old man and a much younger woman. The old man is wearing dirty overalls, with one sleeve tied off at the shoulder.

The three gang members are poking him in the stomach, laughing at him as he tries to shield the woman. She's twig-thin, her head completely bald. One of the gang members reaches over, and taps her on the dome of her skull, laughing. She shrinks up against the old man, who whirls around, screaming threats.

"Come on," says one of the others. "I seen you in the market before. You gotta have some food."

The man says something back, spit arcing from his mouth. A dot of it lands on the gang member's shoulder, and he flicks it away.

"You spat on me," he says, and shoves the old man in the chest. He slams against the corridor wall, dropping to his knees. The woman screams.

"Hey!" Prakesh says.

They all turn to stare at him. Prakesh is walking towards them, a few feet away. There's no possible way he can do what he's about to do, but he keeps coming, bearing down on them.

The gang member who shoved the old man gives Prakesh a crooked smile. "Keep walking, man."

Prakesh grabs the front of his shirt, pulling him in close. As he does so, he sees that he's just a kid. So are the others – the oldest one looks like he's barely scraping sixteen.

"Hey, what—" the kid starts.

"You think what's happening gives you the right to beat up old men?" Prakesh says. His forehead almost touches the gang member's, their skin so close that he can feel the heat baking off. "I don't give the tiniest shit who you are, or what you think you can do. You'll run, and you'll keep running, and if I see you again before this is all over I'll take that rag off your arm and stick it down your throat."

He lets go. The boy stumbles backwards, only just managing to keep his feet. The other two are shocked back to life, and the older one takes a step towards Prakesh.

Don't quit now, Prakesh thinks, deliriously. He screams in the older boy's face. "*Go!*"

It breaks them. They move away, not quite running, but not quite walking either. The one Prakesh took hold of looks back over his shoulder, his face threatening payback. Prakesh holds the boy's gaze until they vanish, disappearing round the corner. His heart is hammering in his chest, and he can't quite describe what he's feeling. It's not quite surprise. It's more like awe.

"Thank you," says the old man. Prakesh turns around and holds out a hand, pulling the man up. His skin feels hypersensitive, as if some weird drug has been injected into his veins.

The woman wraps her arm around the man, her huge eyes taking in Prakesh.

"Bastards," the old man spits. "All of them. Take and kill, all they do." The woman nods, a venomous look crossing her face.

"Yeah, I know," Prakesh says. The adrenaline is draining away, replaced by the cold glare of reality. Those three were kids. The next ones might not be.

"Madala," the old man says.

Prakesh turns to him. "Huh?"

"Name's Madala," the man says, thrusting out an ancient hand. Prakesh takes it, and the man pumps twice, then jerks his head at the woman. "This Indira. She not talk much, but she says hello."

The woman blinks at him, and nods.

"Sure," Prakesh says. "Listen, you two need to get inside. It's only going to get worse out here."

"Ha," says the old man, barking the word. "Inside? No. We come with you."

Before Prakesh can protest, Indira and Madala have grabbed him by the arms, and are marching him down the corridor. He tries to say something, but Madala talks over him. "You tell us what to do, we do it."

Well, OK then, Prakesh thinks.

63

Darnell

"Where are you?" Darnell says, his eyes on the screens.

His words are barely coherent, blurring together in a husky whisper. Around him, the control room is silent. He doesn't know where Okwembu is, and he doesn't care.

He has the Apogee entrance to the Core up on the screen. The protection officers guarding it are restless and worried, pacing with their stingers out. No Hale.

He selects another camera view – the Apogee gallery, the camera under the Level 1 catwalk, pointing down. It shows a gallery strewn with burning trash, wreathed in smoke. He's lost count of how many times he's pulled up the feed, hoping to see Hale being burned alive. Not for the first time, Darnell curses the cameras that no longer work, the blind spots in his vision.

Pain lances through him, driving a pointed tip through his torn ear, his shoulder, the scabbing burn on his arm. He growls in anger. After he was shot, the pain felt like it belonged to someone else. Now it's everywhere, ferocious, biting. He can't get away from it.

He should be savouring these last few hours, using

the control room to create as much fear as possible. Instead, he's obsessing over Hale. The stompers who came through the Core provided a momentary distraction, but she keeps returning to the front of his mind. He knows that she's a minor threat at best, that she can't run forever, but it doesn't help. The fact that he can't do anything about her is infuriating. It makes him feel useless.

Like before.

And in the years following the controlled burn, he *was* useless. He was placed with different families. He had counsellors. But those years are a dark, indistinct smudge – he doesn't remember a single thing anyone said to him.

Darnell didn't feel sorry about his mother – she would have died soon anyway, and at least this way she'd been useful. Why couldn't they understand that? Why couldn't they see that the plants were just doing what was needed to exist?

He tried to rationalise it, tried to understand why they'd destroyed the plants, and why nobody had stopped them. He couldn't. It was too big, a monstrous truth that he couldn't comprehend.

And it wasn't just the plants in his hab. The Earth below them was wrecked, its environment destroyed. Humans had done that too. *And they didn't learn*. Even as they clung to existence, spinning around the Earth, they committed the same mistakes.

Darnell was a minor when he was put into the system. When he was eighteen, in accordance with Outer Earth law, his record was wiped clean. He moved to a distant sector, where no one recognised him. By that time, he had his size, and he found work in the Food Lab, toting sacks of fertiliser. It was there that he had his revelation, which arrived so suddenly that it stopped him in his tracks, the sack he was carrying swaying in his grip.

He would fix it.

A species that could destroy something so pure and beautiful didn't deserve the world they were given, so Darnell would take it away from them. Without humans, nature would reclaim the Earth. It would take millennia, but that didn't matter.

There would be no place for him in that world, either. When he realised that, the relief was exquisite, like he'd been thirsty for years and had finally found cool water.

He would have to be careful. Blend in, make contacts, accumulate power and influence. It would be immensely difficult. If his plan was going to work, it would need to be total – not a single human survivor could be left alive. He would have to wipe out Outer Earth in one go. He accepted that there was little he could do about the asteroid catcher ships, but without Outer Earth to sustain them, where would they go? The humans on board would die too, even if it took a little longer.

And it had worked. His patience, his self-control, had all been worth it. In a matter of hours, Outer Earth would be utterly destroyed. Hale couldn't stop that, no matter what she did. So why is he fixating on her? What keeps him watching the screens?

"We don't have much time left."

Okwembu is behind him; her mouth is set in a thin line.

Darnell ignores her. He's still scanning the screens.

"I know there's no point treating those wounds," she says. "But I can give you something for the pain, if you like."

Darnell opens his mouth to tell her that he's fine, but his eyes are drawn to movement on the feed. He quickly maximises the camera, zooming in.

Something is happening at the core entrance in Apogee.

64

Riley

"Ten stompers," says Carver. "This isn't a break-in, Riley, it's suicide."

I bite my lip, staring at the entranceway to the Core. We're off to one side, in the shadows of the corridor. We managed to run up the levels without encountering too much resistance; there was a group of teens looking for a fight, but they weren't armed, and even undermanned we got through them easily. Now, as I stare into the room, half of me is tempted to agree with Carver. But with less than ten hours left before Darnell destroys everything, we don't have a choice.

The entrance is pretty much as I remember it: a massive open space, stacked with pallets for transporting equipment. The walls are lined with rows of lockers, each capped with an oversized keypad. There's no overhead lighting. Instead, harsh spotlights at floor level point upwards at the roof, directed at the colossal blast doors themselves. They take up nearly the whole ceiling, reaching from one wall to the other. The seal between the two halves is like a giant set of metal teeth, decayed with age until each tooth is black with rust. The doors aren't flush with the roof, but sit slightly below it. Painted across them in enormous black letters are the words *Reactor Access*.

I can see the control panels on either side of the room. I'd like to get a closer look, but even if I could understand the readouts – about as likely as being able to grow eyes in the back of my head – there's no way I'd get near them. The stompers in the room are on edge, pacing back and forth. It doesn't look as if anybody has tried to breach their defences yet, but from the way they're fingering their guns I'd guess they're expecting an attack any minute.

And now, it seems, their first one's going to come from three exhausted tracers. Lucky them. They'll probably see it as a warm-up.

Kev squats down next to me, whispers, "Still think this is a good idea?"

"Not really. But it's the only one we've got. You ready to go?"

He grunts, hefting his backpack.

"Remember," Carver says to him. "The second it kicks off, hit the ground. They'll be shooting, and you'll be the last thing they see."

Kev nods. I busy myself with pulling on the gloves Carver gave me. They're thick, made of a stiff outer material stuffed with shreds of old fabric. They're too big for my hands. I give them an experimental flex, dismayed to find that I have to exert real effort to make even a clumsy fist. Climbing with these on is going to be nearly impossible. But they'll protect my fingers from the cold. What happened to Amira won't happen to me. *In more ways than one.*

There's a dirty black scarf wrapped around my neck. I've already padded myself out under my jacket, pulling on two of Carver's shirts and a hooded top belonging to

Kev. The clothing is threadbare, barely holding itself together. The under-layer is soaked in sweat from the run. I'm worried that the sweat might freeze, drawing body heat, but I can't think about that now. It'd be great if I had a full thermo-suit to wear, but it'd just slow me down. For now, I'll have to live with the discomfort.

"Last chance to back out, Riley," says Carver.

I shake my head. My heart is thudding in my chest, and there's a curious metallic taste in my mouth. But I push it away, forcing myself to focus. "We're doing this," I say.

"I always knew being a tracer would get me killed," says Kev. And with that, he stands and walks straight into the room. I have to remind myself to breathe.

Kev walks slowly, his hands up, his pack hanging loosely from his shoulders. The stomper nearest to us – a stocky woman with a ponytail – looks up at the sound of footsteps. "Stop!" she barks. In half a second, she and every other stomper in the room have their guns out and locked on Kev.

He gives a nervous smile, his hands raised above him. "Cargo delivery," he says. "Speed run from the mess. Someone sending up food for you."

The first stomper's expression doesn't change, but behind her I see a couple of the others lower their guns very slightly, their expressions hopeful. My guess was good: they've been up here for hours, maybe days, and chances to eat will have been slim. A shipment of food would be a welcome prospect.

I'm almost sorry that we'll have to disappoint. Almost.

"Since when did the mess start using tracers for food deliveries?" says the first stomper.

Kev shrugs, and I marvel at how calm he seems. "Not my problem," he replies. "But if I go back, they probably won't bother sending another one." At this, the stompers glance at each other nervously. I can almost hear their stomachs rumbling. Still the woman with the ponytail doesn't move.

"Tell you what," says Kev. "I'll take out the cargo, and put it on the floor. Nice and easy." He keeps his hands raised, not wanting to provoke.

After a long minute, the woman says, "Take off the pack."

Kev slowly reaches behind him, pulling the pack off his shoulders and holding it out in front of him at arm's length. The stomper nods. "Good. Take the cargo out," she says.

"OK," says Kev. And tears out the hidden panel at the bottom of the bag.

The chemicals inside react to the air immediately. Kev hits the deck just as the lead stomper fires, but his body has already vanished into the huge, billowing cloud of smoke gushing from the pellets.

This was what Carver had been working on when he locked me out of the Nest for kicks. Turns out he'd been trying to build this smoke system, hoping to give us an extra escape route if we ever ran into trouble. He'd been struggling with it, not able to get the formula right. But it turned out that quicksleep – the stuff Arthur Gray used to grab his victims – was the missing ingredient. Distil it down, add a few other chemicals into it, then combine it with Carver's original recipe. Expose it to air, and you've got something that could easily help a Dancer evade someone hunting them.

With the quicksleep, and the scraps he and Kevin managed to scrounge from the Nest, there was just enough left to make a single batch. It took Carver less than twenty minutes to mix the chemicals and transfer them to a pack, storing them inside a modified water container. He had to do it pretty quickly to stop smoke filling up the hab, but he managed it.

We dash from our hiding places into the noxious smoke, the room filling with confused shouts and gunfire. It's clear that for a few seconds at least, we won't be noticed. We've got scarves wrapped around our faces, but the thick smoke still worms its way in, burning my throat. I sprint towards where I think the control panel is, and a bullet ricochets off the floor in front of me; I duck, but keep running, heading towards the far end of the room.

There's a yell from behind me. Carver? No way to tell. The smoke is everywhere now, filling the room; a stomper materialises out of the gloom in front of me, his gun raised, but I'm moving too fast. I clock him across the throat, and he gives a loud, strangled cry as he flies backwards. His gun fires, the bullet dancing off the ceiling. I wince, but keep running.

A split second later, I slam into the wall, my fingers bending back painfully where they've made contact. I bite back a cry of pain, not wanting to give away my position. I force my throbbing fingers to feel along the wall to my right, hoping desperately that I've picked the right direction.

It's impossible to see now. I'm breathing too fast, inhaling too much smoke, expecting a bullet in the back at any second. But then the surface under my fingers changes, from cold metal to the smooth glass of a screen, and I know I've found the control panel. My hands feel downwards, exploring the panel. It juts out of the wall at waist height, a bank of buttons capped with the screen, which I can now see glowing dimly through the smoke.

I dig into my pocket, fighting with the thick gloves, and pull out Carver's second gadget.

It's almost too simple to work. A tiny plastic box, filled with a small blob of explosive putty. Inside the box, above the putty and pointing right at it, is a short spike. On its tip, another chemical, harmless – until you place the box on a flat surface and slam your hand onto the lid, driving the spike into the putty, combining the chemicals. Then you have about a second to dive away before the explosion takes your hand off.

When the bang comes, it's so loud that my hearing goes completely, leaving nothing but a ringing that burrows into my skull. I've thrown myself to the side, away from the explosion. It's small, but bright and hot, and enough to blow a hole the size of a man's head in the control panel. A moment later, I feel a second thud reverberate around the room. Carver must have detonated his own device.

My hearing slowly comes back. The room is louder now, filled with the terrified shouts from the stompers, telling each other to fall back. I want to yell that they're not under attack, that we don't mean to hurt them, but with the smoke and the explosions, I think I'd just earn myself a volley of stinger bullets. Lying on the ground, my ears throbbing and my lungs burning with hot smoke, a tiny thought in the back of my mind says that this is absolutely the worst idea ever.

And then I hear it. A high-pitched mechanical whine.

The blast doors are opening.

I jump to my feet, and start running, ignoring the nausea brought on by the smoke. It occurs to me that I have no idea how you actually get through the doors: does a ladder drop down? Stairs? I curse myself for not thinking about it before. I'm looking upwards through the smoke, searching for the opening. But then, no more than five seconds after the doors started opening, the sound changes: it gets lower, more throaty. As if…

My heart sinks. The doors are closing. Some failsafe, some little electronic gatekeeper, has kicked in, and there's no way of telling how far the doors opened before they started to shut.

A figure explodes out of the fog. It's Carver, blood pouring down his face, mouthing something I can't hear. He has to say it twice before I hear him: "Jump!"

Without breaking my stride, I push off with my left leg, launching myself upwards. At the same time, Carver drops to one knee, cupping his left hand under my foot. My body acts before I can think about it, and I push into his hand even as he forces me upwards, my own arm raised. He cries out, putting every ounce of effort he can into pushing me up with his one arm. I force my eyes to stay open in the stinging smoke, hunting for an opening.

The edge of the door takes me in the forearms, almost causing me to fall backwards, but I swing my arms down, and then I'm hanging from the blast doors by my elbows. The whine is louder now, burrowing into my head. If I can't pull myself up, the doors will cut me in two.

My legs are dangling in space, and at any second I expect a bullet to slice through them. But Carver hasn't let go of my foot, and he starts pushing upwards, standing, lifting me from below. Groaning with the effort, I haul my way upwards: first my chest, then my waist, and then my legs are up and over. I catch a brief glimpse of Carver's face through the gap in the blast doors: soaked red with the blood, but with eyes burning bright. Then the doors slam shut with a huge, echoing boom.

The silence is instant and total. As I lie there, in the semi-darkness, the cold starts to seep in, tongues of ice licking at my exposed skin.

65

Darnell

"She's inside," Oren Darnell says.

His voice is even, quiet, controlled. He grips the back of one of the chairs, his eyes fixed intently on the screen. The camera is looking down on the Core doors. It shows Hale, getting to her feet, hugging herself tightly. On the screen, the clouds made from her breath are grey pixels, blocky and stuttering.

Okwembu stands in the doorway to the control room, arms folded.

Darnell throws the chair. It crashes across the control room, knocking over other chairs as it goes. Okwembu doesn't respond, not even when Darnell walks right up to her. His body is drenched in sweat and blood.

"She's tenacious, I'll give her that," Okwembu says.

"We have to shut her out."

Okwembu shrugs. "The stompers disabled the lock. We can close the doors, but we can't seal them."

"She knows the damn code. If she were to get in the control room—"

"But she won't," Okwembu says wearily. "She isn't wearing a thermo-suit. She'll freeze solid before she gets within a mile of here. And if she does somehow make it through, she'll be far too weak to fight."

Okwembu's eyes glitter, and Darnell sees something in them that he hasn't seen before. Something like excitement.

"We can kill her together. In front of everyone. And then we can tell them what's coming."

Darnell starts laughing, and once he does, he finds that he can't stop. It comes from somewhere deep inside him – an awful, hacking noise, as if a malignant tumour has come loose in his chest. He lifts the knife, points it at Okwembu. His shoulder wound has started bleeding again, and he can feel it throbbing, a deep ache that won't go away.

"You've never killed anyone in your life," he says, between gusts of laughter. "You even had me suck the oxygen out of that amphitheatre for you. You don't *deserve* to kill her."

"If you go in there, you put yourself at risk. But if we meet her here, she'll have two of us to deal with. Let her come to us."

Darnell considers it, but only for a second. Every iota of hatred he possesses has focused down into this one thing. He's not going to *let her come*. He's going to fix it. He's going to fix her.

He steps past Okwembu, and only stops when she puts a hand on his arm.

"You're hurt," she says, gesturing at his mangled shoulder. "It'll only slow you down in there. If you're going to go, then at least let me give you something for the pain."

Darnell looks down. Okwembu is slipping the cap off a syringe, filled with clear liquid. She moves to slide his sleeve up, and that's when he knocks her arm aside. The syringe explodes against the wall.

"It's butorphanol," she says, raising her hands. "Pain meds. That's all. Just—"

Darnell hits her.

Okwembu goes down, collapsing on all fours. Darnell steps over her, striding down the passage. It's only when he reaches the stairs that he wonders if he should kill her. He half turns back, then stops himself, because all he can see is Riley Hale. Okwembu isn't important. There's nothing she can do to him.

Darnell laughs again, turning away. He begins climbing the stairs.

"Oren," says Okwembu from behind him, her voice thick with pain. When he doesn't respond, she says it more sharply. "Oren!"

He barely hears her. Barely realises what he's doing. All he can think about is how every step takes him closer to the Core.

Closer to Hale.

66

Riley

Every breath is visible, as dense as the smoke in the room below me – and every one I suck in cuts deep into my lungs. This isn't like the cold I've felt in the Nest, when I've woken from a deep sleep with the blanket bunched around my feet. That you get used to. This is dry cold, ripped from the absolute zero of the vacuum, channelled and controlled to bring down the colossal heat of the fusion reactor and the superconducting cables that carry its power to the rest of the station.

I'm at the bottom of an enormous cylinder, stretching upwards to infinity, lit with huge spotlights that nevertheless fail to cut through the gloom completely. I count six cables, each as thick as three men, spaced around the cylinder. There's a catwalk, laid around the sides of the cylinder in front of the cables, curling steadily upwards like a coiled spring.

I get to my feet. Six miles from here to Apex. If I can keep the pace up, it should take me about two hours to run the Core.

Of course, I have to do it in sub-zero temperatures, and in a gravity that will get lower with every step.

I head towards the ramp that leads to the catwalk, then stop. How do the Core techs get up there? After all, if you're in a bulky thermo-suit, carrying heavy equipment, you aren't going to walk upwards for three miles every time a pipe springs a leak.

It takes me a moment to spot it, hidden in the shadows behind where I came in. An elevator. A golden ticket right to the top. I can't help cracking a smile.

My footsteps are loud in the vast space as I cross the room. The thought occurs to me that they might have found a way to shut down the elevator after I broke in, but it opens as I touch the button. The lights on the inside flicker to life, illuminating the cramped space. Under normal circumstances, it'd probably be a chore to ride in, but right now, I can't get in there fast enough.

I thumb the Up button, fighting to push it hard enough through my bulky gloves. Despite the padding, my hands are already numb, and my cheeks are throbbing gently, as if I've been slapped. I try to stay as still as possible, hoping to conserve energy. The elevator hums to life, and with an enormous clanking noise, begins to move slowly upwards. I hold my breath, expecting that at any moment it'll shudder to a halt, and start downwards, where a group of heavily armed stompers will be waiting. But the lift keeps moving, slowly making its way up the tube. My chest is still warm, and my sweat-soaked undergarments don't appear to have frozen.

It occurs to me that this is the first time I've been by myself since I was locked in the brig in Apogee. There's nobody to back me up: no Amira, no Prakesh, no Carver or Kev. And the higher the elevator gets, the further I go from everybody else.

The Dancers would get a real kick out of this place. Imagine being able to run as you approach zero gravity. Amira would...

I shut my eyes tight. I take Amira, and Yao, and Grace Garner, and put them in a very small place, deep in my mind. I force myself to do it, *will* them to stay silent. *Later,* I tell them. *Later, when this is over, we can talk.*

At that moment, the lift gives a screeching sound and judders to a halt. I drop to the floor, out of sight, before I realise that there's no way anybody could be aiming at me through the window. Slowly, I get to my feet, but I'm thrown off balance when the elevator jerks downwards. I panic, realising that they've managed to report the attack, the intrusion, and they're bringing me back down.

I hammer on the door release button. Nothing happens. There are two other buttons indicating up and down, alongside another button that looks like it activates a communicator. I'm about to press it, but stop, irritated with myself. Yes, Riley, confirm that you're in the lift.

I try to force the doors open, to push my fingers into the crack, but it's useless with the gloves on. My heart sinks: I'll have to take them off.

I grasp one in my teeth, pull it upwards, shucking it from my hand. I do the other, then tuck both under my arm. My fingers are a pale white. Is it my imagination, or are they turning ever so slightly blue at the tips?

No time. I jam my fingers into the door, hunting for a grip. The metal burns on contact, sending jabs of icy pain through my numb fingers. Ever so slowly, with a hideous creaking sound, the doors separate, and I wedge my body between them. I'm half in and half out of the lift, my hands screaming with pain, no more than a few feet above the catwalk surface.

With a yell, I throw myself out of the lift, landing feet first on the ramp with a boom that reverberates around the shaft. One of my gloves under my arm flies forwards, bouncing towards the edge. A terrified gasp escapes my lips, and I dive forwards, scrabbling for it. My fingers grab it a moment before it flies off the ramp, into space. I lie there, breathing heavily through my nose. Behind me, the lift continues its downward path.

I sit up, and shove the gloves back on. My hands are numb, way too numb. More panic begins to seep in, clouding my thoughts. I force myself to concentrate, trying to put what I need in order. I'm cold, so my body is pulling everything to its own core, diverting blood from my extremities. I need to get blood to my hands. I stand and begin swinging my arms. The tingling that returns to my hands a second later is almost worse than the numbness, but I grit my teeth, forcing myself to push through it. After a few spins, they start to feel a little warmer. Maybe I can get through this.

It takes me a moment to notice the curious sensation in my arms. It's as if, at the top of my windmill movement, I have to force my arms downwards, rather than letting momentum carry them through. And then a small wave of nausea rises in my stomach, and I realise: gravity. I'm starting to feel the onset of zero-G – or microgravity, anyway. The closer I get to the centre of the spinning ring, the less gravity there'll be. I cast my eyes up the ramp, curling up the sides of the shaft, wondering what it will feel like.

Only one way to find out. I start running.

I have no idea how far I have to go before I reach the Core, but I start to feel the effect of the lower gravity on my running instantly. As with my arms, I have to force my feet downwards – I'm exerting less effort on the push-off with each stride, but far more to get it to stick. I try to adapt to the gravity, using it to conserve the energy at the start of each stride, and then release it at the end. But instead, I just tire a lot faster than normal. The nausea ebbs and flows; presumably, the protein bars I ate must be starting to bob around in my stomach. I want to laugh at the thought, but I'm breathing too hard, my breath forming soft clouds of condensation.

After a few minutes, I stop for a rest beside one of the superconductor cables. I run my hand down the casing: it's not metal, more like some kind of rubber, slightly springy to touch. I can feel it humming under my hand, pulsing with energy. Is this how Darnell and the Sons of Earth are planning to destroy us? Maybe they've got some kind of bomb in the reactor. Shut off the power, kill every light and air system and source of heat, turn the station into a tomb.

I tell myself that I won't let that happen.

With a groan, I push myself off the cable, and start running again. The catwalk slopes upwards, running clockwise around the cylinder, spaced a little way from the wall to make room for the cables. The surface is perforated metal grating, uneven and sharp. Every time I take a step, the sound echoes back from the other side of the cylinder. There's a railing on the outside of the catwalk; I trail my hand along it as I run, using it to steady myself against the lowering gravity. I might be running upwards in a circle, without any changes of direction, but I find that my torso keeps tilting too far forwards, threatening to tip me off balance. I have to pull it back consciously, and every time I do so, it saps even more energy.

And there's an even stranger sensation: it's like I'm constantly tilting towards the wall, as if I'm made of metal, and the wall is a giant magnet. It takes me a moment to work out what it is: the spinning motion of the ring. When I'm heading towards the centre, moving in low gravity, the spin will start to have an effect. I'll be pushed up against one of the walls of the shaft. I can only hope it doesn't slow me down too much.

I stop again, my breathing ragged. The Core's not a vacuum, but it feels like I have to force every breath into my lungs. Is that something to do with the change in elevation? Or is it just the run itself? The sweat under my clothes has started to turn cold, and I catch myself shivering. *This isn't working.*

The whole time, I've been fighting against the lack of gravity, struggling to run in a way that I'm used to. Maybe there's a way to work with the gravity.

This time, instead of pushing each stride down, I concentrate all my energy on the upwards spring, trying to push myself higher. The first time I do it, I put so much effort into it that I nearly hurl myself over the outside railing. I grab it with both hands, steady myself and try again – and this time I control the spring, keeping my body steady in the air. The first stride takes me a good ten feet. The next, fifteen. Then, I'm leaping higher and higher, bounding forwards in huge, springy steps, covering twenty feet at a time, twenty-five. It still feels as if the wall is trying to pull me towards it, but I angle my jumps, giving myself some room to move.

The sensation is like nothing I've ever experienced. I close my eyes, and now I do laugh, because for the first time I feel what it's like to fly. For the first time in my life, in the middle of the most impossible circumstances imaginable, I'm airborne.

I've never felt a rush like it. And I know right then that if I survive this, I'm going to spend the rest of my life chasing it.

The catwalk vanishes below me, leaving me hanging in mid-air. My heart jumps, and for a long second I think I'm about to plummet to the bottom. But then I realise that I'm still moving forwards, buoyed by the lack of gravity.

It's an amazing feeling – almost peaceful.

Five seconds later, I collide painfully with the wall of the shaft.

I bounce right off, flying across the gaping centre of the tube towards the opposite wall. I flip my body around in the air, so my legs are facing the wall.

This time, instead of smashing into it, I let my legs take the impact, then push upwards, launching my body up the shaft. Not hard enough. I shoot out a few feet, and then the wall catches up with me. I bend my legs again, then push upwards even harder. This time, I propel myself into the middle of the shaft.

Looking down, I spot the catwalk, which does indeed end abruptly just before one of the cables. Of course: techs wouldn't need it any more. Not when they could just push upwards, and fly.

It's an odd sensation. The gravity is low enough that I can fly down the middle of the shaft for lengthy stretches, but every few hundred feet, I find the wall rushing up again as the spin catches up with me. Without the act of running, I start to get colder, and before long I'm shivering. I'm painfully aware that I need to get through the Core as quickly as possible. I don't know how long my body can take this cold, and I'm already going to be dangerously weak by the time I get out the other side.

An unsettling thought occurs to me. How do I actually get through the doors on the other side? Will there be a panel that controls the door? Or can it only be accessed from the outside? I didn't even stop to check at the Apogee end of the shaft, which seems like a colossal oversight.

The sound in the shaft changes, the rumbling getting deeper, more hollow. I crane my neck upwards, and there, silhouetted from behind by a dozen huge beams, like something coming out of the sun, is the Core Reactor.

It's enormous, far bigger than I'd ever expected. The shaft opens out into a massive spherical chamber; the reactor is in the centre, an angular block, running from one wall to the other, cocooned in cables and control panels. I almost expect to see jets of steam being vented into the room, but any real moisture in this cold would be lethal to the electronics. The hum coalesces, and it's unlike any other sound I've ever heard. Like this thing has a stomach, and it's rumbling.

I'm flying out of the mouth of the shaft, heading straight towards it. I look back over my shoulder, and see that the shaft entrance is moving to the side. I'm at the centre of the ring now, and everything is rotating around me. The movement is slow, more than enough for me to deal with.

I swing my body around – it's harder with so little gravity, but I just manage it – and my legs make contact with the reactor, sending a dull clang echoing around the chamber. There's a set of handgrips to my right, and I reach out for them, letting my body come to rest. I'm about to throw myself outwards again when I hear a cry of triumph from above me.

Oren Darnell flies out of the darkness, clutching an enormous blade.

67

Riley

A scream dies in my throat, choked off by the memory of those rough, damp hands. All that emerges is a terrified mewling.

I'm frozen in place, watching Darnell bear down on me. His face is like something from the other end of the universe.

At the very last moment, just before he reaches me, I finally find the strength. I piston my legs, hurling myself towards the wall of the chamber. But Darnell was ready for the move; he grabs the handgrip I was holding on to not two seconds before, then uses it to swing himself after me, his legs making contact with the reactor and pushing outwards. I'm moving away fast, but not fast enough – his push-off was more powerful, and as we race towards the wall, he starts to gain on me.

How? How did he know I would be running the Core? How long has he been waiting for me?

The part of the wall we're heading towards is fitted with several screens, all trailing power cables. When I make contact a second later, it's knees first, and I feel one of the screens crack and buckle under me, spitting glass and sparks.

Darnell is right behind me. I throw myself off the wall, aiming over his head. But instead of trying to catch me, he swings around in mid-air, bracing his left shoulder for impact as he jabs the blade upwards, slicing through my jacket and tagging my side.

It's like a red-hot piece of metal being held to my skin. I jerk away, another scream tearing itself from my lips, as a tiny bubble of blood appears and starts to spread out, floating in mid-air between us. His strike has changed my direction, knocking me back towards the reactor.

Darnell roars, and launches himself after me, but this time I have a head start, and his direction is slightly off. He's moving underneath me. He turns his face upwards, and the sight of his smile almost causes me to lose control completely.

"I saw you come in through the Apogee entrance," he calls out. "You thought I'd just let you walk into Apex?"

The cameras. That's how. It doesn't matter if not all of them work any more; the one outside the Core does. Maybe even one in the Air Lab control room. How else would he have known that Amira had failed?

He spreads his arms wide. The movement sets him spinning slowly in the other direction, but his eyes never leave me. "Now it's just you and me, Hale. And what better place for us to have a rematch than the centre of Outer Earth itself? It's almost poetic."

The mewling is back, stuck in my throat. My side is on fire; I don't think I've been cut deeply, but I leave a glistening trail of blood as I move through the air.

I hit the reactor and scrabble at it, hunting for a hold. But this section of the surface is smooth, and with nothing to hold on to, all I do is put myself into a spin. A rolling wave of nausea spurts through me, and the tumble causes my arms and legs to flail. Darnell's also trying to get a grip on the reactor. He's taken his eyes off me, hunting for a hold.

There are cables passing below me, a tangled mess of wires spewing out of their black insulation sheaths. I reach out and snag one of them, praying that I don't rip it out of its socket; the last thing I need is to cause a reactor shutdown myself. Holding on to the cable swings my body around, until my head is pointing back towards Darnell.

I can't beat him. Not when he's armed and I'm not. And in near-zero-G – no way. I barely survived in normal gravity. I'm breathing too hard, the cold beginning to lock down my body heat. There's an odd tingling sensation in my hands.

The cables. There's a big tangle of them, positioned slightly away from the reactor, held apart at intervals by steel brackets. The gap behind the cables looks just wide enough for me to squeeze into.

I pull myself towards the opening, trying to be as quiet as possible. I wedge myself into it, the cables pushing against my bulky jacket.

If Darnell saw me enter, he'll have me trapped, able to pick me off whenever he wants. I can see the blade shooting from between the cables, skewering me in the chest, but there's nothing, just the hum of the reactor against my back. I can't even hear Darnell any more, and when I peer through the mass of cables, he's vanished. I slow my breathing, try to remain still.

There he is, drifting slowly across my field of vision. His eyes scan the room, passing across my hiding place. I hold my breath and draw back against the wall, worried that a stray puff of breath from my mouth will give me away.

He stares for what feels like an eternity.

But then he turns his head, looks away. And I notice something. He's breathing heavily: I can hear it, a tired, wet rumble. His blade hand is shaking slightly too, as if he's gripping it too hard, and his enormous shoulders are also shaking, rising up and down with each breath. He's not as fit as I am, and his body is burning too much energy too quickly. He's injured too, with blood soaking his shoulder. His jacket doesn't fit him, and the shirt underneath looks thin and insubstantial.

He came into the Core because he wanted to take me down himself, right here. It's the kind of twisted logic that would appeal to someone like him. But he didn't think. Didn't realise how much the cold would affect him.

For the first time, I may just have the edge.

Could I wait him out? Stay here until he dies of hypothermia? It sounds so ridiculous I have to force myself not to laugh. Even if I was able to somehow not die of cold myself, and even if he kept missing my hiding place in a room with very few hiding places, there's just no time. Okwembu is still out there, and the heat convectors are still inactive.

What are you going to do if they come after you in the Core?

What I always do, Prakesh. I run.

I have to wait until he's far enough away. He's getting agitated, moving towards the bottom of the reactor. I force myself to keep breathing, to flex my fingers and toes, to keep the blood flowing. The seconds stretch into minutes.

"Where are you?" he yells.

Slowly, I slip out from behind the cables. I can see him; he's below, and won't see me unless he looks straight up. Moving very quietly, I position myself on the reactor, ready to push off towards the shaft leading to Apex as soon as it comes into view. Under me, the reactor hums, the vibration gripping the soles of my shoes.

I see the shaft entrance. With one movement, I push myself off the reactor, floating towards it.

Darnell bellows as he spots me. I sneak a glance back. He's still below me, but – no – he's gaining. Maybe he pushed off harder. I will myself forwards, tucking my arms, streamlining my body. Behind me, Darnell raves. There's no joy in his voice now; just pure hatred.

The first part of the shaft is hard. The wall rises up to meet me again, and I have to push off it, adjusting to the gravity as I go, willing myself not to look back. I can see the ramp below me. Slowly, I change my aim, bring my body around – it's hard without anything to push off, but I do it. He's got closer, no more than a few yards away. The blade glints in the dim light, and I can hear his breathing, deep and hard, echoing around the shaft. I'm shivering uncontrollably now – whether from fear or the cold, I don't know.

Then I realise: the gravity. It's coming back as we get further away from the reactor, and I can use it to my advantage. Like the Apogee shaft, the ramp here curves downwards, circling the walls. I don't have to run down the whole catwalk. I can jump from side to side, letting the low gravity cushion my fall. And the lower I go, the less problematic the station's spin will be.

"You're mine, Hale," he says.

I look back over my shoulder.

"You'll have to catch me first."

I hit the ramp, and almost immediately bounce back upwards. But this time, I push myself out over the shaft aiming for a lower part of the catwalk on the far side. The low gravity means that I can drop down a few levels of the ramp each time.

The move surprises Darnell, but he recovers quickly. I can hear him in the air behind me as I drop onto the catwalk below. My heart is pounding, but I force myself to run, to jump down again, this time back to the other side of the shaft. When I look back over my shoulder, I see Darnell: he didn't quite reach the catwalk, and is scrambling over the railing on the far side, cursing with the effort. The knife is jammed in his waistband.

"What's the matter, Oren?" I shout. "Can't jump high enough?"

He doesn't say anything. He just roars. I don't waste any more time gloating, just start moving down the ramp. It's not long before I start running. The gravity is still low, so I have to control my strides, but almost immediately I start to leave him behind. He's running now, moving down the ramp behind me, but before long I'm far ahead of him. His panting gets softer and softer. When I get to the bottom, maybe I can get out and trap him in here, somehow…

I still have no idea how I can get the doors at the bottom of the shaft open. If they can only be opened from the outside, I'll be dead in minutes.

No choice. I have to keep running.

It's an age before I reach the bottom of the shaft. The last few minutes are a haze of exhaustion and pain, coursing through my body and sizzling in the cut on my side. As I reach the floor, my feet tangle up, and I crash to the ground, crying out.

I force myself to get up. I can't hear Darnell any more, but I have to move. I'm colder than I've ever been in my life. I can no longer feel my feet, or my hands.

The bottom of the shaft here is similar to the Apogee end. Same elevator, same cable points. There's got to be a way to open these doors. Whatever's on the other side – even if it's Okwembu, waiting with a stinger – I have to get out of here.

I spot a control panel, tucked away by the elevator, and my heart leaps. As I approach, I can see it's simple enough: a small digital readout, and a single switch. There aren't any labels, but I don't need them. I hit the switch, scarcely daring to breathe.

The doors clunk, sputter and begin to open. At that same instant, I hear Darnell above me.

He's coming down the last few coils of catwalk. Without thinking, without even looking, I drop through the opening doors, into Apex.

I land heavily and roll, my side flaring with pain. The temperature changes so quickly that pins and needles cascade through my body. The room is brightly lit, a huge space with white walls and glaring fluorescents. But I don't have time to take in the details. I'm looking for the door controls. There. One on either side of the room, just like back in Apogee, much newer and better maintained than their partners on the other side.

I can still hear him, panting, as he moves towards the open doors. How close is he? No way to tell. I have to lock the doors. I spring to the first control panel, jab at the touch-screen, searching for the option to close.

Seal Reactor Access? asks the panel. I hit *Confirm* so hard that a spear of pain shoots back into my finger. No time. Run. I'm pushing my body to the limit, but I still feel as if my legs won't move fast enough, like the cold has sealed my bones in place. Then I'm at the other panel, hunting through the options.

Above me the doors start to close, grinding shut. I look upwards – just in time to see him come down the last part of the ramp. The doors are closing too slowly. He'll be through them in seconds.

Move, I tell myself, but it's like I'm back in the reactor, watching him fly towards me. My legs have turned to lead.

The doors move towards each other, inch by inch. Darnell hits the floor and makes one last desperate jump towards them.

68

Darnell

Darnell is halfway through the doors when they close on his torso.

The metal teeth bring his descent to a shuddering halt, first slowing him, then holding him, then biting down as the enormous, grinding motors try to push the doors closed.

He feels his ribs break – the sound is a soft snap, like pulling a twig off a tree. He almost blacks out from the agony. He's upside-down, clawing at the air, his face twisted with pain. Something below his ribs gives way, and he screams. The darkness rushes in.

Before it closes on him completely, he sees Riley Hale. She's standing below him, her eyes wide, staring in mute horror. No more than a few feet away.

You're mine.

Darnell starts to twist his body. He can feel his legs flailing at the air above the doors, and he plants his hands on the other side of them, begins to push. He feels bone scrape bone, and he screams again, the thick cords of muscle in his neck tight enough to snap. The doors' motors are stuck in a high-pitched whine, and he can smell the sharp stench of burning electronics.

With a final wrench, Darnell rips his body free of the doors. When he hits the ground, it's as if an enormous hand has torn away his midsection. His legs have stopped working, and a dull pain emanates from the base of his spine.

Hale is slowly backing away. As Darnell screams her name, she turns and runs.

His hands still work. He can still do something. His knife has slipped out of his waistband, and lies in arm's reach. Darnell grabs it, groaning as the world turns grey and scarlet. But he can still see her. She's directly ahead, her back to him, presenting a perfect target. Darnell summons all the strength he has left, raising his arm as high as he can, crooking his elbow.

You always pull to the right, he thinks. *You have to adjust for that.*

His muscle memory is perfect, each movement sliding into place, and his arm is fully extended when he releases the knife. It's a perfect throw.

The blade spins through the air, heading right towards Riley Hale, a flickering star in an impossibly bright universe. For an instant, Darnell thinks it's going to hit its mark. Right when it counts, he's found his aim.

The knife goes wide.

It ricochets off the wall with a clang, the blade flickering as it bounces away. Hale looks back, startled, and the stupid, animal confusion in her eyes fuels Darnell's anger. He starts to pull himself across the floor, slamming his elbows into it, his ribs tenting the fabric of his shirt. If he can just get to her…

His arms give out. His face slams into the ground, all the strength draining away at once. He lies there, heaving, his hands balled into fists. He's not supposed to die here. He's supposed to die with everyone else, the only one laughing in a sea of screams. This isn't fair.

He lifts his head once more. The tracer is still staring at him.

"You cuh. You can't imagine," he says, and then stops. His throat has forgotten how to form words, and kicking it back into action nearly wipes him out.

"You can't imagine what you'll find in there," he says. A spray of blood shoots out from between his teeth as he speaks. "You can't run from it. No one can."

His eyes find hers.

"It's going to burn you alive."

The grey and scarlet turn black, like a piece of silk in a fire, and then there's nothing at all.

69

Riley

For the longest time, I can't move.

I'm expecting him to twitch, for him to look up and come for me again. He doesn't. I should retrieve the knife, plant it in his heart, make sure, but the thought of being close to him again makes me shudder.

Crushed. His organs turned to pulp. The old Riley would have felt something.

The new one doesn't care.

After a minute, my legs give out. I go down on one knee, breathing hard. The shivering is back, stronger now, and needle-jabs of pain are ricocheting through my body. The temptation to close my eyes and drift away is so strong that I have to will my eyes to stay open. *Focus on something. Anything.*

That's when I see it. A water point. Standing in the corner, gleaming under the lights. I'm up so fast that it's a full second before the pain in my side kicks in. I ignore it, stumbling over to the water point, fumbling with the switch. The tap clicks, whirrs, and falls silent, dry as my throat.

I hang my head, more furious than I'm willing to admit,

but as I do so the tap whirrs again, startling me, and begins to gush water. I let out a small cry of relief, and stick my head under the tap, greedily sucking it in, gulping in huge mouthfuls of water. I drink, and drink, and drink.

After a while, I drink too much. Coughing and spluttering, I collapse against the water point, but I'm surprised at how good I feel. Amazing how a little water can change things around.

I wipe my mouth; I'm still shivering, but the tremors are smaller now. Slowly, I strip myself of my gloves and undo my jacket. I'm no expert on frostbite, but it looks as if I managed to protect my hands for just long enough. Before long, they're flaring with powerful, reassuring pain, flushed with red.

I'm alone. No Okwembu. Or anyone else. Every surface is a gleaming white, lit by strips of lighting where the walls meet the ceilings and floors. There aren't any crates or pieces of equipment that I can see, or even any control panels on the walls. Unlike Apogee – or any other sector – it's quiet here. I can still hear the groaning of the hull, but I have to strain to do so.

And then I notice something. It's cooler here.

When I was on the other side of the station, the temperature was almost unbearable. But here, it's actually pleasant. Darnell – and Okwembu – must have kept the convection fins active for Apex. I've got to find a way to turn the rest of the station's convectors back on. How much time do I have left?

No way to tell.

I don't look at Darnell's body as I leave. I'm done with him. Trying to be as quiet as possible, I make my way to one of the corridors running off the main room. The light is dimmer here. There are doors recessed into the walls; I'm curious to know what's behind them, but there's no time.

The small, dark place where I put Yao, Amira and everyone else pulses. I fight it back. I can't be scared now, can't afford to be scared. Darnell is out of commission – I hope – but that doesn't mean his plan is. And it doesn't mean Okwembu isn't still out there.

I hit a T-junction. As I reach it, I flatten myself against the wall and close my eyes, listening hard. If Okwembu wasn't waiting for me when I came out of the Core, then there's every chance she'll be in one of the corridors, just waiting for me to show myself so she can put a bullet in my chest. I suddenly remember Darnell's knife, and curse myself for not retrieving it.

I can't hear anything: just the quiet hum of the lights, and behind them, like a ripple in a puddle of water, the sound of the station. I slip round the corner and pad quietly down the deserted passage, almost breaking into a run, deciding that it's better to be quiet.

There are stairs at the end of the corridor. Again, I hesitate before stepping onto them, wary that Okwembu could be waiting above or below me. Again, I hear nothing. Scarcely daring to breathe, I step into the stairwell, and start down it.

It's a few levels before I'm breathing again. I'm oddly reassured by just how much noise the stairs make when stepped on, giving off odd clangs every time my feet come down. Anybody listening would be able to hear me coming – but I'd be able to hear them, too. After a few levels, there cease to be any more corridors leading off. I'm getting close.

A few minutes later, I reach the bottom level. Ahead of me is a single small corridor, and at the end of it what must be the door to the control room. I don't know what I was expecting – a set of blast doors, maybe, or some complicated locking mechanism – but it's like every other door in the station.

I walk up to it, glancing nervously over my shoulder. There's a small keypad on one side of the door. Under the usual circumstances, there'd probably be several heavily armed elite officers on guard here, so other security measures in such a tight space probably wouldn't be necessary.

Still, the sight of the keypad gives me pause. There'll be no way to guess the code. Does this mean I've got to find Okwembu? Force the code out of her? My shoulders sag. I can't spend time tracking someone in an unfamiliar sector, where they know the layout and I don't, where they're armed and rested and I'm exhausted and defenceless.

It's then that a little green light blinks at the bottom of the keypad, so quickly that I nearly miss it. I freeze, hardly daring to believe I've seen it, but after thirty seconds or so it blinks again.

The door's unlocked.

This is too easy. Okwembu is waiting inside, knowing that I'll come to her. She'll shoot me the moment I'm through the door.

But there's no other choice. I have to get in there. I cast around for something to hide behind, anything to give me cover, but there's nothing in the corridor.

What if I didn't have to take cover out here? What if I could surprise her, and get behind something inside the control room before she shoots? It might buy me a few crucial seconds. And while Okwembu might fire in the direction of the corridor, she might be a little more hesitant to shoot if she could hit the controls.

Which would be a bit more relevant if she wasn't so intent on destroying the station.

I shake off the thought, and take a step back from the door, breathing hard. I rest my finger on the keypad's Enter button, tell myself to push it, but I hold back. Every cell in my body is screaming for me to turn around, to go find somewhere dark and warm and safe, and let everything disappear. I have to remind myself that there's nowhere like that any more.

I push the button.

The door whooshes open, and I throw myself through, tucking into a roll. I catch a blurred glimpse of several terminals, and then I'm in the roll, my heart in my mouth, expecting to hear the awful bang of a gunshot. I swing my head to the side, preparing to dive behind the nearest bit of cover. But as I do so, I get a look at the room, and I check my movement, coming to a stop on all fours.

The control room is deserted.

Terrified, I flick my head from side to side, hunting out hiding places, anywhere that she could be waiting. But there's no place to hide. Slowly, I stand, gazing around me.

Wherever Okwembu is, it's not here. The main control room of Outer Earth is narrow, barely wider than the corridor outside. The walls on either side of me are crowded with banks of screens, bathing the room in an orange glow. There aren't any keyboards or control pads, so I'm guessing the screens are touch-based. Several chairs are scattered around, overturned.

Slowly, I wander down the room. It's tiny. There's not even a viewing port: just bank after bank of terminals. There's no retinal scanner that I can see, nothing that Darnell would use Foster's eyeball on. It must be hidden away somewhere.

By now, I'm expecting to hear klaxons, computerised voices reading off dire warnings, but the room is quiet. I turn back to the door, hoping against hope that there's a way to lock it. There's another keypad, but it's also blinking green, and without the code, I won't be able to close it. I walk back and thumb the Enter button, and the door shuts with a hiss.

Okwembu's absence nags at me. Where is she? I can't think of a single reason why she wouldn't be in the control room. Maybe she's watching from a distance, or listening. Waiting for me to trigger a trap.

There's nothing I can do about it now, not unless I'm willing to waste time searching the sector for her. With one eye on the entrance, I scan the screens again. I'm looking for a login box, something that requires a password, something I can input the word Iapetus into and find out what it does.

But each screen I look at appears to be logged in already; they all display various options, ranging from Dock Access to Thruster Management to Aeronautics. Most are in English, but several seem to be in Hindi and Chinese as well. One of them shows a static radio frequency, and there's a little dust on the controls, like no one has used them for a long time. Can't say I blame them; in the decades after the nuclear war, we could still pick up radio signals from Earth. One by one, they all faded. Fifty years ago, the planet went completely silent.

I stop in front of one of the screens. I debate pulling a chair upright, but decide to stand – if Okwembu comes through that door, I want to be ready.

Hesitating – but only for a second – I place my finger on one of the touch-screens and start to navigate through the system. There are lots of false starts, and I find myself staring at incomprehensible readouts and dead-ends of reactor kilowatt graphs. Cursing, I find my way back to the main menu screen, and methodically begin to trawl through the options. It's strange to think that right now I have an enormous amount of control over even the tiniest details of Outer Earth. No wonder Darnell and Okwembu wanted to take this place for themselves.

It takes me a lot longer than I want, but I find it, hidden in a sub-menu: *Convection Systems*. I tap the option, and the screen flashes with even more graphs and readouts. One catches my eye. *Average module temperature: 46C*.

Forty-six degrees Celsius. I've got to turn these things back on now.

Forcing myself to be patient, I scan through the display. I find it at the bottom of the screen. *Convection fin status: Inactive.* I tap the option, hoping that's all there is to it. My heart sinks as another menu opens up: a circular diagram of the station, showing the location of each convection fin with a small green triangle. There look to be about a dozen, scattered across the station hull.

I lean forwards, squinting to make out the detail. Each little triangle is empty. I reach out, tapping one, and it turns solid green. On the bottom of the screen, a text box flashes up: *Fin 6E1 active.*

Smiling, I start hitting all the triangles, breathing a huge sigh of relief as they turn green. But the breath catches in my throat as an error message flashes up, freezing my finger halfway to the screen.

Warning: ice crystals detected in convection system. Temperature at sub-optimal levels.

Numbers and letters pop up underneath the message. They must be convection fin locations. The error message is slightly transparent, and as I look closely I can see that all of them are on one side of the station, covering Gardens, Chengshi, half of Apogee.

Convection pump system may malfunction if exposed to extreme temperatures, reads the message. *Continue?*

I rest my head on my arms, growling in frustration, and I can feel helplessness pulling at me.

I raise my head, looking at the screen. The ice in the pipes…it has to be there because the pumps are shut down. The liquid that was on the outside when they got turned off hasn't moved. It's been exposed to the cold in space for too long.

I can't pump it back into the system yet. But what if I can melt it somehow? Raise the temperature of the liquid in the convection fins just enough so I can circulate it back in?

Circulate…

Maybe it's not the liquid in the pipes that I need to get moving.

Maybe it's Outer Earth itself.

70

Riley

It takes an age to find. I have to keep moving between touch-screens, looking for the right menu, and on the one occasion I glance at the heat readouts, I see that the internal temperature of the station has risen another half a degree.

"Come on," I say, cutting through a tangle of readouts and obscure options. "I know you're here."

I actually scream for joy when I find it. *Rotation speed*. I know that thrusters on the hull keep us spinning, slowly turning like a wheel. If I can increase the spin rate, I can move those iced-up pipes into direct sunlight.

It'll ramp up the gravity. The G-forces will increase, pushing me into the floor. But what other choice do I have?

Another model of the station has appeared, showing position relative to the Earth, moon and sun. I spot the controls for the rotation rate, and I crank them right up.

I expect to hear something – a dull boom, perhaps, as the thrusters power up. Instead, I feel a pressure between my shoulder blades. It goes from mild to excruciating in seconds, forcing me to my knees. There's no pain, but my hands are heavy – like I'm having to force them down simply to keep them sliding off the control panel. Raising my head – it feels like my neck is going to split down the sides – I see that the on-screen station has begun to rotate faster. I need to spin it a full one-eighty to get the frozen pipes in the sun.

The gravity seems to get even heavier, and this time there's real pain: a headache so intense that I cry out. I lose my grip on the controls, and my body thuds to the floor, sending an arrow of pain into my arms when they hit the deck.

It would be so easy just to lie here. My entire body feels as if huge weights are pinning it to the floor. But I push myself up, groaning with the effort. I get my right forearm on the control panel, and raise my eyes to the screen. Chengshi has moved – it's in direct sunlight. But the station is still spinning too slowly. If I don't make this happen faster, I'm going to pass out. There'll be nobody to slow the spin rate.

Gritting my teeth, I reach upwards – it feels like my wrist is connected to the floor with huge rubber bands – and push the spin control right up.

71

Prakesh

Madala is more spry than he looks, hobbling along in an odd, loping gait. Prakesh and Indira have to jog to keep up. And he has friends. As they move down the levels, he stops to rap on hab doors. Their little group swells. First it's joined by a family – husband and wife, their teenage son – and then a thick-set man with long, pale dreadlocks falls in alongside them, shouldering a steel bar like it was made of foam rubber.

Dreads passes around a canteen, and everybody takes a long swig. Sweat is running into Prakesh's eyes, stinging hot, and he has to keep blinking it away.

"So what we do?" says Madala, turning to Prakesh.

"What do you mean?"

There's a shout from behind him. They all turn to see two men fighting, slamming into the corridor walls, tangling over what looks like a single protein bar.

Madala gestures. "That. What we do about that? About everything?"

"I don't..." Prakesh says, but he can feel everyone looking at him. He drops his eyes for a second, and only raises them again when the man with the dreadlocks speaks.

"Madala says you saved him," the man says. "He trusts you. That means I trust you. Tell us where to go."

The rest of the group murmurs assent. Indira nods vigorously, pounding her fist into her palm.

The words are on Prakesh's lips, out before he can stop them. "We can't do anything about the big fights. But maybe we can break a few of the smaller ones."

"What good will it do?" The question comes from someone Prakesh didn't even know was there, a skinny young woman with a stern face and short, spiky hair. She reminds him of Riley a little, and he has to force himself to answer.

"We stop a small one, we get more people. Maybe we can stop one of the bigger ones."

"You heard Darnell. We're all gonna cook. We should be heading up to Apex and—"

"No," Prakesh says firmly. "Apex is taken care of. Our job is down here."

Dreads says, "Why don't we go down to the mess? It was crazy when I was there earlier."

Prakesh nods. "All right."

The woman with the spiky hair shrugs. "Whatever you say, boss."

The Apogee mess hall is on Level 2, a square room with lurid orange walls – a misguided attempt, early on in the station's life, to make the place cheery. There are big metal tables and benches scattered across the room. Some of the tables have been overturned, as if to act as barricades. And there are people, dozens of them, clustered around the long food service counter and spilling out of the kitchens at the back of the room. The noise is cacophonous – the sound of people gone beyond fear and rage, into a kind of helpless panic.

Once more, Prakesh feels everyone looking at him, and when he reaches inside himself to figure out what to do, he's surprised to find the answer waiting for him.

He turns to the two biggest people in the group – the man with the dreads, and the teenager. "You two. Go break up as many fights as you can. Don't hurt anyone who doesn't try to hurt you. Everyone else, find something to make noise with. Pots, chairs, utensils."

For a moment, nobody moves. Then Dreads grabs the boy and starts jogging towards the kitchen. Madala and Indira and the others begin hunting, picking up anything that looks like it can make a noise.

Prakesh rights a table, kicking it down with a bang. The sound cuts through everything, but not one of the looters so much as glances in his direction. Ignoring the sick feeling in the pit of his stomach, he climbs up on the table, cupping his hands around his mouth.

"Everybody – listen to me," he shouts. He tries to be as strident and authoritative as he can, but he might as well be trying to shout a message to Jupiter. Nobody pays him any attention.

He looks back at Madala, intending to tell everyone to start making as much noise as possible to focus the looters' attention. He feels a twinge in his shoulder blades as he turns, ignores it, and then the twinge grabs on and pulls.

Prakesh cries out, dropping to one knee on the table, his hands flying to his neck. At first, he thinks someone hit him with something, but through sweat-stung eyes he can see that everyone else is feeling it too. The looters are screaming in pain. Madala and Indira are flat on the floor, reaching for each other.

The pressure increases, pushing Prakesh down onto the metal surface of the table. His head is pounding. *It's the gravity*, he thinks. *Darnell's going to spin us out of control.*

Just when it seems like the pressure can't get worse, it does. As his vision shrinks to a tiny bright spot at the end of a dark tunnel, Prakesh hears glass cracking, and the pained sound of metal beginning to bend.

72

Riley

The weight between my shoulder blades pushes down harder, and my raised hand slams back onto the panel. What must it be like in the rest of the station? People pushed to the floor. Metal beginning to kink and grind as the gravity forces it outwards. The trees in the Air Lab, bending under the pressure, branches snapping.

One of the screens on the other side of the room is flashing red. A calm voice echoes through the control room: "Warning. Horizontal thrusters overheating. Reduce rotation rate immediately."

Come on.

For the second time, I push myself up. My muscles feel like they're going to tear apart. One arm. Two. Even raising my eyes to the screen takes an effort, like they're being held in a vice.

And as I look, I see that Apogee has slipped into the sunlight. Gardens and Chengshi are already there. With a final burst of energy, I slam my finger onto the screen, pulling back the rotation rate.

This time, there is a noise – like a giant fan powering

down. I slide to the floor, gasping for air. Gradually, the weights that have been placed across my body lift off.

It's a few minutes before the gravity is back to normal. When I get to my feet, I realise that my legs are trembling. I have to steady myself using the control panels, and it takes me a little while to get back to the other side of the room. The temperature has risen another degree, to 47.5 Celsius.

I try to activate the convection fins again, tapping the tiny triangles. The same error flashes up. Extreme temperatures.

I force myself to wait. A minute passes. Two. I try again.

This time, there's no error message. The green triangles all flick to solid. After another long minute, the average temperature reading drops to 46.

I've done it. The fins on the hull will be working again, venting the heat back into space. It'll take a while, but the temperature will come back down. The enormous amount of heat generated by the million or so people here will vanish. Whatever happens now, we're not going to roast to death.

I'm too exhausted to cheer. I just smile. And all I can think is: *you might make smoke bombs, Carver, but I bet you've never spun an entire space station.*

But something nags at me. I haven't had to use Iapetus, the piece of information Grace Garner and Marshall Foster died for. I'm missing something.

I need to get the Apex doors open – if I can get some stompers in here, this will all go a lot faster. I'm more confident now, and it doesn't take me long to find the screen which controls the doors. A wireframe model of the sector appears on screen, with red markers for where each door is. I tap the option to Open All.

The screen flashes red, firing up another error

message. I very nearly put a fist through the glass, but instead, I take another deep breath, and make myself read the message.

Temperature imbalance detected.

The names of the sectors are scrolling underneath it – all over 40 Celsius, except for Apex, sitting at 22.

Access to sector will remain restricted until temperature balance has been restored. Lift restriction when this occurs?

I hit *Confirm*. No telling how long that'll take, but it's a start. As soon as the convection fins have done their work, the doors to Apex will spring open. Now I just have to figure out what to do until then.

I'm about to step away from the screens when one of the other menu options catches my eye. *Comms*.

I open it up. A list of sectors appear – numbered, not named – and they're all set to Inactive. I change that, then speak as clearly as I can. There's no way of knowing if my words are going out – there's no microphone visible. But I say the words anyway.

73

Prakesh

Prakesh comes back.

He's lying on the floor of the mess, and the pain between his shoulder blades is slipping away. The inside of his mouth is dry, as if he's woken up with a killer hangover.

He raises his head, blinking against the light. Madala and Indira are unconscious, splayed out next to each other. Prakesh gets to his knees, fighting off a sudden burst of nausea, and sees Dreads slumped against an upturned table. The man is staring up at the ceiling, as if daring it to fall on him.

Prakesh uses a chair to pull himself up. His legs feel like they're made of mashed potato, and for a second he's not entirely sure where he is. Then he catches sight of the serving area and the kitchen beyond, packed with groggy people swaying to unsteady life, and it all comes rushing back.

Prakesh grabs the table he kicked upright, and pulls himself onto it. It's all he can do not to lose his balance – the world goes woozy for a second, and the black tunnel threatens to come back, feathering the edges of his vision. He pushes past it, raises his hands to his mouth.

"Everybody – listen to me."

In the stunned silence of the mess hall, his voice is impossible to ignore. Dozens of eyes turn towards him, surprise and hostility pinning him to the spot. He pushes past those, too.

"This is what he wants," he says, jabbing a finger at the ceiling. He should have pointed at the comms screen, sitting in a top corner of the room like a malevolent god, but it doesn't matter. They know who he means.

"He wants us fighting. He wants us to hurt each other. And if we keep doing it, then he wins. Simple as that. There's enough food for everybody, if we work together."

More silence meets him. The crowd is recovering from the effects of the gravity increase now, and he can see them starting to mutter to one another. One or two are even turning away, back to the kitchens and stores, as if to get a head start on the others.

"I know everyone is scared," Prakesh says, but it's no use. More and more of them are turning away. In desperation, Prakesh hunts through the faces of the crowd, eventually stopping on a young woman. She's about Riley's age, with a red shawl wrapped around her shoulders. She's got a child pulled close to her, a little boy, her hands on his shoulders. Both of them are looking back at him, and it's not anger that Prakesh sees in their eyes. It's confusion, and fear.

He tries again, speaking to the mother, to the little boy. "I know everyone is scared. You want to feed your families. You want to get back some control. You want to protect the people closest to you."

He pauses for a second. The table creaks under him, and he feels someone moving to his side. Dreads. He glances at Prakesh, and gives a short nod.

"Right now," Prakesh says, "the woman I love is in danger. She's risking her life for us – for you – to stop Oren

Darnell. And that scares the hell out of me, because I don't know how to help her, and she might not make it back. But you can't just care about the people closest to you. That's what Outer Earth has been about for so long: look out for you and yours, and screw everyone else. We can't do that. Not now. The only way we make it through this is if we help each other."

For a long second, Prakesh is sure he's blown it, that the crowd is going to ignore him. But the silence stretches on, and even those who were heading back towards the kitchens are staring at him.

The comms system crackles to life.

A horrified gasp ripples through the crowd. Even Prakesh jumps, glancing up at the comms screen, expecting Darnell's face to appear. But there's no image. There's just a voice. And as Prakesh hears it, his heart almost explodes out of his chest.

Go, Riley, go.

74

Riley

"This is Riley Hale. I'm in the control room in Apex. Oren Darnell is dead, and I've turned the heat convectors back on. I . . ."

I swallow. My next words were about to be: Okwembu is responsible. She did it all. But before I can utter the words, I realise that they won't help. People won't believe me. I have to find her. I have to *make* her tell them herself. Somehow.

"Whoever's listening, none of this was my fault. I am not responsible. But I will find the person who is."

I can't think of anything more to say. I step away from the screen, and cast another glance around the room. All the readouts seem to be OK, and the warm orange light from the screens seems oddly reassuring.

I'm about to leave to search for Okwembu when something catches my eye. One of the screens at the end of the room, showing a view that I haven't seen in years.

The Earth.

Scorched brown land, dull blue ocean. Swirling, simmering clouds, flecked brown and white. It's almost unchanged from the last time I was shown a picture of it, years ago.

But there's something else there.

Something horribly familiar, hanging in the middle of the camera's view, stark against the curve of the planet.

Every muscle in my body is paralysed. My mouth has gone completely dry, my thoughts frozen in place. I know that silhouette. I know it because I've seen it more times than I can think of. On broadcasts, in pictures. On the Memorial wall in Apogee.

It's the *Akua Maru*. The ship from the Earth Return mission.

I tell myself to stop being ridiculous, that it can't be the *Akua*, that this is archive video, something set up by Okwembu as a cruel, cruel taunt.

My hand moves without me telling it to, touching the screen gently. An orange square blinks around the form of the *Akua*. An option appears at the bottom, displayed in the orange light. *Ship broadcast frequencies: Inactive.*

I touch the screen, and the broadcast activates. I manage to say one word.

"Hello?"

For a long moment, there's nothing. Then there's a burst of static, emanating from speakers somewhere in the room. And I hear a voice, twisted with time and distance, as familiar as my own.

"Janice?" says the voice. "Is that you?"

I don't know what to do. My hand is still on the screen, and I can't pull it away.

"Are you there?" the voice continues. An edge of anger has crept into it. "Answer me. We don't have much time, and everything must be ready for my return. Respond."

With my eyes on the ship, I manage to speak one more word.

"Dad?"

75

Riley

At first, there's just silence, broken by the crackle of the radio signal in the empty room.

I can't take my eyes off the screen. I can see the *Akua* more clearly now: the curve of her hull, the swept-down fins jutting off the sides, the cylindrical body. It doesn't seem real.

The static swells and roars. "Who is this? Who are you?" The voice fires a bright line back down the years to a man standing tall in his captain's uniform, looking down at me, with a gentle half-smile on his face.

"It's me, Dad," I say, my voice shaking. "It's Riley."

There's contempt in his voice when he replies. "I don't know that name."

"Dad..."

"And I don't know your voice either. Whoever you are."

"Dad, I promise, I'm—"

"No!" The transmission is so loud and so sudden that I nearly fall backwards in surprise. The voice is warped now, malformed, not just by distance and signal quality, but by something else. "Riley is dead. She's dead. You're a liar!"

"No," I whisper. "I'm not dead." And then, louder: "Please, Dad. Please listen to me."

"Don't call me that," he snarls, and the venom in his voice burns a horrible, ragged hole in my mind. "You're not my daughter. Do you hear me? You're not her."

The static vanishes, plunging the room into silence.

I hammer the touch-screen, desperately trying to raise him, my voice cracking and turning from a harsh whisper into a full-on scream. Every fibre in my body wants me to run; to run and run and never look back. But I can't run from this.

It's some time before I can raise him again. When the static returns, I don't hear anything for a long time, nothing but my breathing. Someone has taken the world I knew and turned it inside out. There is so much I want to say, but every time I try, the words won't come.

Eventually, he says, "Whoever you are, it doesn't matter. You'll all pay for what you've done."

I can't make sense of his words. It's like I can hear them individually, but not connect them. There's no way my father could be the one speaking them.

I force myself to stay calm. "Dad," I start, but then my voice cracks again. "Dad, how is this possible? You're still alive – how . . ."

"Why do you keep calling me that?" he says, but there's something else in his voice beyond anger. A tiny, desperate note of hope.

I close my eyes, and slowly say, "Your name is John Abraham Hale. You were born on December Tenth, in Apogee. You married Arianna Tahangai on Outer Earth when you were twenty-one years old."

"None of that means anything. That doesn't prove who you are."

I keep my eyes closed. "When I was five, you showed me one of your space rocks. You got it from your missions on the asteroid catchers. Mom didn't want you showing it to me – I think she thought it was radioactive or something. But when she was away you took it out and let me hold it, one night when you were putting me to bed. The rock had so many colours in it – we tried to name all of them, and then we made up names for the colours we hadn't seen before. Afterwards, we—"

"Stop," he says, and this time his voice is quiet. "This... this is impossible. You can't be her."

"No, Dad. I'm here and I'm alive and please, please talk to me."

"Riley" – and, at last, it's his own voice that cracks, see-sawing between fear and disbelief – "how are you doing this? Where are you?"

"In the main control room in Apex."

"Is Janice Okwembu with you?"

Okwembu. I'd forgotten about her. I look over my shoulder at the door, but it's still shut. "No, Dad, she's not," I reply.

Something catches my eye. A tiny lens, positioned at the top of the touch-screen. "Dad," I say. "There's a camera in the control room. Do you have one too?"

"Yes," he replies. His voice has a new note of strength in it. "Yes, of course. I'll try to establish a link."

It takes a little while, and a lot of navigating through sub-menus to do it, but eventually a tiny blinking icon appears in the bottom right corner. I touch it; the *Akua*, and the stars behind it, vanish. The screen is black, and for a moment I think the link has failed – but then the blackness moves, and I realise it's his body close to the screen, blocking out the light. The feed glitches and stutters, but it works. He moves into view, and for the first time in seven years, I see my father.

The man staring back at me is a ruin, a scarred, wrinkled old man, his face ringed by a dirty, matted shock of hair. His eyes – at first, they're as dull and lifeless as the planet he travelled too. But when they meet mine, recognition dawns, flaring like a tiny star. And in the crags and furrows on the face, I recognise him too.

He's wearing a tattered tunic. I can just make out a piece of faded red piping on the shoulder. Behind him, the cabin of the *Akua* is dark, with a few flickering lights illuminating black metal and coiled cables.

"Oh, Riley," he whispers. "I – I thought you were – she told me you were dead," he finishes, and a single tear falls down his cheek.

I had defences up the moment I first heard his voice. I didn't think about it, but I did. When I see the tear, every one of them cracks and collapses. My own tears come, too late, seven years too late.

"I'm here," is all I can get out, before the sobs come, thick and fast. Now it's not the world that's ended. It's me. Every memory I've ever had of him swims to the surface, one by one: him picking me up, holding me above his head. With my mother, smiling at me from the door of our quarters. And that last goodbye, before the Earth Return mission, standing above me, the smile on his face warm and genuine. I can't connect them to what I see on the screen.

"You're alive, Dad," I say after a time, wiping away tears. "You're alive! How? How did you do it? What about the rest of the crew? Where have you—"

He holds up a hand, and for a fleeting moment I catch a glimpse of the captain he once was.

"The first thing you need to know, my darling, is that this ship is on a course for Outer Earth. It's coming, and in less than two hours it will collide with you. The whole station will be destroyed."

"What?" I say, confused. "Dad, is there a problem with the engines? We can fix it. We can come to you."

"No!" His face twists with fury. I physically recoil from the screen; I can't understand the look on his face. "This is how it has to be. This is how it's meant to be."

"Why?"

"Because," he says, speaking through gritted teeth, forcing himself under control, "you left us to die. Everyone on Outer Earth turned their backs on us."

"I don't understand. They said the *Akua* burned up in the atmosphere."

He laughs, a sound tinged with bitterness. "We didn't burn up. The reactor malfunctioned during the entry process. We had to crash-land, bring the whole thing down manually. And everyone, every single person on Outer Earth, let it happen. You did nothing. You just went on with your lives."

My hands are gripping the edge of the control panel, the knuckles white. I release them slowly, keeping my eyes on the figure in the screen, watching him as one might watch someone wielding a knife. What he's saying can't be true. There's no possible way a ship could crash, spend seven years on a broken planet, and then somehow manage to find its way back.

"Tell me what happened," I say. "Tell me from the beginning."

My father appraises me, his eyes locked on mine. After a minute, he says, "It took years to develop all the machines needed to establish a colony back home. Earth's biosphere was a disaster, and we had to try and fix it. Outer Earth couldn't hold us forever."

He pauses. "I should have been home in two years. With you. With your mother."

"What went wrong?"

"Something happened in the reactor. An explosion of some kind. How we didn't burn up in the atmosphere, I'll never know. We managed to put down in a place called Kamchatka, in what used to be eastern Russia. It was a miracle that we were alive. Nearly all the basic functions of the ship just shut down."

"Then why did they tell us that the ship had been destroyed? Why lie to us?"

"A man named Marshall Foster was Station Command for the mission. He—"

"I know who he was."

He gives a harsh laugh. "Then imagine if a rescue mission had been mounted. There'd be a chance to investigate the cause of the explosion properly. If it turned out that Foster was in some way responsible for what happened, if it was down to something he missed or a calculation he got wrong, then his reputation would be ruined."

"Dad, that doesn't make any sense."

"It does, if you knew Foster. He was always obsessed with his own legacy. He wanted to be on the right side of history. Better that the mission failed because of an unknown mechanical issue than because of something he might have done. He wouldn't risk it. He thought we could be forgotten about. And you – all of you – believed him. You're as guilty as he is."

"Dad, that's not true. If we'd known, if everybody had known, we would have done something. We would have sent help."

"We sent endless messages. Activated our distress beacons. And we got nothing. We thought someone would come for us. But as each day went past, and each year, we realised that Foster had left us to rot, locking our signal away, and everyone on Outer Earth just stood back and let him do it."

"No. We were lied to. All of us. If anybody had known, a ship would have been sent. You have to believe me."

He turns away from the camera. I can hear him muttering something, but I can't make out the words.

A thought occurs to me. "Dad, how did you survive? How did you eat?"

"Oh," he says dismissively, still staring at something I can't see. "A lot of our terraforming machinery was destroyed during the crash, but we managed to get some of it working again. Eventually, I worked out how to turn the power back on. How to rebuild the ship."

"But food..."

There's a long pause. Eventually, his eyes meet mine, and the face that turns back to me is filled with anguish. "I've done terrible things, Riley. Things you can't imagine. We turned on each other, and I did what I had to. I survived."

I raise my hand to my mouth, all the blood freezing in my veins.

"I worked for years to repair the system," he says. "It was so hard. And there was no one for a long, long time. I forgot how to speak, for a while. All I did was work on the reactor. I was convinced the *Akua* could fly again. But even if I did get it working, I couldn't have gone anywhere. Our guidance system was damaged. Without precise data, there was nowhere we could go. I'd almost given up hope.

"And then one day, there's a signal. And it's *her*. Telling me she knows I'm here. That she wants to help, that she wants me to use the *Akua* to destroy the station."

"But why? You stayed alive for so long..."

"The only thing that kept me going," he says, "was you and your mother. As long as you were alive, I would stay alive too. I would get back to you – that's what I told myself. But Janice said...she told me you were both dead."

"You could have come home."

"For what? The only reason for keeping myself alive was gone. Outer Earth and the people inside it hadn't just left me to die. They'd taken the ones I loved the most. I wanted them to suffer."

I don't want to picture what he must have gone through, but it's impossible not to. Seven years in the cold, alone, barely hanging on. Aware that the people orbiting the Earth could save you – and believing that they chose not to. And then, right when you've lost the only thing that keeps you going, you're handed a way out. A way to make your death mean something.

"She gave me data," he says. "Schematics, flight paths, positions in space. I'd worked out how to get the *Akua* moving again, but I couldn't steer it. Not without her help. But we did it. It took two long years, but eventually I could point the ship towards Outer Earth."

"Dad, that's impossible. You couldn't..."

"Oh couldn't I?" he says. His voice has turned to ice. "I've spent my life in space. And I've spent years on this ship. All I needed was Outer Earth's projected flight path, and I could line us up exactly."

"But she'd die too."

"Don't you see? That was her goal all along. She told me that there was no place for humans in the universe any more."

"You believed her?"

"What did I care?" he says. "She was giving me everything I needed. Her beliefs were none of my concern."

All at once, everything comes together. I see the *Akua Maru*, travelling at thousands of miles an hour, colliding with Outer Earth. I see the station tear apart, cracking in two, see it consumed in fire. No one will survive.

Your world's going to end.

I pull my jacket around me. No, not my jacket: his. The one thing he left me. I push back the urge to tear it off, to hurl it on the ground and never look at it again. He must see the look on my face, sense the horror I feel, because his own expression softens a little. "Riley, if I'd known you were alive...if I was told..."

Deep in the hurt, in the fear and the confusion swirling in my mind, there's a tiny core of hope. I lean close to the camera, forcing myself to stare into those eyes. I hunt for something beyond the hatred.

"Yes, they lied," I say eventually. "They lied about everything. About you. About the ship. Foster lied to us. But Dad, I'm telling you the truth. I'm alive. And I love you. I love you. Please don't do this."

For what seems like an age, he stares at me. Then his face falls, and something in my heart shatters. John Hale, so proud, so courageous, has reached the end.

"I can move the station," I say, desperation in my voice. "I know how to turn it – I can figure out how to move it away from the *Akua*."

"Riley, I'm sorry," he says. "The ship's reactor is still active, but the main thrusters have died. Even if I kill the reactor now, I can't slow us down. Moving the station out of its orbit will take too long. It's too big. There's nothing we can do."

76

Riley

I expect to feel something. But there's nothing there. I find myself not wanting to look at him, my eyes fixed on the control panel instead. Looking at its lights. Its clean metal surface. It can control an entire space station – turn the lights on or off, cut the oxygen supply, kill the water or make it flow freely. All that power. And it means nothing.

Again, I search for something to hold on to. But even when I focus on the faces of Prakesh, of Carver and Kev, there's no reaction.

On the screen, my father says, "Your mother. Is she…"

My voice is flat. "She died a year after you…after we were told what happened. She just gave up."

I look at him. Sadness etches his face. "Who…" He licks his cracked lips, and won't meet my eyes. "Who took care of you?"

"Nobody. Myself. But I survived." I pause, weighing up how much he deserves to know, but then decide that I don't care any more. "I became a tracer, Dad. One of the best. Someone good taught me. She showed me how to run."

I see Amira, holding her hand out to me. Again, nothing but a creeping numbness.

"I am so proud of you," he says, and the sadness in his voice bubbles over. He's crying openly now, the tears streaming down his face. "Riley, I wish..."

"No." The hardness in my voice startles me. But I grasp that tiny thread of steel, hold it close. "It's over. We're done."

My legs give out, and I collapse to the ground, leaning up against the console. Behind me, the man on the screen tries to talk, pleading with me. I shut my eyes. Maybe if I keep them closed for long enough, I won't even feel it when the ship hits.

But something tugs at the edge of my mind. It takes me a minute to find it.

Iapetus.

Slowly, I pull myself up. My father has gone silent, but he's still there, staring at me, leaning back in his chair. He opens his mouth to say something, but I cut him off.

"There's something you're not telling me," I begin, struggling to find the words. "Marshall Foster's dead. He was killed a few days ago. But there was something he wanted to keep secret, something he locked away. A word. Iapetus."

His face, which darkened at the mention of Foster's name, creases with puzzlement. "Iapetus?" he says – then surprise turns to recognition, a brief flash across his face. He tries to hide it, but I catch him too soon.

"You know what it means, don't you?" I say.

He shakes his head. "A safe-word, that's all. Something to secure communications." But he avoids my eyes.

"Dad," I say. The word feels strange in my mouth. "You have to tell me what it means."

"It's nothing."

"You're lying," I say. "Is this what Mom would have wanted? For you to lie to your daughter?"

"Don't you talk about her."

"Why, Dad? She's gone. She's been gone for a long time. It's just me, and I'm asking you. What does it mean?"

He looks as if he's about to smash his camera, cutting off communications all together. But then he takes a deep breath. "It's an override. One half of a dual fail-safe."

"Overriding what?"

He seems to weigh up the question, deciding how to answer. When he does, his voice is resigned. "On every mission, the station command and the ship's captain choose code words. You can't use one without the other. Foster chose his, I chose mine. In the event of…in the event of an accident, when a ship malfunctions or looks like it might damage the station, both code words can be entered into the system."

I wait for him to continue, but he seems to be searching for the words. "What happens then?" I ask.

He seems to take an age to form the words. "It sends a signal which causes a reactor override. Detonation."

Detonation.

Before I'm even aware I'm doing it, my fingers are navigating through the on-screen controls. I catch the look of alarm on his face as understanding dawns. "Riley," he says, his voice thick. "What are you doing?"

"Whatever I can," I mutter. My fingers seem to work of their own accord, flying through the menus, flicking through *Capacitor Control* and *Reactor Data* and *Network Variance* until it alights on *Ship Communications*, and then – *Override.*

"Riley, please," comes the voice from the speakers. His eyes are serious now, hunting mine down, until eventually I'm forced to look at them. "I have to finish the mission."

Something snaps. We both start screaming at each other at the same time, our voices cut with anger and fear. It takes me some time to understand the words coming out of my mouth. "You want to kill us all!" I yell. "You say you love me, but you're going to destroy us. Destroy me. Is this what you want? What Mom would have wanted?"

In a rage, I stab the screen, activating the Override option. The computer begins flashing up data on the *Akua*: ship reactor temperature, rate of rotation – and trajectory. On the bottom left of the screen, a little icon appears: an exclamation mark, surrounded by a small triangle, blinking on and off. Somewhere in the control room, a calm voice quietly says: "Warning: proximity alert."

Outer Earth, it seems, has finally worked out that it's in danger.

Next to the icon are the words: *Transmit override command*. With my father still yelling in the background, I activate the option. Every bit of text on the screen vanishes, replaced by an on-screen keyboard, and the words: *Confirmation Code 1*.

I don't think. I enter the word Iapetus and hit the confirm option, wanting everything to be over, wanting the world to go away. Not wanting to face the man on the screen.

The word on the screen turns green, blinks for a moment, and vanishes, replaced by a text box labelled *Confirmation Code 2*.

Foster chose his, I chose mine.

No.

"You're like your mother," he says. The words are a shard of ice, and the chill that sweeps through me is so intense that I find I can't move my fingers. I can't move anything. "She was strong. Stronger than I ever was. She would never have wanted this. Any of it. I'm sorry. Oh gods, Riley, I'm sorry."

I want to say something. Anything. But nothing will come. Every last bit of emotion is dried up, gone, as empty as space itself.

Eventually, he says, "It's asking you for a second code, isn't it?"

I whisper, "Yes."

"I waited so long," he says, as if he's speaking to himself. "And all this time, you were right there. You were alive."

It takes me more than one try to get the words out, but as I do, I'm surprised by the strength in my voice. "Whatever you left behind, it's not like that any more. There are things on this station worth saving. Things I could show you if..." The words catch in my throat. "Things that I love. People that I love. You have to tell me the second code, Dad. Please."

"Riley, no."

"I am your daughter, and I am begging you not to do this. You wanted to die? This is your chance. You were lied to for so long. You were controlled and manipulated. Both of us were. But you can choose, Dad. You can choose."

The agony pulsing in my heart is reflected on his face. "I love you," I say again, my voice tiny, almost buried in the thrum of the electronics.

Finally, his hand touches the camera, a single finger pressing against it. It has to be soon. It has to be soon, or every ounce of me will turn to dust.

"The second code is *Riley*," he says, holding back the words, as if trying to keep them from escaping. "You need to enter your own name."

What?

"Why, Dad?"

"Because I thought that if everything went wrong, the last thing I wanted to say was your name."

It takes me a few tries to punch the letters into the display, but in what seems like no time at all, my name is on the screen, glowing in orange text over his face. Below the word blinks the option: *Confirm?*

His hand is on the monitor again. "Riley... I love y—"

My finger touches the screen for the last time.

77

Riley

I don't know how long I lie there. Time passes, but I don't know how much. I feel tears streaming down my face, and I desperately want to cry out, but nothing comes.

After a while, there are strong hands lifting me up. It occurs to me that I might be dead. The thought is vague, distant, like a shape at the end of a dark corridor. I find I don't care all that much.

I'm not aware of opening my eyes, or even of focusing on my surroundings. There are shapes, and light, but it's a long time before they resolve into something I recognise. Janice Okwembu is sitting in a chair opposite me, her hands in her lap. She looks expectant, as if I'm supposed to say something.

Hate. That seems to be the appropriate response. But there's nothing there. The numbness I felt earlier is total. My wounds don't hurt. My stomach is a hollow drum. My mind is blank. It's not that I can't hold on to any feeling; it's as if there's nothing there to hold on to.

"Can you hear me, Ms Hale?" Okwembu asks, her head tilted slightly to one side. "I want you to listen very closely to what I'm about to say."

My eyes fix on hers. Her words stir something deep in my gut, and slowly, ever so slowly, hate begins to uncoil.

If she sees it in my gaze, she ignores it. "You'll want to hurt me. That's understandable. But I can't let you do that." She raises her hand, and I see she's holding a stinger.

"Now, I could simply kill you, right here and now," she says. "But I think you deserve better than that. You've performed brilliantly. Better than I ever could have hoped. And so, I'm going to give you a choice."

I have to will my lips to form the words. "A choice?"

She nods, and throws something at my feet. A knife. Polished steel, with a black handle. It clatters on the steel floor, spinning in place. I reach down to pick it up, keeping my eyes on her the whole time.

"You're going to die, Ms Hale. Whether you die a hero or a traitor is up to you. That's your choice. If you try to attack me, I'll put a bullet right through you. You'll die, and I'll make sure everyone knows that you were working with Darnell, that you were part of the Sons of Earth, that you brought back the *Akua* to destroy us. The name Hale will come to mean traitor. You'll be the daughter who betrayed her own father. Your friends will be too scared to speak your name. I will destroy everything you stood for."

"They won't believe you," I whisper.

"They'll believe what I tell them. They always do. But if you take your own life – I'd suggest cutting your wrists – then I'll make sure that you're remembered as a hero. You'll be the one who made the ultimate sacrifice to save Outer Earth. And while you couldn't live with yourself afterwards, your name will be written into history. When we return to Earth, they will build cities dedicated to you."

When we return?

She dips her head slightly. "I'm offering you this choice because I respect you, and I respect what you have gone through. I'm going to lead Outer Earth into a new era of peace, but for that to happen, you have to die. Your only choice is how you are remembered."

I touch the blade to the skin of my left wrist. It's sharp. The cuts will be clean.

I can't possibly do this. I can't do what she says.

But then that quiet voice whispers, *Keep her talking. Buy some time.*

I think about attacking her, or diving away. But I know that I won't be able to move fast enough. There's only one way this can end.

In two quick movements, I cut shallow slashes across my left wrist. There's pain, but it's not the stinging agony I expected. It's a distant ache, like something felt by someone else. The blood blooms instantly, a steady, pulsing flow, running into my palm and dripping downwards. The drops drip gently onto the floor.

I try to transfer the blade to my left hand to cut my other wrist, but it too falls to the floor, the clang echoing around the control room.

Okwembu nods. One wrist seems to be enough for her. "You're going to be a hero," she says. Incredibly, she smiles.

"Why?" I ask, and it's then that the pain really comes, a stinging so intense that I have to bite my lip to keep from crying out.

"Because sometimes the only way to restore order is to create chaos," she replies, speaking slowly, as if to someone very young.

The realisation dawns gradually. "This was never about saving the Earth from humans, was it?"

"The Earth is none of my concern – not yet. I wanted to save this station."

"Save it? From what?"

"From us." She's quiet for a moment. Then she says, "The council had been losing control of Outer Earth for a long time. Gangs. Crime. One riot. Two. Then war. The station would destroy itself, and I knew that if we left things as they were, it would fall away from us. When that happened, there'd be no hope."

"So you decided to rescue Outer Earth by trying to kill everyone on it? Help me out here."

She continues as if I hadn't spoken. "So I created the Sons of Earth. A terrorist group, hell bent on wiping out humanity. When I defeated them – or helped defeat them – then the entire station would unite under me. My power would be absolute. I could fix it all. Get rid of the gangs, empower the protection officers, control the tracers. I could rule, and not as a council member, not as someone held back by others, having to put every decision to a committee of fools."

"You're insane."

"It might seem that way, but only because you don't yet understand. I've learned a few things about power."

"Like?"

"Nothing unifies people like a common enemy, and fighting through hardship which can be blamed on that enemy will forge them in steel. And Darnell did have such useful ideas about human extinction. It was so easy to let him believe that I wanted the *Akua Maru* to collide with us, for the good of the Earth."

There's a lot of blood now. It forms a dark pool at my feet, draining into the seams of the plating. The blankness has been replaced by a faint dizziness.

"Foster hid your father's beacon transmission deep in the system," she says. "It didn't show up in the logs. Until one day, I saw something in the sub-routines, deep in the code. When I realised that the *Akua* wasn't only intact but potentially still functioning, I saw the opportunity."

Another stab of pain shoots up my arm, and without thinking, I clutch my wrist. I cry out, and let go of the wrist as if it's on fire.

"Did you hear me, Ms Hale?" she says. When I look up at her, she seems to flutter in and out of existence in front of me. "I managed to keep my communications with your father private, and with the information I gave him two years ago, we were able to plot his course exactly."

"But Foster…"

Okwembu leans forward slightly, and looks right into my eyes, like she badly needs me to understand. "For every ship mission," she says, "an override code is locked away behind a retinal scanner. The only person who has access to it is the mission commander. Standard procedure, in case a ship malfunctions and endangers the station. Foster could hide the *Akua*'s beacon transmission, but to try and erase the override code would have invited suspicion, so he just left it there. I don't believe he ever thought it would need to be used."

She smooths out a crease in the leg of her jumpsuit, picking at an invisible speck of lint.

"I knew he'd never tell me the override code. I asked anyway. He claimed he didn't remember, which was a lie. He was suspicious, of course, but he would never do anything to dig up the past. Same old Foster – always hoarding information, like little stores of food he could put away for when he needed them most. He was a real politician, that one."

"And you're not?"

She just smiles, totally serene.

It's an effort to get the words out now. "Why not just hack it?"

She shakes her head. "That's the point of a retinal scanner. It's completely isolated from the rest of the network. It can't be hacked." Okwembu smiles to herself. "Not by digital means, anyway. In any event, for everything to go as planned, I had to make Darnell believe that we had to unlock the scanner, and destroy the code."

She leans back in her chair, the gun resting in her lap. "You will never know the terror I felt when I heard how Darnell had botched the retrieval of Foster's eye – by the time I found out, the protection officers had recorded it, and incinerated it." She exhales slowly. "I should have got that eye a lot sooner."

"Why didn't you?"

"Darnell. If he'd had Foster killed too soon, the stompers might have had time to investigate, and link it back to him. He'd never allow that. It had to happen when everything had been set in motion. At any rate, it didn't matter. Garner saved us all. *You* saved us all."

"You used me."

It takes a long time for her to answer. When she does, there's something in her voice – not regret, but sadness. "If I'd had my way, you'd have survived along with everyone else, and never been a part of this. But I came to suspect that you knew where Garner was. If only you'd told me, all of this would have been easier. But you would never have given in. You're stubborn. Like your father."

"Don't you dare talk about him." I'm stunned to hear a version of my father's words fall so easily from my mouth. The pain in my wrists flares again.

"Once Foster's eye was found and destroyed, so was every hope of us accessing the retinal scanner," she says. "Garner was our only hope, and it would have taken too long to search the entire station."

"Amira."

"A shame," she replies, and my coil of hate seems to tighten. "She believed that fiction of Darnell's far too easily. If she'd shown a little vision, then she would have made an excellent second-in-command. Darnell wanted me to torture the whereabouts of Grace Garner out of you, but I preferred a more subtle approach. Amira provided it."

The dark place I've put Amira, Yao and Garner into is threatening to blow open, to spill its terrible memories into my mind. I push it back.

"I should have known that she wouldn't have the strength to kill you," Okwembu says. "It seems I'm not as good a judge of character as I thought. Still, every desperate situation will have an opportunity hidden in it. And you – oh, you – when you survived Amira, you provided the greatest opportunity yet. Because what better way to preserve order than to create not just an enemy, but a martyr to destroy it?"

I catch sight of one of the screens behind Okwembu. I can just make out the message on it. *Temperature equalised. Sector access granted.*

Doesn't matter. They'll never get here in time. And even if they do, they'll never believe me.

"When we realised that you were running through the Core to get to Apex, I knew how the sequence of events would have to play out," Okwembu says. "Darnell, of course, still wanted the *Akua* to destroy us. He was convinced you needed to die, and went into the Core to kill you."

"And you let him?"

"You must believe me, Ms Hale. I never, ever wanted you to go through that," she says. "I underestimated just how far gone he was. I tried to inject him with an overdose of pain medication, but it didn't work. I should have taken a more direct approach. For that, I'm sorry."

I have to force myself to speak now. I've lost all feeling in my arm; the pain is a memory, but there's a lightness there that leaves me afraid. So I find that little coil of hate in my heart, and hold on to it, mentally wrapping fingers around its scales.

"You let Darnell murder the council."

"They were weak," she says. "None of them would have had the strength to go through with the plan."

It's then that I realise that she's more insane than I could ever have imagined. Her eyes show nothing: not triumph, not reason, not elation. Just a horrible, green madness. The madness of someone who views people as playthings, as pieces in a game to be moved around at a whim.

"They would have backed out, eventually," she says. "When they saw what had to be done. And after all, one person can rule just as well as many."

A thought tugs at me. "The second code," I say. My voice is croaky, and my breaths are coming too fast. My heart is pumping quickly, far too quickly. I repeat the words, then say, "There was no way you would have got it out of him. My father. He'd never have given it to you." Even as I realise the implications of my words, a fierce pride burns in my chest.

She actually laughs. "Ms Hale. Your father gave up the code willingly."

"What?"

"The ship colliding with us would be devastating, but there was a slim chance that some parts of the station would survive. Your father knew that. So I told him that I planned to detonate the *Akua* the instant that I felt it collide with Outer Earth. Maximum destruction. He believed me, and gave me what I needed."

Those insane, empty eyes fix on mine. "You saved Outer Earth, Riley Hale. And no one will ever forget you."

Her words are drowned out by the pounding of my heart. There's a blackness at the corners of my vision, and all I want to do is close my eyes. Close my eyes and slip away, go somewhere with no pain and no memories. I can't focus on Okwembu any more; the edges of her form keep blurring, though whether it's because of tears in my eyes or not, I can't say. There's no time left.

Noise. Banging. Something outside the room. Feet on steel plating. With an effort, I lift my head.

There's a shadow in the doorway to the control room, silhouetted against lights that seem far too bright. It's a man – he's holding a stinger, pointed right at us.

No – not at us. At her.

The man speaks. "Janice Okwembu – get on the ground. Now!" Other shapes appear behind the man, blocking out the light.

Okwembu is looking around, first confused, then fearful. She turns to me, and her expression darkens with anger.

"You're right," I whisper. "You're not a very good judge of character."

Realisation dawns on her face. Maybe she sees something on the screens, or maybe the dots just connect in her mind, but she suddenly understands.

The comms system.

The one I turned on, and never turned off. The one which broadcasts to the entire station.

I guess it really was working.

I hear the men entering the room, heading right towards us. But by then, my eyes are closed, and I've fallen sideways off the chair. The coil of hate has come loose, slipping free. There's nothing to hold on to now.

My body doesn't slam into the cold steel of the floor. Instead, I just fall.

Forever.

78

Riley

First, there's nothing.

And then, after some time has passed – hours maybe, or decades – there's something.

Voices. They're muffled, and I can't make out the words. I want to speak to them, to let them know that I'm here. But then the voices fade, and I sink back into the warm darkness.

My eyes are open, and I'm looking at a body, slumped in a chair. The head is lolling on the shoulder, the mouth slightly open. I blink, still unsure of how much time there is between when I close my eyes and when I open them. But when I do, the body is still there, and I see it's Aaron Carver.

As I watch, he stirs, then stretches, yawns, and rubs his jaw, his hand scraping on stubble. I try to say his name, but my throat is as dry and smooth as old rubber.

I must make some noise, or a movement, because suddenly, he's looking in my direction, his eyes wide. "Riley," he says in astonishment, and his voice is so loud that it causes my ears to ring. I squeeze my eyes shut, and it's at that moment that the pain strikes, stabbing into my body in so many places that I feel like I'm being ripped apart.

At the edge of my vision, I see Carver step forward and adjust something next to my head. Immediately, something cool and wonderful floods through me, first halting the pain, then turning it back. As it dwindles into nothingness, I stare up at Carver, my eyes blurring. I mouth a silent thank-you, and he reaches across and places a hand on my stomach.

It's an odd gesture, but then I remember Okwembu. Cutting my wrist. Pushing the grogginess away, I sit up, my back creaking with the effort.

"Hey, slow down, Ry. Easy," says Carver.

I'm in a bed, with crisp sheets bundled around my waist. I cough. "Where am I?" I ask. I barely recognise my own voice. It's not just croaky and dry, but older somehow.

"The hospital in Apogee," he replies. As he does so, the rest of the room snaps into focus. White, and brightly lit, filled with humming machines and clean lights.

"I didn't..." I falter. "I thought I was dead."

"You came pretty close," he says, flopping back down in the chair. "You must have had some extra blood stashed behind a lung or something, because apparently you were right on the edge. That's without talking about your other bumps, like that little opening in your side. Or the borderline hypothermia."

I catch sight of my left wrist: heavily bandaged, and quite numb.

"Oh, you'll have plenty of scars," says Carver, a weird smile on his face. "But hey, wear 'em with pride, right?"

He leans forward in his chair. "You did good, Riley. We heard you on the comms. Everybody did. I don't know how you managed to get through to Apex, but after you turned the convectors back on, everybody stopped fighting."

"Okwembu? Is she..."

"In the brig, under some serious armed guard," he says. "They're talking about keeping her there for a while, trying her when there's a new elected council. But we heard everything, the whole story. You're a genius."

I close my eyes. I suppose I should feel happiness. Or at least, relief. But instead, the coil of hate, which I thought had gone, suddenly unwinds itself, flexing deep in my stomach. I wanted her dead. I wanted her to suffer.

I push it away. "And Darnell?"

"They found his body at the Core entrance in Apex."

Suddenly, my eyes widen. "Prakesh. Kev. Where are they? Are they OK?"

Carver laughs. "Would you relax? They're fine. They're both fine. Prakesh has been kind of amazing, actually. He's taken over food distribution for, like, three sectors. You should see him, Ry. It's scary. He came to visit you a few times, but you were out of it."

"And Kev?"

"Please." He spreads his arms. "You think a few fat stompers are going to stop us? After you went into the Core, we outran them in about five seconds. Kev's all good. He's back to running cargo. Although if he hasn't made some decent trades, I'm going to kick his ass."

"How long have I been here?"

"Two days, just about."

Something he said earlier tugs at me. "You heard me on the comms system. Did you hear..."

He's avoiding my eyes now, and I know that he doesn't have to answer. The conversation with my father seems like something out of a dream. I can't recall all of it, only snatches, expressions, odd words.

I swallow. "The *Akua Maru*. Is it over?"

He stares at the floor. "The pieces missed us. Riley, I'm so sorry."

And that's when the small, dark place at the back of my mind bursts open. It's the place where I put my memories of Amira and Yao and Garner and, I now realise, my father. It fractures so suddenly that it's as if someone has punched me in the chest. The scream claws its way up my throat, ripping itself out of me like some kind of horrible, angry animal. When it finally tears free, it's as if the fracture in the dark place has spread everywhere, ripping my very soul in half. I scream, and scream, and scream, until there's a tiny jab in my neck and I sink into the darkness again, the scream dwindling to nothing.

When I come back, both Carver and Kev are there. Kev has some nasty bruises, but when he sees me, his face lights up, and he walks to the edge of the bed and hugs me. Behind him, Carver hangs back, a worried look on his face.

There's less pain than before. I manoeuvre myself into a sitting position and swing my legs off the edge of the bed. There's a dull ache, but nothing more. Can we ever run together again? Will the Dancers still exist without Amira, without Yao?

The scream, born from that coil of hate, has left behind its offspring, squatting in my gut. They'll always be there.

But I show none of this. I can't.

Instead, I stick a smile on my face, look Kev in the eye, and say, "Help me up."

He lifts me to my feet, his huge arms taking the weight of my slender frame easily. He grimaces, more in amusement than anything else. "What are you wearing?"

I look down. It's a smock of some sort, reaching to just above my knees. Slowly, I reach behind me, and feel the back of it. Or rather, where the back should be.

"Please tell me someone saved my clothes," I mutter, as Carver and Kev collapse in howls of laughter. Soon, I'm laughing too, even as I keep one hand scrunching up the fabric firmly behind my back.

They find me some trousers, a loose shirt, a spare pair of shoes. There's no sign of my father's jacket, and neither of them mention anything. For a moment, I want to ask them about it, but then I realise that if I had it back, I'd never wear it again. Maybe it's best that I don't know where it is.

The guys try and support me as we leave the room, but I shrug them off, walking hesitantly at first, and then with more confidence. Two doctors try to stop us, but I wave them aside, muttering that I'm fine.

We leave the hospital, walking down one of the corridors in the direction of the gallery. Apogee is a mess. There's trash everywhere: overturned crates, pieces of equipment, smashed lights, crumpled trays from the canteen. But oddly, it doesn't feel like a bad place. Nothing like it was when we had to escape the crowds who wanted to tear us apart. The thought is a strange one, another memory that feels like it happened in a different lifetime.

The people we pass make a pretence of ignoring us, but I catch them staring at me as we walk by. A few of them whisper to each other, and one or two even point. I guess I'm going to have to get used to that. But more than once, I'm smiled at, and one old woman even pushes aside Carver and Kev to pull me into an awkward, fumbling embrace. I'm so surprised I nearly burst out laughing, but I return the hug, and she squeezes me briefly before wandering off.

"What's happening in Apex?" I ask Carver.

He shrugs. "The council's finished. Okwembu was the only survivor, and she's in lockdown. There are some people running things, I hear. Techs mostly – nobody making any big decisions or anything, just guys keeping an eye on the main systems. I was expecting some of the gangs to try and step in, but there's been nothing."

"What's going to happen now?"

"Nobody knows. I'm kind of hoping it stays like it is for a while. I can't describe it, Ry, but I've never felt the station like this. It's almost..." he searches for the right word: "Peaceful."

"Yeah," says Kev, speaking for the first time in a while. "No fighting. It's weird."

Someone behind me barks my name, and I smile when I see who it is. Royo, limping up the corridor towards us. He's as beaten up as Apogee itself, a mess of bruises and bandages. One covers his right eye, and his arm is bound up in some kind of complicated sling. He's limping too, but still manages to look as if he could throw a punch at any moment.

I'm about to throw my arms around him, but stop just in time. He seems to catch the gesture, though, and smiles. "Nice work, Hale," he says.

"Thanks. How're you holding up?"

"Flesh wounds, is all," he says, the smile still on his face.

The moment passes, and he clears his throat gruffly, all business again. "If you're going to the gallery, I hear they're short of hands for shifting soil. She's excused from duty, but you two" – he points at Carver and Kev – "you're able-bodied. Get in there."

Carver rolls his eyes. We turn to leave, but then Royo says, "On second thoughts – give us a minute?"

He's staring over my shoulder at Carver, who frowns. "She just got out the hospital, man. Leave her be."

"It's OK," I say. "I'll be right there."

Royo puts an arm around my shoulders, turning me away from Carver and Kev. It's an unexpectedly protective gesture.

"You need to be ready," Royo says.

"Oh yeah? For what?" It's hard not to laugh at his words, at his overly serious tone. After everything I've been through, it's hard to imagine something I wouldn't be ready for.

Royo glances over his shoulder at the impatient Carver. "You did the right thing. I wouldn't have you change any part of it. But—"

"Even the part where you – you know." I gesture to his wounds.

"*Listen to me.* That doesn't matter. I could give you some bullshit about cause and effect, but you're smart enough to figure that out on your own. It's just... I'm going to give it to you anyway. You don't just remove a council leader like Janice Okwembu, and expect things to go right back to normal."

"I don't care who takes her place."

"Forget that. What I'm worried about are the things you won't see coming. The consequences you can't plan for, no matter how hard you try."

"And those are?"

"Stupid question, Hale."

He lets me go, nodding towards Carver and Kev. "Keep 'em close. They'll have your back."

I look right into his eyes. "What about you, Royo? Do you have my back?"

He looks right back at me, and a ghost of a smile darts across his face. "Never stopped."

We leave Royo behind, and walk into the main gallery. The noise and movement is intense. People carrying huge sacks of soil, hefting the bags between them. Others yelling instructions, telling people to form lines. But even through the chaos, I see Prakesh immediately.

He's standing with a white-coated tech, looking over a clipboard, his expression serious. The moment I see him, it's as if the noise in the room drops away.

I don't know how he senses I'm there. All I know is that one moment he's looking at the clipboard, and the next he's staring straight at me. The expression on his face is a mix of relief, of sorrow, and of joy.

I'm running, my body sloughing off the pain like old clothes, my arms pumping, my feet in perfect rhythm, the rush building. Running towards him.

And then we're in each other's arms, and we kiss, and the world disappears.

The story continues in

ZERO-G

by

Rob Boffard

The clock is ticking down again for Riley Hale.

he may be the newest member of Outer Earth's law enforcement eam, but she feels less in control than ever. A twisted doctor bent on revenge is blackmailing her with a deadly threat. If Riley's to rvive, she must follow his orders, and break a dangerous prisoner out of jail.

But this isn't just any prisoner – it's Janice Okwembu, the former ouncil member who nearly brought the space station to its knees. To save her own skin, Riley must go against all her beliefs and break every law that she's just sworn to protect.

Riley's mission will get even tougher when all sectors are thrown into lockdown. A lethal virus has begun to spread through Outer Earth, and it seems little can stop it. If Riley doesn't live long nough to help to find a cure, then the last members of the human race will perish along with her.

The future of humanity hangs in the balance. And time is running out.

REDHOOK

meet the author

Rob Boffard is a South African author who splits his time between London, Vancouver and Johannesburg. He has worked as a journalist for over a decade, and has written articles for publications in more than a dozen countries, including the *Guardian* and *Wired* in the UK. *Tracer* is his first novel.

Find out more about Rob Boffard and other Orbit authors by registering for the free monthly newsletter at www.orbitbooks.net.

interview

What was the inspiration behind *Tracer*?

I've always been obsessed with space, and what it's like to live up there. I got to thinking about what it would be like if huge numbers of people lived on a giant, self-contained station. Obviously, that's been done before, but what happens if those people have been there for hundreds of years, without any external contact?

The place would be a mess. It'd be broken down, rusting, falling apart. Social order would be tenuous at best. Public transport would, in all probability, be non-existent, so couriers would emerge to ferry packages and messages from place to place.

The more I thought about the couriers, the more I couldn't get them out of my head. They'd have to be fast and quick-witted, and they'd need to be good fighters – especially since they probably carry sensitive packages from time to time. What would they be like? What was their story? From there, it was a short leap to writing some of it down.

The name "tracer" came a lot later. A *traceur*, in real life, is a practitioner of parkour – something Riley and her crew are very good at. I just mangled the word for my own purposes.

What was the most challenging thing about writing this novel?

Tracer has a really intricate plot. Keeping all the parts in my head at once, and making sure that there were no logical inconsistencies or plot holes, was an enormous task.

I also had absolutely no idea how to write a novel – seriously, up until *Tracer*, the longest thing I'd written was a long-form magazine story. I knew nothing about plot structure, character development or any of the techniques that would-be novelists are supposed to know. I just went in cold, with nothing but a very loose plot outline to guide me.

How much research went into the novel?

Huge amounts. I'm a journalist, and as pompous as it sounds, I believe in accuracy. *Tracer* was always going to be set in the real world, so getting the science right was important to me. I love gravity guns and portals and aliens and lasers, but they didn't have a place in the world of *Tracer*.

My best source was a genuine rocket scientist, Dr Barnaby Osborne, who let me come down to his lab at Kingston University and ask him lots of questions. He's the architect of Outer Earth – thanks to him, it works properly. I get a big rush from solving problems, always have, and figuring out a cool solution to a complex science problem gets me buzzing.

I spoke to plenty of other scientists too: fusion experts and entomologists and orbital physics specialists. They helped set me straight on a few things.

Which was your favourite character to write?
You know that cliché, about bad guys being more fun? Totally true. Oren Darnell was a blast to write. He terrifies me, because in his mind, human beings are absolutely worthless, and so he sees them as entirely expendable, whether they're friendly to him or not. Figuring out why he thinks the way he does took me to some deliciously dark places.

And while we're on bad guys, the only one who terrifies me more than Darnell is Janice Okwembu. Darnell's a nuclear weapon who will leave nothing standing, but Okwembu is a very precise surgical strike. She's going to be very important in the next few books...

What we can expect from the next Outer Earth novel, *Zero-G*?
I don't want to say too much. I will say that it takes place six months after the events of *Tracer*, and that Riley is going to face off against an enemy who makes Oren Darnell look like a kitten. This guy's got a vendetta, and Riley is going to have to push herself further than ever to survive. Everybody's back: Royo, Carver, Prakesh, Kev, Okwembu, plus some new faces. I refuse to say who'll make it out alive...

What do you get up to when you're not writing novels?
Being a writer is a fairly sedentary activity, so the one thing I try to be as obsessed as possible with is snowboarding. As of yet, I've injured nobody but myself.

Despite being South African, I'm a die-hard fan of the Chicago Bulls basketball team, which is unfortunate as they've spent the past few years not being very good. I'm also a massive hip-hop fan, and spend a lot of time hunting down obscure music from around the world, then playing it on my podcast, *20/20*.

introducing

If you enjoyed
TRACER,
look out for

ZERO-G
by Rob Boffard

Prologue

Outer Earth

A huge ring, six miles in diameter, its cooling fins slicing through the vacuum. The Core at the centre of the ring, the sphere containing the station's fusion reactor, shines in the glowing sunlight. Three hundred miles below it, the Earth is dark and silent.

To generate gravity for the million people who live on board, Outer Earth spins—just fast enough to keep everything inside Earth-Normal. The spin is almost imperceptible, the rockets on the station firing at intervals to maintain it. It has been in orbit for over a hundred years.

The side of the station explodes.

A great wound opens up in the hull, like skin parting under a knife. The hole expands faster than the human eye can register, ripping apart until the gash is half a mile long. The pressure loss rips out everything inside, forming a cloud of glittering debris. Shreds of metal collide, bouncing off one other.

And there are bodies. Dozens of them. They tumble through the wreckage, crashing into the larger chunks of debris as they hurtle away from the station. Some of them are still moving, limbs clutching at nothing, fingers hooked into claws. One by one, they go still.

All of this happens in the purest silence.

1

Riley

Two days earlier

"We've got hostages."

Royo's voice echoes around the narrow entrance corridor. The big double doors to the Recycler Plant are behind him, shut tight. A rotating light spins above them, casting flickering shadows on the assembled stompers.

"Roster says twenty sewerage workers were on duty today when it happened," Royo says, jerking his thumb at the double doors. "It's our job to get 'em out."

"How many hostiles?" I say.

A few of the stompers look round at me, as if they can't quite believe I'm actually wearing one of their uniforms. I can't quite believe I am either. Six months ago, I'd be doing my best to get as far away from the stompers as I could. I've never liked cops.

Royo glances at me. His bald head reflects the spinning light perfectly. "We don't have any intel on the situation inside. That's the problem."

"What about the cameras?" says a voice from behind me.

I turn to see Aaron Carver jogging up, the top half of his black stomper jumpsuit tied around his waist, his perfectly styled blond hair swept back. He's wearing a bright red vest, exposing his toned upper arms. Behind him is Kevin O'Connell, a head taller than any other stomper here, with a closely shorn head and dark stubble across his cheeks.

All three of us used to be tracers—couriers who took packages and messages across the station. That was before Royo got us onto the stomper corps.

Royo shakes his head. "Nice of you to join us, Carver."

"Wouldn't miss it for the world, Cap."

Royo turns back to the group. "There were two working cams on the floor, but whoever did this shot 'em to pieces the second they got in there. Locked down all the exits, too.

Carver comes to a stop alongside me, breathing hard. "Was over on the sector border when I got the call," he says to me between breaths.

"Worried about us starting without you?" I say, out of the corner of my mouth.

He puts a hand on my shoulder, uses it to pull himself upright. "Only worried you'd make us look bad. Lucky I got here when I did."

"You got something you want to say, Carver?" Royo shouts. Heads turn to look at us. My stomper jumpsuit is made of thin fabric, but right then it feels too tight around my shoulders.

Carver gives a huge smile. "Not at all, Cap. Carry on."

"What are their demands?" says one of the other stompers, a heavily muscled woman named Jordan, leaning up against the corridor wall. Her ponytail is pulled back so tightly that it looks like her hairline is going to tear her face apart.

"Before they killed the camera," Royo says, "they held up a tab screen with a name written on it."

"A name?" says Jordan, her eyes narrowing.

But I know already. We all do. I grit my teeth, without really meaning to.

"Okwembu," says Kev. His voice is quiet, but it cuts across the hubbub in the corridor.

Royo gives him a crooked smile. "Big man gets it in one."

Janice Okwembu. Our former council leader, who nearly destroyed the station in a twisted attempt to gain more control for herself. A lot of people want her dead. More than a few have tried to break into her maximum security prison to do just that.

I guess whoever took the plant got tired of waiting.

Royo raises his voice. "We don't negotiate with hostage takers. Never have, never will. But, right now, what we don't have is— *Hey!* Get those people out of here!"

I look back towards the entrance. The corridor leading to the Recycler Plant backs out onto the main Apogee sector gallery, an enormous space with multi-level catwalks running all the way up the station levels. This much stomper activity has attracted a crowd, blocking up the entrance to the corridor. They're craning their necks, looking for action. I see workers in mess kitchen uniforms, tech jumpsuits, a few people with tattoos who look like they run with a tracer crew. One man on the side is covered in filthy rags, holding on tight to a pushcart full of gods know what. Three stompers break away from our group, shouting at the crowd to fall back.

"As I was saying," Royo says. "We need intel. That means we need people inside. So while Jordan here takes point on the assault, I need our new tracer unit"—he points at us, and I feel a nervous prickle shoot up my spine—"to get inside, and see what we're dealing with."

"All right," says Carver, rolling his shoulders. "About time we had some action."

"Wait, hold on," I say, raising my hand. "You said they locked down the exits, right? So how *do* we get inside?"

Royo smiles that crooked smile again. A few of the other stompers are sniggering.

"That means the only way in..." I trail off, and, as one, Carver, Kev and I look down at the floor. The metal plating is perforated, and just then I realise what's below it.

Pipes. Conveying human waste from every hab in the sector to the plant. Pipes which we're now going to have to pull ourselves through.

Carver raises his eyes to Royo. "You have *got* to be kidding me."

introducing

If you enjoyed
TRACER,
look out for

ARTEFACT
The Lazarus War: Book 1
by Jamie Sawyer

In the twenty-second century, mankind has spread out into the stars, only to find themselves locked in eternal warfare with the insidious Krell. On the farthest edges of known space, a stalemate has been hard won, and a Quarantine Zone is being policed by the only people able to contain the Krell menace: the brave soldiers of the Simulant Operation Program, an elite military team who remotely operate bioengineered avatars in the most dangerous theaters of war.

Captain Conrad Harris is a veteran of the Sim Ops Program, a man who has died hundreds of times running suicide missions inside his simulants. Known as

Lazarus, Harris is a man addicted to death, and driven by the memory of a lover lost to the Krell many years before. So when a secret research station deep in the Quarantine Zone suddenly goes dark, there is no other man who could possibly lead a rescue mission.

CHAPTER ONE

NEW HAVEN

Radio chatter filled my ears. Different voices, speaking over one another.

Is this it? I asked myself. *Will I find her?*

"That's a confirm on the identification: AFS New Haven. *She went dark three years ago."*

"Null-shields are blown. You have a clean approach."

It was a friendly, at least. Nationality: Arab Freeworlds. But it wasn't her. A spike of disappointment ran through me. *What did I expect?* She was gone.

"Arab Freeworlds Starship New Haven, *this is Alliance FOB* Liberty Point*: do you copy? Repeat, this is FOB* Liberty Point*: do you copy?"*

"Bird's not squawking."

"That's a negative on the hail. No response to automated or manual contact."

I patched into the external cameras to get a better view of the target. She was a big starship, a thousand metres long. NEW HAVEN had been stencilled on the hull, but the white lettering was chipped and worn.

Underneath the name was a numerical ID tag and a barcode with a corporate sponsor logo – an advert for some long-forgotten mining corporation. As an afterthought something in Arabic had been scrawled beside the logo.

New Haven was a civilian-class colony vessel; one of the mass-produced models commonly seen throughout the border systems, capable of long-range quantum-space jumps but with precious little defensive capability. Probably older than me, retrofitted by a dozen governments and corporations before she became known by her current name. The ship looked painfully vulnerable, to my military eye: with a huge globe-like bridge and command module at the nose, a slender midsection and an ugly drive propulsion unit at the aft.

She wouldn't be any good in a fight, that was for sure.

"Reading remote sensors now. I can't get a clean internal analysis from the bio-scanner."

On closer inspection, there was evidence to explain the lifeless state of the ship. Puckered rips in the hull-plating suggested that she had been fired upon by a spaceborne weapon. Nothing catastrophic, but enough to disable the main drive: as though whoever, or whatever, had attacked the ship had been toying with her. Like the hunter that only cripples its prey, but chooses not to deliver the killing blow.

"AFS New Haven, *this is* Liberty Point. *You are about to be boarded in accordance with military code alpha-zeroniner. You have trespassed into the Krell Quarantine Zone. Under military law in force in this sector we have authority to board your craft, in order to ensure your safety."*

The ship had probably been drifting aimlessly for months, maybe even years. There was surely nothing alive within that blasted metal shell.

"That's a continued no response to the hail. Authorising

weapons-free for away team. Proceed with mission as briefed."

"This is Captain Harris," I said. "Reading you loud and clear. That's an affirmative on approach."

"*Copy that. Mission is good to go, good to go. Over to you, Captain. Wireless silence from here on in.*"

Then the communication-link was severed and there was a moment of silence. *Liberty Point*, and all of the protections that the station brought with it, suddenly felt a very long way away.

Our Wildcat armoured personnel shuttle rapidly advanced on the *New Haven*. The APS was an ugly, functional vessel – made to ferry us from the base of operations to the insertion point, and nothing more. It was heavily armoured but completely unarmed; the hope was that, under enemy fire, the triple-reinforced armour would prevent a hull breach before we reached the objective. Compared to the goliath civilian vessel, it was an insignificant dot.

I sat upright in the troop compartment, strapped into a safety harness. On the approach to the target, the Wildcat APS gravity drive cancelled completely: everything not strapped down drifted in free fall. There were no windows or view-screens, and so I relied on the external camera-feeds to track our progress. This was proper cattle-class, even in deep-space.

I wore a tactical combat helmet, for more than just protection. Various technical data was being relayed to the heads-up display – projected directly onto the interior of the face-plate. Swarms of glowing icons, warnings and data-reads scrolled overhead. For a rookie, the flow of information would've been overwhelming but to me this was second nature. Jacked directly into my combat-armour, with a thought I cancelled some data-streams, examined others.

Satisfied with what I saw, I yelled into the communicator: "Squad, sound off."

Five members of the unit called out in turn, their respective life-signs appearing on my HUD.

"Jenkins." The only woman on the team; small, fast and sparky. Jenkins was a gun nut, and when it came to military operations obsessive-compulsive was an understatement. She served as the corporal of the squad and I wouldn't have had it any other way.

"Blake." Youngest member of the team, barely out of basic training when he was inducted. Fresh-faced and always eager. His defining characteristics were extraordinary skill with a sniper rifle, and an incredible talent with the opposite sex.

"Martinez." He had a background in the Alliance Marine Corps. With his dark eyes and darker fuzz of hair, he was Venusian American stock. He promised that he had Hispanic blood, but I doubted that the last few generations of Martinez's family had even set foot on Earth.

"Kaminski." Quick-witted; a fast technician as well as a good shot. Kaminski had been with me from the start. Like me, he had been Alliance Special Forces. He and Jenkins rubbed each other up the wrong way, like brother and sister. Expertly printed above the face-shield of his helmet were the words BORN TO KILL.

Then, finally: "Science Officer Olsen, ah, alive."

Our guest for this mission sat to my left – the science officer attached to my squad. He shook uncontrollably, alternating between breathing hard and retching hard. Olsen's communicator was tuned to an open channel, and none of us were spared his pain. I remotely monitored his vital signs on my suit display – he was in a bad way. I was going to have to keep him close during the op.

"First contact for you, Mr Olsen?" Blake asked over the general squad comms channel.

Olsen gave an exaggerated nod.

"Yes, but I've conducted extensive laboratory studies of the enemy." He paused to retch some more, then blurted: "And I've read many mission debriefs on the subject."

"That counts for nothing out here, my friend," said Jenkins. "You need to face-off against the enemy. Go toe to toe, in our space."

"That's the problem, Jenkins," Blake said. "This isn't our space, according to the Treaty."

"You mean the Treaty that was signed off before you were born, Kid?" Kaminski added, with a dry snigger. "We have company this mission – it's a special occasion. How about you tell us how old you are?"

As squad leader, I knew Blake's age but the others didn't. The mystery had become a source of amusement to the rest of the unit. I could've given Kaminski the answer easily enough, but that would have spoiled the entertainment. This was a topic to which he returned every time we were operational.

"Isn't this getting old?" said Blake.

"No, it isn't – just like you, Kid."

Blake gave him the finger – his hands chunky and oversized inside heavily armoured gauntlets.

"Cut that shit out," I growled over the communicator. "I need you all frosty and on point. I don't want things turning nasty out there. We get aboard the *Haven*, download the route data, then bail out."

I'd already briefed the team back at the *Liberty Point*, but no operation was routine where the Krell were concerned. Just the possibility of an encounter changed the game. I scanned the interior of the darkened shuttle, taking in the faces of each of my team. As I did so, my suit streamed combat statistics on each of them – enough for me to know that they were on edge, that they were ready for this.

"If we stay together and stay cool, then no one needs to get hurt," I said. "That includes you, Olsen."

The science officer gave another nod. His biorhythms were most worrying but there was nothing I could do about that. His inclusion on the team hadn't been my choice, after all.

"You heard the man," Jenkins echoed. "Meaning no fuck-ups."

Couldn't have put it better myself. If I bought it on the op, Jenkins would be responsible for getting the rest of the squad home.

The Wildcat shuttle selected an appropriate docking portal on the *New Haven*. Data imported from the APS automated pilot told me that trajectory and approach vector were good. We would board the ship from the main corridor. According to our intelligence, based on schematics of similar starships, this corridor formed the spine of the ship. It would give access to all major tactical objectives – the bridge, the drive chamber, and the hypersleep suite.

A chime sounded in my helmet and the APS updated me on our progress – T-MINUS TEN SECONDS UNTIL IMPACT.

"Here we go!" I declared.

The Wildcat APS retro-thrusters kicked in, and suddenly we were decelerating rapidly. My head thumped against the padded neck-rest and my body juddered. Despite the reduced-gravity of the cabin, the sensation was gut wrenching. My heart hammered in my chest, even though I had done this hundreds of times before. My helmet informed me that a fresh batch of synthetic combat-drug – a cocktail of endorphins and adrenaline, carefully mixed to keep me at optimum combat performance – was being injected into my system to compensate. The armour carried a full medical suite, patched directly into my body, and automatically provided assistance when necessary. Distance to target rapidly decreased.

"Brace for impact."

Through the APS-mounted cameras, I saw the rough-and-ready docking procedure. The APS literally bumped against the outer hull, and unceremoniously lined up our airlock with the *Haven*'s. With an explosive roar and a wave of kinetic force, the shuttle connected with the hull. The Wildcat airlock cycled open.

We moved like a well-oiled mechanism, a well-used machine. Except for Olsen, we'd all done this before. Martinez was first up, out of his safety harness. He took up point. Jenkins and Blake were next; they would provide covering fire if we met resistance. Then Kaminski, escorting Olsen. I was always last out of the cabin.

"Boarding successful," I said. "We're on the *Haven*."

That was just a formality for my combat-suit recorder.

As I moved out into the corridor, my weapon autolinked with my HUD and displayed targeting data. We were armed with Westington-Haslake M95 plasma battle-rifles – the favoured long-arm for hostile starship engagements. It was a large and weighty weapon, and fired phased plasma pulses, fuelled by an onboard power cell. Range was limited but it had an incredible rate of fire and the sheer stopping power of an energy weapon of this magnitude was worth the compromise. We carried other weapons as well, according to preference – Jenkins favoured an Armant-pattern incinerator unit as her primary weapon, and we all wore plasma pistol sidearms.

"Take up covering positions – overlap arcs of fire," I

whispered, into the communicator. The squad obeyed. "Wide dispersal, and get me some proper light."

Bobbing shoulder-lamps illuminated, flashing over the battered interior of the starship. The suits were equipped with infrared, night-vision, and electro-magnetic sighting, but the Krell didn't emit much body heat and nothing beat good old-fashioned eyesight.

Without being ordered, Kaminski moved up on one of the wall-mounted control panels. He accessed the ship's mainframe with a portable PDU from his kit.

"Let there be light," Martinez whispered, in heavily accented Standard.

Strip lights popped on overhead, flashing in sequence, dowsing the corridor in ugly electric illumination. Some flickered erratically, other didn't light at all. Something began humming in the belly of the ship: maybe dormant life-support systems. A sinister calmness permeated the main corridor. It was utterly utilitarian, with bare metal-plated walls and floors. My suit reported that the temperature was uncomfortably low, but within acceptable tolerances.

"Gravity drive is operational," Kaminski said. "They've left the atmospherics untouched. We'll be okay here for a few hours."

"I don't plan on staying that long," Jenkins said.

Simultaneously, we all broke the seals on our helmets. The atmosphere carried twin but contradictory scents: the stink of burning plastic and fetid water. *The ship has been on fire, and a recycling tank has blown somewhere nearby*. Liquid *plink-plink-plinked* softly in the distance.

"I'll stay sealed, if you don't mind," Olsen clumsily added. "The subjects have been known to harbour cross-species contaminants."

"Christo, this guy is unbelievable," Kaminski said, shaking his head.

"Hey, watch your tongue, *mano*," Martinez said to Kaminski. He motioned to a crude white cross, painted onto the chest-plate of his combat-suit. "Don't use His name in vain."

None of us really knew what religion Martinez followed, but he did it with admirable vigour. It seemed to permit gambling, women and drinking, whereas blaspheming on a mission was always unacceptable.

"Not this shit again," Kaminski said. "It's all I ever hear from you. We get back to the *Point* without you, I'll comm God personally. You Venusians are all the same."

"I'm an American," Martinez started. Venusians were very conscious of their roots; this was an argument I'd arbitrated far too many times between the two soldiers.

"Shut the fuck up," Jenkins said. "He wants to believe, leave him to it." The others respected her word almost as much as mine, and immediately fell silent. "It's nice to have faith in something. Orders, Cap?"

"Fireteam Alpha – Jenkins, Martinez – get down to the hypersleep chamber and report on the status of these colonists. Fireteam Bravo, form up on me."

Nods of approval from the squad. This was standard operating procedure: get onboard the target ship, hit the key locations and get back out as soon as possible.

"And the quantum-drive?" Jenkins asked. She had powered up her flamethrower, and the glow from the pilot-light danced over her face. Her expression looked positively malicious.

"We'll converge on the location in fifteen minutes. Let's get some recon on the place before we check out."

"Solid copy, Captain."

The troopers began a steady jog into the gloomy aft of the starship, their heavy armour and weapons clanking noisily as they went.

It wasn't fear that I felt in my gut. Not trepidation,

either; this was something worse. It was excitement – polluting my thought process, strong enough that it was almost intoxicating. This was what I was made for. I steadied my pulse and concentrated on the mission at hand.

Something stirred in the ship – I felt it.

Kaminski, Blake and I made quick time towards the bridge. Olsen struggled to keep up with us and was quiet for most of the way, but Kaminski couldn't help goading him.

"I take it you aren't used to running in combat-armour?" Kaminski asked. "Just say if you want a rest."

The tone of Kaminski's voice made clear that wasn't a statement of concern, but rather an insult.

"It's quite something," Olsen said, shaking his head. He ignored Kaminski's last remark. "A real marvel of modern technology. The suit feels like it is running me, rather than the other way around."

"You get used to it," I said. "Two and a half tonnes of machinery goes into every unit."

The Trident Class IV combat-suit was equipped with everything a soldier needed. It had a full sensory and tactical data-suite built into the helmet, all fed into the HUD. Reinforced ablative plating protected the wearer from small-arms fire. It had full EVA-capability – atmospherically sealed, with an oxygen recycling pack for survival in deep-space. A plethora of gadgets and added extras were crammed onboard, and Research and Development supplied something new every mission. These versions were in a constantly shifting urban-camouflage pattern, to blur the wearer's outline and make us harder targets to hit. Best of all, the mechanical musculature amplified the strength of the wearer ten-fold.

"You can crush a xeno skull with one hand," Kaminski

said, absently flexing a glove by way of example. "I've done it."

"Stay focused," I ordered, and Kaminski fell silent.

We were moving through a poorly lit area of the ship – Krell were friends of the dark. I flicked on my shoulder-lamp again, taking in the detail.

The starship interior was a state. It had been smashed to pieces by the invaders. We passed cabins sealed up with makeshift barricades. Walls scrawled with bloody handprints, or marked by the discharge of energy weapons. I guessed that the crew and civilian complement had put up a fight, but not much of one. They had probably been armed with basic self-defence weapons – a few slug-throwers, a shock-rifle or so to deal with the occasional unruly crewman, but nothing capable of handling a full-on boarding party. They certainly wouldn't have been prepared for what had come for them.

Something had happened here. That squirming in my gut kicked in again. Part of the mystery of the ship was solved. The Krell had been here for sure. Only one question remained: were they still onboard? Perhaps they had done their thing then bailed out.

Or they might still be lurking somewhere on the ship.

We approached the bridge. I checked the mission timeline. Six minutes had elapsed since we had boarded.

"Check out the door, Blake," I ordered, moving alongside it.

The bridge door had been poorly welded shut. I grappled with one panel, digging my gauntleted fingers into the thin metal plates. Blake did the same to another panel and we pulled it open. Behind me, Kaminski changed position to provide extra firepower in the event of a surprise from inside the room. Once the door was gone, I peered in.

"Scanner reports no movement," Blake said.

He was using a wrist-mounted bio-scanner, incorporated into his suit. It detected biological life-signs, but the range was limited. Although we all had scanners – they were the tool of choice for Krell-hunters and salvage teams up and down the Quarantine Zone – it was important not to become over-reliant on the tech. I'd learnt the hard way that it wasn't always dependable. The Krell were smart fucks; never to be underestimated.

The bridge room was in semi-darkness, with only a few of the control consoles still illuminated.

"Moving up on bridge."

I slowly and cautiously entered the chamber, scanning it with my rifle-mounted lamp. No motion at all. Kaminski followed me in. The place was cold, and it smelt of death and decay. Such familiar odours. I paused over the primary command console. The terminal was full of flashing warnings, untended.

"No survivors in bridge room," I declared.

Another formality for my suit recorder. Crewmen were sprawled at their stations. The bodies were old, decomposed to the point of desiccation. The ship's captain – probably a civilian merchant officer of some stripe – was still hunched over the command console, strapped into his seat. Something sharp and ragged had destroyed his face and upper body. Blood and bodily matter had liberally drenched the area immediately around the corpse, but had long since dried.

"What do you think happened here?" whispered Olsen.

"The ship's artificial intelligence likely awoke essential crew when the Krell boarded," I said. "They probably sealed themselves in, hoping that they would be able to repel the Krell."

I scanned the area directly above the captain's seat.

The action was autonomic, as natural to me as breathing. I plotted how the scene had played out: the Krell had come in through the ceiling cavity – probably using the airshafts to get around the ship undetected – and killed the captain where he sat.

I repressed a shiver.

"Others are the same," Blake said, inspecting the remaining crewmen.

"Best we can do for them now is a decent burial at sea. Blake – cover those shafts. Kaminski – get on the primary console and start the download."

"Affirmative, Cap."

Kaminski got to work, unpacking his gear and jacking devices to the ship's mainframe. He was a good hacker; the product of a misspent youth back in Old Brooklyn.

"Let's find out why this old hulk is drifting so far inside the Quarantine Zone," he muttered.

"I'm quite curious," said Olsen. "The ship should have been well within established Alliance space. Even sponsored civilian vessels have been warned not to stray outside of the demarked area."

Shit happens, Olsen.

I paced the bridge while Kaminski worked.

The only external view-ports aboard the *Haven* were located on the bridge. The shutters had been fixed open, displaying the majesty of deep-space. *Maybe they wanted to see the void, one last time, before the inevitable*, I thought to myself. It wasn't a view that I'd have chosen – the Maelstrom dominated the ports. At this distance, light-years from the edge of the Quarantine Zone, the malevolent cluster of stars looked like an inverted bruise – against the black of space, bright and vivid. Like the Milky Way spiral in miniature: with swirling arms, each containing a myriad of Krell worlds.

The display was alluringly colourful, as though to entice unwary alien travellers to their doom; to think that the occupants of those worlds and systems were a peaceful species. Occasional white flashes indicated gravimetric storms; the inexplicable phenomenon that in turn protected but also imprisoned the worlds of the Maelstrom.

"Your people ever get an answer on what those storms are?" I absently asked Olsen, as Kaminski worked. Olsen was Science Division, a specialised limb of the Alliance complex, not military.

"Now *that* is an interesting question," Olsen started, shuffling over to my position on the bridge. "Research is ongoing. The entire Maelstrom Region is still an enigma. Did you know that there are more black hole stars in that area of space than in the rest of the Orion Arm? Professor Robins, out of Maru Prime, thinks that the storms might be connected – perhaps the result of magnetic stellar tides—"

"There we go," Kaminski said, interrupting Olsen. He started to noisily unplug his gear, and the sudden sound made the science officer jump. "I've got commissioning data, notable service history, and personnel records. Looks like the *Haven* was on a colony run – a settlement programme. Had orders to report to Torfis Star..." He paused, reading something from the terminal. Torfis Star was a long way from our current galactic position, and no right-minded starship captain would've deviated so far off-course without a damned good reason. "I see where things went wrong. The navigation module malfunctioned and the AI tried to compensate."

"The ship's artificial intelligence would be responsible for all automated navigational decisions," Olsen said. "But surely safety protocols would have prevented the ship from making such a catastrophic mistake?"

Kaminski continued working but shrugged non-committally. "It happens more often than you might think. Looks like the *Haven*'s AI developed a system fault. Caused the ship to overshoot her destination by several light-years. That explains how she ended up in the QZ."

"Just work quickly," I said. The faster we worked, the more quickly we could bail out to the APS. If the Krell were still onboard, we might be able to extract before contact. I activated my communicator: "Jenkins – you copy?"

"Jenkins here."

"We're on the bridge, downloading the black box now. What's your location?"

"We're in the hypersleep chamber."

"Give me a sitrep."

"No survivors. It isn't pretty down here. No remains in enough pieces to identify. Looks like they were caught in hypersleep, mostly. Still frozen when they bought it."

"No surprises there. Don't bother IDing them; we have the ship's manifest. Proceed to the Q-drive. Over."

"Solid copy. ETA three minutes."

The black box data took another minute to download, and the same to transmit back to the *Liberty Point*. Mission timeline: ten minutes. Then we were up again, moving down the central corridor and plotting our way to the Q-drive – into the ugly strip-lit passage. The drive chamber was right at the aft of the ship, so the entire length of the vessel. Olsen skulked closely behind me.

"Do you wish you'd brought along a gun now, Mr Olsen?" asked Blake.

"I've never fired a gun in my life," Olsen said, defensively. "I wouldn't know how to."

"I can't think of a better time to learn," Kaminski replied. "You know—"

The overhead lights went out, corridor section by corridor section, until we were plunged into total darkness.

Simultaneously, the humming generated by the life-support module died. The sudden silence was thunderous, stretching out for long seconds.

"How did they do that?" Olsen started. His voice echoed off through the empty corridor like a gunshot, making me flinch. On a dead ship like the *Haven*, noise travelled. "Surely that wasn't caused by the Krell?"

Our shoulder lamps popped on. I held up a hand for silence.

Something creaked elsewhere in the ship.

"Scanners!" I whispered.

That slow, pitched beeping: a lone signal somewhere nearby...

"Contact!" Blake yelled.

In the jittery pool of light created by my shoulder-lamp, I saw *something* spring above us: just a flash of light, wet, fast—

Blake fired a volley of shots from his plasma rifle. Orange light bathed the corridor. Kaminski was up, covering the approach—

"Cease fire!" I shouted. "It's just a blown maintenance pipe."

My team froze, running on adrenaline, eyes wide. Four shoulder-lamps illuminated the shadowy ceiling, tracked the damage done by Blake's plasma shots. True enough, a bundle of ribbed plastic pipes dangled from the suspended ceiling: accompanied by the lethargic *drip-drip* of leaking water.

"You silly bastard, Kid!" Kaminski laughed. "Your trigger finger is itchier than my nuts!"

"Oh Christo!" Olsen screamed.

A Krell primary-form nimbly – far too nimbly for something so big – unwound itself from somewhere above. It landed on the deck, barely ten metres ahead of us.

A barb ran through me. Not physical, but mental

– although the reaction was strong enough for my med-suite to issue another compensatory drug. I was suddenly hyperaware, in combat-mode. This was no longer a recon or salvage op.

The team immediately dispersed, taking up positions around the xeno. No prospect of a false alarm this time.

The creature paused, wriggling its six limbs. It wasn't armed, but that made it no less dangerous. There was something so immensely *wrong* about the Krell. I could still remember the first time I saw one and the sensation of complete wrongness that overcame me. Over the years, the emotion had settled to a balls-deep paralysis.

This was a primary-form, the lowest strata of the Krell Collective, but it was still bigger than any of us. Encased in the Krell equivalent of battle-armour: hardened carapace plates, fused to the xeno's grey-green skin. It was impossible to say where technology finished and biology began. The thing's back was awash with antennae – those could be used as both weapons and communicators with the rest of the Collective.

The Krell turned its head to acknowledge us. It had a vaguely fish-like face, with a pair of deep bituminous eyes, barbels drooping from its mouth. Beneath the head, a pair of gills rhythmically flexed, puffing out noxious fumes. Those sharkish features had earned them the moniker "fish heads." Two pairs of arms sprouted from the shoulders – one atrophied, with clawed hands; the other tipped with bony, serrated protrusions – raptorial forearms.

The xeno reared up, and in a split second it was stomping down the corridor.

I fired my plasma rifle. The first shot exploded the xeno's chest, but it kept coming. The second shot connected with one of the bladed forearms, blowing the limb clean off. Then Blake and Kaminski were firing too – and the corridor was alight with brilliant plasma pulses. The creature collapsed into an incandescent mess.

"You like that much, Olsen?" Kaminski asked. "They're pretty friendly for a species that we're supposed to be at peace with."

At some point during the attack, Olsen had collapsed to his knees. He sat there for a second, looking down at his gloved hands. His eyes were haunted, his jowls heavy and he was suddenly much older. He shook his head, stumbling to his feet. From the safety of a laboratory, it was easy to think of the Krell as another intelligent species, just made in the image of a different god. But seeing them up close, and witnessing their innate need to extinguish the human race, showed them for what they really were.

"This is a live situation now, troopers. Keep together and do this by the drill. *Haven* is awake."

"Solid copy," Kaminski muttered.

"We move to secondary objective. Once the generator has been tagged, we retreat down the primary corridor to the APS. Now double-time it and move out."

There was no pause to relay our contact with Jenkins and Martinez. The Krell had a unique ability to sense radio transmissions, even encrypted communications like those we used on the suits, and now that the Collective had awoken all comms were locked down.

As I started off, I activated the wrist-mounted computer incorporated into my suit. *Ah, shit.* The starship corridors brimmed with motion and bio-signs. The place became swathed in shadow and death – every pool of blackness a possible Krell nest.

Mission timeline: twelve minutes.

We reached the quantum-drive chamber. The huge reinforced doors were emblazoned with warning signs and a red emergency light flashed overhead.

The floor exploded as three more Krell appeared – all chitin shells and claws. Blake went down first, the largest of the Krell dragging him into a service tunnel. He brought his rifle up to fire, but there was too little room for him to manoeuvre in a full combat-suit, and he couldn't bring the weapon to bear.

"Hold on, Kid!" I hollered, firing at the advancing Krell, trying to get him free.

The other two xenos clambered over him in desperation to get to me. I kicked at several of them, reaching a hand into the mass of bodies to try to grapple Blake. He lost his rifle, and let rip an agonised shout as the creatures dragged him down. It was no good – he was either dead now, or he would be soon. Even in his reinforced ablative plate, those things would take him apart. I lost the grip on his hand, just as the other Krell broke free of the tunnel mouth.

"Blake's down!" I yelled. "'Ski – grenade."

"Solid copy – on it."

Kaminski armed an incendiary grenade and tossed it into the nest. The grenade skittered down the tunnel, flashing an amber warning-strobe as it went. In the split second before it went off, as I brought my M95 up to fire, I saw that the tunnel was now filled with xenos. Many, many more than we could hope to kill with just our squad.

"Be careful – you could blow a hole in the hull with those explosives!" Olsen wailed.

Holing the hull was the least of my worries. The grenade went off, sending Krell in every direction. I turned away from the blast at the last moment, and felt hot shrapnel penetrate my combat-armour – frag lodging itself in my lower back. The suit compensated for the wall of white noise, momentarily dampening my audio.

The M95 auto-sighted prone Krell and I fired without even thinking. Pulse after pulse went into the tunnel, splitting armoured heads and tearing off clawed limbs. Blake was down there, somewhere among the tangle of bodies and debris; but it took a good few seconds before my suit informed me that his bio-signs had finally extinguished.

Good journey, Blake.

Kaminski moved behind me. His technical kit was already hooked up to the drive chamber access terminal, running code-cracking algorithms to get us in.

The rest of the team jogged into view. More Krell were now clambering out of the hole in the floor. Martinez and Jenkins added their own rifles to the volley, and assembled outside the drive chamber.

"Glad you could finally make it. Not exactly going to plan down here."

"Yeah, well, we met some friends on the way," Jenkins muttered.

"We lost the Kid. Blake's gone."

"Ah, fuck it," Jenkins said, shaking her head. She and Blake were close, but she didn't dwell on his death. *No time for grieving*, the expression on her face said, *because we might be next*.

The access doors creaked open. There was another set of double-doors inside; endorsed QUANTUM-DRIVE CHAMBER – AUTHORISED PERSONNEL ONLY.

A calm electronic voice began a looped message: "Warning. Warning. Breach doors to drive chamber are now open. This presents an extreme radiation hazard. Warning. Warning."

A second too late, my suit bio-sensors began to trill; detecting massive radiation levels. I couldn't let it concern me. Radiation on an op like this was always a danger, but being killed by the Krell was a more immediate risk. I rattled off a few shots into the shadows, and heard the impact against hard chitin. The things screamed, their voices creating a discordant racket with the alarm system.

Kaminski cracked the inner door, and he and Martinez moved inside. I laid down suppressing fire with Jenkins, falling back slowly as the things tested our defences. It was difficult to make much out in the intermittent light: flashes of a claw, an alien head, then the explosion of plasma as another went down. My suit counted ten, twenty, thirty targets.

"Into the airlock!" Kaminski shouted, and we were all suddenly inside, drenched in sweat and blood.

The drive chamber housed the most complex piece of technology on the ship – the energy core. Once, this might've been called the engine room. Now, the device contained within the chamber was so far advanced that it was no longer mechanical. The drive energy core sat in the centre of the room – an ugly-looking metal box, so big that it filled the place, adorned with even more warning signs. This was our objective.

Olsen stole a glance at the chamber, but stuck close to me as we assembled around the machine. Kaminski paused at the control terminal near the door, and sealed the inner lock. Despite the reinforced metal doors, the squealing and shrieking of the Krell was still audible. I knew that they would be through those doors in less than a minute. Then there was the scuttling and scraping overhead. The chamber was supposed to be secure, but these things had probably been on-ship for long enough to know every access corridor and every room. They had the advantage.

They'll find a way in here soon enough, I thought. A mental image of the dead merchant captain – still strapped to his seat back on the bridge – suddenly came to mind.

The possibility that I would die out here abruptly dawned on me. The thought triggered a burst of anger – not directed at the Alliance military for sending us, nor at the idiot colonists who had flown their ship into the Quarantine Zone, but at the Krell.

My suit didn't take any medical action to compensate for that emotion. *Anger is good.* It was pure and made me focused.

"Jenkins – set the charges."

"Affirmative, Captain."

Jenkins moved to the drive core and began unpacking her kit. She carried three demolition-packs. Each of the big metal discs had a separate control panel, and was packed with a low-yield nuclear charge.

"Wh-what are you doing?" Olsen stammered.

Jenkins kept working, but shook her head with a smile. "We're going to destroy the generator. You should have read the mission briefing. That was your first mistake."

"Forgetting to bring a gun was his second," Kaminski added.

"We're going to set these charges off," Jenkins muttered, "and the resulting explosion will breach the Q-drive energy core. That'll take out the main deck. The chain reaction will destroy the ship."

"In short: *gran explosión*," said Martinez.

Kaminski laughed. "There you go again. You know I hate it when you don't speak Standard. Martinez always does this – he gets all excited and starts speaking funny."

"*El no habla la lengua*," I said. You don't grow up in the Detroit Metro without picking up some of the lingo.

"It's Spanish," Martinez replied, shooting Kaminski a sideways glance.

"I thought that you were from Venus?" Kaminski said.

Olsen whimpered again. "How can you laugh at a time like this?"

"Because Kaminski is an asshole," Martinez said, without missing a beat.

Kaminski shrugged. "It's war."

Thump. Thump.

"Give us enough time to fall back to the APS," I

ordered. "Set the charges with a five-minute delay. The rest of you – *cállate y trabaja*."

"Affirmative."

Thump! Thump! Thump!

They were nearly through now. Welts appeared in the metal door panels.

Jenkins programmed each charge in turn, using magnetic locks to hold them in place on the core outer shielding. Two of the charges were already primed, and she was working on the third. She positioned the charges very deliberately, very carefully, to ensure that each would do maximum damage to the core. If one charge didn't light, then the others would act as a failsafe. There was probably a more technical way of doing this – perhaps hacking the Q-drive directly – but that would take time, and right now that was the one thing that we didn't have.

"Precise as ever," I said to Jenkins.

"It's what I do."

"Feel free to cut some corners; we're on a tight timescale," Kaminski shouted.

"Fuck you, 'Ski."

"Is five minutes going to be enough?" Olsen asked.

I shrugged. "It will have to be. Be prepared for heavy resistance en route, people."

My suit indicated that the Krell were all over the main corridor. They would be in the APS by now, probably waiting for us to fall back.

THUMP! THUMP! THUMP!

"Once the charges are in place, I want a defensive perimeter around that door," I ordered.

"This can't be rushed."

The scraping of claws on metal, from above, was becoming intense. I wondered which defence would be the first to give: whether the Krell would come in through the ceiling or the door.

Kaminski looked back at Jenkins expectantly. Olsen just stood there, his breathing so hard that I could hear him over the communicator.

"And done!"

The third charge snapped into place. Jenkins was up, with Martinez, and Kaminski was ready at the data terminal. There was noise all around us now, signals swarming on our position. I had no time to dictate a proper strategy for our retreat.

"Jenkins – put down a barrier with your torch. Kaminski – on my mark."

I dropped my hand, and the doors started to open. The mechanism buckled and groaned in protest. Immediately, the Krell grappled with the door, slamming into the metal frame to get through.

Stinger-spines – flechette rounds, the Krell equivalent of armour-piercing ammo – showered the room. Three of them punctured my suit; a neat line of black spines protruding from my chest, weeping streamers of blood. *Krell tech is so much more fucked-up than ours.* The spines were poison-tipped and my body was immediately pumped with enough toxins to kill a bull. My suit futilely attempted to compensate by issuing a cocktail of adrenaline and anti-venom.

Martinez flipped another grenade into the horde. The nearest creatures folded over it as it landed, shielding their kin from the explosion. *Mindless fuckers.*

We advanced in formation. Shot after shot poured into the things, but they kept coming. Wave after wave – how many were there on this ship? – thundered into the drive chamber. The doors were suddenly gone. The noise was unbearable – the klaxon, the warnings, a chorus of screams, shrieks and wails. The ringing in my ears didn't stop, as more grenades exploded.

"We're not going to make this!" Jenkins yelled.

"Stay on it! The APS is just ahead!"

Maybe Jenkins was right, but I wasn't going down without a damned good fight. Somewhere in the chaos, Martinez was torn apart. His body disappeared underneath a mass of them. Jenkins poured on her flamethrower – avenging Martinez in some absurd way. Olsen was crying, his helmet now discarded just like the rest of us.

War is such an equaliser.

I grabbed the nearest Krell with one hand, and snapped its neck. I fired my plasma rifle on full-auto with the other, just eager to take down as many of them as I could. My HUD suddenly issued another warning – a counter, interminably in decline.

Ten... Nine... Eight... Seven...

Then Jenkins was gone. Her flamer was a beacon and her own blood a fountain among the alien bodies. It was difficult to focus on much except for the pain in my chest. My suit reported catastrophic damage in too many places. My heart began a slower, staccato beat.

Six... Five... Four...

My rifle bucked in protest. Even through reinforced gloves, the barrel was burning hot.

Three... Two... One...

The demo-charges activated.

Breached, the anti-matter core destabilised. The reaction was instantaneous: uncontrolled white and blue energy spilled out. A series of explosions rippled along the ship's spine. She became a white-hot smudge across the blackness of space.

Then she was gone, along with everything inside her.

The Krell did not pause.

They did not even comprehend what had happened.